BALL *of* STRING

BALL *of* STRING

Gary Lee Martinson

GARY LEE MARTINSON

TATE PUBLISHING
AND ENTERPRISES, LLC

Published by Tate Publishing & Enterprises, LLC
127 E. Trade Center Terrace | Mustang, Oklahoma 73064 USA
1.888.361.9473 | www.tatepublishing.com

Tate Publishing is committed to excellence in the publishing industry. The company reflects the philosophy established by the founders, based on Psalm 68:11,
"The Lord gave the word and great was the company of those who published it."

Published in the United States of America

ISBN: 978-1-62295-490-2
1. Fiction / Romance / General
2. Religion / Christianity / Church Of Jesus Christ Of Latter-Day Saints
13.04.18

DEDICATION

I would like to thank the Independence Public Library for their assistance in my research for this book. I would like to thank my daughters—Amanda, Kimberly, and Madison—for understanding my need to write from time to time. I thank my wife, Janet, and my sister, Tina, for assisting me in this endeavor.

CONTENTS

Innocent Secrets _____ 11

Life in the Amish World _____ 32

A Sister's Confession _____ 50

The Day of Reckoning _____ 64

Time Does Not Heal the Wounds _____ 82

A New Look for Linda _____ 95

Dream or Nightmare _____ 123

A Lasting Good-Bye _____ 144

Getting on with Life _____ 167

Ready for a Family _____ 178

The Need for a Child _____ 192

Happy Family _____ 211

Controlling the Joy _____ 227

The Power of Water _____ 241

The Working Girl _____ 250

The First Day on the Job _____ 263

Learn, Teach, and Experience _____ 284

Too Close for Comfort _____ 305

The World Comes Crashing Down _____ 319

Truth and the Consequences _____ 330

FROM THE AUTHOR

I grew up near a strict Amish community and have the greatest respect for the people and their beliefs. This novel, *Ball of String*, is as accurate a depiction of Amish living that I could portray. I don't pretend to be an expert on their way of life, but accuracy was a priority. It is not my intention to exploit or teach the Amish way of life to the secular person. I simply want to give you a glimpse into the world of these wonderful people. I believe theirs is a good way to live, possibly a better way than in the secular world. We worldly people get so wrapped up in our electronic gizmos and fast-paced lives that we have little time left for our family. I remember when I was a child, stores were closed on Sundays, giving families time to be together, to really interact with one another, on the Sabbath. Our worldly world has taken the Sabbath and made it an ordinary, profitable day.

There are many Amish settlements around the country, each made up of one or several charters. A charter is an established geographical area with landmark boundaries, such as roads, streams, or farm property. The charter would cover the area that would allow a reasonable distance for a family to travel for church meetings. Since the main transportation by the Amish is the horse-drawn buggy, a charter is generally between four to six square miles. Each charter sets its own Ordnung, or rules. The

Ordnung is not a written set of rules but rules lived and practiced by all members of a charter.

The Amish isolate themselves from other religions and traditions that don't conform to their own beliefs. Their lifestyle may appear simple but, in reality, it is hard work. Their living conditions are similar to those in the late 1800s. They wear dark clothes without any patterns or embellishments. They are not permitted to enjoy such modern conveniences as indoor plumbing, electricity, and gas powered machines. They plow their fields with horses and cows are milked by hand.

Large families are needed in order to have enough hands to work the farm, which means women are expected to bear many children. Boys grow up doing heavy farm work while girls took care of domestic chores. The wealth of an Amish family is not measured in monetary terms. What matters most is the efficient manner in which the farm is operated. A well-kept farm with a healthy crop and a well-fed family is considered wealthy.

All cultures in the world today have their problems. Just because I depict an instance of abuse in my novel does not mean the Amish are any more abusive than people of any other culture.

Linda, the main character, is a very honest, innocent soul, but she gets involved in a situation for which there is no clear solution This story is purely a work of fiction; it does not in any way depict anyone I know or have met. I had so much fun writing it, and I hope you have as much fun reading it. You deserve to enjoy *Ball of String*.

CHAPTER ONE

Innocent Secrets

I t was the first warm and sunny day of the year in America's heartland. Spring fever tugged at every living thing to get out and enjoy the day. Trees were still bare, grass damp and brown, yet shades of green had begun to appear in many places. Fields were soft and muddy. Remnants of snow filled the bottom of road ditches and other shaded areas. A gentle southerly breeze carried warm air across the land and fueled the first real warmth of spring. Robins had returned from their winter residence in the South. Red-winged blackbirds chirped mating calls to one another from fence posts and tall grasses. Small animals emerged from their winter quarters to welcome long-awaited warm breezes.

A young girl ran from a farmyard through the damp earth of a harvested cornfield. She wore the apparel of her Amish heritage, a heavy, dark-blue dress with a white apron covering the front and whose hem flapped at her ankles. Her thick, black shoes grew heavy as mud clung to the bottoms. She had a smooth and round face, whose most striking features were a pair of deep-brown eyes. Her hair was the same deep brown, tucked under her white bonnet.

She was slightly smaller than most girls her age, but she carried herself proudly. Hours earlier, she had risen before dawn to feed the chickens and collect their eggs. She helped her mother and her older sister prepare and serve breakfast for her father and brothers, who then went out to feed the livestock. Mother and the daughter scrubbed the kitchen clean, mended torn pants and shirts and then prepared the noon meal. She was anxious to be off to her special place and enjoy an afternoon of solitude.

She lived in a square two-story house. To the north stood a large, red barn. The family called it Big Red. Bales of hay were visible through the high gable doors. Next to the barn stood two tan-and-gray silos, each forty feet tall. A windmill turned briskly between Big Red and a short, narrow white barn. There was a smaller, white version of Big Red on the opposite side of the house, with chickens scratching the ground around it. Next to that was a three-sided building surrounded by a wire fence. Inside the fence were nearly fifty pigs of a variety of piggy colors and sizes.

The house was surrounded by a white three-rail fence, which separated it from the farm buildings. In the backyard, a bucket hung from a water pump. A large area of tilled ground would soon be planted with enough herbs and vegetables to see the family through another year. Opposite the garden was a large tree with a wooden swing hanging from a low branch. In front of the house, a large flower garden waited for warmer days to begin anew.

It was important to her that no one knew where she went that afternoon. She hurried toward the row of trees that lined the field, hoping to spend a few hours by herself by the stream that bordered the family's farm. She found solace in the periodic secluded bliss.

Once she had gotten into the trees, she looked back at the farm to see if anyone had seen her. Not seeing anyone, she felt that her secret will remain a secret. However, she could not see through the kitchen window, where her mother, Clara, had watched her run across the field.

The mother turned around to speak to her oldest daughter in German, "All right, Linda is in the wooded area. Susan, go tell the men they can work in the north field now."

"Yes, Mother," Susan said in English. She was trying to speak English without a German accent, so she always spoke in English. She wanted to go to an English college so she could come back to teach Amish children. Susan was twelve, a year older than Linda. Both sisters had the same hair color, although the older girl had a thinner chin line. "I don't know why we have to play hide-and-seek in order for Linda to get away," Susan said.

Clara and her older daughter were mixing bread ingredients into large bowls. "It makes her happy," her mother answered in English. "She doesn't want us to know she goes there." Clara was a big, round woman with a round, pink-cheeked face. She always had a pleasant disposition. Her smile charmed the hearts of anyone who caught a glimpse of it. She ran a very clean, organized kitchen and orchestrated meals that were envied by many of the Amish families in the area.

Clara's five-year-old daughter, Mary, was sweeping the wooden kitchen floor with a broom twice her height. There was a large kitchen table in the middle of the large kitchen. The old, worn floor had a few crevices, which irritated the little girl as she swept. Her mother assisted in moving chairs around so the little girl could easily sweep under them.

"Since she gets special treatment, why can't the rest of us?" Susan asked with an air of frustration.

Clara smiled at her and said, "You do."

"I do not get special treatment."

"Of course you do." Clara's charming smile broadened. "Remember the doll the English neighbor girl gave you several years ago?"

"You mean the doll Trish gave me?" She weakly responded.

"Ya."

"But you and Father threw the doll away." She didn't want to admit she still had the doll. She and Linda undertook a rescue mission one night after everyone was in bed. They had retrieved the doll from the garbage. Amish girls had dolls, but they were all handmade of cloth.

These particular dolls had tiny pieces of clothing made by a manufacturer. Susan had quite a collection of those clothes from Trish. All types of English clothes to dress her doll in. She had kept the continued existence of the doll a secret.

"Ya, Trish's doll." Clara nodded her head and smiled to herself. She stopped peeling a potato and thought for a few seconds, "What did she call that little thing? Started with a *b*..."

Susan admitted in a quiet tone, "Barbie."

"Ya, that's it, Barbie." Clara chuckled. "It was funny you rescued Barbie out of the trash. I figured this doll was important to you since you went against our wishes. I had to confess knowledge of it at our next confession." She laughed. "Well, don't let your father find out."

"What is so funny?" Susan asked.

"I remember when I found it between your mattresses. You had B..."

"Barbie," Susan assisted her.

"That's it! You had her made up in Amish clothes."

"I got the pile ready for you," Mary informed her mother. "Can I go out and swing now?"

"Ya." Clara took the broom from Mary.

"Well, it was bad enough I kept the doll, I had to at least dress her up properly." Susan looked at the floor. "In case Father did discover her, at least she'd be in Amish clothes."

"I remember finding little, tiny clothes in a box in your dresser drawer." She tilted her head slightly. "Cutest little things. Oh, and the little tiny shoes." She laughed and swept the dirt into a dustpan.

"Ya." Susan was not amused at the realization that her big secret was no secret at all. "I used to dress her up in bright colors. But I made sure she was dressed in Amish clothes when I put her away."

Clara turned to get knitting material from a hutch. "Once the yeast is set out, we'll have a few hours to knit."

Susan wasn't thrilled with the idea of knitting but joined her mother in the task. They were making a lap blanket for Grandfather Levi.

As Linda approached the stream, she saw how it flowed fast and deep with the melting of winter's snow. She enjoyed the warmth since it had been such a cold and snowy winter. There were plenty of muddy spots to avoid along the bank. She hoped not to startle any wildlife nearby and was disappointed to see no deer. Brown grass crunched under her feet. She found a dry, dead, grassy area to sit in under the sun and enjoy the peaceful spring day.

She sat for several minutes basking in her delight when she was startled by rustling noises in the weeds on the other side of the stream. The underbrush was thicker on that side, so she could not see what was making the noise, although she was certain it was a large animal. She leaned back into the brush around her, hoping to stay hidden from whatever wild thing was approaching her. She was even more startled when the wild animal turned out to be a boy about her age emerging from the brush.

She had never seen another human at the stream before. She didn't know this boy. He didn't look mean or menacing, but he was certainly not dressed like an Amish boy. He wore a bright red cap that had a bill like a duck over his face and an oversized, thick red shirt. His long, dirt-blond hair covered his ears. He wore dirty, rubber-soled shoes with red-and-blue stripes on the side. In his right hand, there was a long, thin red stick with a pulley device on one end. The stick looked similar to a whip but was stiff, as if it was frozen. He carried a small green metal box in his left hand.

Linda was disappointed and angry that this worldly person had shown up to interrupt her peaceful visit to the stream. She didn't want to be discovered, so she remained still, hidden behind the brush. She was annoyed when he found a place to settle down on the bank of the stream right across from her. Her curiosity of this boy prompted her to make herself comfortable and observe him. She had never truly met a worldly boy and wondered if boys like this one were all that different.

The boy opened up the green metal box and pulled out a small white carton, which he set down next to him. He then started to pull on an invisible thin string that appeared to be coming out of the end of the stick. He then picked up the carton next to him and started to shake it slightly as he looked intently into it. He reached into the carton and pulled out a short, brown string. She was surprised to see the string curl up on its own. She then determined that it was a worm. She cringed when he tore the worm in half.

She watched as he fastened the worm to the end of the thin string. He again reached into the metal box and pulled out a tiny, bright, red-and-white ball. He attached this ball somehow to the thin string a few feet above the worm that had been strung at the end of the string. He dropped the ball into the stream. The ball settled into the water and created a tiny ripple. The boy sat quietly, watching the ball in the water. Linda watched the ball in the water too, expecting it to do something since the boy was watching it so intently. She knew no animals would come to the stream while the boy was there. He lay back against a small tree trunk, content with the way things were working out. However, when Linda shifted, she broke a twig, and the boy lifted his head and looked intently across the stream in her direction. She lay silent and still. When he relaxed again and stretched his legs, she knew he was going to be there for some time.

After nearly fifteen minutes of this, Linda was beginning to get restless. But the boring, serene scene was interrupted as the ball in the water began to bob slightly. The boy sat up excitedly, clutching the stick firmly in his hands. He slowly got to his feet while watching the ball. Suddenly, the ball disappeared completely, and he snapped the stick upward. He slipped on the stream's muddy edge and fell butt first into the water. He began to splash around, the stick whirling around wildly. He eventually found his footing, he stood there wet, with his hat crooked on his head. He straightened it quickly as if he didn't want anyone to see it crooked. Linda couldn't help but laugh at the sight. She was sure he could hear her.

The boy did not respond to her laughter as he stood chest high in the stream. He tried to walk up to the bank but slipped again, and his head went under. Linda worried he may be in trouble. But his head popped back up out of the water. He spat out some water and grabbed his hat just as it began to float away from him. He threw his hat up on the stream-bank and then tossed his stick after it. Then he struggled to pull himself out of the water.

Linda was surprised to see the stream was as deep as it appeared. She thought this might be a good opportunity to let her presence be known to this boy. She spoke English to him with an air of sarcasm and a slight German accent, "Did you have a nice swim?" She didn't think it was a very nice thing to say, but she wasn't very happy he was there anyway.

He abruptly turned around to see who had spoken to him. He caught a clear glimpse of Linda just as her foot got tangled in a tree root and she fell forward. She was able to stay on her feet, but she couldn't help feeling embarrassed.

"Did you have a nice trip?" he taunted.

Linda couldn't help but laugh out loud at herself. Then suddenly, the ground gave way beneath her, and she fell on her butt, sliding into the muddy-bottomed stream. The boy was concerned she would be hurt or might panic and drown.

Linda's world suddenly went from a warming, sunny day to a frightful, quiet, cold, wet, muddy world. Amish were not encouraged to swim, so she didn't know what to do or expect. The weight and length of her garment made it so cumbersome that she could barely move. When she tried to push off the muddy bottom of the stream, her heavy-shoed feet stuck deep into the mud.

The boy did not hesitate to come to her aid even before she could completely disappeared under the water. He jumped back into the cold water and frantically swam toward her.

He had very little trouble finding her when her hand suddenly popped out of the water, splashing water into his face. He grabbed for her under the surface and found her shoulder. He quickly grabbed an arm and pulled as hard as he could. He was unable to lift her, and the force he used pulled him under the water instead. His grip slipped away from her. He reached down again and got a better hold of her this time. He pulled once again just as she pushed herself up. This time she broke free from the muddy bottom.

Once her head popped out of the water, she immediately began to spit out water in his face. She was coughing and trying to apologize for spitting on him at the same time.

He understood what she was trying to say. "It's all right," he comforted her just as she coughed, spitting more water in his face.

"Sor—" she coughed out, trying to apologize once again. He gently clasped his hand on her chin and turned her head away from him just as she coughed up more water.

They eased their way to the bank on her side of the stream. There was a pile of rocks and a tree branch they were able to get a grip of. They pulled themselves out of the water. She was so heavy with the thick, wet clothes she needed his assistance.

They sat down and she looked at her feet. "I lost my shoe."

"It's probably stuck in the mud," he solemnly told her as he looked back at the stream.

Her face went pale. "I'll have to get it."

"What?" the boy asked.

"I will need my shoe."

"Don't you have another pair of shoes?"

"These are the only shoes I have," she said sadly.

The boy looked puzzled. "You only have one pair of shoes?"

"Ya," she said, puzzled by the question. "One only needs one pair of shoes."

"Well, because of recent events, it is obvious a person needs two pairs of shoes, don't they? Don't you wear different shoes for different occasions?"

She looked at him blankly. "No."

"Well"—he thought about it a moment—"I must have twenty pairs of shoes." He thought again for a moment. "No, I have twenty-one pairs of shoes."

"Really? Why?" she asked.

"Well, when I play baseball, I wear special shoes with cleats," the boy said to her. "I have three pairs of tennis shoes I wear to school, like these." They both looked at his dirty, wet shoes. "Well, the rest of them are cleaner than these are. These are just my crappy, knock-around shoes. I have two pairs of dress shoes I wear to church." Linda looked at his tennis shoes again. He noticed this and clarified, "Well, they are different shoes than this type. They are dress shoes similar to your shoes. I also have a pair of sandals to wear to the pool or the beach."

Linda counted the number of pairs of shoes this boy said he had. "That isn't anywhere near twenty-one pairs of shoes."

The boy smiled coolly. "Well, I may have exaggerated a bit."

"By about fifteen pairs," Linda said.

"Fourteen," the boy spoke up. "I forgot about my lawn-mowin' shoes."

Linda shivered violently as a breeze swept by. "Why would you want all those shoes?"

The boy began to laugh uncontrollably. "Listen, girl, I'm not the one that only has one shoe for two feet to her name."

She smiled briefly. "Oh…well…you've got me there."

"I have never met an Amish girl before," he said seriously. "You seem to be pretty normal. You talk a little funny, and dress a bit oddly and only have one pair of shoes."

"It is our religion and lifestyles that are different. We are all God's children."

"Yeah, okay, whatever," he said. "So what is your name?"

"Linda," she answered while looking at the stream.

"My name is Allen Barber." He extended his hand as if to shake hers in greeting, but she stared at it blankly. He withdrew his hand quickly, hoping he had not offended her.

"Linda Hershberger," she said.

"Hershberger." He chuckled. "Sounds like something that ought to be on a menu somewhere." She looked at him blankly once again. The smile quickly left his face as she shivered again. "You had better get home and out of those wet clothes."

"I can't go home like this," she said in a tone of panic.

Allen was confused. "Why not?"

Linda shook her head as she spoke, "If I go home like this, they will know that I was here at the stream. They won't let me come back here ever again. This is the only place I can go to find solitude." Her eyes widened into a dreamy look. "I love coming here. It is so peaceful and serene. They don't know I come here. I just couldn't go home like this."

"Stop with the sophisticated words."

"What words?"

"Forget it." Allen changed the subject back to her well-being. "You have to go home because you will get very sick if you stay in those wet clothes. That's no lie either."

"I can't," she said, turning her head toward the stream. "Besides, I have to get my shoe." Linda got up while continuing to look at the cold, muddy stream.

Allen looked across the stream. "I have some matches in my tackle box. I'll start a fire."

"No," she quickly shouted. "My family will see the smoke and will come to find out what is going on."

Allen rolled his eyes and thought for a moment. "I will go to my grandfather's house and get a blanket and dry clothes for you to wear until your clothes dry." He looked to her in hopes to get a positive response. "Does that sound like a plan?"

"I guess," she agreed. "Hurry please. I only have a few hours. I will try to get my shoe while you are gone."

"No, I will get your shoe when I get back, okay?"

Linda was greatly relieved. "That will be fine."

"You may want to start getting out of some of those layers of clothes."

He stepped carefully into the stream and made his way to the other bank. He quickly picked up his metal box and stick. He started to run through the trees and brush toward his grandfather's farm. Linda listened with an amused smile as he stumbled through the brush.

She only felt comfortable removing her bonnet, apron, shoe, and socks. She laid these garments over a small tree in the sun to dry. She again began to shiver from the cold. She shifted slightly into the sun.

Soon she heard rustling in the brush and Allen popped out of the brush, carrying an armload of clothes and blankets. Linda shivered again more violently than before. He dropped the handful of clothes in a pile on the ground.

"Get those wet clothes off now!" he ordered as he sorted through the pile of clothes. He found a pair of blue soft, baggy cloth pants, a large thin-cloth shirt, and a sweatshirt.

"You need to go away or something."

"Right, sorry," Allen picked up the blanket, threw it over his head, turned his back to her, and spread his arms out, extending the blanket fully. This assured her that he could not see her undress. She disrobed quickly and tried to figure out how to put the shirt on. She had never attempted to put on any items of clothing like these before.

After several minutes, Allen asked her, "Are you about done?" He was getting a bit tired of holding the blanket up. He also shivered as he stood exposed to the cooling wind.

"I can't figure it out." She held the shirt out, looking it over.

"Figure what out?"

"How to put this shirt on." She was panicky, cold, and exposed to the world.

Allen, who was unable to assist her physically, tried to assist her verbally. "There are three holes in the shirt."

"Ya," she acknowledged.

"Your head goes through the middle one, and an arm goes through the other two."

"Should I do the arms first or the head?"

"Put your head through the middle hole, and then work the arms up."

She poked her head through it. She folded the tube part of the shirt over her and found plenty of room to maneuver her arms through the side holes. "I got it." The shirt went down nearly to her knees. "This is a big shirt."

"It is my grandfather's shirt. He's a big guy."

Linda felt very uncomfortable wearing an old man's shirt. In spite of having something to cover herself with, she still felt very exposed. The feeling of a breeze under her clothing was very unnerving.

She studied the pants and then asked, "All right, how do boy's do this?"

Allen was getting very weary of holding the blanket up much longer. He desperately explained, "One leg at a time, and hurry please."

Linda observed the pants had a rip between the two legs. The rip was lined with metal teeth. "There is a rip in them." Allen turned around briefly, not thinking of the situation. He saw she was looking at the pants with a tremendously puzzled look on her face. She noticed he had turned to look at her.

"Hey," she yelled at him.

Allen chuckled and rolled his eyes. "That's not a rip. It's a zipper."

Linda looked at them. "We don't use zippers. I don't think I am supposed to wear these."

"Don't use those? Why?"

Linda twisted her face a bit. "I don't know."

"Well," Allen said in frustration, "you don't have much choice. Just put them on, please." She remembered how she would help her two-year-old brother get dressed once he started wearing pants. He had worn dresses until he was trained to go to the little barn. Linda finished putting everything on, and she felt funny wearing them. It was a very different feel to her. Besides, they were way too big. The legs bunched at her ankles, and she had to hold them up at the waist.

"Do I have to wear these pants?"

"Are you well covered otherwise?" Allen asked. "It might be cold on your legs."

"No." She stood up looking at herself. "Are these your grandfather's pants?"

"Yes, they are." He put down the blanket and then turned to look at her. "Holy cow!" Linda looked around to see where this special cow was. "Put on these boots to keep your feet warm." She rolled up the pants, sat down, and slid her feet into the large boots. He tried to control his laughter as he watched her clog toward him with his grandfather's clothes seemingly dripping off her. She took her hair out of its tight wrap and shook her head. Her straight brown hair fell out around her head, covering her shoulders. He could see she had very beautiful hair. He was amazed at how normal she looked, except for the hideous outfit he had bestowed upon her.

"You couldn't have gotten me some of your clothes?"

"Mine were in the wash," Allen explained. "Stay there. I'll hang your clothes up." He hung the clothes on low tree branches that were exposed to the sun. He could not help himself from studying them for a moment. He looked back at her and began to chuckle.

"What are you laughing at?" she asked.

"You look so much like a clown. A clown that isn't made-up yet," he said.

She was not sure exactly what a clown was. She had a vision it may have been a certain fluffy dark cloud or something, but the words *made-up* threw her for a loop.

He could sense by her vacant expression she didn't know what a clown was. "A clown. You surely know what a clown is?"

She didn't want to seem stupid to him, so she answered, "Sure I do. I am just not amused at the comparison."

"Sorry," he said sympathetically.

"Why were you looking at my clothes earlier?" Linda asked.

Allen was ashamed that he was caught looking at her underwear. "I'm terribly sorry. "They're just different."

Linda took a long, deep breath. "I have to be home in an hour," she stated. "Do you think my clothes will be dry?"

"I doubt it," he said. "They are so thick it would take a long time to dry. If there was a stronger wind…"

Linda looked very sad. "I guess they will find out."

"Well, we know your shoes certainly won't be dry." He got up and started for the stream.

"Where are you going?"

"To get your shoe," Allen answered.

"What about you getting sick?"

"I'll put on dry clothes after I get your shoe."

"I am sorry I lost my shoe. You really don't need to do that. I will just have to get another pair of shoes soon." Linda knew it would not be easy getting a new pair of shoes, not to mention the telling of how it was lost.

"You need to wear shoes, Linda."

"I don't want that shoe. It didn't fit anymore anyway. It was too small." She was trying to deceive Allen so he would not go after her shoe. Her shoes were actually new shoes, and they were still a bit big for her. She figured it wouldn't have come off so easy had it fit properly.Allen began to laugh again. "If they were too small, how did it happen to come off your foot?" He picked up the shoe that was lying out in the sun to dry. He placed it close to her foot and looked carefully at it. "This shoe is too big, if anything. They look like new." He looked into her deep, beautiful brown eyes. "You're not a very good liar. Wow, you have cool eyes."

"How can you tell they are new? They are all wet and muddy."

"They aren't worn at all." Allen questioned, "Do you still have your old shoes?"

"Forget it. I don't want you to go back into the water."

"Very touching. You care more about me than you do an old shoe." He smiled. "It will be fine." He stepped into the stream, and quickly the water was up to his waist. He was walking slowly to the area where she fell in. He moved slowly so he would not stir up mud. "If I don't come up right away, don't panic. I can hold my breath for a long time." He looked back at her and chuckled. "In other words, keep your pants on."

Soon he slipped completely under the water. Linda waited for a time. She could never live with the thought of something happening to him. Then his head bobbed out of the water to her great relief. He shook his head to get his hair out of his eyes. He smiled and raised his hand, holding a very muddy shoe. He washed the mud off it and then threw it onto the shore. Linda reached out to assist him; one hand extended toward him, and the other holding up her pants. He waved her away. "No, you might fall in again."

He climbed out of the water and moved away from Linda several feet. Then he shook himself like a dog, splattering water everywhere. A drop of water flew into Linda's left eye. She blinked and rubbed at her eye.

"Sorry," Allen said.

The wind blew, and Allen noticed her shivering a bit. He got the blanket and put it around her. He felt flushed when he had his arms around her.

She also felt a flush of emotions as his arms encircled her. "Thank you," she said. The Amish don't often say the words *thank you* among themselves. They do to others outside the religion out of politeness for the worldly modern English people. She had seldom said it before. The Amish will show gratitude and affection to each other through acts of respect and kindness, not through the simple words *thank you*. It is much more meaningful and honest to express affection through physical acts rather than with words that can be so easily spoken and not truly meant.

"Not a problem," he said. "I hope you don't mind if I change into dry clothes now."

"No," she said, "I think you should right away." She took the blanket from around her and stood up to turn her back.

"That's all right. You stay wrapped up. Just turn your back. I trust you," he said as he spun his hand around to indicate to her to turn around. As soon as she turned around, he began to change into dry clothes.

"What were you doing with that stick?" she asked.

"Stick?" He had to think for a moment of what she was talking about.

"That thing with the string," she explained, "and the red-and-white ball."

"Oh, that," Allen laughed. "That's a fishing pole."

Linda soon figured it out. "Oh, you were trying to catch a fish."

"Yeah."

"Are there fish in this stream?"

"Sure there are."

"Have you ever caught any?"

"I've never fished here before." He chuckled. "And the one time I get a bite, I have to abandon it to save a girl from drowning," he answered as he pulled on his jacket. "I'm visiting my grandfather's for the weekend."

"Really," she said. She adjusted her Amish clothes to sit more comfortably on a branch to dry while she kept one hand on Allen's grandfather's pants. Her shoes lay at her feet. "I guess I will be going home with wet shoes. They will never dry in time." She adjusted her pants with both hands to give her a better grip on them.

"Well"—he tried to help her with a solution—"take your shoes off when you get home."

"If it were warmer out, I would be barefoot so I could carry my shoes without bringing on much attention to myself," Linda said.

"Do that then," Allen agreed. "Just say that you wanted to feel the grass between your toes. You missed the grass between your toes all winter. However, that may be more suspicious than if you just go in with wet shoes. You could say that you accidentally stepped into a puddle."

They both sat down near the stream's edge, but not too close to the edge. They sat in silence for a few moments. They were finally enjoying the nice peaceful afternoon like they had intended to enjoy earlier.

Linda ended the silence. "So how often do you visit with your grandfather?"

"Well, this is"—he nodded his head—"this is the first time. I will be back from time to time, helping out on the farm. I may be staying here all summer, helping out."

"How old are you?" Linda asked.

"I'm twelve," he replied.

"I am eleven." Linda started to throw small twigs into the stream to watch them float in the current.

Allen asked what he was always asked, "What do you want to do when you grow up?"

Linda looked slowly up at him and honestly answered, "I may not look like it right now, but I am still Amish."

"Yeah," Allen said, unaware of the point Linda was making.

"Well, like all Amish girls, I want to get married and have many children to help work the farm of my husband's family," she said excitedly.

"Sounds pretty definite," he said. "No chance to do something more exciting?"

"You don't know much about the Amish way of life, do you?"

Allen was silent for a moment before he said, "I guess not. I've seen Amish in town, but I have never talked to one before."

Linda explained, "Well, next year I will probably work throughout the day and will not have time to spend here at this stream."

"What do you do all day?" he asked.

"Cook, clean, bake, knit, all kinds of things. Cleaning clothes takes two days." Linda looked to the sky with a smile. "I want to have ten children. My daughters will help me make our home the envy of all Amish families."

"Ten kids!" Allen bellowed. "What a racket that would be."

"Please don't call them kids," Linda said. "I want to always call them children."

"What's wrong with calling them kids?" he asked.

"Kids just sounds so cold, informal, disrespectful. Children just gives them more meaning and respect."

"I see your point," Allen said. "But to always call them children… It's just easier to call them kids."

"Kids, children, kids, children," she said as thoughts whizzed through her brain. "I like children."

"Yeah, well, whatever," he said. "But your life sounds very boring."

"It's only boring when you don't make the effort to make it fun."

Allen thought back. "Well, sometimes I listen to a boom box when I work. Once, a friend and I painted a fence while listening to a baseball game. It was a great time."

Linda did not want to ask what a boom box was. A baseball game was something she had heard of. As for Allen, he did not want to sound like a slacker when it came to doing work. He was starting to like this, girl and he wanted to impress her. "I like building things."

Linda smiled. "Like building barns, maybe a chair or table."

"Yeah," he said, "I want to build stuff, all kinds of stuff."

"That's good." Linda was happy to hear that he liked to work. She had a sudden thought. "If my father finds out I wore English clothes, he will be angry."

"What makes you think that?"

"There are a lot of things we don't tell Father."

"Really, what would he do if he found out?"

"I wouldn't be allowed to do certain things for a while."

"Does he beat you?"

"Oh no." Linda chuckled. "There is no reason to ever do that."

"Is your father the final authority in your home?"

"I suppose so, but I have found that my father is not always right. Besides, it wouldn't be a good idea to question anything he does."

Allen looked at her with concern. "That may not be a good thing."

"What do you mean?"

"Grownups can be wrong. They make mistakes, misunderstand, or are just not into it."

She didn't want to involve herself in any conversation like that with a worldly boy. So she changed the subject. "So what do you want to do when you grow up?"

"Me? I have changed my mind about a hundred times."

"Well, what do you want to do at this particular time?"

Allen looked at her. "I want to be an architect. You really need to have good, high grades to be one, though."

"Ark-i-tect." Linda pronounced it slowly to make sure she got it right.

"Yeah, that's right."

"You want to build an ark." Linda laughed. "That's already been done."

Allen thought she was being silly. "I like drawing plans of things to make. Right now, I make some small things, but when I get older, I want to build buildings, or maybe be an artist. Being an architect is like being an artist, kind of. I have done some paintings in school. Do you like painting? I'll make you one, maybe one of this stream and some wildlife around it?"

Linda shook her head. "We don't have paintings in our homes. We decorate our homes and yards with God-made beauty. Mostly, we use flowers."

Allen addressed her more seriously than he had before, "Linda."

"Ya."

"Do you come here often?"

"Every chance I get, I actually come here to be alone."

"I sort of ruined that today, didn't I?"

She smiled. "I really don't mind too much. It has been a very interesting day."

"Do you think you may be here tomorrow?" he asked quietly. "I want to find out what happens with you at home. I mean, not that it is any of my business."

"I'll try. If they find out what happened, I won't be allowed to do anything forever." She got up to check if her clothes were dry yet. "They are still damp, but I can't wait much longer." She started to pull them off the branches.

There was a cooler breeze chilling the air as the sun was lowering in the horizon. Allen got up after her and began to shake the clothes one by one to try to dry them quicker. Only her bonnet, socks, and apron were dry.

Allen held the blanket to his back so she could get dressed. Linda was not as hesitant to change as she was before. She put on her moist clothes and soggy shoes. She left her dried socks off to use when she took her shoes off. "Wish me luck."

"Good luck."

CHAPTER TWO

Life in the Amish World

L inda ran back through the field and entered the yard as inconspicuously as possible. She removed her shoes in the back porch and slipped on her socks. She shivered slightly when she entered the kitchen. She was hoping her long dress would cover her feet enough so no one would notice her stocking feet. Her mother was pulling a beef roast out of their wood-burning cooking stove. The room was very warm from the heat of the stove, which was a welcome surprise. She wore her damp clothes that clung on to her like leaded weight.

It was common for Amish children to go barefoot in the summer when it was warmer. However, this early in the spring, it would be unlikely for anyone to go barefoot. The other problem was that with shoes, she would clunk across the floor whenever she would take a step. But because she was stocking footed, the clunking wouldn't be heard. She tried to make a hard foot-pounding sound with her feet. The best she could do was a very painful, muffled sound.

Her mother noticed her. "Linda, you're late. I need you to set the table." Dinner is nearly ready, and the men will be in from the fields soon. The Hershbergers' kitchen was similar to a kitchen you would have found in the late 1800s. The old woodburning stove, with several doors, looked as if it had been used a lot. There was an icebox sitting in a corner with three doors on it. There was a windup clock on a shelf near the stove.

The walls were a pale-green color bare of pictures or patterned wallpaper. There were two areas of cabinets and counter, an icebox, a woodburning oven/stove, and a very large, sturdy, white kitchen table. There were eleven chairs around it, two of which were raised obviously for children.

Clara noticed that Linda was walking along the floor and wasn't making the normal noise of shoes to the floor. "Linda." Her mother bent over to look at her feet. She pulled up slightly on her dress, exposing her stocking feet. She also noticed the dampness in her dress. "Where are your shoes?"

Linda was silent with fright for a few seconds. "They got a little muddy outside. I'm sorry I didn't pay attention and stepped right into a mudhole." She technically wasn't lying since she had stepped in many mud puddles.

Her mother glared briefly at her and nodded. "All right." She stood up and addressed her youngest daughter. "Mary, will you please go ring the bell."

"Ya, Mama," the five-year-old Mary said as she dropped the broom where she stood and ran out of the kitchen through the backdoor. Linda was reaching up into the cupboard to get the plates when the school bell outside started ringing. She felt chills as she stretched as far as she could for the plates. She shivered, which rattled the plates she held. Her mother glanced up from removing the baked potatoes from the oven.

Linda set the plates out as she went around the large table. Even though the kitchen was warm, she felt a cold shake course through her body.

Mary came back into the kitchen. "Ding dong, ding dong," she chanted. Then she saw Linda shake. "Mama, why is Linda shaking?"

Linda quickly turned to Mary and put her finger to her mouth. "Shhh!"

"Why should I shush? You are shaking." Their mother turned away from the heated food she had placed on the counter. She walked toward Linda while she removed the oven mitts. Linda tried not to shake, but she could not stop herself.

Clara placed her hand on Linda's shoulder, noticing her clothes were damp. Linda stopped placing silverware on the table but did not turn around to face her. "What is it dear?"

"Nothing, just a chill."

"Really?" She pulled Linda around to face her. Linda knew it was over for her. "Why are you all wet? Your cheeks are freezing. You take yourself straight upstairs and get changed into some dry clothes before your father sees you."

Linda did not hesitate. She ran from the kitchen as her mother yelled out to her, "Then later, we will talk."

She brushed past Susan who was making her way into the kitchen.

Susan looked to Clara and asked, "Why is she all wet?"

"Fell into the stream, I would guess," her mother replied. "But let's not let your father know, shall we? That means you too, Mary. Do not tell Father that Linda was wet."

"Why not tell Father?" Mary asked.

"I will tell him when the time is right, in my own way," Clara explained firmly.

Both daughters understood that they should do as they were told. They weren't intimidated; they knew their mother knew best.

Susan looked at Mary and quietly spoke as three of their older brothers entered the kitchen through the back-porch door. They were in their normal work attire: pants, shirt, suspenders, and straw work hats. "We women need to stick together. Men want to know everything, but they can't handle it."

The two girls quickly went to work, setting the table and bringing in the food. There was fresh-baked bread. Mary put out two cakes of butter and one cake of apple butter. Susan used two hands to put out a large platter of baked potatoes. Then she got two bowls of gravy. Mary tried to carry a tray of vegetables, but it was looking a bit tipsy to Clara. "Mary, let Susan get that."

"But I want to help."

"You are helping. Why don't you get the salt and pepper."

"All right."

There was a large plate of cheese, homemade crackers, and a dish of baked beans. Finally, the mother of this Amish family brought over the large plate of steaming roast beef. A surprise dessert sat on the table under a clean cloth. The boys began to sit around the table. The boys all had brown hair that lay flat on their heads.

It would be important that Linda returned from changing her clothes before her father arrives. The rest of the family would not be concerned, but her father, John, would have questions. Clara was soon relieved to hear the clomping footsteps on the steps. This was obviously Linda descending the stairs hastily.

Linda came into the kitchen as inconspicuous as possible, a far cry from her hasty descent down the steps. She had put on her old shoes that were painfully small for her. So she walked noticeably awkward through the kitchen. She grabbed a bowl of gravy from the stove but quickly put it right back down because it burned her hands. She refrained from saying anything so as not to draw attention. Using hot pads, she was able to place it on the table. The boys were confused as to her odd behavior but were content to watch silently.

Her mother understood Linda was trying to make up for her absence and said calmly, "Sit down, Linda." Linda sat down quickly and quietly as if she had been chastised. She squirmed a bit as she worked diligently to partially remove the tight shoes from her feet. Soon, their father, John, came into the kitchen through the backdoor with their seven-year-old brother, Paul.

John would sit at the end of the table, with Paul to his right. Lanky thirteen-year-old Aaron will sit to Paul's right. To Aaron's right was seventeen-year-old Jacob, the strongest and largest of the boys. To Jacob's right was stocky, eighteen-year-old Isaac, the oldest of the boys, but shorter than Aaron and Jacob. His brothers respected his authority, and he was certainly in charge when their father was not around.

The women in the family would sit on the other side of the table. The next child to sit at the table between John and Clara was the youngest member of the family, Joel. He was a busy two-year-old that normally would fuss and be disruptive at dinner. He was between Clara and John, so they can both look after him. Continuing clockwise around the table, Mary would sit next to her mother. Linda would sit next to Mary then Susan. Next to Susan would be Grandfather Levi, who had not yet come in from the fields.

It was traditionally the firstborn son of the family who would be given the family farm when the father gets older. John was the firstborn son of Levi and Martha, who had died a few years earlier. Levi had inherited the farm when his father died at an early age. John and Clara were married twenty years earlier and worked for Levi for several years. John was given the farm a few years earlier.

"Levi will be a few minutes." John pointed his son to the sink to wash his hands. "He had to use the little barn." John poured water from a pitcher onto his sons hands and then onto his own. The rest of the boys saw the gesture, and they all got up to wash their hands as well.

"I don't know whether to be thankful about that," Clara said in regard to Levi's use of the little barn. "We're not waiting for him, are we? You know how long he can be."

"He said not to wait for him," John informed her.

The seats around the large table filled up as the family members sat down one by one.

Linda sat quietly, not speaking as the rest of the family was involved in small talk with one another. The conversation subsided as they gave thanks to their Lord. After giving thanks, there was a sudden mass of hands, plates, silverware, bowls, and baskets moving over the large table.

A few minutes later, Levi entered the kitchen, washed his hands, then took his seat. This evening meal was quieter than the noontime meal. The noon meal was full of talk of what was accomplished and what still needed to be done that day. The next day's duties would be discussed later that evening.

By the time the family had finished their meal, darkness had fallen over the farm. Aaron and Paul took two kerosene lamps and went upstairs to their room to read. The older boys went out to the barns with their father to milk the cows.

The older boys were excited to finish their chores, which would leave them free to leave the farm. They were old enough to have steady girlfriends. It was a Saturday night, and there was no church meeting the following day. This is a typical time for young Amish men to court young Amish ladies. It is normal for the courting couples to try to keep their affairs to themselves. Oftentimes, close family members will be caught by surprise when a wedding announcement is made.

Jacob and Isaac claimed they were going to a friend's home to look over a thoroughbred horse. The family was sure the two were planning to visit some fine young Amish ladies. Two weeks earlier, on a Saturday night, the two had left to go to a friend's home to help with the birth of a foal. They did not return until early next morning. It wasn't unusual to help with a foal, but the fact that no foal was born that morning drew a great deal of suspicion. Any excuse given, was accepted by the parents to encourage the courting activity. John and Levi passed some of the time speculating about the young boys' affairs. They laughed, reliving their courting times. John was careful to speak softly of the times that did not include his wife. Clara would glare at them when they spoke quietly.

Susan, Mary, and Clara cleared off the table while Linda started to do the dishes.

Clara began to salvage what food was left. Mary pulled the chairs out away from the table and began to sweep the floor. It was normal for Linda to be the last to leave the kitchen after doing the dishes. She didn't work quickly as she washed dishes, pans, bowls, and utensils. As she doodled along, she tried to think of all the excuses why she was wet. She should have been thinking about an excuse all afternoon. She blamed Allen for distracting her thoughts. Then she convinced herself that it was his fault she was in this situation. She laughed at her own thoughts of Allen. She knew her mother and sister would not tell her father. Still, she did not want to tell them the truth. Then it occurred to her. Why not tell the truth? She had gotten too close to the bank of the stream and slipped in by accident. She did not have to tell her anything about Allen.

She knew the truth would work, just as she had always been told it would. She just had to leave out the complete story. She found the dishes were cleaned much easier when one was happy than when one was in deep thought.

John came in the kitchen through the back porch door and called to his wife, "Clara!"

"Ya," Clara answered, "I'm coming." Clara came into the kitchen and joined her husband standing at the back window to watch the two boys. They got the buggy hitched up and were quickly trotting the horse out of the driveway and down the gravel road.

John and Levi took the two youngest children, Mary and Joel, in the parlor to read them a Bible story before sending them to bed. They turned the kerosene lanterns up as high as the flame would go. Susan grabbed a lantern and went up to her room to read.

Clara watched Linda as she was finishing up with the last few dishes. "You are a bit slow this evening."

"I wasn't concentrating on my work," Linda said. "I was concentrating on coming up with a believable, dignified reason for being wet."

"And what story did you decide on?" Clara asked with a kindly smile.

"The truth." She turned to face her mother.

"Does the truth give me any reason to be concerned for your future?"

Linda had to think for a moment in still silence. By the tone of her mother's voice, she was almost certain her mother knew she met an English boy or something odd. "No, nothing that will happen again. I just went down to the stream, and I got a little close to the edge of the water and slipped in. It's still muddy in places."

Her mother heard the words and believed she certainly fell into the water by accident. But the fact that some of her clothes were completely damp and some were as dry as they were, she knew she had to have hung them up to dry. "Just want to be sure you don't start a tangled ball of string."

Linda was confused by her mother's words—tangled ball of string. She wondered deep inside her mind whether her mother may have known more than she was letting on. She thought that maybe it was just a trick to get her to confess more. "Why do you say that?"

"Say what?" Clara asked.

"Say 'don't start a tangled ball of string.' What do you mean by that?"

Her mother chuckled. "It is a symbol of life. As we conduct ourselves in life, it is like wrapping string around and around into a ball. The more thought and patience you put into wrapping the string, the better the ball. If you wrap your ball carelessly, you will create tangles."

Linda wondered if the events that day did create a knot in her ball. "I understand."

"I am not saying that you have done anything to have created a tangle," Clara said.

"I understand," Linda responded, trying to end the conversation before she confessed to the whole truth.

Her mother assisted her with putting away the last of the dishes into the cupboard. Then she gestured for Linda to retire for the evening. Linda asked for permission to use the little barn before going to bed. Her mother chuckled. "Of course you can."

Linda woke the next morning, well before the sun had risen in the sky. She wanted to get her Sunday chores done early in hopes of getting the afternoon free right after the noon meal. She quickly checked the chickens' nests for eggs and then fed them. She thought about her upcoming time at the stream, but she was also thinking about how wonderful it would be to see Allen. She absentmindedly started to check the same nests a second time as her mind wandered in anticipation. She couldn't figure out if she was more excited to go to the stream for seclusion or to see Allen once again. She wondered if she should feel obligated to be his friend since he had saved her from the depths of the stream. She wondered if she should feel obligated to be his friend because he was such a good gentleman, taking care of her when she was so wet. She then wondered if she should be his friend because he was so interesting and fun to talk to.

She thought it couldn't hurt to have one friend that wasn't Amish. Meeting Allen has stirred up curiosity to learn more about the people from the worldly modern world.

Her education, like that of all other Amish children in the area, was conducted out of a small country school. These schools were very reminiscent of the old country schools scattered around the rural country in the 1800s. The education was normally through the eighth grade level. It had been a tough battle for the Amish in the past to allow their schools to be separated from the local public schools. After a court-defying act by an Amish community in Iowa, they secured the right to teach their own children.

Some charters in the Amish communities had state-certified teachers, but others, like Linda's, had an Amish teacher who had attended a teacher's college but was not a certified teacher. Linda liked her teacher very much and often thought of becoming a teacher herself. However, she also just wanted to be a mother and cook for her family, just as her mother did.

She had collected nearly a full basket of eggs, which she took to her mother. "Good work, ladies," she told the chickens, as she normally did. "You filled the basket. I will come back and give you your treats." She enjoyed talking to the chickens because she thought they actually reacted to her.

While she recounted the eggs, she heard a buggy wheeling down the road toward the farm. It was Isaac and Jacob returning from the night's activities. She walked across the yard and went into the barn while Jacob and Isaac unhitched the horses. They hung the harness on the wall. Isaac went to get a bucket of water, while Jacob filled a bucket with oats for the horse.

"I'll bring some carrots out when I take the eggs in the house," Linda told them. The boys both nodded without saying anything. She could not help but ask, "So how was your night? Were you successful with your quest?"

Neither of the boys offered up a response right away. Finally, Isaac said, "Ya." He was hoping the short answer would not lead to any further questions about the night's activity.

"Why are you two blushing?" she asked, knowing that neither one of them was blushing. Both of them looked at each other out of the corner of their eye.

Isaac could see that neither one of them was flushed. But with the thought, both the boys flushed for real. "We aren't flushed."

Linda smiled broadly. "You are now."

Isaac made a quick move toward Linda. She screamed and ran out of the barn, trying hard not to damage any of her eggs. She began laughing halfway to the house. The two boys later joined the other men milking the cows.

Linda came into the kitchen. "Linda," her mother said, "don't run with the eggs."

"Sorry, Mother," she responded in defense, "I was being chased by Isaac."

"If you wouldn't torment them about their adventures, they wouldn't chase you." Clara took the eggs out of the basket and broke them into a pan.

"How do you know I tormented them?"

"I would have, and you are my daughter, so it just makes sense that you did."

Her mother was happy to receive a good number of eggs for that morning's breakfast, as well as some available for the baking she had planned for the next day. The kitchen was filled with the smell of sausage cooking. "Did the boys tell you anything about the night's activity?"

Linda sadly replied no.

"No?" Susan asked as she rolled the sausage on a large iron skillet.

"No," Linda said.

"You must not have tormented them enough."

"Oh! I told them I would bring out some carrots for Ginger." She quickly went to a box in the corner of the kitchen and got two fresh, unclean garden carrots. "I'll get some information out of them." She ran out of the house.

"She'll get locked in the toolshed if she annoys them too much," Susan told Clara.

There was fried cornmeal mush cooking on the stove. Mary was having trouble feeding Joel cooked-up oatmeal. He was fussing and knocked the dish on the floor. The oatmeal stuck to the bowl, so it did not create a terrible mess.

Susan Chuckled. "I don't think they will be able to stay awake long enough to eat."

"Sure they will, but they'll miss dinner," Clara said. Linda strolled into the kitchen.

"Did you find anything else out?" Susan asked. Linda just shook her head.

John, Levi, and Aaron came into the kitchen after milking and feeding the cows. Clara turned toward her husband. "We will need a block of ice tomorrow."

John responded, "Ya, I have already made arrangements."

Breakfast went well; however, John and Levi couldn't help making jabs at the two boys for their excursion the night before. The boys took the comments calmly without saying anything.

When breakfast was finished, the older boys went to bed while Aaron went horseback riding. The comments after his departure indicated they expected Aaron to be anxious to start courting. The family suspected he rode around the area farms in hopes to arouse a conversation with some young Amish girl.

Linda wanted so badly to ask her mother if she could skip dinner and stay at the stream all day. "Mother," she addressed her tentatively.

"Ya," her mother responded as she placed the last of the dishes next to the sink for Linda to clean.

"Would it be all right if I take a picnic for lunch?" Linda was unsure her mother would allow her to go back to the stream after she had fallen into it yesterday.

She responded, "Sure, but you have to pack it yourself. And you must be back before we start to prepare supper tonight. We will be eating around sundown."

"I understand," she happily answered.

"Susan won't be here, so I will need your help with Joel," she said, adding urgency to the command.

"Where is Susan going?" Linda asked.

"It's not where she is going, it's where she has gone," Clara explained. Linda looked around noticing Susan had left. "She is going to spend the day with Rachel." Rachel was an Amish friend that lived a half mile south of their farm.

"They aren't going to a singing, are they? They're too young," Linda asked her mother with interest. Singings were held at nearby farms home to encourage young couples to the courtship process. There would be a group of fourteen to eighteen year olds gathering at a farm home to sing and play games.

"No, they are not going to a singing. I don't really know what they are planning."

"But if Susan is gone, you will be preparing noon dinner by yourself." Linda looked to her mother. "I will stay and help you."

"No," Clara told her firmly. "I used to feed everyone before on my own, before you and Susan were old enough to help. Besides, the way it is looking, there won't be many to prepare dinner for."

Linda felt guilty, but she did not want to miss meeting Allen or having time at the stream. She couldn't decide what was more important to her. "Are you sure? I don't have to go."

"Ya, go enjoy your youth," she said. "I might enjoy having the whole kitchen to myself for a change."

Linda cleaned the dishes and the kitchen very quickly yet very efficiently. She prepared sandwiches with many chips of cornbread to snack on. She filled a plastic bottle with lemonade. She grabbed two plastic cups.

Her mother looked at her. "Expecting to have guests?"

Linda felt caught and flushed a bit. "Just in case I get one dirty," she answered. She felt a bit guilty deceiving her mother in that way. She thought to herself that she did not technically lie to her mother. If Allen showed up, one of the cups would certainly get dirty. She also thought to herself, the boys lied all the time about where they go on Saturday nights, why couldn't she lie about meeting a boy at the stream? She debated to herself that the boys lied because they were expected to. She would be lying because she was meeting someone she probably shouldn't be meeting.

When she had finished, she asked her mother, "Is there anything else to do?"

"Sweep the floor. Then you may go." Her mother left the kitchen to join her husband, John, and his father, Levi, in the parlor to read Bible stories to Joel, Mary, and Paul. Linda quickly swept the floor, grabbed her prepared basket lunch, and scooted out the door. She also had her favorite book, *Swiss Family Robinson*. She made her way through the wooded area.

She did not see Allen, so she decided to make herself comfortable near the peaceful stream. She took the book from the basket and started to read it from where she had left off the last time she had read it. The day was clear, and a warm sun penetrated through the bare trees. The grass was tan and crisp as she sat down in the sun. She was very content to enjoying the outdoors even if Allen didn't show up. Soon her mind was entrenched deep in the words of *Swiss Family Robinson*.

As she was reading chapter five, she heard a rustling noise in the weeds on her side of the stream. She got up, anxious to see if it was Allen."

She was tempted to call out for him, but if it was not Allen, it could cause a situation for her. She was relieved to see his head briefly through the brush. "Allen."

"Yeah." He emerged from the brush smiling.

"I'm glad you came."

"Sorry I'm late. I did the chores as fast as I could."

"I brought lunch."

"I brought an extra set of clothes. Just in case you decide to go for another swim." Allen held up a bag with straps. "So what did you bring to eat? I'm starving."

"I have sandwiches."

"Ham?"

"No."

"Turkey?"

"No."

"Chicken?"

"No."

"Don't tell me you're a vegetarian?"

Linda smiled. "No, of course not. We raise cows to eat, along with chickens and pigs."

He got up and quickly ran into the brush. Linda turned quickly toward him in fear he was leaving her. She softly said to herself, "What did I say?" Before she could get too upset, she saw Allen coming back out of the brush. He was carrying two long sticks, like he had the day before, in his hands.

"You're going to fish?" she asked, as if she was disappointed.

"Yeah," Allen said excitedly. "I got a pole for you."

"I can't fish," Linda said.

"Why not?"

"I'm not sure, but I know I shouldn't."

"Is it something to do with your religion?"

"Ya," Linda answered.

Allen began to loosen the line from his pole to bait it with a worm. Linda looked at it with some distasteful thoughts. When the worm oozed some puss, she made a moaning sound. It did not seem to bother her appetite since she opened the basket to get out something to eat. She pulled out a roast beef sandwich with gravy, wrapped in wax paper.

She offered it to Allen, who had just dropped his baited line into the water. He set the pole down and tucked the end of it under his thigh so it would not fall in the stream. He took the sandwich from her. He took time to see what the sandwich was.

"It looks pretty good."

"Wait till you eat it."

He separated the bread to reveal the contents of the sandwich. He looked at it for a few seconds. "What is it?" Before she could answer, he had eaten half of it.

Linda was used to her family eating fast but was impressed and surprised at the way Allen ate the sandwich. "It was roast beef and gravy. But I'm sure you know that by now." Linda said.

"I am a picky eater, but that was really good."

"Ya," she said, "anything my mother makes is good."

"Do you always wear such heavy, dreary clothing?"

Linda looked at herself. "Ya."

"I liked you in the sweatshirt much better."

"That was not a good thing for me to wear. I could get in big trouble."

"Oh yeah, how did it go for you yesterday when you got home?"

"My sister Mary noticed my clothes were wet. Mother didn't tell Father though."

"It apparently is a good thing your father didn't find out then." Allen threw his sandwich wrapper into the water and watched it float downstream.

"What are you doing?"

"What?"

"You threw the wax paper into the stream."

"Sorry, did you want it?"

"Ya," Linda said. "You have desecrated the beauty of God's earth with that wrapper."

"You mean littering. It is against the law, but I don't think anyone will catch us out here."

"I caught you," Linda chastised him. "It isn't that you get caught or not but to keep the earth pristine and clean. You don't do it because it is the right thing to do."

"Are you going to turn me in?"

"Well, no." Linda thought and then scolded him with a smile. "I won't turn you in *if* you promise never to do it again, ever!"

"All right, never again. I will forever look after God's beautiful earth."

Linda said seriously, "I will hold you to it."

"Yeah, never again," Allen agreed. He wanted to change the subject, so he asked, "So what did your mother say to you? Or should I ask, what did you say to your mother?"

"Are you not going to pick it up?"

"Huh?"

"Pick up the wrapping," she demanded.

"You're kidding, right?"

Linda did not say anything, but Allen understood. He got up and started to walk along the stream-bank to try to locate the wrapping. "Boy, it is way downstream. I will be right back."

Linda looked around for the dogs. "It's all right. You don't have to find it, please."

"All right. Are you sure?"

"Ya, it will just be one of thousands of others spread around the countryside."

"I will not litter again."

"Good."

They talked for the rest of the afternoon while Allen fished. They laughed and poked at each other as if they were good friends all their lives.

The time went quickly, and the sun seemed to get lower into the sky before they wanted it to. Linda was disappointed. "I will have to go home soon."

Allen watched her beautiful brown eyes looking at him. He turned away from her and blushed slightly. "Oh, I know our time together would have to end sometime," Allen said sadly. "I will be going back to my parents tonight. But I will be back in two weeks."

They talked about unimportant subjects. Linda noticed the sun low in the sky. "I really have to go now. We meet here again in two weeks then?" Linda got up quickly and gathered up her basket.

"Saturday, early afternoon," Allen said with excitement. "I am sure I'll have to help with chores in the morning but could be free in the afternoon."

"Great!" She smiled and walked away into the brush.

CHAPTER THREE

A Sister's Confession

When Linda had finished cleaning in the kitchen after supper, she decided to read the Bible with the rest of her family. When Susan got home, it was getting late. She and Linda cleaned up and retired to their bedroom.

Their room was a small room that had been intended to be a nursery for a farm family when it was built in 1895. They had twin beds with feather mattresses. There was one small nightstand between the two beds. They each had a small trunk under their beds and shared a four-drawer dresser in the corner.

The two girls changed for bed. Then knelt next to their beds to give thanks to the Lord. The days started early, well before the sun cast a glow in the eastern sky. Their chores and breakfast must be done before the long walk to school. Linda was annoyed by Susan's exuberance. She knew they would be up for a while, talking. There was a few seconds of silence, giving Linda false hope.

Susan broke the silence. "I had a very interesting day."

"Can you tell me tomorrow, while we walk to school?" Linda pleaded quietly. She opened her eyes to see Susan looking at her.

"No," she said, "I don't want anyone to know about it."

"Then why tell me?" Linda asked. She really was interested but not at that time.

"I know about your secret at the stream." Linda could see a coy smile in the eerie moonlight through the window.

Linda was horrified but made it a nonissue. "Tell me about it later."

"I went over to Rachel's house last week, and we went to visit Trish, you know, the English girl. They have the farm just north of Rachel's farm. So we conveniently went for a walk and stopped at Trish's house. She is thirteen, and she has such beautiful dark-toned skin. Her eyes are blue, her eyelashes are dark, and she has long, wavy, blonde hair. I noticed when she closed her eyes, her eyelids are baby blue. I thought she was sick or dying or something, but she is really that way." Susan talked quickly and quietly. "I asked her if we should come back another day, when she was feeling better. She said she felt fine."

"Was she born colored like that?" Linda was concerned about Trish's health. "She doesn't sound very healthy. Does she eat properly? Is there anything we can do?"

Susan got out of the bed and knelt down next to Linda. "I'm getting to that." Linda quieted down and listened intently. "She makes herself look like that."

Linda was surprised. "Why?"

Susan shrugged her shoulders. "I'm not exactly sure, but apparently, worldly girls are insecure about themselves and feel they must pretty themselves up to attract boys. That's what Rachel and I concluded later."

"They want to appear half-dead?" Linda asked in amusement.

"No, they think it makes them look beautiful, all the colors and stuff."

"Really?"

"Ya. We watched a television, and I noticed some programs have women all colored up worse than Trish was. Some of them even had sparkly stuff on their faces."

"You watched television?"

"Ya. We watched a game being played by girls dressed in less than undergarments. They were jumping around on sand, hitting a ball back and forth over a net."

"Did the game have a name?"

"Bitch volleyball, is what Trish called it, but I don't think that was correct," Susan said.

"Were there dogs there?"

Susan thought for a moment and then said, "I didn't see any." Susan chuckled. "We must have looked funny because Trish laughed at our expressions when we were watching the television. Rachel was watching it with her mouth wide open in shock. I mean, those girls didn't have clothes on."

"Wow." Linda was unenthusiastic.

"Trish pressed buttons on a plastic hand pad, and the picture on the television changed. There was a man talking, telling us about a murder. There was another game that had one man with a thin stick hitting a small white ball. Then he would find it and hit it again until they find a hole to tap it into."

"That sounds dumb."

"We didn't watch that very long." Susan thought for a moment. "Then she pressed a button, and the television went blank. She said we should listen to the radio and talk about boys." Susan flipped over on her back. She began to wave her hands in the air. "We listened to a silver box that made weird sounds. Trish put in a small plastic thing, and it played some really awful noises. Trish said that the sound was rad, apparently their kind of music. But if you listen enough, the sounds seem to make you want to shift around and dance. Trish said it was are-eh-owe."

"Are-eh-owe? What does that mean?"

"I don't know"—Susan thought for a second—"must be what they call the plastic thing."

"Radical expression of oddity," Linda thought out loud. "It appears to me, if anything forces you to do something, it must be the devil's helper."

"I know it is silly, but Trish was moving around the room making funny, jerky movements. Then her sister Tasha came in and started to do the same thing. They tried to get us to move like them. Rachel and I didn't want them to feel bad, so we—"

"You didn't fall to the temptation and moved funny too?" Linda interrupted.

"Ya, like this." Susan stood up and started to move silently in a dance motion between the beds. "You just kind of want to move."

"I don't want to hear any more about it."

"Trish is boy crazy too. She wants to date a boy she goes to school with. He is, according to Trish, 'a real butt.'"

"Is there such a thing as a fake butt?" Linda asked.

"I don't know."

"Well, apparently, if she likes him, then she calls him a butt."

"A real butt."

"All right, a real butt." Linda thought hard. "Then butt must be a good thing."

"I don't know. We listened to more weird R-E-O thing, danced, and sang songs. Later, she wanted to make us up."

"Make you up? What does that mean?"

"I don't know. We weren't sure either, so we said no."

"You are going to get into trouble if anyone finds out what you were doing."

Susan sighed. "Don't you get it?"

"Don't I get what?"

"There is a whole different world out there, a world we know nothing about. I haven't been to town since I don't know when."

Linda was getting the impression that Susan felt she was interested in finding out more about this other world. "It sounds scary to me."

"It isn't really scary, just different and wild," Susan said with great enthusiasm. "So tell me about your day at the stream."

The reality of the activities earlier in the day was coming back to haunt Linda. "Quiet and peaceful," she said. She was hoping to elude the situation of the truth by making the events of the day seem routine and trivial. Still, she really wanted to talk about it to someone.

"Right," Susan said in a tone that said she was asking for more detail and expecting it. Linda thought it was bold of Susan to tell her about what she had done. It showed great confidence that her sister trusted her to keep her secret. Linda knew Susan could not have known anything about Allen. "So why were you all wet yesterday?"

"I fell into the stream, slipped on the mud."

"And what else? Mother thinks there is something you are not talking about."

"All right." Linda decided to tell the truth. She told Susan the whole story, including the fact she really liked the English boy, Allen. In the faint moonlight, Linda could see Susan's eyes were wide open in astonishment.

When Linda had finished, Susan said, "You did not."

Linda knew now that Susan did not know what had taken place. "I thought you said you knew all about what I was doing."

"I knew you fell in the stream. But this. You can't see him again."

Linda was mad at herself for confessing. "You better not say anything."

"I made up my story so you will tell me yours."

"Well, it will be hard to convince Mother that you didn't go over to Trish's," Linda reasoned. "You know too much about their world for it not to be true."

"I'll say you learned all that stuff from your new butt friend." Susan flipped on her back. The next morning, their mother noticed tension between them as they prepared breakfast. They assisted their mother, cleaning the kitchen before leaving for school. They avoided each other all day.

Linda couldn't take the tension between them. She showed her affection for her sister by punching her softly on the shoulder in passing. Susan knew Linda was too nice to carry a grudge for very long. Their mother could see things had worked out when they prepared dinner. Things could not have been going better for the two of them.

Just as everyone was finishing their meal, Susan blurted out, "I want to know what happened to Linda Saturday." Linda immediately went red in the face as the whole family went silent.

Linda's father, John, asked cordially, hoping to hear an amusing story, "Please tell us of your adventures. Did you see any deer this time?"

Clara could see Linda was upset. "Linda doesn't have to tell us if she doesn't wish to." She gave a slight, respectful bow to her husband.

John nodded. "I will not press the subject." The rest of the family remained quiet and began to go about their business. Linda looked at Susan sternly, giving her a warning not to say anything more.

"She's meeting an English boy there." Susan was satisfied this would get the story plenty of attention. She knew her family would make fun of Linda, especially their older brothers.

Linda's heart sank when the family looked to her for an explanation. She was angry at Susan but knew better then to lash out at her. She sat in solemn silence, offering no defense to the accusations.

Clara broke the silence. "We will talk about this later."

"No, Mother," John said, "we will talk about it now. I think the family has a right to know what is going on." His penetrating glare at Linda frightened her. The rest of the family was also seeing a side of their father they had not witnessed before.

Susan looked at her sister in a desperate attempt to say she was sorry to have brought it up. Linda did not look her way and, without delay, began to tell the story. She had to remind herself to tell the truth. "I went to the stream yesterday, and there was a boy there. He was fishing and fell into the water. When I got up, I slipped into the water, over my head. My foot got stuck in the mud, and I couldn't free it. He pulled me out of the mud and probably saved my life. Then he went to get dry clothes for us. I didn't want to come home wet because you may not let me go back there ever again. I lost my shoe in the mud, and Allen—"

"You call him by name," her father interrupted.

She hung her head. "Sorry. The boy dove down in the water to retrieve my shoe. I waited until my clothes were nearly dry before I came home." The family looked to their father to appraise his expression to the story. "The next day, I thought I might meet the boy again, so I took an extra sandwich. We spent the rest of the day talking and fishing. He fished. I didn't fish at all."

Linda got up and began to clear the table. Jacob and Isaac began to laugh, thinking that she had made up the story. They were sure she didn't just about drown.

The rest of the family began to laugh, seeing the humor the older boys saw. Their father, however, perceived the story as the truth. "How did you get your clothes dry?"

Linda answered without hesitation to Susan's surprise, "I told you, Al—the boy went to get dry clothes for me to wear." Linda could sense the rage building in her father. It got strangely quiet as the rest of the family could feel it as well.

Her father's face reddened as he barked, "You undressed in front of him?"

"No," she said abruptly, with a slight tone of obstinate disrespect. Her father leaped up, knocking a chair over.

Her mother stood up in an attempt to calm him. "Please, John." He did not heed her calming words. He grabbed Linda roughly by the arm. Linda lost her balance and fell into a chair. Her father held her up and then dragged her out of the house through the kitchen door. The rest of the family sat at the table in stunned silence. Levi got up and calmly followed his son and granddaughter.

The smack of the door snapped the family out of their trance. Susan began to cry uncontrollably from fear of what she had sentenced her sister to. Mary cried in distress, not understanding what was going on. No one thought Linda had done anything that would result in such a violent reaction. Clara looked at Susan with a touch of anger.

Jacob said, "I've done worse things but never got whipped for it."

Isaac, the oldest, said, "I have never seen Father so angry."

Clara explained in an unwilling defense of her husband's reaction, "Boys are supposed to be mischievous and curious, but girls are to respect morality above all else."

The boys all turned to look at Susan. "I didn't know this would happen," she said.

Soon Levi and John returned to the house. John informed Susan and Clara, "Linda will do the after-dinner chores for the next two weeks. No one is to talk to her." He looked at his wife. "You go and relax with your family."

"I don't believe I will be able to relax," Clara said as she threw the dishtowel down on the kitchen counter. Linda slowly came into the kitchen through the back door. Her eyes were swollen and red. She moved slowly through the chores of cleaning the kitchen. Right now, she hated everything. She hated people, she hated her father, she hated her family, and she hated Susan. Surprisingly, she wished Allen was there to save and protect her.

Mary came into the kitchen. She stopped and looked at Linda. Mary was not afraid of Linda, but she was afraid of crossing her father. Linda looked up, smiled at her little sister, and decided she did not hate her.

A few moments later, Clara got up and looked at her husband. "I am just getting a glass of water."

She quickly grabbed some dishes and leftovers from the table and put them away. She squeezed Linda's shoulder gently. She quickly put away a few dishes. She returned to the parlor without her glass of water. She turned right around and put a few more items away before returning to the parlor with her glass of water. Linda decided she didn't hate her mother anymore.

After everyone had gone to bed, Linda finished up. She went up to her room and silently changed so as not to wake Susan, who had not been able to sleep knowing she was responsible for Linda's ordeal.

After giving thanks to God, Linda crawled into bed.

Susan broke into tears and hugged her. "I am so sorry. I didn't think you would get into so much trouble."

"Neither did I," Linda said. "I don't think I will ever tell the truth again."

Susan chuckled between sobs. "You will. It isn't in your nature to lie."

"Yeah, that's a flaw in my character."

"Why didn't you say something about me?"

"I don't know."

"Sorry," Susan said sincerely "Are you hurt bad?"

"Remember the time I got bucked off Hooves?"

"Ya."

"This is much worse."

"I'm so sorry. I will never tell anything about anyone ever again," Susan said.

"You won't tell anyone I plan to meet Allen again?"

"Are you still going to meet him?"

"Ya," she said. "Ow."

"Sorry."

The next two weeks dragged on for Linda with the extra chores. She battled within herself the emotions she felt for Allen. She knew that someday she would get married to a really nice Amish boy. Would she have the same feelings for an Amish boy that she has for Allen? Her only experience with boys has been teasing and pranks from her brothers and their friends. Maybe Allen treating her kindly encourages another kind of feeling.

She looked forward to meeting with Allen at the stream. She was not allowed to go to the stream for two months. Since she promised to meet Allen, she had to find a way to go to the stream. With only a day left to come up with a plan to get away, Linda's father lifted the rule. He had been feeling a bit bad for what he had done. He had one condition, though: she had to take the family dog, Wally, with her.

Wally was a cross between a yellow lab and something nobody could determine. The dog was big, hairy, and as gentle as a dog could be. Despite his gentle ways, he could be trusted to defend to the death anyone in the family.

Linda spent the afternoon at the stream hoping Allen would show up. While she waited, feelings tore at her insides where Allen was concerned. She knew they could never have any kind of a relationship. Maybe it was best when Allen did not show up that day.

The next day, Linda hurried through her chores once again in hopes of meeting Allen. Linda left the farmyard with her picnic lunch and a book to read. She took a deep breath as she patted Wally and encouraged him to follow her to the stream. Wally followed as if he knew his job was to protect her. Her mother watched through the kitchen window as she trod through the fields of tiny corn seedlings being tickled by the wind. The day was warm with light, puffy clouds lazily moving across the sky. Susan had gone to her friend's house again for the afternoon. This time, Susan was supposed to be home early enough to assist her mother with Sunday night's meal.

At the stream, Wally wanted to roam around the bushes. There was a noticeable green life sprouting from the ground and trees. Allen was already there fishing when Linda popped out of the brush. Wally was frolicking around with no interest in Allen.

"Allen," she said cautiously.

He looked at her and smiled broadly. He was wearing loose cotton pants and a big sweatshirt. "Linda, you showed up. I hoped you would."

Wally must have heard the discussion and figured he should attend the party. He bounded through the brush and placed himself between the two of them, gently pushing Allen aside. He sat down and panted. Allen did not hesitate to put down his pole and pet Wally. Wally sucked up the attention.

"He likes you," she said happily.

"All dogs like me."

"What's his name?"

"Wally," she answered, petting the dog.

"Hi, Wally, are you a good boy?" He patted his head gruffly. "It is good to see you again. I wondered if you would remember me."

"Of course I remember you. You saved my life"—Linda smiled.

"Well, I am glad to see that you have someone to look out for you now. Just in case I'm not around." Allen pointed to her. "I like your outfit."

She looked at herself, trying to see what he was referring too.

"Your clothes. You look nice."

"These are the same clothes I had before."

"Yeah, but now they are dry."

"Oh."

"I'm sorry, I'm just nervous trying to make conversation."

Linda was flattered that he was nervous to be with her. "You don' have to be nervous around me."

Allen settled back, picking up his pole. "It is a much nicer day than even the lovely day when we met."

"Yes, it is." Allen looked into the sky toward the sun, which felt very warm when it shone through the clouds. Allen was tempted to remove his sweatshirt. He remembered he had a cutoff T-shirt under it that offend Linda. "So how have you been?"

Linda just stared at him with the warmest of feelings. "I have been good."

The conversation started out slowly but quickly grew to cover a great may topics. Allen was interested in learning about the Amish way of life. Linda was not interested in learning about his way of life, so she ended up doing most of the talking. Allen loved to listen to her. She did not tell him about being punished for seeing him. She did not want him to blame himself for what had happened.

They made plans to meet again the following Thursday night after supper. They both wanted to be together as much as they could. Linda knew she could get away under the pretense that she wanted to go for a walk, which was the truth. They were going to meet at a roadside park about a half mile from her farm.

Clara was preparing dinner for the family, and Susan had not returned as expected. She saw Aaron in the backyard, causing a ruckus chasing chickens. "Aaron!" she called out. She figured it would save the farm by giving Aaron a task. It would certainly quiet the place down and save the chickens from further torture. It would also get her second oldest daughter to the house to help with supper. "You know the chickens won't lay as well if they get all worked up like that."

"Ya," he said as he sadly quit chasing them. He hung his head and kicked at the ground as a young boy might after being scolded.

"I need you to get Linda. I need her to help with dinner right away."

"Ya," he replied as he made one last leap toward a chicken, who seemed to be tantalizing him by staying just out of his reach.

"Is she by the stream or in it?" he asked smartly.

"Who knows. Get along quickly. I need her right away."

He picked up the pace and jogged across the field toward the wooded area of the stream. He heard Linda's voice and silently made his way toward her. He got close enough to see Linda and Allen sitting together on the bank. Wally noticed Aaron, got up, and bounded toward him with great excitement. This interrupted the conversation as Linda and Allen looked intently into the brush.

Aaron called out to them, "Mother needs you to help with supper, Linda." Linda's heart sank, knowing it was Aaron who was there with them. She felt bad that Aaron was now involved with her indiscretions. Allen could sense this.

She looked at Allen. "I'll try to meet you on Thursday. If I don't, I will try every Saturday or Sunday until we meet again." She looked intensely at him as she got up to leave. He nodded in agreement.

Allen followed Linda through the brush. Linda stopped. "Where are you going?"

"I want to meet your brother."

Linda knew it would not be a good idea for him to meet Aaron. However, Aaron could become a friend if they did meet. Aaron was waiting for Linda on a path. He saw Allen following her. Aaron looked away from him, unsure of what to do.

"Hello, Aaron." Allen extended his hand to shake Aaron's. "It is nice to meet you."

"Ya," Aaron responded simply without looking at Allen. Wally ran ahead of them, leaping and running with great excitement. Allen did not say anything else. Linda gazed briefly back to Allen as she and Aaron made their way back home.

"Are you going to tell Father?" Linda asked Aaron.

"No, but I will have to tell Mother. She will have to figure out what to do."

"I understand," Linda said with some reservation.

"I am sorry," Aaron said. "He seems like a very nice boy."

"You hardly even talked to him."

"Don't need to talk to him. I can just tell."

CHAPTER FOUR

The Day of Reckoning

Susan showed up shortly after Linda did, and Clara chastised her for her tardiness.

After dinner cleanup, Linda noticed Aaron discussing something with her mother. She went upstairs to bed, hoping Aaron had changed his mind about telling their mother. As she lay in bed, she thought about talking to Susan. She felt confident Susan would not say anything since she had promised never to tell anyone anything ever again.

Susan started the conversation. "I went over to Trish's again today."

"Really," Linda said, irritated at herself for being interested.

"Ya," Susan said excitedly, "we got all dressed up in colorful clothes, and we got made up in cream and paint that makes your face pretty." Susan was talking as if it were the most delightful activity on the planet.

"Really. Pretty."

"Ya, and I have some pictures of me all dressed up."

"Really," Linda said, this time with true interest. The Amish generally do not have pictures of themselves, nor do they have pictures on the walls of their homes. Pictures are considered worldly decorations. The Amish homes are plainly decorated with neutral-color-painted walls or wallpaper with bland patterns. They may decorate the house with flowers grown from their gardens because they consider flowers as God's decoration that can be used to beautify their lives.

Susan leaped out of bed and lit the ceresin lantern on the bedside table. She dug deep into the bottom drawer of their dresser and retrieved an envelope. Linda sat up anxiously as Susan handed her one of the pictures.

Linda studied it for a few seconds. "Who's that?"

"That's me."

"Wow, that's you? You don't look like yourself. You look like a worldly person." Linda said as her eyes widened with amazement. Susan was wearing a tight-fitting red dress with no straps over her shoulders. The dress showed much of her undeveloped chest area. Linda was amazed that the dress could stay in place. "Where's the rest of it?"

"No, that is it. There is no rest of it."

"The dress"—Linda looked at it carefully, tipping her head from one side to the other—"the sleeves, what happened to the sleeves?"

"That's it. There are no sleeves."

"Didn't it fall?"

"What fall?"

"The dress."

"Oh, it never really fell, but it kept inching down. I had to keep pulling it up. It felt weird wearing it. It was very lightweight and silky smooth. It sort of tickled my whole body."

Linda noticed Susan's skin tone was darker in appearance. Her eyes appeared bolder and darker. Linda thought her eyes made her look devilish. Her cheeks were reddish, and her hair hung freely with unnatural waves over her bare shoulders. Susan's bright-white teeth gave Linda the impression she really enjoyed having her picture taken looking like that. "You look really different."

"Ya, Trish says that if I were at her school, all the boys would want to go out with me." Susan looked at herself in the picture with a wild-eyed look on her face.

As Linda observed Susan's reaction to seeing herself in the picture, she wondered if this girl next to her was really her sister. Susan then handed her the next picture. This picture showed her wearing a tight-fitting white T-shirt. She was also wearing a pair of shiny red shorts that exposed her legs nearly to the crotch.

Linda's eyes popped open, and her hand went up to her mouth. "Susan, you are in someone else's hideous undergarment."

"It's not undergarments." Susan laughed quietly. "They're just shiny, short pants." Susan then placed the next picture of her on the bed.

Linda gasped and turned her head away quickly. "Oh my goodness," she said in a squeaky whisper. "You're naked."

"No, I'm not," Susan said. "I have a swimsuit on, a bikini." Just as she got those words out, the door to their room began to open slowly. Susan quickly grabbed the pictures and hid them under her nightgown.

Their mother peeked around the edge of the door. She came into the room and closed the door behind her. "I see that you're still up." She looked at Linda, whose mouth was still open from seeing Susan in the bikini. "I'm sorry. Did I frighten you?"

"No, not really," Susan answered.

"I'm glad. Susan, could you leave us please?"

Susan was surprised that she was the one asked to leave home. Linda was not surprised, and she sank back down into her bed and stared at the ceiling. Linda lay in silence as her mother approached and sat down at the foot of her bed. "Aaron told me you met the boy at the stream again today. Is this true?"

In the past, Linda had always told the truth, but the last time she told the truth in a situation similar to this, she was severely punished. She had vowed to herself that she would lie if she felt it necessary to avoid punishment like that again. Yet she knew if she lied, it would be the same as calling her brother a liar, and she could not do that. "Ya, I met him again."

"I thought your father had forbidden you to see this boy again?"

"Ya," Linda answered solemnly.

"Why do you wish to go against your father's wishes?"

Linda was not sure whether or not to tell her mother how she felt or say what she wanted to hear. "Because they are his wishes, not mine." She spoke her mind as politely as she could while making this defiant statement. This was even more contemptuous because she was an eleven-year-old girl.

Her mother seemed to disregard her insolence. "What does this boy mean to you? You certainly do not have much in common with him. He is worldly and worships devilish things."

Linda tried to tell her mother that Allen was not the devil. "So what if he is not Amish? He is not a bad person. We have good talks together and—"

"But you can never marry a devil boy," her mother stopped her flurry of excuses with a calm and peaceful voice.

"Don't call him that. Besides, I do not want to marry him. He is my friend."

"You have others that are your true friends."

"I know I do, but he is different."

"You are too young to be seeing this boy, even if he was Amish."

Linda could sense her mother's growing impatience, but she wanted to make her point. "I am not seeing him for love or marriage," she said with mixed resolve she did not understand.

"This is not a good thing, Linda. You must not get involved. He will change you, and you will not be able to fulfill your commitment to God."

"He has not changed me, nor does he want to. He talks about trying to understand our religion and respecting it."

"He does not talk of his world and all its evil ways?" Clara asked, expecting Linda to say that he had not, whether he had or not.

"Sure he does, but he recognizes the evil and the good for what they truly are."

Clara was proud of her daughter's resolve but knew it would get her into trouble. She decided to defuse the situation. "It sounds like he is a very good boy, but if your father finds out about this, you know what will happen." She wanted to save her child from any further punishment. She knew Linda could not be reasoned with any further, but wanted to curve her thoughts to the consequences.

"Ya, I know what will happen," Linda said firmly. "I still choose to see him again."

Clara sighed, "I will not tell your father if you promise you will not see this boy again." She looked deep into Linda's eyes. "You must promise me." Clara now had cleared her conscience of anything Linda does is of her own choice.

Linda thought for only a few seconds. "No, I will not promise." She felt a cold sweat run through her body.

Clara was disappointed but impressed by her daughter's decision. "All right, with this choice, you will suffer the consequences."

Linda could feel the stings of pain she would have to bear once her father learned of the incident. She closed her eyes to try to think of something else, something pleasurable. She thought of being free in the fields, running after a beautiful butterfly.

After a few moments, Clara gave up hope that her daughter would change her mind. She slowly got up and left the room.

Susan quietly returned and put her pictures deep into the bottom dresser drawer. Linda's eyes began to fill with tears of fear. "Aaron just told me what he saw," Susan said kindly. "I am glad she didn't tell Father about it."

"Mother is going to tell him," Linda said sadly. "I must find a different way to see Allen. Maybe I could meet him at night after everyone has gone to bed."

"Have you made arrangements to see him again?" Susan asked with surprise.

"Ya, Thursday night after supper."

"That will be tough, but we can figure something out."

Linda was surprised Susan was willing to help her. "You know you will get into big trouble if you help me."

"Only if we get caught." Susan sat down at Linda's side and embraced her. "It's my fault you got into this mess."

"No, it isn't." Linda leaned her head on Susan's shoulder. "I am the only one to blame."

Linda had mixed emotions about her sister. Allen had never said anything to try and discourage her from her faith. Yet Susan was visiting a worldly girl's home and playing the part of a worldly person. She wondered if bringing up the subject of Susan's indiscretions might take some pressure off her. She slowly shook her head, knowing that she would never tell on Susan.

Clara decided not to tell her husband. Instead, she decided to take time out the following day to visit the next-door neighbor, the Barbers. After breakfast, Clara loaded up a basket of various foods to take to the Barbers as a gift. Clara did not tell Susan or Linda where she was going. Clara requested Aaron to hitch up the horse and drive her to the neighbors' home.

Susan was left in charge to begin preparation of the noontime dinner. She and Linda worked on preparing the meal together for the first time without their mother's guidance. As soon as Clara had left the driveway of the farm, Susan immediately began ordering Linda and Mary around like a tyrant. Mary was chastised to tears almost immediately when she could not reach the cups in the cupboards.

Linda understood Susan's obsession, so she took Mary aside and explained to her quietly, "Don't be upset. Susan is having a mental episode right now. She needs our help to get through it." That calmed Mary down enough to accomplish the task at hand. She also was very sympathetic of Susan's terrible problem. Even though she had no idea what a mental episode meant.

When Clara and Aaron arrived in the Barbers' driveway, there were two gentlemen leaning on a fence near a large barn. Both gentlemen began to stroll over to greet them.

"Well, hello, Clara," Gerald Barber greeted her. He nodded to Aaron. "Aaron." Aaron nodded politely.

"Good Morning, Mr. Barber," Clara politely responded. Gerald was a small, wiry man dressed in a blue flannel shirt and overalls. He had a thinning head of gray hair, and it was obvious he hadn't shaved for several days. He was wearing an old, beat-up, white cowboy hat.

Clara began to step out of the buggy. Aaron remained in the buggy, making no attempt to get out. Gerald hurried to assist her out of the buggy. Clara visited the Barbers' home from time to time, so this visit wasn't a complete surprise. Once she got her footing, she reached back into the buggy to get the basket of gifts.

"Clara, this is my grandson, Allen, Barry's boy."

"Hello," Allen said politely. He did not know that this woman was Linda's mother. Clara did not respond to Allen in any manner. Allen was not upset by her actions. Once Allen saw Aaron, it became obvious Clara was Linda's mother. "Hello, Aaron."

Aaron raised his hand to the front of his black, round-rimmed hat and tipped his head slightly. Allen then raised his hand to the brim of his baseball cap and tipped his head slightly as well. He thought this must be the proper way to greet Amish people.

"What brings our good neighbor to us this morning?" Gerald asked pleasantly.

"I need to have a talk with you for a few moments."

"Sure," Gerald said as he gestured her to the back door of the house. "We sure have had some great weather lately, haven't we?"

"Ya, it has been a fine spring," she said. "I have a few things for your family."

"Well, thank you." He took the basket from her. He opened the back door to the porch leading to the door to the kitchen for her. "Milly!" he called excitedly. "We have a visitor."

"Oh, how wonderful," Milly said from inside the house. "I'll get the coffee poured." Milly was wiping her hands dry with a dish towel when Clara and Gerald entered the house. She was a portly, short woman with a friendly round face. She had a dark-blue bandana wrapped around her head covering most of her short, gray hair. "Good morning, Clara, would you like a cup of coffee or tea?"

"Ya, coffee would be nice," Clara answered. "I have a few things for you." She opened the basket Gerald had set on the kitchen table and pulled out a fresh apple pie and two jars of apple butter.

"Oh my," Milly said, "that really isn't necessary. Clara, you're always welcome to visit without having to bring any gifts."

"I wanted to—" she looked at Gerald—"I know how you like apple butter."

"I sure do," Gerald said happily as he grasped the two jars of apple butter. "Thank you."

Clara and Gerald sat down at the kitchen table. The Barbers had two sons and two daughters that had grown up and moved on with their lives. They have been neighbors for nearly thirty years and never had any dispute of any kind. Mrs. Barber gathered up two cups of coffee and served them before serving herself.

Clara stated her business, "Your Allen, the boy staying with you."

"Yes."

She got right to the point. "According to my daughter, he has saved her life twice down by the stream."

"Really," Milly answered, "I don't believe I have heard that story." She looked out of the back kitchen window to see the young hero.

"Apparently, he saved her from drowning," Clara said.

Milly was proud. "Well, let me get him so you can meet him."

Gerald held up his hand to stop his wife from getting up. He got up, went to the back door, opened it up, and yelled, "Allen! Come on in here!" He looked around but did not see Allen. He did not see Aaron sitting in the buggy either. He called again, "Allen!" When he heard no response, he went back into the house. "I guess he and Aaron are off somewhere."

Clara felt she could talk more freely without Allen present. "I want to express my gratitude to you for your grandson saving my daughter's life."

"Well, you should tell this to Allen," Gerald suggested.

"I intend to," Clara said, "but I must express the problems of Linda and Allen becoming too close." Gerald and Milly could tell it was a very important subject to her. They listened carefully and with respect. "I have much respect for your way of life. But my husband will not like the fact our daughter is meeting with your grandson."

Milly defended her grandson, "I can assure you, Allen is a fine young man. He would not do anything to hurt your daughter. You even admit he saved her life."

Gerald chimed in with more positive regard for Allen. "He has been helping me out around here. I tell you, it has been hard for me the last few years to keep the farm running. Allen is going to be here this summer. He's trying to earn money for college. He is a good boy."

Clara agreed, "Ya, he is a fine young man. Linda would not have risked her well-being if he wasn't a fine young man. The fact he did save her life may place her in a situation that she may feel obligated to him."

"I'm sure he wouldn't take advantage of her in any way," Milly said firmly. "We certainly will have a talk with him about it."

"I agree," Clara said. "I just don't want a bad situation to continue. If my husband finds out they are meeting, he will not be as understanding as we are. Please forgive me, but listen to my warning."

There were a few moments of silence before Milly spoke. "I think I understand the situation. What should we do?"

"If Allen stayed away from the stream, they would not meet."

"He likes to fish at the stream," Gerald said.

Clara did not want to push the subject but felt cornered to point out a few facts they were all aware of. "The stream is technically on our property, so I can force you to comply. I really don't want to do that, but this is important."

"I know it is technically on your property, but we have always agreed it a joint stream between us," Gerald said.

Tears began to fill Clara's eyes. "I know we have, but it just has to be this way." She got up to leave. "Please," she made a final plea, hoping not to escalate any hostilities.

"Please"—Milly gently touched Clara's hand—"Clara, stay and finish your coffee. You are our neighbor, and we will always have our door open to you. Please stay."

"Absolutely," Gerald said as he gestured for her to sit down once again. He looked out into the backyard. "I believe we will have trouble rounding up the two boys anyway."

Clara felt warmed by these kind words. Milly and Gerald understood Clara's position and respected her enough to abide by her wishes and not hold any malice toward her.

"Ya," Clara said with great relief, "I would like that." She had always liked the Barbers and did not want to leave with bad feelings between them.

The rest of the visit was very pleasant among the three of them. All of them seemed to understand the situation did not affect the respect they had for one another.

Meanwhile, Allen had struck up a conversation with Aaron as they watched the two older people going into the house. "Hi, I'm Allen."

"I know. We met yesterday."

"I thought maybe we could start over. Maybe things could be cool between us."

"All right." Aaron nodded. "My name is Aaron." Aaron lifted his hand to tip his hat slightly. Allen quickly moved his hand to his baseball cap and tipped it once again. Then Aaron held out his hand to shake Allen's.

"So you are Linda's brother?"

"Ya," he said quickly. His eyes darted around from side to side. He wasn't sure if his mother was keen on him befriending Allen.

Allen could sense the apprehension Aaron was feeling. He wanted to get to know Aaron in hopes of gaining more favor from his sister. "Wanna see our horses?"

He nodded slightly, tucked the reins to the horse to one side, and climbed out of the buggy. They both walked silently, hanging their heads as they walked toward a large red barn. Their conversation was clinical and only about the horses. After seeing the two horses the Barbers had, they went through the barnyard and other barns looking over all the animals.

They were enjoying a light conversation about a runt pig that was running around jumping on the other pigs. Allen thought he heard a yell from his grandfather. Allen looked to the house but saw no one. They leisurely checked the fields for progress.

After this, Aaron felt he needed to be ready to go whenever his mother was ready. Allen invited Aaron in. Aaron declined the invitation and chose to give his horse some attention. Allen stepped into a small shed just outside the back door to the house and brought out two nice big carrots. "Here, give this to your horse."

"He will like that."

Allen asked, "You brought your mother here?"

"Ya," he responded.

Allen wanted to meet Linda's mother. "It was very nice meeting you."

Aaron cracked a slight smile and said, "It was nice to meet you."

Allen entered the house with a big smile just as the three inside started laughing. "Allen," Gerald excitedly addressed him, "I would like you to meet our neighbor, Mrs. Hershberger. Apparently you have met her daughter—"

"Linda," he interrupted excitedly. It was obvious he was truly excited to meet Linda's mother. She had always talked very kindly about her mother. Linda indicated to him that it would not be a good idea to meet members of her family, yet today he has met another one.

Allen started to hold out his hand but quickly withdrew it and tipped his hat. "Hello, it's very nice to meet you," he politely expressed to her.

Clara did not waste a moment. "I am grateful for your assistance in protecting my daughter. I do not know what you mean to her, but it will be best that you do not see her anymore for her sake. I mean no disrespect to you or your family, but to see her again can destroy her. It must be this way."

"Why?" Allen asked.

"It can only cause hardship and confusion for her. I can't tell you what this could do to her." Clara did not want to admit to the abuse Linda had endured for seeing him.

"Allen, we'll talk about it later. Please trust us with this." His grandfather tried to save the happier moment. He understood Allen was hurt and angry with the words he was hearing.

Allen did not speak any further but looked at Linda's mother with surprise. Then he excused himself and went out of the kitchen.

"You could have been a little more tactful, Clara," Milly said calmly but firmly.

"I know," Clara said sadly. "But he must understand this is serious, for Linda's sake."

Allen did not say anything to Aaron as he passed him on the way to the barn. He started cleaning the stalls vigorously. He wasn't surprised or angry, but he could not understand the reasons why he was prohibited from seeing Linda. He had no intention of ever talking Linda out of embracing the Amish way of life. He did not have romantic ideas about her. However, he did harbor thoughts of deeper feelings he had not felt before. To him, she was a very good friend he could talk to and pass the time with.

Aaron quietly entered the barn. "I know what is happening, Allen."

"Do you?" he said in a sarcastic manner.

"Ya," Aaron said kindly. "For Linda's sake, she must stay away from you."

"That's what everyone keeps saying."

Aaron stood firm in front of him and told him straight out, "My father beat her badly for meeting with you. If it happens again, he will beat her worse. I am afraid for her." Allen was stunned as Aaron turned away and walked out of the barn.

Allen chased him down angrily. "Why did you tell on her?"

"She was beaten two weeks ago. I told Mother because she would not beat her," Aaron said. "It is important she not see you anymore."

The thought of Linda being punished that way, tore at Allen's insides. Then to think she was still willing to take the chance to see him again filled him with tremendous emotion. "Aaron," Allen pleaded, "I must see her one more time." He nodded at him in hopes to gain a favor.

Aaron was not sure what Allen wanted from him. After a few seconds, he came up with an idea. He pointed down the road to the east. "Be at the four corners at seven tomorrow night. You won't have much time."

"I understand," Allen said as he clutched Aaron's forearm in a grateful gesture.

Allen watched from the barn as Clara and Aaron left the farm. He noted that Linda's mother appeared to be a kindly person. He could find no reason to dislike her.

Allen saw his grandfather was coming, so he went back to shoveling manure and tried to ignore his approach. Mr. Barber explained to him how the Amish religion was very strict about certain things they could and could not do. He explained that mixed relationships would never work.

"But we are too young to be romantic. Wow." Allen shook his head in wonderment.

"Things will change soon." He remembered his sons. "You kids grow up so quickly."

Allen looked away toward the stream. "You're right. We won't be children much longer."

Gerald had to tell him, "The stream is on the Hershberger farm. You are not to fish there anymore. You can fish off the bridge."

Later, Aaron took it upon himself to make the arrangements to get Linda to the four corners the following evening. The next morning, Aaron asked his father, "Can I take the buggy to the Miller farm for Bible study tonight?" This surprised John since they normally had to force Aaron to go to the studies, but he was agreeable to the request. Aaron looked at Linda and winked. She didn't think anything about the wink, except that he must have gotten something in his eye. "Linda wants to go as well. Is that all right if she goes with me?"

Linda's eyes popped completely out of their sockets. He quickly gave her a killing stare that frightened her. "Oh please, may I?" She answered, faking an excited reaction. She was afraid Aaron would tell Father if she didn't agree.

"What has gotten into the two of you?" their father asked with great delight.

"Renewed interest," Aaron explained.

"Renewed?" John asked with a smile. "Well, of course you may."

Linda didn't really want to go to the reading, but it seemed to be very important to Aaron. She was not very upset since it would not interfere with her seeing Allen on Thursday night.

After supper, Aaron was certainly showing signs of being nervous about what he had planned. She worked hard to finish quickly; Clara had to excuse herself to leave on time.

It was a three-mile trip to the reading. There was only a sliver of moon to light the way. Aaron had two lamps lit hanging on both sides of the buggy.

"So should I try to get you a seat next to anyone in particular?" Linda asked coyly.

"What?" he asked blankly. He was so nervous he wasn't listening properly to Linda.

"Maybe next to Rachel?"

"Rachel?"

Linda was confused at his blankness and decided to ask him directly, "Why were you so insistent about me coming along with you?" They were approaching the four corners. Aaron pointed out of the buggy toward the four corners. Linda looked carefully and saw a small figure of a person in the darkness. She looked more intently at the figure. As the slightest light from the lamps hit the face of the human figure, she knew in an instant it was Allen. Her heart leapt with excitement.

She remained calm and collected, however, so she wouldn't alert Aaron to her feelings. She smiled at him, and Aaron knew she was grateful to him.

"Hello," Linda said cordially to Allen.

"Hi," Allen replied. She started to climb out of the buggy, but Allen held his hand up to stop her. She sat back down disappointed. Allen then began to talk in a serious tone, "I'm sorry if you got into any trouble over me. I really didn't think it would be such a big deal."

"It shouldn't be a big deal," she answered. She knew it was a big deal and was surprised he knew of the trouble she had gotten into.

"Yeah," he said, "you would think we were lovers or something."

"I believe that is what they are afraid of."

"It's funny because I don't even like girls." When he said this, he could see a hurt look on her face. "I mean, except you. You're different." It was then that he realized that he did like her for more than a friend.

This thought crossed Linda's mind as well. She wanted to get out of the buggy and talk to him alone. She didn't want to involve Aaron in her problems any further than he already was. She started to get out of the buggy; this time, Allen helped her down.

Aaron began to squirm in his seat. "Don't be long."

"Just a few minutes, Aaron," she stated sincerely to ease his mind.

As Allen helped her down from the buggy, she accidentally fell into his arms. They were face-to-face, and Linda quickly spoke to break the intense moment. "These overgrown shoes, they are too big for me." He set her on her feet and backed away cordially. They walked away from the buggy until Linda was sure Aaron could not hear her. "Thursday night is all set. I have to bring my sister, though. Is that all right?"

Allen took a deep breath. "No, I can't see you then."

"All right, how about Saturday night?" Linda said excitedly.

"No." He stiffened his resolve to fight his feelings. "I can't see you ever again." She was confused. "Why?" she asked with some anger.

"I don't want you to get into trouble over me."

"I won't get in trouble. We'll just be more careful not to get caught. It isn't as big a deal as it may appear." Linda thought hard of how to convince Allen it would be fine. "The worst thing they would do is give me extra chores."

79

He couldn't live with himself knowing she would get beaten for seeing him. He had to do something to convince Linda not to want to see him. He wanted to see her very much, and it would be a lie to say otherwise. He had to do something drastic to put an end to their relationship.

What he was about to do would tear his heart out. He laughed. "I got you hooked, didn't I? You really thought I liked you. You thought that I would like a stupid little hooky girl. I hooked a hooky." He started to fake an evil-sounding laugh. "Get back in your pathetic little cart and go home, hooky girl."

Linda's smile fell from her face at these false words. Aaron also heard it, and at first he was mad, but then he understood what Allen was doing.

Linda looked him in the eye. "I know you don't mean that."

Allen could not look at her. "I mean it, stupid girl. Get out of here. Leave me alone." Linda stared at him. Her big round eyes did not blink but filled with tears.

"Why?" she asked.

Allen could no longer continue the horrible pretense he was acting out. He had to turn and walk away from her. As he walked away, he could hear her quietly calling out his name. His stomach turned, and his knees went weak. He never thought he would shed a tear for a girl, but his eyes blurred with moisture.

Aaron got out of the buggy and pulled on Linda's arm in an attempt to get her back into the buggy. She could only stand and watch Allen walk away, horrified at the sudden turn of events. "You can't mean that!" she said, tears streaming from her eyes down to her cheeks. Allen did not acknowledge her final call. "I know you can't mean that!"

Gently, Aaron pulled on her shoulders and kindly said, "I will take you home."

Linda did not want to go home, and Aaron knew they shouldn't return too early. They pulled the buggy into a small roadside park. As Linda cried, Aaron sat patiently, patting her on the shoulder. After a few hours, they returned home.

CHAPTER FIVE

Time Does Not Heal
the Wounds

Linda didn't believe for one minute that Allen really felt that way. She did her best to forget him for the next months and then for the next few years that followed. Even after years since she last saw him, she would often think of him. She wondered what he was doing and where he was. It was hard for her to stop thinking about him even though they had only met a few times. She could only remember he was the only boy she had a real friendship with, and it was wonderful.

Linda stopped attending school when she turned fourteen, which was normal for the Amish, and stayed home to participate in more chores in the house. She soon was doing meal preparations, much like Susan had done the last several years. Mary was taking care of the chickens, and Susan was doing more baking and sewing. Clara was still the main cook; she would often oversee the meal preparation but did less actual hands-on preparation.

When Linda was fifteen, she started to attend singings after Sunday church meetings. She would occasionally be courted by a boy, but most of the time, she was a tagalong with Susan. Linda was generally indifferent to any boy courting her. The boys took this indifference to mean she was not interested in them. Linda was reclusive and was often overlooked by the boys of courting age.

Susan often left home to visit friends and family. She would always be out on Saturday nights, even on church weekends, courting Amish boys. Linda asked about her relationships, but she was normally quiet about them. Linda noticed from time to time that Susan would say things that she had never heard before. She once described a garden a neighbor had grown as "sweet." Another time, she described one of their meals as "awesome." There were other things Susan did that were different, such as the way she walked. She did not say anything to anyone about the observations.

When Aaron was eighteen, he was baptized and took his first communion. The family was expecting an announcement of an engagement to a fine Amish girl, Rachel Miller.

Jacob married a very wonderful girl and moved away to Ohio to start a farm. Her family had two uncles living there. One of them had never married and wanted to have Jacob and his wife take over his farm someday. They had one son and were expecting another child soon.

Isaac, the oldest of the brothers, married Ruth Lapp and would be expecting the farm to be given to him when their father retires. Isaac worked extra hard on the farm, but with that, he worked with a bit of arrogance, irritating Aaron. Isaac and Ruth had two children, two and three years old, and were expecting another in a few months.

Clara ran her kitchen as usual but with the addition of Ruth to the family. Ruth took it upon herself to order the others around. Susan hated her. It was not that she was mean, obnoxious, or bossy, it was the authority given to her in the kitchen. Linda was understanding of Ruth's situation, which further irritated Susan.

Grandpa Levi had a stroke and could no longer work the farm. He did a few things he could and was cared for by the rest of the family. Joel was still too young to work the fields, so he assisted Grandpa.

When Linda was sixteen, another Amish family moved into the area. They had a son named Luke. Luke was a year older than Linda, and he took a fancy to her right away. Linda found he was very nice and a good conversationalist. He talked about nature in the same way she did. Hearing Luke talk about the water and wildlife brought back memories of the serenity of the stream. The first singing they went to was delightful for her. This was the first time she felt happy again with a friend that was a boy.

Luke found himself infatuated with Linda and often would meet her on Saturday nights when there was no church the following day. Susan and Linda were both being courted by gentlemen at the same time.

One warm summer Saturday night, the two girls waited in their rooms after dark for a signal. They watched carefully out the window, with the wind blowing in their faces. It felt as though they were being brushed with a feather. They could hear trees rustling in the wind and crickets calling through the still night. They could hear croaking from frogs in a distant pond.

Their parents went to bed early when there was no church to allow the girls their opportunity to be courted. Courting was a private, personal thing between the young couples. The parents would encourage the process by staying out of the way.

Susan didn't always wait with Linda for her courter. She would often, in the past, take off on her own before it got dark to meet her courter halfway. She informed Linda that they had more time together if they would rendezvous somewhere. This was one night Linda wanted Susan to wait with her. It was a quarter moon, so there was just a hint of moonlight cast over the front yard.

Soon, they could see a lantern being waved back and forth near the front gate. The lantern went from side to side and then up and down. "That's Jobe," Susan said. Earlier that day, Susan had cleared a nice place for them to lie in the grass to watch the stars. She leaned out the window and waved at him. She left the bedroom very quickly and quietly. Linda watched out the window to see them walking across the lawn toward a secluded area behind the barn.

It was not very long before another lit lantern appeared by the front gate. Unexpectedly, the lantern went out. She looked intently out the open window for her courter. The house cast a deep, dark shadow in the front yard, so dark she couldn't see anything below her. She was leaning out the window to get a better look when her face was pelted by tiny rocks. There were tinkling sounds all around her. There were now little tiny pebbles all over the bedroom floor.

She yelled out softly, "Stop it, Luke. You're pelting me with rocks."

"Sorry," a voice emanated from out of the vast darkness below. She made her way down the stairs and out the back kitchen door.

Luke waited outside the back door. "Where should we go tonight?"

"Follow me. I have a great place," she said excitedly.

"Sorry about the pebbles," Luke said.

"Not as sorry as I am." Linda laughed. "It probably woke everyone in the house."

"It was just a few pebbles," he reasoned.

"They're all over my floor," Linda scolded him. "Couldn't you have just whistled a happy tune or something?" Linda led him through the backyard to a field with shoulder-high corn. The leaves of the tall, wet stalks had collected a great deal of summer dew. It splattered in their faces and soaked their clothes. She held tightly to his hand as she led him through the corn. They reached the grove of trees that lined the stream, and Linda dragged him through the brush and branches.

"I'm sopping wet," he complained.

"So am I," she agreed with great excitement. "Isn't it invigorating?"

"Well, there is a little pain involved."

She abruptly stopped and faced him. "Man or mouse?"

"Huh?"

She turned and looked him straight into his eyes. "Are you a man or a mouse?"

"Man," he said firmly, knowing he dare not admit anything else. The eerie darkness made him feel like a mouse, ready to be preyed upon by a cat, or maybe a large owl.

"Good." She dragged him farther through a brushy area toward the stream. She had not been there since Allen, and she was determined to create new memories. This adventure has now become a quest to share time with Luke. He followed blindly into the abyss of Linda's past.

"How do you know where you're going?" he asked her.

"I just know," she said. She had never been to the stream at night, and she was disoriented. She looked around, hoping to get her bearings. "It doesn't matter. We'll get there." She clutched his hand harder, pulling him in the most logical, torturous direction.

They got through the brush and found themselves on the edge of the stream. The trees didn't look familiar silhouetted in the pale moonlight, but she knew they were there. Feelings of peace and freedom washed over her. Luke quickly understood why Linda had dragged him there. The rustling of the leaves in the trees, the crickets, the frogs made up nature's song. Moonlight shimmered in the small ripples on the water.

Linda pointed to her left. "There is a place we can dangle our feet in the water. It's not very deep." They stepped carefully through thick brush at the stream's edge. She found the perfect spot to sit and flattened the grass with her hands. The weeds made a comfortable cushion to sit on.

Luke joined her as she unlatched her shoes, removed her socks and dangled her feet in the water. "That's cold." Luke said. Linda felt more awake and alive than she had been in years. She looked at Luke in the shadows next to her, and memories of the past seemed to fade away. They dangled their feet in the water and talked all night. Their adventure came to an end when they saw a dim glow in the eastern sky. Luke found Linda to be fun. "Wow," he said, "you're not like what everyone said."

Linda looked at him. "Why do you say that?"

"Oh nothing." He shrugged his shoulders. "It didn't matter to me what they said."

"What were they saying?" Her voice was stern. The leaves from the corn in the field slapped at them as they walked through it.

"They just thought you weren't very exciting, that's all."

"Specifics please."

"Huh?"

"Come on, more details." Luke did not know what to say. "Oh, forget it," she said. The night had been wonderful. As they approached the barn, they heard the rooster crowing.

Before Luke departed, he placed his hands on her shoulders, pulled her face toward his, and whispered, "I think I like you." He turned and walked down the driveway and then down the country road. She watched his figure shrink down the road and thought she might like him too. Now she knew there was a chance for her to love and be loved.

Luke visited Linda whenever he could. They became good friends and talked about someday having a big family and running a farm together. Linda was seventeen by now and nearing the age to be baptized and devote her life to God.

Her older sister, Susan, was reluctant to devote herself to God and her religion. Her parents understood this was an important step in her life. They were confident she would make the expected commitment when the time came.

One night, as they lay in bed, Susan whispered, "I have to tell you something."

Linda turned on her belly and raised her head. "You sound scary."

"It is scary. I've"—she stopped talking as tears welled in her eyes—"I've decided to leave home and move in with Trish."

"What!" Linda sat up in her bed. "Do you understand what that means?"

"Ya," Susan answered coolly, "I have thought about it for a long time."

"Do you *really* understand what that means?"

"Ya." Susan got out of the bed and began to twirl around the room. "You need to realize there is a whole wonderful world out there that we can't have here. I can't live like this the rest of my life."

"Do you know what you're saying?"

"Of course I do. I'm the one saying it."

"I mean, I will not be allowed to talk to you anymore. None of us will be allowed to talk to or look at you ever again. You will be shunned by all."

Susan stopped her happy dance, and her arms fell to her side. "That's the only thing I don't like. I will miss my family."

"Aren't you scared?"

"Ya. It is such an exciting world out there. I want you to come with me."

Linda's eyes popped open. She was stunned at Susan's request. "I know this is a bit sudden for you, but trust me."

"I don't know anything about the worldly world."

"Come with me tomorrow night. I'll show you."

"Luke is coming over."

"Tell him you can't make it."

"What will I tell him?"

"You have to watch Joel while Mom is visiting friends."

"I can't tell him a lie like that."

"Then tell him the truth. Tell him you're going with your sister to a friend's house."

Linda thought it would be the perfect excuse. "I could tell him that." Then she remembered her objective was to discourage Susan from leaving the Amish way of life.

"The fair is in town. It will be fun. I'll take you to Trish's, and we'll dress you up like an English girl." Susan's eyes sparkled.

Linda was appalled. "Dress me up?"

"I met this boy a few weeks ago, and we made out."

"What?"

"We made out." Susan realized Linda didn't understand. "We kissed. If you come along, you might make out."

Linda did not speak for a few seconds. "But I don't want to make out, kiss, or anything."

"That's all right. You don't have to kiss." Susan hopped over to Linda's bed. "You don't have to do anything. You can go where you want, whenever you want. You won't have to live this sheltered backward way of life. You may have to get a job somewhere, of course. But you get paid, and when you are not working, the rest of your time is your own. You can see your beau whenever you want to and not have to worry about seeing him at night in secret. You can see several different beaus if you want. You will love living in the real world. You don't have to walk or ride in a buggy. You can get into a car and drive wherever you want to go in just minutes. Trish has one, and we go all over in it. She has a job at Patty's Pizza Place, and she is going to get me a job there."

"Patty's Pizza Place?" Linda was amused by the name.

"It's a place where they make pizzas. Tasha calls it the Triple P."

"What kind of place is pizza?"

Susan laughed. "Pizza is not a place. It's a food you eat. It's like a big pie, but flat. You eat it hot, right out of the oven. You can even go to different states and visit our relatives. Of course, we won't have any relatives to visit because they won't have anything to do with us."

"Wait," Linda interrupted loudly but then dropped her voice to a whisper. "Stop with the 'us' talk. I haven't agreed to run away."

"It's not running away, Linda. It's called freedom."

Linda knew that if Susan left, it would be as if she died. "You're really going to do this?"

"Ya," Susan said solemnly. "I leave two weeks from today. I won't be back."

"Ever," Linda said sadly.

"I can't come back. You know how it is."

"You can live among the English and still embrace our faith."

"If I were going to embrace our faith, I wouldn't want to live out there. They don't understand it out there." She paused to think. "It just wouldn't work."

"This can be the real world." Linda tried to get control of Susan's thoughts.

"You go out with us, and you will understand. You can't say anything about something you know nothing about. I mean, there are about a billion of them living out there and ten thousand of us." There was a banging on the floor under their feet.

"Quiet up there!" Father's voice bellowed. They had forgotten to keep their words to a low whisper. They were confident the content of their conversation was still secret. Susan lay down and whispered, "Please come with us tomorrow night, just this once."

"I'll think about it," Linda said. "Now be quiet."

A whirlwind of thoughts ran through her head. She understood why her sister was excited, but she wanted no part of the English world. Linda decided that the only way to have any influence on Susan was to go with her the next night. The thought of going frightened her, but the fact Susan was leaving made it imperative for Linda to accompany her.

The next morning, Susan looked cautiously toward Linda so no one else would see. She was anxious to hear if Linda would go.

Finally, knowing the suspense was killing Susan, Linda nodded. Susan smiled. She was ecstatic to have the opportunity to show her sister the real world. Susan informed her parents she was going for a long walk after dinner and wasn't sure where she would end up.

She then looked to Linda and asked her in the presence of the whole family, "Linda, would you like to accompany me?"

"I would love to," Linda replied exuberantly.

Mary asked, "Can I go?"

"No," her two older sisters replied together. Mary was disappointed, but Grandfather Levi reminded her they were going to read that night. The two older sisters flew through their chores and then were off to Trish's.

Susan began to talk so quickly it appeared to Linda that she never took a breath. "I usually wear something of Trish's, but the last time I was there, I gave her some money to buy some clothes of my own. Trish has a younger sister, Tasha, who may be more your size. She has well-developed bosoms, but maybe we can fill you in a bit."

"Fill me in?" Linda looked down at her chest.

"You know, make them bigger," Susan said. "We'll stuff something in there."

Linda peered down at her chest once again in wonderment. As they approached the house, a buggy came over the hill toward them.

"We'll just keep walking past the house until they are out of sight," Susan said. The girls both smiled and waved as the buggy passed them. The passengers politely nodded to them. Once the buggy was well past them, they stopped and backtracked to Trish's house. Susan was trying to get Linda to pick up her pace.

As they reached the front door to Trish's house, Susan said, "Listen carefully." Susan pushed a small lighted button on the doorframe. Linda could faintly hear two bells ring inside the house. She refused to be impressed about anything on this ill-advised adventure. Susan said, "Isn't that cool." Linda then pushed the button. She did not feel any cool feeling, so she pushed the button again. Susan noticed her pushing it again. "Stop that."

Soon, a young boy about twelve years old opened the door. "Knock it off. We hear you, all right," he said coarsely. When he saw them, a disgusted look came over his face, and he said, "Oh god, there are two of them." He turned around and walked off, leaving the door half open. Susan opened the door the rest of the way and escorted her sister in. Linda was hit with a blast of cool air from inside the house. She then understood what the cool Susan mentioned earlier was about. She was reminded of a cool blast on her face when opening the icebox at home. Only this immersed her whole body in cool air.

"That's Justin, Trish's brother. He doesn't like me," Susan said. "He doesn't like anyone that is associated with his sisters."

"I see," Linda said. She could hear and feel a deep, steady, thumping noise that made the house vibrate. The pulsating noise ominously emanated from above them. There was a brightly colored painting in the entry hall, which caught Linda's eye. It was a picture of a large body of water on the right side of the picture and a sandy beach with trees with large, drooping leaves. As she walked, she felt something squashy under her feet. She was walking on a spongy surface of multicolored yarn. It felt like she was walking on soft grass.

They entered a kitchen and heard a man's voice. Linda looked around but didn't see any man, only a device built into the wall where the voice seemed to be coming from. There was a multicolored wall with little pictures of exotic animals all over it. The kitchen was much brighter than Linda was accustomed to. It seemed nearly as bright as if they were outside in the sun. She noticed a lit-up replica of the moon on the ceiling.

A middle-aged woman entered the kitchen. "Oh, hello."

"Hello, Mrs. Jared," Susan greeted her.

Mrs. Jared smiled. "Who's your friend?"

"This is my sister, Linda."

"Hello, Linda," Mrs. Jared said. There was a loud crash and screaming from somewhere in the house. Mrs. Jarred rolled her eyes. "Sorry, it's just the kids fighting again." She stepped out of the kitchen and screamed, "Knock it off! We have company!"

"Isn't this great." Susan looked to Linda with the greatest excitement.

"Ya, I can't wait to see more." Linda regretted being there. She recalled the crushed look on Luke's face when she told him she wouldn't see him that night.

"I know," Susan said excitedly. "You never know what is going to happen next. Can you see Mother yelling out like that? They are so free-spirited." Linda was indifferent to Susan's overenthusiastic rhetoric.

What kind of free spirit do they have? Linda thought to herself. "She wouldn't have to yell at us like that because we wouldn't be acting like that," she retorted. Susan paid no attention to her comment.

When Mrs. Jarred no longer heard any screaming, she turned back to the girls. "Trish is upstairs, listening to her stereo, as if you couldn't tell. I'm thankful it's not Pink Floyd again."

"Come on," Susan said as she pulled Linda back down the hall over the spongy floor and up the stairs. The steps were a shiny oak wood that Linda thought for sure were wet. She hesitated a moment as Susan started up the steps. "They're not wet. They're always like that."

Linda gingerly took one step, then another and, since she didn't want to get separated from Susan, quickly ran up the rest of the steps. The steady pounding noise was getting louder as they proceeded down a hall. Linda noticed a small room that she had only heard about being in houses. "Susan, is this an outhouse, inhouse?"

"Ya," Susan raised her eyebrows a bit. "Crazy isn't it?"

"Ya," Linda sniffed the air. "Do they use it?" Susan smiled at her and continued down the hall.

CHAPTER SIX

A New Look for Linda

Susan stopped at the door where the constant thud was emanating from. There was a sign on the door that read *Enter and Die*. Linda's heart pounded in fear after reading the sign.

Susan shouted so Linda could hear her over the thumping noise, "She wouldn't hear me knock. Plug your ears!" As Susan opened the door, they were blasted by a noise that vibrated their insides. Linda could barely hear Susan yell out "Turn it down!"

A girl dressed in bright yellow-and-orange clothing flashed by the door. Soon, the pounding subsided to a mere annoyance. "I love the Arrhythmics," the girl said. She was slightly taller than both Susan and Linda. She was full-figured, with stringy shoulder-length, blonde hair. Linda thought the girl must be Trish, but she kept quiet. This girl popped back into view with a bright smile, and her eyes fixed on Linda. "Is this who I think it is?"

"Ya, I mean, yes, yeah, or whatever," Susan said. "She wants to go out with us tonight. So do you think you can fix her up?"

Trish looked at her wrist, which Linda could see had a watch with a strap around it. "We had better get started right away." She gestured for them to enter the room. "Come on in." As Linda passed her, Trish stuck her head out the door into the hall. "Tasha!"

There was a faint, distant yell from down the hall. "What!"

"Get in here. I need your help!" Trish closed the door without waiting for an answer. She quickly crossed the room to a silver-and-black box, turned a knob, and the noise that had been coming from it went silent. She turned back to face Linda. "First of all, we have to get your clothes off." Linda looked to Susan, who was already removing her apron and bonnet. Linda was reluctant to do anything. Susan looked at her, knowing Linda wasn't privy to the procedure to be exposed to the other world as a worldly person.

Susan had changed over several times over the last few years and had not given much thought how she would introduce Linda to the procedure. "Take off your basics. Then you can change in the bathroom." Linda looked puzzled, so Susan added, "The indoor little barn, it's in there." She opened the door and pointed to a room across the hall. Susan shook her long, brown hair out of its tight bun. Her hair fell lazily over her shoulders and down her back.

"It doesn't smell like a little barn," Linda expressed.

Susan closed the bedroom door. "I know," Susan said excitedly, "you're going to love this world." She asked Trish, "Did you get my clothes?"

"Yup, check it out." She crossed the room to a dresser, opened the bottom drawer. She pulled out a pair of short dark-blue pants. "These will show off your nice butt. Guys like a nice-lookin' butt." She smiled. "I got a nice, modest blouse. Just like you wanted."

"These are great." Susan looked over her pants. "They have pockets. That is so cool."

Trish carefully pulled out a neatly folded blouse out of the bottom drawer. It was light green, short sleeved, and with buttons up the front. Linda turned and was shocked to see her sister completely naked. Trish threw some thin material that looked like a pink handkerchief to Susan. Then she threw her a garment with thin white straps and two small round cups. Linda had never seen her sister naked outside of a bathtub. And the fact that Trish was in the room was awkward for her. There was a knock on the door.

"Who is it?" Trish called out.

"Tasha."

"Is Justin out there?"

"No," Tasha replied.

"Come on in then."

Susan, to Linda's surprise, was placing her legs in holes that appeared to be in the pink handkerchief. Tasha entered the room and saw Linda had come along. "There's two of them? Justin said there were two of them, and I called him a liar." She looked at Linda pleasantly. "Hi." Linda's eyes were drawn to Tasha's chest, having been warned earlier about it. She now understood what Susan was talking about. Tasha was very chesty, and there was no way she would be able to fill out any of her clothes.

Tasha was shorter and huskier than her sister. She was wearing a tight-fitting white top showing a substantial amount of cleavage. Linda's eyes seemed drawn to her chest. Tasha noticed her gaze with great amusement. Linda embarrassingly averted her eyes from Tasha's chest. "It's okay," Tasha said, "everybody has to check them out."

Linda's eyes shifted to her sister wrapping the strappy thing around herself. She was impressed when Susan reached around behind herself to fasten it.

"This is my sister, Linda," Susan informed her, then stumbled getting into her pants.

Linda was amazed that her sister knew how to put on men's pants.

"Hi, Linda," both Tasha and Trish said together. They looked at each other. "Sisters!"

Tasha looked at Linda. "I don't know if we'll have a pair of pants to fit you. You are so skinny."

"She would probably prefer a modest dress, if you have one." Susan was looking out for her sister, to some extent.

"A modest dress," Trish said blankly, not very confident they had a modest dress. "Sure, not a problem."

"How about the green dress I wore about a month ago," Trish suggested. "You know, the one that I wore to the church social?"

"The dog got it," Tasha said bluntly.

"How about that purple skirt of yours and a nice white blouse? You know, the one you wore for the play."

"It got ripped the other night." Trish looked at her blankly. "I told you about it yesterday."

"Oh yeah, Bobby," Trish remembered.

"Is there anything else that would work?" Susan hoped to reaffirm modest apparel.

"I don't know. Let me look." Tasha shook her head. "She's so skinny." She abruptly left the room.

"You can undress down to your undergarments," Susan instructed quietly, and Linda proceeded to remove her outer garments, shoes, and socks. "We'll need to get her some shoes, maybe those red pumps. I think they will fit."

Linda mouthed the word *pumps* and thought what kind of pump they were talking of.

"Yeah, they may work. I'll get 'em." Trish turned and walked into a large closet.

Susan had her worldly clothes on now and looked completely out of character as far as Linda was concerned. She could hardly recognize her own sister, whom she had grown up with. Trish returned from a closet carrying a pair of slippers. She placed them down at Linda's feet.

"I am going to wear slippers?" Linda asked.

Tasha laughed. With a smile on her face, she said, "They're not slippers. They're pumps." Linda thought she had heard her right but could not imagine pumping anything with them. She quickly realized that it was a name of a type of shoe.

"You will have to go braless. There just wouldn't be anything that would fit properly," Trish said.

"What?" Linda asked blankly.

Susan reached into her shirt and pulled out one of the straps of her skimpy top. Linda saw what she meant and looked down at herself. "What's wrong with this?"

"Honey," Trish said, "women don't wear girdle things anymore."

Trish stopped for a moment and studied what she was wearing. She tipped her head a bit. "Well"—she continued to think—"you could always tell him you broke some ribs. I don't think any guy would know what a rib-wrap thing looks like."

Linda's eyes opened widely at the thought of telling "him." She thought to herself, *Why would I be telling a person anything about my under things.*

Trish added, "We'll make sure you have a blouse that covers you nicely. Then you won't have to say anything unless you get lucky."

"That will work," Susan said. She knew what Trish meant by getting lucky but did not want to upset Linda.

Linda, on the other hand, was totally lost. "What do you mean lucky?"

Trish looked at her sweetly, suddenly remembering these girls were pure in nature and not familiar with certain terms and behavior. "In case you score."

"We are going to play games?" Linda asked, which was followed by a great burst of laughter from Trish. "What would that have to do with my undergarments?"

Trish chuckled while raising her eyebrows. "Strip poker maybe." She realized Linda needed reassuring that everything would be all right. "I'm sorry, but we are just going out to have fun. We're not going out to get lucky or anything."

Linda nodded meekly and quietly said, "Good." She still did not understand but did not want to appear to be so uninformed. There was a knock on the door; then it opened. Tasha quickly entered with some clothes in her hands.

She looked at Linda. "You'll have to take off the bloomers, sweetie." Linda's lost look amused Susan.

"Your undergarments," Susan explained.

Linda looked down at her bottoms and slowly unhitched them, and they fell down at her feet. Tasha held up a red skirt in one hand and a white blouse in the other. She took one look at Linda's legs and blurted out, "Oh my, girl, we are going to have to shave your legs."

Trish looked more closely at Linda's legs. "Wow!" Trish looked astonished. "They are worse than yours were, Susan."

Linda looked at her legs. She said meekly, "Shave my legs? I can't shave my legs."

"Don't worry, Linda," Susan reassured her sister. "Look, I shaved mine nearly three years ago." Susan stuck out her clean-shaven leg.

"My legs are always covered. No one ever knew."

Tasha said, "If we don't shave them, you will have to wear really dark nylons."

"Well, it may be dark enough that no one will notice," Trish reasoned.

"It would probably be best to use nylons for tonight," Susan said. "If she chooses to be a permanent member, that's when she should shave."

Trish then asked Tasha, "Is that Mom's skirt?"

"Yupper," Tasha said. The skirt had a shiny black belt around it. The blouse had a pattern in it made from black thread stitching. Tasha looked at Linda's full undergarment apparatus and said sympathetically, "I didn't know you were hurt. Is it your ribs?"

Trish got excited about the comment. "See, the broken-rib story would work great. You would get a lot of sympathy that way."

"The granny panties aren't good," Tasha said. "If you are going to wear them, you had better make sure you keep this skirt down. And, if things get going, you had better get them off before they are discovered. It would be a big turn-off."

Linda looked to her sister for an explanation. Susan looked at her and shrugged her shoulders. Susan knew what they meant but didn't want to tell her. She feared that Linda would choose not to go with them. Linda studied the belt for a minute and discovered how it worked. She had watched her sister button her blouse earlier, and from that, she figured out how to button her own buttons. She fumbled around with each button until she got to the top one. There was a hole for a button but no button to go into it.

She quietly said to Tasha, "There's no top button."

Tasha looked her over. "You're all twisted, sweetie." She reached over and began to unbutton her shirt. Linda felt really weird about that but went along. Tasha then buttoned the bottom button. "Okay, you're all lined up." Linda buttoned up again and came out even.

Tasha reached behind Linda to detach the clip holding her hair up. The long, brown hair fell neatly over her shoulders. "Wow, you have very beautiful hair. We have just a few knots to get out."

Trish looked quickly at the clock. "We may have time."

"Tasha," Trish directed, "you take care of her face, and I'll work on her hair."

Linda looked to Susan once again. "Why do we have to go through all of this?"

"We can't have anyone recognize us."

"Oh. There wouldn't be anyone we know at the fair, would there?"

"Not necessarily. There may be some non-Amish people that may recognize us," Susan said as she dabbed at her eyes with a stick. "There are some modern farmers that may know us."

Trish started running a hairbrush through Linda's hair. Linda grimaced a few times as the brush caught a few loose knots tugging her hair back. Tasha brought out some thin, dark-brown stockings.

Linda looked at the all-shrunk-up stockings. The stockings appeared to be a size that would fit a large doll. "I'll never fit into them."

Tasha smiled. "They expand, sweetie, trust me." The phrase "Trust me" gave Linda a sense of instability. She stretched the stockings in a gesture to demonstrate their elasticity. She then handed Linda the stockings. "Point your toes into them and work it up to your thigh then to your waist over those granny panties. The whole process should take three minutes and fifteen seconds." Tasha looked at her watch. "Go!"

Linda jumped in fright and quickly tried to put her foot in the nylon. "It's all right. I was just kidding about the time. But you need to hurry."

Linda continued to try getting the nylons on properly. She would pull up on the stockings, but they would bind up. She was not having much success, and after several minutes, Tasha had to help her. Once they got the nylons on, Tasha pulled gently on Linda's arm. "Sit over here."

Trish brushed at her hair as they walked a few feet to the edge of the bed. Linda kept pulling down on her skirt in fear that she may be revealing something. She could only get the skirt to stretch down to her knees. It seemed to ride up her thighs when she moved the slightest bit. This was very uncomfortable for a girl who only wore long-length clothing.

"This isn't going to work," Tasha said. "I need better lighting." She looked to Susan. "How are you coming along, Susan?"

"I am about done, I think."

"Do you think we can borrow the seat and mirror please?" Tasha asked.

"Of course," Susan answered.

Susan got up from a stool in front of a mirror. Susan moved the chair to one side of the large mirror. Tasha guided Linda across the room to the dressing table. There was a mirror and a row of bright, glowing white spheres hanging on the wall. As Linda sat down, she drew her legs together and pulled her skirt down. She started to look at the mirror, interested in seeing what she looked like. Before she could get a good look at herself, the chair spun around. Tasha pulled her around to face her. "Close your eyes."

Linda closed her eyes and then felt a brush going over her eyelids.

"You are the homeliest girl I have ever seen."

Linda wished she was home.

Trish spoke, "Where's the curling iron?" To these words, Linda had visions of a curled iron stake. They used them at the farm to stake down things sometimes. She reassured herself that Susan would not let any bad things happen to her. "We are running out of time." Trish had a metal pipe in her hand. She handled it like a knife with a kinked-up black string. When Linda first saw the curling iron, she thought for sure that it was a very clean small cattle prod.

"We really need to clip the eyebrows," Tasha said.

"No, you can't do that," Susan said firmly. "I know we have been doing it to me for a few years. But Father may notice it, and Mother would certainly notice it."

Trish asked, "I thought you were encouraged to experience the English ways so you would be sure you want to devote yourself to God?"

"That is true that we need to be sure of our convictions. But we keep it a secret as to what we do so we are not judged on our actions. Well, that is the way I figure it should be."

"Okay," Tasha said, "how about we just clip these really long ones? Maybe we can just trim it a bit."

Linda felt a painful tug on her forehead, and her skin snapped back on her head. "Ow."

"Sorry," Tasha sympathized. "Gotta do it."

Linda muttered "Ow" after each tug. Soon, tears trickled down her cheeks.

Tasha then started to rub Linda's forehead with a soft flesh-colored pad. "Close your eyes please." Linda closed her eyes once again. Then Tasha moved the pad around her eyes and cheeks in a circular motion. Meanwhile, Trish played with her hair. Tasha's hand rolled over her chin and ended with several long strokes down her neck. The tugging on her hair was accompanied by a clicking noise behind her.

"Your hair doesn't curl very easily," Trish informed her.

"Sorry," Linda said weakly.

"I wish we had time to wash your hair. It would be more manageable."

"You have very pure skin. It is a bit darker than Susan's," Tasha said as she started to brush Linda's cheeks with a soft brush. "You have no freckles or pimples. Just a small mole, right there." Tasha grabbed something from the table. She felt a dab of a cold substance on her mole.

"I would leave it alone. Moles are sometimes considered sexy," Tasha said.

"I feel a bit chilled," Linda said as she tugged at her skirt once again. She certainly was not accustomed to wearing so little clothing. Her legs felt really strange, a bit tingly with the thin see-through stockings.

"You will feel warmer once we get outside," Trish said. "How's Susan doing?"

"Fine," she said as she looked at herself in the mirror, "you better have a look."

"Are you going to put your hair in a ponytail tonight?" Trish asked Susan then addressed Linda. "It's no use trying to curl your hair. We'll just put some nice waves in it."

"Yes, that will be much easier," Tasha agreed.

Linda then felt another softer brush touch her cheeks like Tasha was painting on her. Then she used a smaller, stiffer brush on the eyelids once again. She felt a poky thing just below her eye. This startled Linda, and she opened her eyes, and Tasha's face was within inches of her own. She felt more comfortable keeping her eyes closed.

Linda opened her eyes to see Tasha smiling. "Oh, hi again. Now hold very still." She was holding a black hairy stick nearly to her eye.

"What's that?" Linda asked in a frightened manner.

"Just eyeliner," Tasha said calmingly. "Now close your eyes once again and hold still please." Tasha tipped Linda's head back. "Hold still."

"Trying," Linda said. She felt the soft touch of a liner move across her eyes.

"Okay, open your eyes and hold very still." Linda pointed to Trish, who was deep in thought of curling her hair. "Trish, can you stop for a moment please." Trish stopped, and Tasha quickly began to brush very close to Linda's eye. Tasha could tell Linda was apprehensive about the proceedings. "Mascara, it darkens your lashes." Linda did not know why it was so important to darken the eyelashes, especially when they wanted to get rid of her eyebrows earlier.

"Linda, you have to be very particular to wash all this stuff off before you go home tonight," Susan explained to her.

Trish started to tug on her hair; that made Linda open her eyes. Tasha, whose face was just a foot away from Linda's, puckered her lips. "Do this, like a fish." Linda was amused at the face Tasha demonstrated and mimicked the ungainly, fish-looking face. Tasha took a pink stick and rubbed it on Linda's lips. "Now do this." Tasha put her lips together and tucked them in and out. This amused Linda again, but she did as she was told even though she felt silly doing it.

Tasha finished with her work on Linda's face and turned to Susan to check her face out. Tasha then said, "You did a very good job, Susan."

A few moments later, Trish said, "That is about the best I can do." The three of them stood back and looked at Linda. "Wow," Trish said, "you look absolutely hot."

Linda did feel a bit flushed. "I actually still feel cool."

Tasha looked at her. "That's precious."

"You do look beautiful," Susan said. "You are prettier than I am, by far." Both Tasha and Trish silently nodded in agreement.

Linda slowly turned to look at herself in the mirror, both excited and scared of what she might see. When she saw herself, she wasn't sure it was her. She moved her hands and arms around to make sure it was her. She felt guilty using the mirror, especially to see herself looking so artificial. She wasn't sure if she was beautiful or scary. She liked the way she looked. Her face felt numb and coated with frosting.

"Let's get going," Trish said. "Tasha, are you coming?"

"I hadn't planned on it." She looked at Linda. "It may be a very interesting night. I would hate to miss it."

Linda could not keep from looking at herself in the mirror. Susan noticed and asked, "You like it, don't you?"

"I'm hideous," Linda lied. "But in a nice way."

"Come on," Susan said as she helped her sister off the seat.

"I'll meet you all downstairs in the car," Tasha said as she left the room.

"Susan," Trish said, "I got you a purse." She brought out a dark-blue bag that looked very much like Tasha's.

"Great," Susan said, "thank you."

"What is that for?" Linda asked.

"You carry your necessities in it."

"Necessities?"

"Yeah," Trish explained, "money, makeup, pads, condoms, all the everyday things."

Tasha then came into the room with two small bags. "You can borrow one of my purses. Put your personals in it." Tasha handed Linda a small, red bag, again very similar to those that Susan and Trish had.

They made their way down the shiny steps to the front door. Linda felt very insecure about herself dressed the way she was. She tugged at her skirt several times before they even got to the front door. She flushed with embarrassment when Justin came around the corner from the front room.

He looked up and down at Linda. "You sure changed." Linda flushed even more but did not say anything to him. "By the way, Mom said you guys have to take me to the fair."

"She did not," Trish insisted.

"Yes, she did. Ask her."

"Where is she?" Tasha asked.

"She's not here. She went to the Morrises."

"Well, that leaves me in charge, and I say you are not going."

"I'll tell on you," Justin snotted out. He picked up an empty cardboard paper-towel tube. He put his mouth at one end and spoke through it. His voice bellowed out like a megaphone. "I'm tellin' on you."

"Shut up, you little twerp," Trish said.

"No," Justin megaphoned out, "I have to sell you something you really need. You need the Ronco fart filter. That's right, folks, the fart filter. You stick this wad of toilet paper up your ass, and voilà, it not only—"

Tasha wanted to stop her brother from saying anything else. "Shut the f—"

"Tasha!" Trish broke in.

"No siree, Bob," Justin continued to speak, "the fart filter will not only suppress your fart so it comes out slow and silent, it will also dissipate the deadly fumes from your colon."

"Will you knock it off," Trish insisted.

"Take me to the fair."

"No!" the two sisters said together.

He continued to speak into the tube megaphone. "The one great medical achievement of the fart filter is that it will relieve you of the nagging urge to take a crap. This could be good, if you have the diarrhea."

Tasha and Trish both grabbed an arm of Justin's, picked him up, and carried him out into the front yard toward a shed. "You asked for it, you little twit," Tasha said.

"No!" he yelled. "No! You can't do that."

"We are doing it," Trish said while she smiled. "You'll be fine. I will call Mom sometime and let her know that you are in the shed, again."

"No!" he kept screaming, "Mom said she would ground you if you did it again."

"We'll risk it," Trish said. They lovingly threw him into a shed, slamming the door quickly before he could get back on his feet. Tasha flipped the hasp and put a screwdriver through the hole to lock the shed door shut from the outside.

"That ought to hold the little jerk," Trish said. Linda was silent through the whole ordeal. Susan was impressed at how they calmly handled the situation. "Tash, remind me sometime tonight to call Mom and tell her."

"Yeah, maybe."

"No really, we can't leave him in there for very long."

"Okay," Tasha said disingenuously.

"You can't leave him in there," Linda pleaded.

"We have to, Linda," Trish explained. "He needs to be taught a lesson." Linda decided to give up even though she could hear Justin pounding on the shed door. She was convinced this was the way they did things in the English world.

The four of them walked over to a two-door red automobile. She remembered her father calling automobiles like that evil carriages. He referred to the trucks he rode in as work-related carriages. It was not allowed by the Amish religion to own automobiles, but they could ride in them. Susan went to the other side of the car with Trish while Tasha opened the door. Tasha reached in, and suddenly, the back of the seat tipped forward. This allowed a small path for Linda to get into the car's backseat. Linda looked at the car carefully before she got in. She had seen cars before but had never ridden in one like this.

Tasha gestured for her to get in. "Watch your head, sweetie." She placed her hand on Linda's head and pushed down on it slightly. "That's how the police do it. You can learn useful things when you get busted. "

Linda bent her body down and instantly felt she was exposing her backside when her skirt rode up her thighs again. She quickly put her hand behind her to pull her skirt down over her buttocks. She realized the skirt had covered her properly, but she wanted to be sure.

She lost her balance and fell face-first into the backseat. She scrambled to get her butt down in the seat. She didn't feel comfortable in any position at this time. Suddenly, the back of the seat in front of her came back toward her, startling her. Linda felt trapped in a deep pit. She forced herself to take a deep breath and closed her eyes.

"Belts," Trish called out as Susan fell back into the seat next to her. Linda was confused about belts, so she watched her sister pull a belt magically out of the seat over her shoulder. She then connected it to another belt that lay on the seat next to her. Trish looked back, "Fasten your seat belt, honey. I'm a terrible driver."

Linda looked over her shoulder to see if she had a belt to pull out of the seat. She grabbed it and pulled, but it slipped out of her hand snapping back into the seat.

"It's all right. Try it again," Trish said.

Linda grabbed it once again and pulled it out. This time she did not let go of it. She pulled it around her until it was long enough to reach the receptacle. "Now what do I do?"

"Boy meets girl," Trish said as she looked back at her.

"That goes in that," Susan pointed out. "Push till you hear a click."

Linda slid the one end into the other; there was a click as the belt latched. She was relieved and felt a bit safer to have the seat belt fastened.

Linda could see into the front of the car, where Trish was holding keys in her hand. She watched as Trish stuck the key in a hole, twisted her hand, and the car cleared its throat and began to vibrate slightly. There was a T-shaped stick protruding from a hump between the two front seats. Trish moved the stick back. Then suddenly, the car lurched forward, throwing Linda's head back against the seat. The car moved swiftly and powerfully down the short driveway, hitting a few bumps, making Linda gasp. She was thankful the seats in the automobile were much softer than the seats in their family's buggy.

The car turned out of the driveway and onto a county gravel road. There was a sudden burst of speed forcing Linda to sink back into the seat. She could hear gravel hit the sides of the automobile. Her first instinct was to get out of there as quickly as possible. That was not an option since she was strapped in a belt and Tasha was blocking the nearest exit. The other girls, including her sister, didn't seem to be too excited about anything. She decided if she was going to die, she wasn't going to complain about it.

Tasha had her window open, and the wind was blowing back into the car. The wind blew in her face, and her hair whipped around her head. Linda never had her hair down like this except to wash it. Now, having it so free gave her the strangest feeling. They seemed to glide along so fast that it made Linda feel like she was in a dream.

She saw Susan looking at her laughing. "Isn't this great?" she yelled.

Tasha yelled to be heard over the noise of the open window, "She has to drive really fast on these roads so dust won't stick to the car! We don't ride around in a dirty red Mustang!"

Linda wanted so badly to say she wanted to go home. It was too late to let her sister down now. She grabbed a handle she found above the window to her right.

"Roll 'em up!" yelled Trish. The two windows closed. The noise of the wind suddenly died. The noise from Trish's room returned surrounding her, thumping her insides.

Tasha looked back at Linda once again. "Your hair fell. I was afraid of that." Linda panicked and grabbed her hair in fear it had fallen out. She was relieved nobody appeared to have noticed her panic. Tasha turned around again. "I wouldn't be too disappointed. It still has some body to it, and it still looks all right, just a bit windblown, which is kind of cool." Linda noticed how cool the car was getting.

As she watched the trees, bushes, poles, and fences flying by her, she began to get a bit queasy. She determined it would be best not to look out the window at the fast-moving world. They slowed down a few minutes later, and the car stopped. Linda could see a small green light blinking on a panel in front of a round hoop Trish was using to steer the car. The hard left turn pushed Linda into the side of the car. This time, Linda emitted a gasp the others heard.

Susan and Tasha looked at her, and Tasha asked, "Are you all right back there?"

"Just lost my breath, that's all."

Tasha chuckled, "You're gonna love the rides."

"Great," Linda responded blankly, hoping to sound enthusiastic. The car was gliding along much smoother since they had turned on a hard-surface road. Linda was not sure what Tasha meant by rides, so she leaned over to Susan. "Where are we going?"

"The fair," Susan answered with a big smile.

"What exactly is the fair?"

"I don't know. But they say it is a lot of fun." She said excitedly.

The car sped down the road toward the nearby town. Trish said, "You can see the Ferris wheel." Trish pointed to a spider-webbed looking structure that was lit up in a great variety of bright colored lights. The sun was setting in the west, and it reflected off the metal structure of the Ferris wheel. Linda noticed a large red-and-white-striped, three-pointed tent to the right of the Ferris wheel. The sight of the Ferris wheel was impressive to Linda. Linda thought of how big, tall, and beautiful it was. She watched it intently as they drove slowly through a field where many automobiles sat neatly in a row in. Trish turned their automobile between two other automobiles. Linda was impressed on how beautiful the Ferris wheel looked. She could not stop looking at it as they drove through a mass of automobiles neatly set in rows. Trish drove her car in between two large trucks and stopped.

"It will be hard for anyone to see our car between these honkin' monsters," Trish said.

When the car came to a stop, Tasha swung the door open. She bopped out of the car with great excitement. Linda immediately noticed a great array of noises when Tasha had opened the car door. These noises seemed very strange to her, making her feel uneasy. She looked to Susan, whose belt snapped back into the backseat. She felt confident her sister would not get her into anything that would hurt her. She also reminded herself this was her only chance to save her sister from this world of mysterious things.

Tasha looked around briefly before she turned back to lift the seat forward for Linda to crawl out. Linda started to pull at her belt.

"Here, honey." Tasha leaned over Linda, her face just inches from Linda's. She reached down, touched the belt holder, and the belt magically retracted back into the seat. Linda squeezed her way out of the car and looked around. The place was bustling with people, lights, machinery, and noises of all types. There were couples of all ages, families, children of all ages, groups of girls, and boys. They were dressed in all colors and all types of thin clothing.

Linda did seem much cooler in a worldly person's clothing than the heavy Amish clothes. It was a pleasant feeling for her. She still could not help the feeling of being undressed and everyone looking at her. She pulled down on her skirt.

She felt if she loosened her belt, she could move the skirt down lower on her hips. Trish looked at her. "We should have gotten you a blouse that shows off your middle."

Linda nodded slightly. "Ya."

There was a group of boys sitting several cars down from them. They seemed to be watching the group of girls getting out of the red Mustang. One of the boys yelled to them, "I heard about you and Jeff, bitch!"

"Oh god," Trish said to Tasha when she realized who had yelled.

"Eat it, Phil!" Tasha yelled profanely back at the group of boys.

"Tasha!" Trish yelled at her, "please watch yourself in front of our friends."

"Sorry," Tasha said calmly, "he just pisses me off."

"Tasha!"

Tasha placed her hand over her mouth and sincerely stated, "Sorry, I'll just keep my mouth shut for the rest of the night."

"Like that will happen," Trish said mockingly.

Linda had no idea what they were discussing. She knew what *bitch* meant and agreed Phil should eat manure.

It warranted a response of some kind. The four of them walked closer to the lighted area.

Susan spoke to Linda. "It is normally not this vulgar, really." Linda nodded.

"We're getting a late start tonight," Tasha said.

"Nonsense, the night is still young," Trish expressed.

Linda could hear men yelling words she couldn't understand. They didn't appear to be angry yells. In fact, they had an excited tone to them. There were many other noises surrounding the fair. There were many sounds of rumbling motors and music of many types. She could hear a magnified voice saying things that didn't make sense to her although she could understand each word. "B fifteen" and then "G fifty-eight."

The variety of lights overwhelmed Linda, who was used to candles and kerosene lanterns. She knew some of the modern farms and many houses in town would be decorated in brightly colored lights like these in early winter.

The four young girls walked by a tent that appeared to have stuffed toys lined up behind a table. Linda looked right at the man yelling behind the table. He was dressed in a dirty, sloppy white shirt that had no sleeves. She could see sweat stains on his shirt. He appeared to not have bathed or shaved for several days. She wondered if he had just gotten married recently because he had a rough short beard. He looked directly at her. "Three tries for a buck, pretty lady." He pointed at her with a dirty finger. "I bet you could win! I'll give you one try for free. Come on, sweetie." He motioned for her to come to him. She began to walk toward the man.

Trish saw that Linda was reacting. She quickly grabbed her. "Don't listen to the carneys. It's the rides we want."

Linda thought it strange he would want her to give him a large deer. She was sure it meant something else, so she whispered to Trish, "What did he mean by *buck?*"

Trish smiled. "It's another word for a dollar."

Linda thought for a few seconds. "Slang word?" Linda had studied some slang in school and the use of slang by people in the English world.

"That's it exactly."

Linda was mesmerized, looking around seeing people screaming with looks of horror as they flew by her on the various noisy metal monsters. She was appalled at the sight of these people being tossed around and in such pain. What was most disturbing to her was that they seemed to be willing to be tortured with these large metal things. They were waiting in long lines to get tortured. She was most disappointed to see the victims were mostly younger children.

"Come on, let's get some tickets," Tasha said. The four of them went to a small building that had a sign saying Twenty Tickets for $10. Susan and Tasha both dug into their purses, pulling out some paper money. They handed this money to Trish.

Linda felt bad that she didn't have any money to give. She looked inside her purse, but there was nothing in it except a blue, foil-wrapped square item. She brought it out of the purse and began to study it. It was about two inches square and flat. There appeared to be an impression of a ring or something inside the wrap. Linda began to read in a whisper what it said, "Ultrasensitive, lubricated, protection that feels awesomely good."

Tasha saw what she was doing and quickly grabbed the pocket. "My God, girl, keep that under wraps." Tasha looked around. "And don't lose it. They are like gold." Linda backed away in shame. Tasha said, "I'm sorry, sweetie, I didn't know that was in there."

"I am sorry. I didn't bring any money," Linda said sadly.

Susan saw Linda was ashamed she had nothing to contribute. "It's all right, Linda. We all agreed to include you equally."

"You're our guest tonight," Trish said.

"Yeah," Tasha said. "Let's take a ride on the Scrambler." Linda smiled gratefully at the thought of being thrown around on one of the loud metal monsters, even though the monster ride's name resembled an egg meal.

Susan looked around at all the activity, noise, and excitement. "Isn't this exciting!"

Linda tried but could only meekly smile. "It is wonderful."

Susan could tell Linda was trying to enjoy herself but was truly uncomfortable. She dropped her smile. "It really means a lot to me that you are willing to do this."

Linda smiled more convincingly. "The night is young."

The four of them lined up at a gate to one of the motorized metal monsters that Linda thought was especially nasty. She continued to subconsciously pull down on her skirt, afraid she was showing too much leg. There was a two-rail metal ring around the metal monster. It also appeared to her that if you leaned on it, it would fall over. As they waited in line to get thrown about by the monster for several minutes, she watched people on the ride screaming in complete frightful terror.

Linda studied the apparatus as they waited to get on. It resembled a large, skeletal-looking metal spider. There were four large legs spread out over an area about the size of one of her mother's gardens. At the end of each of the four legs were four more legs. Each of those legs supported a metal box. Each box was filled with several screaming people, their faces distorted and blurred as they whizzed by. Many of them were girls whose long hair were wickedly being tossed about. That seemed tame compared to the sight of the victims' necks being snapped about like a rag doll.

Soon, the ride slowed down and eventually came to a stop. Linda began to get nervous as the people began to flip up the restraining bars imprisoning them in the seats. She noticed that many of them were happy and smiling. She was convinced they were relieved to have survived the ride. One boy asked the dirty man running the dirty motor if he could get right back on the ride. The dirty man gruffly told him to go around and get in line. The boy ran around to get in line. She concluded these people actually wanted to be thrown about in this manner.

The man came back to the line and began to take the tickets from people at the gate. Many of the younger ones would run to their seats. Trish handed the man several tickets and pointed at all three of her companions. Linda found herself running to keep up. She was afraid to get separated from the rest. If she were going to die, she didn't want to die alone.

Trish led them to one metal box then said, "Not this one."

"What's wrong with that one?" Tasha asked.

"It's missing the side pad," she explained as she darted for another one close by.

"Oh sure," Tasha said, "my big sister, always looking out for our best interest."

"Are we all going to get into the one box?" Susan asked.

"It will be tight but should be less bruising," Trish answered.

They were able to get to the next box just before a group of three younger boys. The boys didn't appear to be too disappointed; they just ran to another one. The four girls climbed into the box. It was apparent they were very tightly packed with Linda on the outside. Tasha pulled the restraining door shut. She had to lean over Linda to engage the locking mechanism, her breasts pressing against her shoulder. Linda lowered her shoulder as far down as she could to avoid the contact. There was no escaping the monster now.

The seat was metal and didn't feel very comfortable to Linda. Her arm was pinned against the side of the box. She was very thankful there was a pad there. The scrubby man came around and checked to make sure the latch was secure. Once he got back to his seat, he pulled back on the lever with two hands. Their box began to move slowly in a circular motion.

The ride slowly gained speed, and Linda felt herself being pushed into the side of the seat. They went around in a circle. Figures of people milling around at the fair came into focus, and just as quickly, they were gone. She felt her hands clenching to the side of the box while being crushed into the side of the box. She felt her hair flopping all over her face, and she noticed Tasha was being whipped by her hair from time to time. She saw the people in another seat coming right at her, and then they suddenly disappeared. The side of the seat began to dig into her arm as the speed of the ride continually increased. The weight of the other three girls was getting unbearable for her. Faces of people and objects were flashing in and out of her sight. The noise of the fair seemed to revolve around her. The whirling sight and sound began to make her dizzy.

Then the machine achieved a steady pace. She wanted to pray to God to get her off this thing safely. She dared not pull her hand away from the side of the metal box. Then, a few hours later, it seemed to her the motor and the spinning motion began to slow. Tasha, who had been screaming, was now moaning in disappointment that the experience was about to end. But the speed slowed very gradually.

Linda was anxious to get out of the seat before the machine stopped, but she didn't know how.

When the machine finally stopped, Tasha reached over to unlatch the door. "Let's head for the Tilt-A-Whirl."

The other three leaped out of the box and started to run toward the gate labeled Exit.

"You mean the Tilt-A-Hurl, don't you?" Trish said. Linda was slow to get out of the metal box. She walked slowly toward the exit, hoping to keep her balance.

Susan stopped and came back for her and asked, "Are you all right?"

"Ya," Linda said as she recovered from her dizziness."

"Isn't this great!" Susan turned away and ran off, not truly waiting for an answer.

They all walked over to the gate to get on the Tilt-A-Whirl. "You people are sick in the head," Linda announced loudly to the three other girls.

"You will like this one. It isn't as violent, but it's different," Trish reassured her.

As they stood in line waiting to board the ride, Linda noticed this one seemed to move a bit slower, and the seats appeared to be more comfortable. She might enjoy this one better than the last ride. She had to admit to herself that the ride was more tolerable as it went on. She might have even enjoyed the ride if it hadn't been so crushing.

Trish said, "This is the ride Jeremy got sick on last year."

Linda started thinking this ride may not be as good as she thought. She was overwhelmed and nervous with her adventure so far. She was feeling slightly queasy from the previous ride. She was beginning to hate her sister more for each minute that passed. This monster had several red-colored shells placed around the center circle. The shells were on small wheels similar to miniature railroad wheels on tiny tracks. These wheels would allow the shell to spin on a platform that moved around the middle circle in a mild wave.

The Tilt-A-Whirl began to slow. Linda's heart began to race with fear. As it stopped, the people got off. Most seemed happy and safe. Linda thought she was missing something since they all seemed to be enjoying the ride. But why were they all screaming just a few moments earlier when the machine was throwing them about? Once all the people had left the platform, they were allowed onto the platform. Linda found it difficult to walk on the uneven platform. She followed the three other girls to a shell, which they barely fit into. Trish pulled down an oval-shaped bar that went over their legs.

Tasha and Trish eagerly grabbed the bar in front of them. Susan grabbed the bar, which prompted Linda to do the same. Linda realized this was a new experience for Susan. She was excited at the prospect Susan may not be enjoying this. In that case, she would have a better chance to convince Susan not to leave the Amish life. Linda took hold of the rail tightly with a different sense of eagerness. Linda was hoping that it would be hell on earth for Susan and a pleasant experience for her.

The man operating the ride came around and checked if their bar was down and locked. Linda lost sight of him as he walked away. Soon, a motor roared, and the shell began to move, rolling freely around the circular track. Views of the surrounding fair began to whiz by.

Linda found herself leaning forward, pulling herself up by the handlebar covering their legs. Tasha yelled to her, "Sit back, relax!" Linda sat back and found it much more comfortable and relaxing. Soon, the ride got faster, and the shell they were in began to twirl around and around. Tasha and Trish both started screaming as they leaned one way; then they would shift another way in hopes to get the shell to spin faster. Susan began to shift with them as the twirling of the shell went around and around. Linda's back and head seemed to press against the back of the shell.

This ride seemed to last forever like the last ride. She was again greatly relieved to hear the motor slow its pace. As the ride ended, their shell began to spin around again and again.

When they were departing that ride, Tasha said, "Wow, we were really spinning that time. Jeremy would never have survived that."

"They seem to get shorter all the time," Trish stated, referring to the rides' time.

Linda didn't say anything until she was out the exit gate of the ride. "That was fun," she said as she proceeded to vomit violently on the grass. The three girls stood astonished at the sight. They looked on sympathetically. Susan felt bad, being responsible for her presence.

"Jeremy didn't throw up that badly," Tasha said.

Trish punched her sister on the arm. "Don't say that."

Tasha said with compassion to Linda, "We're going to get something to eat. Do you want anything?"

Linda nodded her head slightly as she continued to look toward the ground, and with misery and unusual sarcasm, she said, "Sure, love some." She had a cold sweat breaking out on her face. There was a stinging, nasty taste in her mouth. She felt absolutely miserable, embarrassed, and now she really wanted to go home. But she had no way to get home. She couldn't ask them to take her home after seeing how much they were enjoying this adventure. Her eyes began to tear up as she hunched over in complete misery. This was the worst day of her life.

Susan put her hand on her shoulder. "I'm sorry, Linda. I wanted you to have so much fun, and you are probably having a terrible time."

Linda weakly nodded. "It's all right." She took a deep breath before continuing. "I know how important it is for you to show me how great this life is."

Susan truly did feel bad and was going to ask Trish if she could please take her home. Tasha and Trish had left them to get something to eat. "I'll see if Trish can take you home."

"No," Linda lied, "I want to stay."

"Well, maybe you shouldn't ride any more rides."

"That would be nice."

"Join us at the food stand when you're feeling better." Susan left to join her friends.

Linda looked up as Susan walked away. Her attention was drawn away from her sister to a young man that was approaching the line her friends were in. She looked intently at this young man that was familiar to her. It had been many years, but she was sure it was an older Allen Barber. She was sure it was him, but she had to find out. She had to get up, compose herself, and find a way to talk to him.

The emotions she had fought to get out of her heart and mind for the last five years came flashing back. They flashed back with a whirlwind more turbulent than any of the rides she had been on. Her stomach was no longer sick with queasiness but sick with the love she once had for a boy who was forced away from her.

CHAPTER SEVEN

Dream or Nightmare

A white napkin blew past her, so she grasped it in her hand. She quickly wiped a bit of the sick from around her mouth. Grabbing a random napkin was certainly out of character, but she was desperate to be presentable to Allen.

He was in line with his friend just behind Trish, Tasha, and Susan. It was a stroke of luck. Linda walked slowly across the median between vendors and rides. She felt much better but still a bit tipsy. She stumbled slightly on some snake-looking black rubber thing that lay on the ground. She had to walk past Allen to get to her friends. Hoping he would not notice, she was not able to keep from glancing backward a few times. His build was smaller than she envisioned, but he was still taller than her. He was handsome with blue eyes that were open and caring, just as she remembered. His dark blond hair was short and stuck out like porcupine quills. Allen's friend, taller and with similar porcupine hair, gestured to a big tent where there was a strong voice that sounded as if God were speaking, inviting all to come inside. "Hey, Allen, want to play bingo?" They both laughed in amusement.

"Not a chance," he said. "That's for old fogies who can't handle rides."

Hearing this, Linda knew for sure this boy indeed was Allen. She was certain he would not recognize her dressed up and with frosting on her face; she didn't know what to do.

Allen checked his wallet for money. His friend noticed Linda's furtive glances and poked him, gesturing his attention to Linda. He looked up, smiled kindly, "Hi."

Embarrassed, Linda blushed and returned the greeting. "Hello," she said quietly then looked away. Her stomach fluttered at the memory of their first meeting when she had fallen into the creek. Then she remembered how he had treated her the last time they met, the hurtful things he had said, but she still felt the burn like a hot brand. She looked to the ground, not sure if she really wanted to be recognized.

Susan turned to Linda and looked at her. "Wow, you seemed to have gotten your color back. Want a corn dog?"

"Ya," she answered.

Susan leaned over and whispered in her ear, "When you are English, you need to say yes or yeah. Corn dog?"

"Ya, sure," Linda responded. She had to say something soon or lose the opportunity, so she blurted out, "What happened to your hair?" She knew immediately it was a stupid thing to ask.

The unexpected comment took Allen by surprise. "What's wrong with it?" he asked, running his hand through it.

Susan interrupted to save Linda from having to answer, "Here's your corndog."

She held up her corndog. "It's a corndog."

Allen smiled, amused at her simple-minded comment. "Yes it is." The girls grabbed her by the arm and pulled her away.

Linda heard Allen's friend say, "She was totally checking you out, dude."

Allen quietly said, "Yeah." He continued to watch her as they walked away. "She would be great if she wasn't mental."

Trish leaned close to Linda. "You were talking to the biggest nerd in town." The three girls snickered and moved away from Allen and his friend.

"What got into you?" Susan asked her. "Talking to a boy."

"I know him," Linda said excitedly.

Susan's eyes opened wide. "How do you know him?"

"I met him a long time ago." Linda was not sure she should tell Susan anything more.

Trish answered, "You know Allen Barber?"

Susan thought deeply for a moment before she started to ask, "How do you—" She paused as it suddenly clicked in her brain where she had heard that name before. Her mouth fell open. "Noooo," she said loudly. Tasha and Trish suddenly became more interested in the sisters' conversation. "Not Allen from the stream?"

"Ya," Linda said. "I mean, yes."

Susan sternly shook her head. "Stay away from him. He will only be trouble for you."

"Allen," Tasha and Trish said together and looked at each other in surprise. "We must be sisters!" Trish exclaimed. They spoke together again, "Allen is a Goody Two-shoes." And both girls laughed uncontrollably. Trish started to gag from all the laughter.

"Are you going to barf too?" Tasha asked.

Trish gagged and hacked out, "No."

Susan and Linda looked at them like they were growing antlers. Then they looked at each other and said at the same time, "Let's never do that."

Trish pointed a finger at them. "You two must be sisters." Trish and Tasha burst into uncontrollable laughter once again. They laughed so hard that both Susan and Linda couldn't help but join in.

Tasha finally calmed down enough to say, "Allen wouldn't dream of doing anything bad or fun with your sister. He's harmless." The group started to walk aimlessly through the fairgrounds, munching on their corn dogs.

"Yeah, a real brain nerd. He aces everything," Trish added.

"He saved my life," Linda said in his defense.

Trish and Tasha stopped walking in pure astonishment at that statement. "Allen!" Trish exclaimed. "But he doesn't even recognize you."

Linda's mouth flew open, and her eyes bugged nearly out of their sockets. "I don't even recognize me. And I see me every day." Linda suddenly got even more excited. "And he must not find out who I am."

"You two have not seen each other in, what, five years," Susan reasoned. Then she began to seriously think about the situation. This might be what could persuade Linda to leave the Amish and join her.

"He saved a life," Tasha said with a starry look in her eyes. Suddenly, she wanted to hear more about Allen. "How did he save your life?"

Linda quickly answered, "He saved me from drowning when I fell into the stream."

"Really?" Tasha said, "Wow."

"What should we do?" Trish asked the group with great excitement. "This is actually kind of romantic, like, real romantic."

"Like a love story," Tasha said. "We could kidnap Bob, leaving Allen by himself. Then Linda can swoop in and sweep him off his feet." Suddenly, she started shouting and waving her hands. "Oh oh oh, we should arrange it that he could save her life again!"

Trish said, "Like saving her from falling off the top of the Ferris wheel."

"Our luck, he would be afraid of heights," Tasha said.

Linda wasn't sure what they were talking about, "sweeping him off his feet." She imagined herself doing some fancy dance past him and then picking him up and carrying him away. She figured it must have been a figure of speech.

Suddenly, Trish gasped, "Oh no, I forgot to call Mom about the little twerp."

"Oh, Trish," Tasha said, "she is going to kill you."

"Me!" Trish screamed. "You helped me."

"Yeah, but you are older and supposed to be the responsible one."

Trish removed a small silver box from her bag. She pulled out a thin metal wire from the end of it then started punching it with her finger. Trish put the open box to the side of her head and soon began to speak. "Hi, Mom. Yeah, we're having a great time... Say, little bro was being a jerk to our guests, so we put him in the shed... Oh, maybe an hour ago... Well, we had to. He was completely out of control. Bad language and inappropriate behavior.... Well, anyway, you may want to let him out. He was doing the fart-filter routine again... Yeah, with the tube... Sorry. Good-bye. Love you, too."

"Was she mad?" Tasha asked.

"A little bit," Trish replied.

Tasha added, "Anyway, back to current events. Remember what I said about those granny panties." Then she reached into her purse. "Here, you might need this." She pulled out the square foiled package and handed it to Linda. "Put it in your purse." Linda placed the small package into her purse, not knowing what it was for.

Susan was grateful that Tasha and Trish had come up with something that might get Linda to leave the Amish. She was hoping Allen would be the love of her life.

Trish told Linda, "Wait here." The three girls left Linda and briskly walked toward the two young men as they slowly walked away from them with cups in their hands. The girls quickly caught the two boys. Trish and Tasha took the arms of Bob, showing great excitement, and soon, they had him separated from Allen.

As they pulled him away, Allen just stood there looking abandoned. Linda felt bad for him because they did not anything to him being abandoned like that. The three girls were bringing

Bob back toward her. Linda saw Allen shrugged his shoulders and proceeded toward the exhibit hall. Linda didn't hesitate to follow him. Trish, Tasha, Susan, and Bob walked past Linda. She heard Tasha say, "We are going to take you on the Rocket Ship." Linda took a deep breath to try and calm herself before approaching Allen.

She went into the exhibit hall several seconds after Allen had gone in. She saw a large open room with a cement floor. There were several long tables full of different items. There were long, bright sticks in the ceiling that appeared to be lighting the large room. She noticed the building was much cooler than it was outside.

Allen was looking at the displays on the tables along the outside wall. Linda moved over toward him and began to look at the same display. She silently stood unnoticed next to him. The display was a miniature farm complete with tractors and animals. There were small signs that pointed out safety rules to follow in farming. She was right next to him when she said, "That is good advice."

Allen turned his eyes toward her without moving his head much. "Yes, it is." He looked at the display for another minute before moving on to the next exhibit. There were a few moments of silence as he looked over the next display.

She looked down the table, noticing several plates of cookies. They had colored ribbons attached to them. "Oh, they have cookies." She moved down the table. "Raisin cookies, I like raisin cookies, do you?" There was a plate of raisin cookies with a blue ribbon tag on it that read Best Cookie Award.

"Yeah, sure," he answered out of politeness, "they're all right."

"I make the best raisin cookies." Linda tried to impress Allen.

"Are these your cookies?" he asked.

Linda looked blankly at the cookies. "No, these are not my cookies."

"Then you don't make the best cookies, do you?" he said as he pointed to a blue ribbon. "These cookies won first prize." Linda picked up one of the cookies and appeared to be about to eat it. Allen looked at her. "What are you doing?"

"I thought I would try one," Linda said. "Nobody seems to be eating them, and they may feel bad that no one ate their cookies."

Allen smiled benevolently. "Noble thought, but these aren't here for people to eat. They are only here to look at." He couldn't believe someone could be so stupid. He thought this girl was a bit abnormal, but he thought she certainly would know enough not to eat the display.

Linda was puzzled. "Why would someone make cookies that aren't to be eaten?" She didn't want to upset Allen, so she placed it back on the plate. She thought it best just to make small talk and not touch anything.

Allen was getting a bit annoyed and uncomfortable around Linda. He thought she must be mentally challenged or something and it was best to avoid her. Yet he was attracted to her in some mysterious way. She was very cute, and it was somewhat endearing that she was so naive. Allen liked girls but never had the overwhelming urge to pursue a relationship. He was more interested in his studies and activities at school mainly because he was not sure he could get a girlfriend. He was intrigued by the attention Linda was giving him and there was just something about her.

He turned toward her and looked her straight in the eyes. When he saw her big round, brown eyes, they seemed eerily familiar. He looked Linda up and down. He got nervous and didn't know what to say to her. He walked down the tables, continuing to look at the displays. A part of him hoped she would go away, yet a part of him hoped she would continue to pursue him. He also thought her friends may have put her up to befriending him to make fun of him.

She knew that things were not going well between them. She continued to act interested in the displays, staying close to him. She saw a very large cucumber. "Wow, look at the size of that cucumber. I wonder if it would taste like a normal cucumber."

"Listen," Allen said facing her, "I know they put you up to this, so just go away."

Linda was lost as far as what he meant by that statement. He continued to look at her for a moment, and he found himself speechless. He turned to walk out of the building without looking over the rest of the displays. Linda asked as a tear trickled down her cheek, "Do you really think that I would ever do that to you?"

He was confused by her statement; she said it as if she knew him. He sensed a tone of remorse in her voice. He turned around and kindly said, "I wouldn't know. We just met."

"Well, we haven't really met yet," she said.

Allen again looked at her like he recognized her. "Who are you?"

Linda only had a few seconds to come up with a name. The only name she could think of in short order was Tanya Tucker. She got the name from a plastic case in Trish's room.

He knew she was lying. "Really," he said, "you don't look like Tanya Tucker. You may be as pretty as she is, but you don't look like her."

"You know Tanya Tucker?" Linda felt she had been caught in a lie.

Allen chuckled out. "No, not personally. It's just strange that you would have the same name. Don't people make fun of you for it."

Linda was confused but decided to go along with the flow of the conversation. "Ya-es, all the time." Linda forced a laugh, trying to cover her slight German accent.

"Well," he said, "it was nice meeting you, whoever you really are." He then began to leave the hall. She felt him slipping away from her. As the door closed behind him, she ran quickly toward the door, holding her skirt down as she ran. She felt awkward running in the shoes they made her wear. She opened the door, looked around to see him strolling toward the big red-and-white tent.

She called to him, "Allen."

He looked back toward her but did not stop walking. When she was closer, he asked, "How did you know my name?"

When she caught up to him, she said, "Trish told me."

He responded, "If she didn't put you up to this and she didn't try to talk you out of it, why are you following me?" He shook his head. "That doesn't sound like Trish."

"I don't know what you mean, but she did say you were the biggest nerd," Linda said, trying to make Allen feel better.

Allen laughed and sarcastically said, "Well, that's the first thing that's made any sense about you." He thought it made sense; she would have told her that. He was sure everyone knew what *nerd* meant, yet this girl appeared to be sincere in the fact she thought it was a compliment. If she did know what *nerd* meant, why would she continue to pursue him?

"Well then, she must think very highly of you then," Linda said honestly.

"Why are you with Trish and Tasha?"

Another question Linda had to think quickly about. "I'm their cousin from Ohio."

"Just staying for the summer?"

Linda said flippantly, "Just passing through. I will only be here for a few days." She knew she couldn't withstand a continued barrage of questions, so she fired one back at him. Linda remembered Allen saying that everyone always asked what he was going to do when he grew up. "So what are you going to do when you grow up?"

Allen was annoyed. "I am grown up."

"Yes, you have. Sorry."

Allen mellowed. "I decided to go to college to be an engineer." He found himself very intrigued by Tanya. He was convinced she was different in a kind of innocent way.

"An engineer on a train," she said excitedly. Linda had ridden the train when the family visited a few relatives in Ohio several years ago. "I rode the train one time. It was fun. I enjoyed it. You must enjoy it as well or you wouldn't want to do it."

Allen was amused at Linda's simple thoughts. "Do you want to go on a ride?"

"We can ride a train now?" Linda asked.

"I meant the rides here at the fair." Allen clarified by waving his hand around them toward the noisy rides.

Linda suddenly had a sick feeling in her stomach. She wanted desperately to get on to a different subject, but the subject now was rides. "I love them." He pulled a roll of tickets out of his pocket and aimed her toward the Tilt-A-Whirl. "Except that one," she insisted as she steered him toward the Ferris wheel. "How about the big glowing wheel," she suggested. He suddenly got a sick look on his face. She remembered he once told her he did not like heights.

"Sure," he said unenthusiastically, "love to."

Linda felt sorry for him and the sacrifice that he was about to give for her. "We don't have to go on the big-wheel thing if you don't want to. As a matter of fact, it looks a little higher than I want to go." Getting high in the sky truly was of great interest to her.

Allen was grateful, "How about the shooting star instead."

Linda looked at the metal machine he was pointing at. It looked tame compared to the first two rides she had ridden. It seemed to just rock from side to side nice and easy. "Sure." As they waited in line, she saw her friends and Bob heading for the Scrambler. She noticed the ride they were lined up for was now twirling around and jerking back and forth. She briefly thought of backing out, but it was too late. She had given Allen a committed agreement to ride on it with him.

Soon, they were being waved to take a seat by a lady that looked much nicer and cleaner than the other people that were running other rides. She followed Allen to a seat at the end of the row of seats. This ride had a padded shoulder harness that came down over them automatically. She felt very secured in the seat once the harness had locked itself down around them. She pulled her skirt down, but when she let go, it rose up again.

A sudden rush of fear flooded through her body as the ride began to sway from one side to the other. She seemed to be handling it well until the ride went high and around and around. Linda's stomach went round and round. Once she stepped onto solid ground, she threw up again. She was embarrassed and flushed in a cold sweat.

She thought for sure Allen would abandon her in disgust of her actions. Allen did not abandon her. Instead, he held her shoulder as she vomited a second time. Then he assisted her to a place to sit down on a wooden bench near a concession trailer. He wiped her mouth with a handkerchief he had in his pocket. Once she was settled, he went to a stand nearby and bought a pop.

She looked at the bubbly dark liquid. As she raised the cup to her face, she felt a timid cold spray on her face. She took a drink and pulled it away as she felt the bubbles tickle her tongue and lips. "That's different," she said with delight.

He looked at her and asked, "Is it bad?"

"What is it?" she asked.

He was amused that she would ask. The cup she was holding had the word *Pepsi* on it. He thought that she certainly has had a pop drink before in her life, even if she were from another country. "Pepsi."

"It certainly is peppy." She did not know what Pepsi was but knew she had to portray herself as more worldly than she was.

"Oh, I guess I didn't take enough to tell." She took another bigger swallow. "Yes, that's a Pepsi all right."

"Must taste pretty well after throwing up?"

"Ya-es. I guess I shouldn't ride any more rides."

"Do you always get sick on the rides?"

"Almost," Linda sadly admitted.

"So we won't go on any more rides." Allen conceded the rest of the night to no rides. It now was important to him to spend more time with this girl.

"Sorry," she said, "if you want to go on some rides, go ahead. I'll be fine. It has been very nice to see you—" She almost said "again" but stopped herself.

Allen sensed this girl did not have all her faculties. "Well, I'll stay. I think you shouldn't be left alone."

"Oh, you are so sweet," Linda said, hoping she would not throw up on him or something. "No, you go ahead and have fun. It won't be much fun around me when I can't seem to handle any of the good rides." She pulled down on her skirt.

He felt hurt that she might be trying to get rid of him. He didn't want to go against her wishes. "Oh, well I guess I better go then." He began to walk away, but he couldn't leave her. She looked as if she were about to cry. He walked back to her. "Want to play bingo?"

She looked up at him sadly but with new hope. "Bingo?"

"Yeah." He shook his head in amusement. He was beginning to get the feeling this girl was from another planet. "It's a game they play at the big tent put on by the band boosters."

Linda smiled and remembered what Tasha had told her earlier. "They did say that I should be able to score easy."

Allen was slightly embarrassed she had said that. Only knowing her for this short time, he got the impression she was not aware of the meaning he, or they had thought.

They sat at a big table with three cards for each of them and a cup of corn kernels. There was a man in the front of the tent standing on a podium. This man spoke into a fuzzy ball on a stick. What he said into it would blast out from all around them. Linda was impressed with how the man could project his voice so well. "How is he doing that?"

Allen asked, "Doing what?"

"Project his voice like that," she said.

Allen put on a face of surprise. "Through the PA system."

"PA system?"

"Public address system." It was freaky that she did not know what that was.

She was revealing her ignorance of the English world. "Oh, of course. Where is my head tonight." She looked briefly into Allen's eyes as he looked into hers.

"You remind me of someone," he said.

She said coyly, "Maybe I remind you of Tanya Tucker?"

He smiled and chuckled slightly, "No, I guess not." Allen still found himself intrigued by her, but he knew there was definitely something screwy about her.

The man with the big voice started to call off the numbers for the next game. Allen placed a corn kernel on one of his cards. He reached over to help Linda, who hadn't caught on to how the game was played. Linda waved him away, insisting she knew how to play. He continued to watch her, and she was doing all right. He noticed her watching other people intently to see what they were doing with their cards and corn kernels.

They played several games of bingo without winning. After an hour, they gave up and turned in their cards. Allen noticed several young couples, many whom he knew from school, holding each other's hand. He noticed a number of people looking at them. He felt proud to be walking with such a pretty girl. He hoped they would not catch on to her weird mentality.

He wanted to grab her hand but did not want to make it obvious. He could not help but notice that it was right there waiting for him to grab. He wondered if he was being too bold to hold her hand so early in their relationship. He also thought if she was only going to be in the area for such a short time, he wouldn't want to get too involved. He thought of the little Amish girl he knew years earlier. He had trouble getting over the feelings he had for her.

Awkwardly, his hand bumped into hers, and he grabbed it. She was not sure what holding hands meant in the worldly world, but she liked it and didn't want to reveal any ignorance.

Allen thought her hand would feel soft and smooth, but it was rough and calloused. They were passing a concession stand that had words on it: Cotton Candy and Funnel Cakes. Allen loved cotton candy but didn't want to show excitement about it. It would be unmanly to be excited about cotton candy.

"Would you like some cotton candy or a funnel cake?" he asked.

Linda didn't know what cotton candy or a funnel cake was. She hoped they weren't rides. She chose the one that sounded the least harmful. "Cotton candy. I love cotton candy."

"Wait here while I get it," he said as he gestured her to a nearby bench. She knew that whatever he brought over was going to be good. She could tell in an instant the pink, puffy, cloud-looking mass on a white stick he was carrying must be cotton candy.

She was not sure just how to eat it. She waited patiently in hopes he would eat some first. He tore away a small bit of it from the side with his two fingers. She did the same. He stuffed the bite thoroughly into his wide-open mouth. It appeared to her to be undesirable to open her mouth so wide. She noticed the cotton was very sticky. She opened her mouth slightly and stuffed the cotton in. The cotton melted quickly in her mouth, bursting with a blissful sweet taste. She noticed the candy was sticking to her fingers and around her mouth. She frantically began to lick her fingers and her mouth before Allen would notice. "A bit sticky, isn't it?"

"Um," Allen moaned in glee, obviously enjoying the taste of the cotton candy. "This is good stuff." He did not notice how Linda was struggling.

Linda felt she had better say something, "Um, it sure is good, nice and sugary." After another bite, more of the sticky stuff stuck to her face and hands. She had a terrible time getting the substance off her hands. The cotton tasted so sweet she did not want to miss out on any part of it, but she was tempted to throw the rest away. Allen was concentrating on his own wad of pink frustration, but he was clean.

Linda worked at eating and cleaning up as quickly as she could. But the more she ate, the messier she got. Suddenly, Allen began to turn his head to look at her, and she blurted out, "I just love this stuff so much. I can't eat it properly."

Allen looked at her and began to laugh. "You should see yourself. You're a mess."

She took another big chunk of candy in her hand and stuffed it hungrily into her mouth. She wanted to make the biggest mess she could.

Allen was amused by the mess she had made on herself. He had a fleeting thought to lick the remnants off her chin, but that would be a bit forward. Linda smiled. "Sorry, you should never feed me cotton sugar. I should have warned you."

He laughed, and the two of them finished their cotton candy as they walked through the fair area a few times. Allen pulled a handkerchief from his pocket and began to wipe some of the sticky candy off her face.

Linda asked him, "Do you ever play the games?"

"A few years ago I did," Allen said somberly. "Never won a thing. They're just a big rip-off." He gave one of the dirty carneys a glare. As they walked, he found her hand once again. This time it wasn't nearly as difficult as it was the first time. He found it uncomfortably sticky. He wasn't going to let go of her hand no matter how uncomfortable it was.

They walked by the Ferris wheel once again. Linda looked up at it with great admiration of its glittering lights and the view she could see from the top of it. Allen looked up at the colorful wheel with great fear. Linda looked at him. "You need to face your fears, young man."

Allen stopped and looked up at the tall, colorful wheel. He pulled at her hand toward the gate. They stood in line in silence. They were next in line to get on when the wheel stopped and a boy and girl got off. The dirty man gestured Linda and Allen to get on board.

Allen tried to separate his hand from Linda to give the man tickets for the ride, but they were there stuck like glue with cotton candy. He was able to extract his hand from hers to dig the tickets out of his pocket. The man gave him a dirty look and muttered, "Rotten candy."

"You won't hurl when we get up there, will you?"

The man taking tickets rolled his eyes. "Great."

"I hope not," Linda answered, almost sure of what *hurl* meant. The dirty man closed and fastened the gate to their seat. The wheel moved slightly as it stopped to board more patrons. It stopped once to let Tasha and Bob on. She saw Susan and Trish walking away toward a ride called the Spider.

Linda was infatuated with the view while Allen was petrified. Linda was excited because they were only halfway to the top. If Allen did not let up on his grip, Linda was afraid her hand would be crushed. When they reached the top of the wheel, Allen looked down at the little people. "Oh crap."

"Isn't it wonderful up here? See how far you can see." She leaned forward, and the seat rocked forward, scaring both of them. They both made a whooping sound in fear as they threw themselves back in the seat. They rigidly sat back, clutching the side handles.

"Don't ever do that again."

"I won't," she agreed quickly. They looked at each other and laughed. They remained still in their seat as they tried to enjoy the view from the top of the wheel.

Soon, the wheel started to move without stopping. They could see out in front of them a whole world of lights and people. Quickly, they were approaching the ground, and the people got bigger. They flew past the base and the ugly, dirty operator. Then they saw the ground fade away, and the people got smaller again. They quickly reached the top and were about to be thrown out, but they just dropped back down. Linda wanted to see the sights from on top, but they were moving so fast she did not have time to take in everything.

They were silent and uneasy the first few times around. But after that, they were more comfortable with the wheel going around and enjoyed the ride. They must have gone around twenty times before it came to a stop. They were stopped at the top.

Allen leaned over to Linda and kissed her on the cheek. Linda smiled with pride. "Thank you," he said to her.

"For what?" Linda asked.

"Making me face my fears," Allen said.

"Oh, what was your fear?"

"Heights."

They got off the ride and found Trish and Susan waiting for Tasha and Bob to get off. Susan looked at Allen and Linda. Linda quickly let go of his hand. "We have to get going," Susan sadly told Linda.

Allen sensed Linda was intimidated by Susan. He turned to Linda, trying to pull her away from the others. "Tanya." Susan raised her eyebrows, surprised Linda came up with the name of Tanya. Hesitating just a moment, Linda went with Allen. "Can I see you tomorrow?"

Linda's eyes darted around. "I can't." She wanted to say yes, but she couldn't. It had been the greatest night of her life. She had so much fun the future was not in her thoughts.

"I thought you had a good time," he said sadly. "I thought we made a good team."

"I am only here for such a short time."

"All the more reason to take advantage of the short time we can have together." He wasn't afraid to fall for this girl. She was worth it. "I haven't got your address or your name."

Linda wanted to see him again, knowing they could never really be together. "One week from tonight, right here, same time." Susan heard her and knew that in one week it would be a night before a meeting, and they would have trouble getting away.

Tasha and Bob got off the Ferris wheel and joined the group. They were holding hands to everyone's surprise. Tasha and Bob would be the oddest couple in school. Trish had only pushed the two together to clear the way for Linda to nab Allen.

"All right," Allen agreed, "one week from tonight."

Tasha gave Bob a very long, passionate kiss. "See you tomorrow, Bob."

Linda was afraid that Allen might want to kiss her like that to say good-bye. But he didn't make any move to kiss her, and she felt disappointed and a bit angry with him. He looked at her with a smile. "I can't wait a week. But if I have to…"

Linda smiled timidly and waved bye as the girls walked away. Linda walked well behind the others and could hear Allen say to his friend Bob, "You and Tasha, what's up with that? She's playing you, man. I'm tellin' ya."

"What about your fox?"

As they approached the car, someone yelled to them, "Tasha and the loser, Bob!" They heard laughter, coming from a group of boys who were hanging out nearby.

Linda could see Tasha wanted to yell back, but Trish put her hand over her mouth. Linda, wanting to help her, yelled out without using Tasha's exact words, "Eat manure Phil! Her three girlfriends looked at her with bewilderment. "Did I not do it right?"

"It was fine. I'm very proud of you, sweetie," Tasha said sweetly. "Except that wasn't Phil. And manure"—she shook her head— "is too soft, too passive. Saying that is like when you go into the field and you see manure. It's no big deal, right?" She then smiled and nodded her head. "You really want to use a phrase like you just stepped in it."

Then Linda halfheartedly yelled in an attempt to correct herself. "You other bad person!" All the girls laughed.

Susan turned Linda around and shook her a bit playfully. "Keep your composure, young lady. Remember who you are." Susan smiled. "Tanya, isn't it?"

"Oh, I don't know who I am or who I want to be," Linda said in angered frustration.

Susan had some hope that Linda may be thinking about joining her in the English world. She asked, "Where did you get the name Tanya?"

"I had to think fast, so I said I was Tanya Tucker," Linda reasoned. "You know, the girl from the little plastic box that goes into the big noisy box at Trish's."

"It's called a boom box," Trish explained. "And he fell for that name? He is so thick."

"Hey, is that a bad thing?"

"Well, if he believed your name was Tanya Tucker, then he is thick," Trish said firmly.

Susan sensed trouble. "It's no big deal if he believed it or not."

"He really didn't believe my name was Tanya Tucker. He said I didn't look like her," Linda said. "He asked me if I got made fun of a lot."

"That sounds like he believed it," Tasha said.

Linda quickly added, "When I said no, he said he wanted my real name, or he wasn't going to talk to me anymore."

Trish said, "He is your typical man. They'll go along with anything if they can get something from you."

"He didn't take anything from me. He was very nice, even though I was lying to him," Linda said.

"Then he has no self-respect," Trish went on.

"Stop it, Trish," Tasha said. "According to you, no man is any good ever since Billy Rat Face dumped you."

"He has a name," Trish said.

"You can't even pronounce it, so shut up," Tasha said in a playful manner. "I call him Rat Face because he looks like a rat. I think Allen is a very good guy."

Trish finally admitted, "Yeah, anyone who will support you when you're hurling the contents of your stomach must be a good person."

"Sorry," Susan told her. She then looked at Linda's nose and began to study it. "I was worried about you, so we kept track of what you were doing."

Linda wasn't upset. "I appreciate your concern. Thank you." Then she blurted out, "He was impressed with your compliment." Linda wanted the three girls to like him.

All three girls tried to remember what the compliment was. Trish then asked, "What compliment?" Susan looked at Linda's nose and raised her hand to touch her nose but stopped.

Linda looked at her blankly but continued to talk. "The one about how he does so well in school and that he was the biggest nerd."

Susan said solemnly, "You really didn't tell him that, did you?"

"Yes, I did." Linda could sense there was something wrong with telling him.

Trish knew telling Linda what *nerd* meant would just upset her. "Well, he really is a good guy. He proved that to me tonight."

"I am glad you like him. I know he likes the two of you." Linda wanted them to like him. Susan looked at Linda's nose again.

"Why do you keep looking at me like that?" Linda asked.

"There's something on your nose," Susan said, moving closer. Linda's eyes crossed as she watched her sister touch her nose. "It's sticky." She squinted harder. "It's cotton candy."

Trish and Tasha laughed again and together said, "You are so sweet."

Susan and Linda rolled their eyes. "We must be sisters." They all laughed.

"Do you two ever argue?" Susan asked them.

"Pretty much never," Trish said, "because we have a common enemy."

"Justin," they said together.

As they walked home, Susan started the conversation, "I am sorry that I made you go out tonight."

"Well," Linda started to say and then stopped for a moment. "Well, I really did have a good time. Too good a time."

"Stirred things up a bit, did it?"

Linda began to shake her head. "I was just getting to forget about him." She paused for a moment. "I wanted to see him again so badly all these years just to find out what had happened to him. Now I have all these feelings inside me that may take several years to get rid of again."

"Sounds like you two should be together," Susan said, hoping to get her sister to leave with her.

"This has been the best night of my life, yet it was the worst night of my life."

CHAPTER EIGHT

A Lasting Good-Bye

The next day, it was life in an Amish family as usual, except for the fact Linda and Susan were both unusually quiet, which aroused their mother to make a comment. "Did something happen last night you want to talk about?"

"No," Susan quickly said, "just tired. We were out late last night."

"Oh, I see," Clara acknowledged pleasantly. "You both going to the singing tonight?"

Linda indicated to her sister that she wanted to go. Linda felt obligated to meet with Luke. She had a feeling of guilt having met with Allen. When they got away from their mother, Susan said, "We need to talk." They worked quickly to finish their noontime Sunday chores. They were free to do whatever they wanted after that. They chose to go for a walk together. Linda wanted to go to the stream to talk privately. Susan was reluctant to go tromping through the wilderness but agreed nevertheless.

They made their way through the waist-high bean field to the stream. Susan asked, "What do you think of the real world? It's a fascinating world of freedom, isn't it?"

Linda considered her answer carefully. "It was interesting, but it was very scary and so different, so gut wrenching."

"Well, now we know you shouldn't ride on spinning rides," Susan admitted sadly. Then she added, "Last night was only a small part of the real world. There is a lot more out there. Great things. Things you will get to understand and love in time." Susan wondered if taking her sister to the fair was too much on her first time out in the real world. Susan continued to talk anxiously, trying to convince Linda that she should leave with her. "There is more. I can tell you all about it, and I'll answer any questions that you have."

"Susan, I didn't say that it was bad. And what is this real-world stuff? There is a real world right here." Linda settled her down from her anxiety. "It is something that someone can get accustomed to. I'm sure I could handle it eventually. Your friends are very kind, and I appreciated their guidance and looking after me last night."

"Ya." Susan was excited that Linda might go with her. "Trish wanted to make sure that you were all right, so we followed your progress. We're sorry you got sick again. Allen seemed to look after you very well."

"Ya, he did, didn't he." Linda smiled dreamily and thought about the night before. She was confident if she left he Amish world, she would pursue a relationship with Allen.

"You two make a cute couple. He impressed Trish with his sentiment. She thinks you are the only girl he ever held hands with." Susan kept babbling on, "She said he has very little interest in girls. That's why they were so anxious to see how well you did."

Linda lost her dreamy feelings of last night. "He was right. They were using me."

"No, no, don't misunderstand me. You wanted to talk to him, didn't you?" Susan asked.

"Ya," she said.

"He was very nice, and he is good-looking."

"Ya, but they were only looking for something to make fun of about him."

"Maybe at first they did, but not after just a few minutes. Bob turned out to be really fun, and Allen warmed up to you so well."

"He didn't at first."

"Do you think he may want you to be his girl?" Susan was trying hard to convince her to leave. "You know, if he isn't interested in girls like Trish said, he sure looked interested in you. I bet you could rope him in forever."

"Maybe."

"When you see Allen again next week, you should try to figure out just how he feels about you. Then you should make your decision."

"My decision?" Linda asked blankly.

"Yes, about coming with me to live in the real world. You would be free to see Allen every day if you wanted. We can get you a job at Patty's Pizza Place."

"I don't know," Linda angrily retorted. "You sprang this on me two nights ago. This is a decision that will affect the rest of my life. I'm not like you. I'm not unhappy here."

Susan felt some guilt for putting her sister through this. "You have always loved Allen, and seeing you with him last night proves it to me."

"I don't know. We were only eleven years old back then."

"Ya, and seventeen last night. You two looked so happy together."

"Ya."

"I decided to move out next week instead of two weeks," Susan said sadly. "I can't make up any more excuses about my baptism to the ministers."

The sisters' conversation was interrupted by the sounds of twigs breaking. They quietly moved into some brush close by in hopes of not being discovered. She hoped the sounds were from a deer or something nice and not from a mean wild dog or a badger. She quickly looked for a stick, but what she could find were too small to use as a defense weapon.

Soon, they saw a figure of a man high-stepping through the brush. He was not Amish and obviously a trespasser. They were concerned that it may be a transient and possibly dangerous. Linda quietly found a bigger stick in which to defend Susan and herself.

The man watched the farm intently for a few minutes. He then looked around, showing his face to the girls. As the man turned toward them, Linda recognized him immediately. "It's Allen," she softly spoke to Susan.

"Allen?" Susan whispered surprisingly. "You're Allen?"

"Ya, my Allen," Linda said with great confusion. She was surprised and concerned about the reason Allen would be stalking their home. *Why?* Linda pondered.

"Is he here looking for you?"

"I don't know. He obviously is looking for Linda."

"You're Linda."

"Ya, I'm Linda."

"Do you think he recognized you last night?"

She thought for a moment as they watched Allen move back through the trees to the bank of the stream. "I thought he did once." She paused, thinking about it. "No, twice." He began to throw something into the stream. He had an old corncob in his hand, and he was throwing the kernels into the stream as he plucked them off the cob one at a time. "He mentioned that I reminded him of someone."

Susan got excited. "He's looking for the little Amish girl. Which of course is you."

"Ya." Linda was confused. "Why would he be looking for me today if he was involved with me last night?"

"You're the other woman," Susan said excitedly. "Interesting." Susan thought about it and said sternly, "That two-timing poop." The two girls studied him for a few minutes silently. "Are you going to talk to him?"

Linda thought for a moment. "No, he may have recognized me from last night."

"If he hasn't already figured it out." Susan suddenly got giddy. "This is so romantic." Linda looked at her, not knowing who her sister was anymore. Susan explained, "That is just something Trish would say." They watched him for a few more minutes. When he started to get up, the two girls ducked back deeper into the brush, making a slight rustling sound. Allen stopped quickly and looked over in the direction of the two girls. The girls did not move, hoping they would not draw attention to them.

He turned from the stream and began to walk quietly away from them. The girls remained where they were, quiet and hidden. They continued to watch him move back through the brush and trees away from their farm.

The girls got back to the house in time to help their mother with dinner. They were much more lively preparing this meal than they were earlier. Their mother noticed. "You two seem to be much more awake now."

"Ya," the two of them answered together. They looked at each other and, speaking softly, said, "We must be sisters." They laughed at themselves as their mother and younger sister, Mary, looked at them with wonder.

Their mother then informed them that the family was going to host the meeting the following Sunday. Both Susan and Linda were shocked at the news. They knew this meant they would not be allowed to leave the house as they had planned. This meant Susan wouldn't be able to move out, and Linda would not be able to meet with Allen. They would be busy preparing the house for the nearly one hundred guests they would expect on that Sunday.

"I thought that we weren't hosting for another two months?" Susan asked.

"This is true," Clara said, "but the Abner Yoder family is having problems, and we are needed to fill in. It is our duty to help out in times of need."

The two girls lay awake, quietly discussing their predicament. Susan planned to get away sometime that week to talk to Trish. "We'll get things worked out somehow."

One afternoon, the girls got a great break. A nearby Amish family baked a dozen loaves of bread for the meeting. Clara asked Susan to go pick up the bread. Trish's house was not far, so she planned to stop by to make arrangements.

"I'll have Paul drive you in the buggy," her mother told her.

Susan knew if Paul drove her, she wouldn't be able to stop at Trish's. "I would love to walk. It is such a nice day."

Her mother responded, "It will be a heavy load for you. You should ride with Paul."

"Bread isn't very heavy. I can handle it."

"It would take too long. We have a lot of work to do." Clara dismissed the thought.

"Oh, Mother," Linda chimed in, "let her walk. It will give her some time to think, relax, come to grips with some life-changing decisions." Linda hoped her mother would think walking could help Susan decide to be baptized.

Clara had been anxious to have Susan baptized and devote herself to God. "All right, I will go along with your request."

Susan left that afternoon and returned nearly two hours later. Clara asked her, "What took you so long? It shouldn't have taken that long."

"Sorry, we got to talking. I thought it would be gracious to spend some time talking with them."

"You're absolutely correct."

Linda looked for a sign from Susan that some kind of arrangement for them to get away that next Saturday night had been made. Susan winked at Linda and smiled.

It wasn't until later when the girls were settled into bed that they were able to converse about their plans. Linda was anxious to hear about them, so as soon as they extinguished the lantern, she asked, "What's the plan?"

"If I tell you, you have to promise not to tell anything even if we are discovered."

"Of course, I won't tell. I am in this as much as you are."

"No, you're not. I won't be coming back." Susan begged, "Come with me."

"I don't know. How will we live without money?"

"I have some money that will last us until we get jobs."

"How did you get money?"

"Don't ask."

Linda asked sternly, "How did you get the money?"

"You are on a need-to-know basis only."

"What does that mean?"

"I don't know, but Trish told me to say that if anyone ever asked something I didn't want to answer. Don't worry about it. It is my money, and the less you know, the better."

"Why would I get in trouble for it? Can you at least tell me the plan?"

"Sure," Susan said as she took a deep breath, readying herself for a long oration of the plan. "Do what I tell you."

"If it is late, Allen may not wait for me."

"Trish and I thought about that, but we remembered you said same time and place. It would be hard to determine what time that really was. Was it the time we got to the fair, or was it the time you two ran into each other, or-was it from the time you said good-bye? So we figured that if he was any kind of a gentleman, he would be there early and wait until the latest time for you to show up. Of course, you know him best. Do you think he will wait for you?"

Linda thought at first and then said with confidence, "Ya, he would wait a long time for me to show up."

"Besides, Tasha and Bob will show up at the fairgrounds at ten o'clock to keep Allen interested enough not to leave," Susan reassured her. "Now don't worry."

"I understand. Susan, please don't leave this week. Can you wait until the next week? It will embarrass the family something awful."

"No," Susan said without hesitation.

"I understand you want to go, and I won't stop you, but you could give our family some dignity if you were to wait."

"I really feel bad about it. But I cannot wait any longer." Susan began to get some tears in her eyes. "Does this mean you aren't leaving with me?"

"I can't leave."

"There is nothing here for us, just rules and restrictions. The English world has everything to offer."

"Living Amish is my world," Linda said angrily.

Susan replied in a harsh whisper, "You have no freedom in the Amish faith."

"No freedom? The only restrictions are not to offend God."

Neither of the girls wanted to end the discussion there. They did not want to argue anymore since their time together was now counting down to just a few days.

Linda was not completely sure she wanted to answer the question. She knew that no matter what she did, it would be devastating. So she put off her decision once again but knew deep down she could not leave. "I don't know."

"Maybe later then." Susan sounded quietly optimistic.

"We'll see," Linda said with a tone of finality to end the night's conversation. Both Susan and Linda girls lay awake for a few hours, too involved in their own thoughts to fall asleep. The next few days went by slowly, and both girls were very nervous about the plan to get away Saturday night. They had to get out of the house unnoticed. They needed to leave as soon as possible after everyone had gone to bed. They spent Friday investigating the best and quietest way out of the house.

When they went upstairs to bed, they tested all the floorboards to find the ones that made noise. They wanted to memorize the ones that were silent. As the girls went down the hall, stepping and slightly jumping on each floorboard to find the ones that creaked, Susan stepped on one that made a moaning sound, a sound that was very eerie, as if someone was hurt and in pain. They froze in near fright. Susan then stepped back on it, and it moaned again. She then started to hop slightly up and down on it, sending the board into a continuous moan. The girls began to laugh heartily at it. Susan then changed her rhythm and the moaning seemed to put on a bit of a gasp along with the moans. The two of them burst into uncontrolled laughter. They continued their inspection of the rest of the floorboards. They planned a practice run that night after everyone had gone to bed and were successful in taking every step in total silence. They found that the kitchen door made more noise than the front door, so they decided to go through the front door. They also determined that the front door squeaked a bit when it was fully extended. They quietly oiled the door that night and planned not to open it fully during the actual escape.

They had to work their tails off the days leading up to the meeting. They were very tired and they did not change into their nightclothes when they went to bed that night. They were wide awake as they lay in their beds. They got out of bed just fifteen minutes after they heard the last sound of human activity. They puffed the blankets up and left their bonnets on the hook on the wall. They carried their shoes in their hands so they wouldn't clunk on the floor.

They slowly opened their bedroom door, which they had oiled just in case it might decide to squeak. They silently glided down the hallway to the top of the steps. They heard their father snoring as they passed their parents' room. They heard their grandfather snoring when they passed his small room. There were four steps that they had to skip as they descended down the steps to the living area. They needed to skip one step at a time twice and two steps at one time.

Linda nearly lost her balance at the end of the steps, bumping a potted plant on a shaky pedestal. They took deep breaths and soon were at the front door. Susan slowly unlocked the front door and turned the knob. The latch gave a release, and she swung it in just enough for them to fit through. They had bent the nail holding the noisy spring to the screen door so they could remove the spring easily.

They had not checked for creaky floorboards on the porch, so they tried to step wherever they could see a concentration of nails. They were successful in getting down the steps, and they walked in the grass without their shoes. Once they got to the country gravel road, they walked along it for one hundred feet or so before slipping on their shoes and walking across the road. They soon approached a car that sat at the designated meeting place. They unintentionally scared Trish and Tasha, who were waiting impatiently in the car.

"Sorry," Susan said.

"It's really creepy out here at night," Trish said as she opened the door to let Susan in. "I can't imagine what it would be like if there wasn't a moon."

Susan looked at Tasha. "I thought you had a date with Bob."

"I told Bob that we can't go out unless he stays with Allen until we get there," Tasha said. "Men are so easy to man-nip-ulate."

As they drove by their house, Linda noticed a lantern light in the window of their grandfather's room. "Grandpa is up."

Susan said, "He is probably headed for the little barn or just getting back."

"Do you think he would check on us?"

"No," Susan said, hoping she was right. She then remembered that it would not matter to her because she was not coming back.

They went to Trish's house to change. It did not take very long to have the two girls changed into their English clothes and makeup. The room was barer than Linda remembered it from the week before. There were not as many pictures on the wall, and there were several boxes laying around on the floor.

They had gotten Linda a pair of pants like Susan's. Linda's pants were slightly oversized for her, however. They had gotten her a bra as well, but she insisted to wear her normal undergarment. They painted her up quickly and put her hair in a ponytail like Susan's. It was getting late, and they felt pressed for time. They hurried down to the car, and off they went toward town. Linda was much more comfortable riding in the car this time.

They arrived at the fairgrounds. Linda was confused that it was dark and there was no lit-up big wheel. She was confused but did not ask about what had happened to the place. She recognized the exhibit hall building she had followed Allen into. She was afraid that Allen would not want to show up at a dark, scary place like this.

Trish stopped the car right in the middle of where Linda was sure that the bingo tent used to be. They sat in the car in the dark. The moon helped light things up around them just a bit. They noticed a man's figure in the shadows of one of the buildings. The figure began to slowly move toward them. It appeared to be Allen, but they were not going to send Linda out there until they were sure it was him.

Tasha yelled out her window, "Bob!"

"No, it's Allen."

"That's him," Linda said excitedly and pushed on Tasha's seat to urge her to get out of the car so she could get out to greet him.

"Are you sure?" Susan asked.

"Ya," she said as she pushed on Tasha's seat again.

"Linda, you need to say yes," Susan warned her firmly.

"Yes," Linda retorted. Tasha hopped out of the car, followed quickly by Linda. She was indecisive whether to run, walk fast, walk slow, be excited, or be calm when she approached him. She wanting to run, but she was content with Trisha's suggestion to not appear to be excited to meet him.

"Where's Bob?" Tasha yelled.

"He is by the building," Allen responded kindly. Tasha looked intently toward the building once again. Another human figure came from around the corner of the building and began to run toward them.

"Where have you been?" Tasha yelled at him when he got closer.

"I had to take a piss. Is that all right?" Bob snapped at her questioning tone.

She was excited at the forcefulness of his statement. "Sure it is, you cute little man." Tasha embraced him as they met. Linda kept her eyes on Allen. Susan jumped out of the car and held the door open. Tasha and Bob slipped into the back of the car, and Susan quickly, with excitement, slipped into the front seat. Tasha yelled out to Linda and Allen, "Remember, you have three hours, Tanya!"

The car sped away, leaving Allen and Linda alone. Allen started the conversation, "I couldn't stop thinking about you all week."

She turned toward the empty fairgrounds. "Where did everything go?"

Allen laughed. "It's a county fair. They don't stay in one place for more than a week. Where did you say you were from, and how do you know Trish and Tasha?"

Linda wanted to answer carefully. "I told you, I am their cousin from Ohio. Have you always lived here?" she asked, attempting to keep him from asking any more questions.

"Yes," he answered politely. Then he fired a question right back, "What city in Ohio?"

"It doesn't matter, does it?"

"Yes," he said, "I want to write to you when you go back home."

"Please don't," she said seriously, trying to stop the barrage of questions.

Allen did not want to start their night off with an argument either. "I'm sorry, but I really like you, and I want to keep in contact with you." He looked at her with great admiration.

"You think we could ever have a life together from a thousand miles away?"

"It isn't a thousand miles," he reasoned. "Listen, I'm sorry, but I have never had a girlfriend, and this is all new territory for me."

"I am just a passing infatuation of yours. I'm not really someone that you love. You don't even know what love is." Linda was trying to convince herself that she didn't love him as well as she was trying to convince him that he didn't love her. Linda thought it was very honest of him to admit he had never had a girlfriend.

She had gotten the impression from Tasha that everyone had many boy- or girlfriends at their age. "You never had a girlfriend even when you were much younger?" Linda was fishing for some confirmation that he really liked her years ago.

Allen laughed. "Nothing that I would like to talk about." Linda was hurt he didn't want to acknowledge their relationship in the past.

"See, so you have loved someone before, haven't you?"

"I don't know. I was only twelve at the time."

"What happened?"

Allen gave a slight chuckle. "Nothing."

"In other words, she sent you away," she said jokingly.

Allen, as a gentleman, responded with a lie. "Yeah, that's what happened." He didn't want her to think he was coldhearted to actually break up with a girl.

Her heart sank as she came to the conclusion that he was talking about someone else. She realized he really meant what he had said back then. "Well, what should we do?"

"Are you hungry?"

"Not really," she said. "We can walk for a while. Maybe I'll get hungry."

"Okay," he said. They started to walk down the gravel parking area at the fairground. "The moon is bright tonight."

"Ya-es," she said, trying to hide her German drawl of the word *yes*. She further hid the slur by pretending to yawn, which turned into a real yawn. Their hands bumped, and he grabbed hers firmly with affection. Linda did not take away; she actually felt delighted about it. She was so affected by the gesture she lost all concentration of the conversation.

Allen wanted to spend all the time with Linda without distractions. "Well, if we were to go somewhere to eat, it would be harder to carry on a conversation. This way, we can get closer." The night was warm, and a slight breeze kept the mosquitoes away. The breeze blew tantalizingly through Linda's few hairs that were dangling in front of her face. "Your hair is straight tonight. I thought it was curlier the other night."

"I used a curling prod last week," Linda said. "This week, it's a ponytail."

"Oh, that's nice," Allen said. "I prefer things more natural—no pretenses, no fake eyes, hair, no lies and deceptions. Some girls fake themselves up so bad that"—he stopped in midsentence—"it's like buying a used car. You really don't know what you're getting until you have driven it awhile."

Linda certainly needed to keep her true identity a secret after that statement. She was not sure why, however. "I agree," she said.

As they approached a large tree near the river, Allen gestured for her to sit under it. "Let's sit here for a while." Linda sat down gingerly because her pants seemed to bind up on her, and she was not comfortable. Allen sat next to her and put his arm around her shoulder. She was sitting up tall and erect using the best posture she could manage. Allen found this made it more difficult for him to keep his arm around her. He sat up as tall as he could.

Linda sensed the awkwardness he was experiencing and slouched down a bit, which made it much more comfortable. She had never had a boy put his arm around her like that before. She surprised herself at how comfortable she felt with his arm around her. Her neck and head seemed to naturally melt into his shoulder. She was flushed with the most beautiful feelings inside her. She felt like screaming that this was what she wanted for the rest of her life.

Allen, who had never dated before, was stunned at how easy it was to pull off. He was nervous and wanted to start a conversation but had so many things running through his mind he didn't know where to begin. He had a nightmarish thought that she might expect him to make out with her. He had never done that, except with a pillow this past week.

Linda shifted again, and his hand came dangerously close to touching her breast. He thought that maybe she shifted herself to try to get him to touch her breast. He then realized that she was wearing something very rough and stiff under her shirt. He was sure her chest was wrapped up for some reason, like cracked ribs or something. He considered asking her but decided it might be too personal and might embarrass her. He figured that if she was wearing something so cumbersome, she certainly would not be looking for any kind of sex. A great rush of relief surged through him with this thought. He moved his hand slightly away from her breast area, just in case there was another shift.

Linda finally broke the silence. "It sure is a nice night."

"Yeah."

"Allen, what are your plans for life?"

"I will be going to college this fall to become an engineer." Allen knew he had told her this before, but he acted as if he hadn't.

"Oh, that's right, ooh ooh," she said as she pulled on an imaginary whistle cord an engineer on a train would pull. Allen began to chuckle, which shook his chest and caused Linda's head to bounce up and down on it. "You're rattling my brain." She laughed.

"I am sorry," he apologized as he laughed and bounced her head even more, "but you are so funny."

"Why?"

"Well, I am going to be an engineer, but not a train engineer as you think. My engineering degree will be in building structures, such as roads, bridges, buildings—you know, big stuff."

She responded lightheartedly, "Oh, of course." She was upset with herself again for being so out of touch with him. "How long do you go to college to become an engineer?"

"Four or five years."

"Oh." Linda's heart sank a bit. She had just been having thoughts of leaving her Amish life to be with Allen. If she did leave for him, he may feel obligated not to go to college. It appeared to her that going to college and becoming an engineer meant a lot to him.

It was a marvelous time as Allen revealed everything he wanted to do in his life. He only mentioned once about getting married and having children. He appeared to be only ready for children after he graduated college and had built several hundred buildings. His conversation stayed mainly with college and building things. Allen continued to talk; she found it to be very wonderful and calming. When she was with him, she was not afraid of anything. She would be happy to stay at home cooking, cleaning, and having babies with him. In the back of her mind, she had visions of being dragged all over the world. It was this thought that scared her even if Allen was there.

Allen looked up into the sky. "Isn't it amazing to think that space is never-ending? It just goes on and on. Planets, stars, galaxies, asteroids, all kinds of stuff out there."

Linda had limited studies of space. "Yes, it is amazing," she said dreamily and with confidence. They had some conversations about space when they were younger, but she could not remember what was said.

"Do you think there are other life beings out there?" he asked.

This question caught Linda by surprise. She had not given that possibility much thought. She was afraid to make a comment. She was afraid that he knew something more. "I hadn't really thought about it," Linda answered. "What do you think?"

"Well"—Allen thought of how to answer—"we are only one planet of ten planets around one sun of billions of suns. I would say that the chances of another planet around another sun having life on it is pretty darn good. In fact, I believe there is probably thousands, maybe even millions, of planets that have life of some kind."

"Really," Linda said earnestly.

"I think it is very arrogant of us to believe we are the only intelligent life-forms in the universe. To be honest with you, I believe there are beings so much more advanced then we are. We could actually be one of the stupider beings in the galaxy." He looked to Linda, expecting a comment.

Linda was interested in hearing more and did not want to say anything for fear of revealing her ignorance. "Go on. I want to hear more about it."

Allen was happy to hear she didn't think he was stupid for thinking that way. He hadn't planned on saying anything else but decided to add. "I mean, what about Roswell? At first, an air force official stated they had found a crashed spaceship. Then suddenly, they call it balloon debris." He went on about a story of this small town in New Mexico. Linda knew nothing about it, but she was intrigued about the story. "I personally have never seen a flying spaceship or anything, but I would love to." He went on to tell stories of people being abducted for study.

The thought of being abducted frightened her. She began to look into the sky, expecting to see some flying object. Her heart began to pound hard in her chest. "When you said people have been abducted, what did you mean?"

The words began to flow rapidly out of Allen. "There have been many people that have disappeared and never came back. Generally, they were in the devil's triangle when they disappear. You know, in the Atlantic Ocean."

Linda had never heard anything in her Bible studies about a devil's triangle and figured it would be a major subject. "The devil's triangle?" she asked.

"Well, it is also referred to as the Bermuda Triangle, since the island of Bermuda is in the triangle area. Have you heard of that?"

"I have heard of Burmuda, but I do not know much about it."

"There is this area in the Atlantic Ocean that ships and planes seem to disappear, or at least the people on them disappear. No one seems to be able to answer the question as to where they have gone." Allen talked in great enthusiasm about this subject. "There are many theories that they traveled into a time-warp thing and were displaced into another time. Others believe they were taken by aliens to spaceships for whatever reasons."

Linda was completely convinced she wanted no part of this crazy, scary world. Allen seemed to sense she was getting frightened. He could feel the tenseness as he felt her stiffen. "What do they do to the people?"

Allen did not want to frighten her any further. "They play with them and treat them very well, I suppose. But anyway, what I am telling you may not even be true. I believe that the aliens are studying us but do not harm us. Several of the people that claim to have been abducted say they don't recall what happened to them." Allen was leaving out the ones that claimed they were treated in a perverse manner. "Have you ever seen the movie *Men in Black*?"

Linda had heard of movies but had never seen one. She had only seen a television a few times in her life. "No, I wanted to see it but never did."

"It showed a secret society of men monitoring aliens from other planets that wanted to live on Earth. It is certainly a fictitious story but interesting nonetheless. How could it be possible for aliens to live among us and we not even know it." Allen raised his eyebrows. "Hard to believe, isn't it? Yet you must have some doubt in your mind about it."

"It doesn't sound all that unlikely," Linda said. "I mean, it could be true." She wanted Allen to feel he would be free to talk to her about his thoughts. She really did not know what aliens from another planet meant and wasn't sure if she wanted to go there with any further conversation. She really felt uncomfortable with Allen trying to make him think she was someone that she wasn't. She found herself very nervous to say anything to him.

As their time together was nearing an end, Linda began to get very nervous. She knew the question of how to get a hold of her was going to come up. She decided to be open and honest with him. "Allen."

"Yes," he said in anticipation of the good-bye that would have to last a lifetime.

"I wish I could stay with you forever. I think we could have a great time together, but I can't see you ever again." Linda teared slightly.

"Why forever, Tanya?" he asked.

"I can't tell you," she said with honest conviction.

"What are you?" he said in frustration. Linda wasn't sure what he meant by the question. He then jokingly added in hopes to ease the tension, "Do you have some secret life that you can't reveal to me or you would have to kill me, like a CIA agent?" He could see even in the dark that Linda was puzzled.

Linda's eyes widened. She was shocked and confused at the thought of having to kill Allen. "No," she said in fright, "I will not kill you."

Allen sensed her fright and reassured her, "I know you won't kill me. It is just a phrase."

"Oh, of course," Linda said. "But I do have a secret life."

"Oh sure," Allen started saying sarcastically. "You really are a secret agent, and your identity must be kept a secret."

Linda did not know what a secret agent was. "No, I am not a secret...person." She had forgotten what the second word Allen had used. Suddenly she thought of the perfect excuse. "I come from another world." She was not sure if this was going to work or not. "Yes," she said with great confidence. "I am from another world that isn't compatible with your world. I must go back to my world to survive." She wanted to be honest, and this was as close to the truth as possible. Susan referred to their two types of lives as worlds, so she thought Allen would certainly understand since he was so smart. "Your world is so different from my world. I am lost, confused, and scared of your world. I must go back to where I belong."

Allen was silent as he pondered what she was saying. He thought she was mocking him for believing in aliens from another world. It all began to become very clear to him. He was now convinced she was put up to mess with him by Trish and Tasha. He got up angrily. "Fine, go back to the rock you come from, and have a happy life." He walked off in silence.

She got up and wanted to call to him, but she knew it would not change the situation. She thought how this was similar to their separation five years earlier but ironically reversed. It broke her heart to do this, she knew it would take a long time to heal.

He got nearly fifty yards away as she stood and watched him, tears pouring down her cheeks. This was the very same scene she had to endure five years ago. He turned around and started to come back to her. Her heart raced, and she began to walk toward him. They instinctively melted together in a strong embrace. She could feel the tears from his eyes soak through her blouse. "I didn't mean that."

"I know," she said between sobs. "Believe me, I cannot be a part of your life. And you cannot be a part of mine. I wish we could be together forever, but we can't. I cannot tell you why. You must trust me." They were suddenly flooded with headlights.

He kissed her passionately even though neither one of them had kissed anyone before this night. Linda felt a surge of emotion race through her body as they kissed. She struggled with herself to let go of him. They said nothing else to each other. She turned to walk to the car. Her knees suddenly went weak, but she caught herself. Susan got out of the car and opened the door for her. Without saying anything, Linda threw herself into the backseat of the car. Susan pushed the seat back and got into the front seat.

Trish looked out of the car and asked Allen, "Will you be all right, Allen? Want a ride?"

"No, thank you," he said, somewhat appreciatively. He turned away and began to walk slowly toward the river.

Trish and Susan were in the front seat. Susan looked back at her sister, hoping to hear her say she wanted to leave with her for Allen. Instead, she saw Linda curled up on the seat, convulsing in tears.

Susan didn't know what to say to her. "Linda, I am sorry I put you through this torture. I should have never tried to talk you into this." Susan reached around as best she could to clutch Linda's knee. She turned back around and realized she and Linda would have to say good-bye themselves in a few minutes.

"Where is he going?" Trish asked about Allen as she saw him in the rearview mirror. Susan looked back at him as Trish said, "Looks like he is going to the river. I hope he isn't thinking of drowning himself."

"Shhh." Susan gestured so Trish wouldn't upset Linda. She drove down the street, watching Allen as he turned away from the river.

There was a weak, nasal voice that spoke up from the backseat. "Is your apartment nice?"

Susan turned around and said calmly, "Yes, it is. I will be very happy there."

"I'm glad," Linda said.

They got back to Trish's house soon and transformed Linda back into an Amish girl. Trish asked Linda, "If Allen wants to know about you, what should I tell him?"

Linda replied in an unenthusiastic tone, "Originally, I was your cousin from Ohio, but I think he really believes that I come from another world."

Trish chuckled. "Another planet. I wouldn't doubt that he believes in that stuff." She shrugged her shoulders. "How did he get the idea that you're from another planet?"

"Another planet?" Linda questioned her own explanation. "I told him I was from another world that was very different from his."

"Really," Trish said. "No wonder he thinks you're from another planet.'"

"No, just another place that is different from his own." Then it occurred to Linda why Allen got so angry about it. "He believes in life on other planets. So he believes I was mocking him by saying I'm from another world or planet."

Trish chuckled, "That makes perfect sense."

Susan looked at her sister all dressed in her heavy, dark-blue Amish outfit. "We'll take you to the four corners, and you will have to walk home from there." Linda only nodded.

Once they reached the four corners, both Susan and Linda got out of the car, both girls fighting back tears as they stood facing each other in the moonlight. Susan opened up the dialogue, "This is really hard for me to do. Leaving you is the one thing that I hate most about leaving. I will miss you so much."

Linda nodded. "I will miss you. We will all miss you a great deal." She sighed, finding it hard to breathe. "Please don't go," Linda pleaded, hoping to get her to come back. "Come back home with me now."

Susan had her mind made up and was not going to change it. "You come with me," Susan pleaded hopelessly to Linda.

"I just can't," she blurted out with tears flowing down her face.

"I know," Susan agreed. "We can keep in touch though."

"How?"

"You know the big rock right over there," Susan began to explain.

"The big rock," Linda confirmed. "All right, I'm listening."

"Behind and under the big rock, I buried a small metal box. In that box is a note." Susan paused. "If I leave a note or if you leave a note, stick a stick in the ground next to it."

"There is a note in it already?" Linda asked.

"Yes, it is a good-bye note."

Linda quietly, sadly said aloud to herself, "A good-bye note." The feeling of this being the final time to see her sister had become a reality. She had hoped it had been a joke and really would never happen, yet here they were.

They hugged, and Susan turned away and got back in the car. Linda could hear her say with an emotional, shaky voice, "Let's go."

Trish said politely, "Good-bye, Linda. Remember to check for the message."

"I will, every day," Linda replied kindly. "Bye," she said weakly. The car pulled away; the red taillights and the sound of the car on gravel drifted away. The night suddenly became eerily quiet and dark.

CHAPTER NINE

Getting on with Life

Afterward, Linda was able to calm herself down from having noisy, sobbing fits so she could sneak back into the house unnoticed. She was already missing her sister. She wanted to see her again tomorrow so she could talk to her about Allen. She now felt completely alone. She had no one to talk to about the situation, no one she could confide in.

She got into bed, knowing that in just a few short hours she would be awakened. It seemed like no time at all before her mother came bustling into their room to wake them up. She noticed that Susan was not in her bed. She did not recall her being downstairs when she came up. "Did Susan go out last night?"

"Yes," Linda said without the German drawl. She dreaded having to tell her about Susan. She knew her mother would certainly be upset. She was too tired and heartbroken to really care about anything.

"I hope she comes home soon," she said as she picked up Linda's clothes that were uncharacteristically lying on the floor. "Did you go out as well?"

"Ya," she admitted.

"When will Susan be home?"

"She's not coming home, Mother," Linda said plainly with a slight sympathetic tone.

The way Linda said it told Clara that it was as true a statement as she had ever heard.

"What do you mean she isn't coming home?"

Linda rolled over on her bed lazily. Clara could see she had been crying. "She has gone to live in the English world."

"English world," Clara was stunned. "She left us?"

Linda was not surprised at her mother's tone but was desperate to get back into her mother's favor. "They're not my words. They're her words."

"Get out of that bed!" she yelled angrily. "We have work to do!" Linda sprang up quickly and got dressed, not wanting to upset her mother any further. She recklessly went downstairs as quickly as she could. They silently worked to get things ready without a word to each other. Her mother did not say anything to the rest of the family concerning Susan. Linda could see the tears gather in her eyes, and once in a while, a tear would roll down her face. When Paul asked his mother where Susan was, she answered, "She will be home later." The first words she said to Linda after they had been working in the kitchen for an hour was, "If you knew she was leaving, why didn't you stop her?"

Linda did not answer right away, hoping to find the words that would exonerate her from the responsibility. But when her mother looked sternly at her, she was compelled to answer. "I don't know. She was very determined."

When the families started to show up for the meeting, many of the women jumped in to help out. As far as Linda could tell, no one knew there was anything wrong. Linda was proud of her mother working hard and putting on a friendly demeanor for her guests.

Linda found inspiration in her mother and was also able to pretend to be happy. She overheard one of the women asking Clara, "Is Susan ill?"

"No," Clara answered gruffly. The woman dropped the subject quickly, and later, Linda noticed the woman speaking quietly to the others. The rest of the day, the women were very kind and supportive of Clara, as if they knew what had happened.

The meeting that morning went very well. Clara and her helpers served the noontime meal with great success. Linda's father asked several family members where Susan was. None of them was able to give him a definitive answer. Clara kept herself busy in the kitchen and was surrounded by women throughout the day, so John was unable to ask her directly. The afternoon service seemed to last forever for the tired Linda. She was almost hoping it would never end. She knew her father would soon be privy to the news.

Soon after the neighbors had left, she noticed her father was upset. She tried to avoid him, hoping not to be blamed for Susan leaving. He might want to punish her in some way. Their relationship had not been the best ever since he punished her for meeting Allen.

As the house emptied out, the anger she had seen in her mother was gone. It was replaced with pure heartbreak. The family would now have to face the fact they must shun their beloved Susan for the rest of their lives. They were bound by Amish rule to turn their backs on her if they saw her and to never speak to her again.

The community would soon excommunicate her, and she would no longer be considered Amish. Susan's only hope would be to return and confess her sins at the next confession. She would then have to take communion. A process Linda knew Susan would never do.

Linda was never confronted by her father about her transgressions concerning Susan's departure. In the days that followed, he treated her very well, almost showing great gratitude that she chose to stay.

The large rock at the four corners just down the road from their farm had now become very important to her. She was anxious to get to the rock to retrieve the letter Susan had left.

Linda met with Luke later; they did not go to the singing. She coerced him into walking past the rock.

"Sorry about your sister," he told her.

"Don't be sorry. We will miss her, but knowing this is what she really wanted and she is happy now eases the pain."

"How do you know she is so happy?"

"I know," Linda sadly admitted.

Luke knew the two sisters were close. "You knew she was leaving, didn't you?"

"Ya, I knew."

"You couldn't stop her?"

Linda thought before answering, "No, I really didn't try to stop her. We talked, and she decided." They were approaching the rock. "You may not want to get involved in this next thing I am going to do."

"Why? What are you going to do?"

"You don't want to know." Linda put her hand on Luke's chest to stop him from moving any farther. She looked all around to see if there was anyone watching them.

"What is this all about?" he asked.

"You cannot tell anyone about this."

"About what?' He held his arms out, palms up.

"That I like to walk in ditches and look behind logs and stuff." She carefully made her way down into the ditch and back up the other side. Luke watched her as she made her way around a large fallen tree trunk.

She soon found the box and dropped immediately to her knees. It was an old, rusty metal cigar box. She retrieved the letter inside and stuffed it into her bonnet. She would read it later when she was alone.

He was surprised at her actions. "Don't you want to read it?"

"No, not yet."

"I don't understand."

"You're not here to understand, but you need to be"—she paused—"understanding."

"I don't understand."

When she made her way back to the road, she looked around. "Remember, you saw nothing and know nothing."

"I don't understand anything."

"That's what I like to hear."

"Is that note from your sister?" Linda stopped and looked at him. "I don't want to know, do I?"

She shook her head. "Nothing." She started walking down the road. Luke said nothing more and went along with her without concern as to what was going on around him.

Later that night, Linda quietly lit a candle and retrieved the note from her bonnet.

Dear Linda,

I realize what I have done is not going to set well with the family. I wish that I can come back to visit, but I know I can't. I hope that I can see you from time to time. We can do that, and no one need ever find out. I don't want to get you in trouble, so if you don't want to, I understand. If you want to see me, leave a note sometime soon. If I don't see you again, remember that I love you more than I can love anyone else. You are and always will be my sister. I will think of you and pray for you every day. I hope you have the life you want and lots of children that you always planned to have.

Love Forever,
Your sister Susan

Linda read through the letter several times before she tore it up into little pieces. She did not dare let anyone suspect there would be any further contact between her and Susan.

The following weeks, her mother's attitude for life had changed. Her fine, upbeat, philosophical personality was gone. She buried herself in her work and often helped out at neighbors' homes more often than before. Linda thought she might have taken it upon herself to make it up to God for Susan's betrayal.

One time, Linda noticed that she cleaned the same floor three times in an hour. She would catch her from time to time crying. It was obvious she could never leave because it would be so devastating to her mother.

For the next several months, Linda would take walks with Luke as often as they could. She would always want to go past the rock to see if the stick was up. He was never annoyed about having to walk past the four corners every time they took a walk. She felt guilty for having certain deep feelings for Allen and not for Luke.

She had grown very fond of Luke. He treated her better than any man could have, even maybe Allen. They were getting along so well she felt confident to tell him that she was receiving messages from Susan. He was not shocked, nor was he upset with her. He often would check for her to see if the stick was up or down by the rock. He respected her privacy and never told anyone.

Susan left messages a couple times a month. The notes pertained mainly about what she was doing and asked how the family was. She missed them very much but wrote about how she was in the "real" world.

Soon after Linda turned eighteen, Susan sent her a message to meet with her. They met at the bridge late one Saturday night. Luke had come over to see Linda that night, and the two of them went to the bridge to meet with Susan.

Susan was there standing next to her car. The car was nothing extravagant but impressive to Linda and Luke just the same.

Linda did not hesitate to give her sister a long, loving embrace when they met.

"Hi," Susan said. She seemed a bit apprehensive about Luke being there.

"Don't worry. Luke has been letting me know when the stick is up," Linda told her.

"Luke, you realize you can get into trouble for talking to me," Susan reminded him. "I've been baptized. I know what I am doing. This is important to Linda, so it is important to me," he said with confident conviction.

"I understand," she said politely. "Can I steal my sister for a moment?"

"Ya," he responded and walked away.

"Thank you," she said. "I have a job for you and a room where you can stay."

"What?"

"I don't work at Patty's Pizza Place anymore. I got a job at Sam's Sizzlin' Steak House. I am a cook and considered a good one. Apparently, Amish make great home-cooked meals people are willing to pay for. I told them my younger sister is a better cook than I am," she said excitedly. "You really aren't as good as me, but I wanted Greg to hire you. You can come right now if you wish. Greg wants to meet you and will build you your own room in the basement."

"My own room in the basement of the restaurant?" Linda asked.

"No," she said, smiling with delight, "at our house, Greg's and mine."

"You got married?" Linda asked in great surprise.

"No, not exactly," Susan said with a coy smile. "We live together. And we sleep in the same bed." There was a moment of silence as Linda absorbed the information. "He wanted to come tonight to meet you, but we discussed it and decided it wouldn't be a good idea." Linda nodded her head slightly, and Susan added, "So how about it? It would be so much fun being together again."

Linda barely shook her head. "I can't," she said mournfully. "You—" She thought about telling her how their mother was devastated when she left. She decided that if Susan knew about it and felt guilty, that was all right with her. "I never told you about Mother."

"What about Mother?" Susan asked. "Is she all right?"

"She hasn't been the same since you left. It has destroyed her." She did not want to hurt Susan, but she wanted her to understand why she could not leave.

"If I could see her and explain how happy I am, she might feel better."

"I wouldn't tell her that you are living with—" Linda had to think for a minute.

"Greg," Susan finished for her.

"Greg," she said. "I can talk to her. She might agree to see you secretly."

"Then she would know I have been in contact with you. Sweetie, you shouldn't say anything, or you will be in trouble," Susan said. "The consequences aren't worth you getting into trouble."

"I believe she would love to see you," Linda said. "I'll check it out."

Luke was invited to join them as they talked for the next two hours, exchanging news of the family. It was hard to say goodbye, but they were able to eventually depart, knowing that they would see each other again soon.

The next morning, while Linda was cleaning up after the family breakfast, she said to her mother, "I wish I could talk to Susan one more time. Maybe I could convince her to come back."

Clara was facing away from her, scrubbing a large fry pan. She stopped scrubbing and raised her head to look out the window. "You can contact her, can't you?"

Linda was not sure how to answer, but she knew the truth would be best. "Ya."

Her mother slumped her shoulders as if she were disappointed. Without turning around, she said, "Linda, you are not to see or speak to her anymore."

"I need to see her and talk to her. She is my sister."

"She gave up being your sister when she left us."

Mary came into the room, which stopped the conversation. This gave Linda a few moments to collect her thoughts. She decided on a simple offer to get them together. Mary eventually left the room.

"Susan wants to see you."

"No, it was her choice to never see us again."

A few weeks later, Linda was baptized, devoting herself to God and the Amish way of life. She was committing a sin by communicating with her excommunicated sister, but she continued to do so anyway. She confessed to seeing her at confession and was allowed to take communion that fall.

She and Luke grew very close over the next several months. That summer they announced their plans to marry in November. Most Amish weddings take place that time of the year. The communication system for Linda and Susan worked so well Susan knew before anyone else. She knew if she went at the right time, she may be able to witness the wedding without anyone noticing her.

It was cold and gray on the day of the wedding. The leaves had all vacated the trees and now decorated the ground in reds, yellows, oranges, and browns. The wedding was held at the Hershberger house. There were people everywhere in the house crowded into every room. While the wedding was taking place, Susan slipped into the back door dressed in a dark dress to mix better with the Amish attire. It was going well until her younger sister, Mary, saw her. She was so excited to see her she could not stop looking back at her. Soon, everyone knew she was there, and they all remained facing away from her.

Linda had looked back to see what the disruption was. She saw Susan and the hurt look that was on her face. She turned to everyone and spoke with confident clarity, "My sister does not wish to show disrespect to us, but she is showing love and respect for Luke and me. Please, everyone, shun her as you must, but please let us continue with the service without any further distractions."

Linda's father stood up, making sure he did not look upon his daughter Susan. "I agree with my daughter. We must ignore the unworthy so it does not disrupt this joyous occasion." He then looked to the ministers and the deacon for an approval to continue. The minster continued with the ceremonies.

Susan stood in the back and watched in silence. Mary often snuck peeks back at her older sister, which was received with great delight by Susan. As soon as the ceremony concluded, Susan exited quickly. She briskly walked back to her car.

When she got to her car, she heard hurried footsteps behind her on the gravel road. She turned around just as Mary, who was fourteen, and Joel, who was eleven, plowed into her. They had outstretched arms and tears in their eyes. Susan began to cry as well. "I miss you two."

Mary pleaded, "Why don't you come back?"

"I can't. I am so sorry."

"Will you come to my wedding too?" Mary asked.

"I sure will," Susan answered.

"Good, I will get married just as soon as I can," Mary said as she cried. Joel was hugging Susan and did not speak a word.

There was a firm yell from the house. "Mary! Joel! Get back here now!" It was apparent their father was upset with them for running after Susan.

"You two better get back," Susan told them. "I love you both."

Joel still did not speak, but she could tell in his eyes what he was thinking. He began to run back to the house while Mary slowly walked back, looking back at Susan from time to time. Susan took one last look at the group of people now standing outside the barn. She saw Linda briefly look at her and give a short wave. It was a great relief to her to have been there when her sister Linda got married.

CHAPTER TEN

Ready for a Family

After the wedding, Linda moved in with Luke and his family. Many of Luke's brothers and sisters had moved away to start their own families and farms. Luke's parents ran a large farm, so they encouraged him to stay with them. It would be several years before he and Linda would have a family large enough to run their own farm.

The next two years were Linda's happiest times. They were trying to start a family while living close to her family's farm. She was able to contact Susan from time to time. The stream was available to her if she wanted to visit it. Luke's family was very grateful to have her in their family, and she liked them very much.

She was particularly entertained by Luke's father, who liked to get the local newspaper. He insisted it was to keep track of the farm markets but seemed to get a chuckle about some of the news stories. He was delighted to read about things people would do to themselves. He would sometimes share stories with the family, or Linda would sneak a read of an article. Things could not have been any better for her.

After a few years of trying to have children, Luke and Linda were encouraged by both mothers to go to the doctor. The couple was reluctant, but they wanted children very badly. Linda wanted to have a meeting with Susan to discuss the topic. But they had not heard from her for several months, and she did not pick up the last note they had left for her. Out of concern for her, the two of them went to town to find her. They went to Sam's Sizzlin' Steak House, where they found out she had broken up with Greg, the owner, and no one knew where she had gone.

On their way home, they stopped to put a letter for Susan back under the rock. After a few months with Linda still not pregnant, they decided to go to the doctor. They still had not heard from Susan.

Luke drove Linda and both their mothers to the doctor's office one fine morning. Linda hoped to see her sister among the people on the street. When they finished with the doctor, neither Luke nor Linda wanted to talk about their situation and actually did not want to talk to anybody about anything. The mothers were all anxious about what the doctor had told them. Linda and Luke remained silent about their experience with the doctor even to each other.

At a follow-up session, the doctor informed them Luke had trouble producing active sperm, and the chance of a pregnancy was very slim. This was devastating news to both of them. Luke wanted to have children very badly, but what hurt him most was his inadequacies destroying his wife's dream.

On the way home, when they approached the mail rock, they noticed the stick was no longer sticking up. Linda's spirits rose as they approached it.

"See if the letter is gone," Linda ordered Luke.

"I was going to," he said. He stopped the horse and jumped out. He patted the horse gently as he nearly fell into the ditch. He was about to reach down for the box when they both heard another buggy coming down the road toward them.

"Luke, the Mangrich's are coming." Luke turned around and walked into the trees behind him. He unfastened his pants and pulled them down slightly. As the Mangriches' buggy neared them, Linda smiled broadly.

Jeb Mangrich stopped the buggy. "Everything all right, Linda?"

Linda smiled happily. "Luke just couldn't hold it." They looked to Luke, who had his back to them.

The Mangrich's both smiled as Jeb Mangrich said, "I see." They all chuckled a bit as he flicked his reins, and the horse began to pull the buggy down the road.

Linda watched as they left the immediate area. "Luke, you can stop now."

"It's still coming," he said. "I had to go more than I thought."

"You were really going?" she yelled out of the buggy at him.

"Ya!" he said as he pulled up his pants. "I seized the moment."

He quickly dug into the dirt for the box and lifted it up so she could see that it was empty. He buried the box then ran back to the buggy.

As he lifted the reins to start the horse, Linda asked, "Do you think someone else may have found the box?"

"I don't believe so," he answered unconvincingly.

They were not positive Susan had received the message. They thought of the consequences if someone else had found the letter. A few days later, on their way to visit Clara, they noticed the stick was up. They were being followed by another buggy, so they could not stop. Linda enjoyed the time with her mother, but the thought of a note from Susan after such a long wait made her uneasy. Clara sensed the tension but did not pursue an explanation.

As they approached the rock, Linda leaped out of the moving buggy. She frantically dug the box out and read the paper inside.

"What does it say?"

"Meet me at the place Saturday night." Linda was excited and could not wait three more days until they were to meet.

Linda decided to go by herself. He gave her a quick kiss when she left that night. She walked along the deserted country road in the half-moonlit night giving an eerie gray glow to the gravel road. The sound of frogs and crickets seemed to scream at her as she walked along. Ahead at the meeting place, she saw a car and two people standing next to it. A woman called out, "Linda?"

"Ya," Linda said wearily. The woman began to walk toward her. "Susan," Linda exhaled as she recognized her. They hugged for a moment and started to walk toward the car.

"I gave your problem some thought," Susan said excitedly. "Did the doctor give you any alternative options?"

"No," she said.

"Well," Susan added, "you could try to adopt a child. You can try artificial insemination."

"I understand what adoption is, but what is artificial insemination?" They had by then come within hearing distance of the man waiting at the car.

Susan smiled. "I am sorry. It is taking a man's semen and implanting it inside your uterus."

The man waiting at the car said, "I can help you out right now if you want me to. You could be pregnant by the time you go home tonight."

Susan said sternly to the rough-looking man, "Shut up."

"Hey, just trying to help," the man chuckled.

"Don't pay any attention to him," Susan said. "By the way, this is Jim."

Jim stepped over to Susan. "See this?" he rubbed Susan's belly. "I helped her. I can help you as well. It would be fun. You will enjoy it."

Linda was confused by this man's words. She looked closer at Susan. "You're with child," Linda said happily.

"Yeah," Susan said happily, and then, in a much sadder tone, "But it is his baby."

Jim angrily said, "You don't want to have my baby. Fine, you can walk home. If you're lucky, you may lose it." He swung his fist, striking Susan, who rolled into the ditch. Linda rushed to assist. Jim got in the car and spun his tires, throwing rocks around. Despite Linda's attempt to cover Susan from the rocks, they were both pelted by several of them. Linda felt a stinging pain on the back of her neck and cheek.

"Are you all right?" Linda asked Susan.

"Yeah," she answered as Linda assisted her standing up. They brushed the dirt from their clothes. "He gets that way sometimes," she said quietly with embarrassment.

"Why was he mad?"

"It was my fault. I made it sound like I didn't want him to be the father," Susan said. She was trying to give Linda the impression she was happy.

Linda watched the car in the distance. "Who is he?"

Susan answered grudgingly, "He's the guy I've been seeing."

"I've seen him, and I don't want to see him again," Linda honestly said.

Susan started to cry. "Me either. But I am stuck with him now."

"Because he is the father?"

"Yes," Susan regretfully said. "Unless I get an abortion or, what he would like, a miscarriage, I'll be stuck with him for the rest of my life."

"You must not say that," Linda added. "This is your child. God's gift to you. It is the most precious thing a woman can do in her life. A child will make your life wonderful."

"Stop trying to cheer me up." She studied Linda's cheek that had a dark spot on it. She could not see what it was in the dark. She placed her hand on Linda's cheek.

"Ow," Linda said.

"You're bleeding," Susan told her as a few drops of blood dripped down her cheek.

Susan began to remove her shirt. "Susan, it's all right," Linda said to her.

"It's all right. I have a tank top under it."

Linda knew she wasn't wearing a tank, so it had to be a type of clothing. Susan took her shirt and dabbed at the blood on Linda's cheek.

"Oh let it go. You don't want to ruin your shirt."

"I can wash it out." Susan passively said. Then she dabbed at her cheek once again. "Linda!" she shouted as a thought came to her suddenly. "Look at me," she said in a serious tone then started babbling rapidly. "I have a child I don't want, and you are trying desperately to have a child you do want. You take my baby. Yeah, I'll have your baby for you! I'll have lots of babies for you! It will be great. You can pretend to be pregnant, and when I have my baby, you can sneak away and come home with a baby. This will be great!"

"Wow, calm down, Susan. Listen to yourself."

Susan calmed down to think properly. "Let's think this out before we get too excited."

"We, get excited!" Linda barked out, defending her calm emotion. "I'm not the one crowing at the top of her lungs. Now, please explain, but do it calmly this time."

"Well, it's simple," she said with a smile. "I have the baby, and you take it as your own."

"Can we do that?" Linda asked. "I don't believe the Amish faith would allow it."

"That is why you are secretly not pregnant but you pretend to be pregnant."

Linda was not excited about pretending to be pregnant. "It would be deceiving God,"

"If we do it secretly, only we will know." Susan thought for a moment. "Jim will get ugly about it."

"He is already ugly enough," Linda said.

Susan was struck by her sister's ridicule of a man she barely knew. "That statement surprises me. It is not like you to be so harsh about anyone."

"I don't like him," Linda said. "He is a bad man."

Susan chuckled. "Anyway, we can't take a chance of something getting in the way. And for this to work, we must start the story now because if we wait, it will not work."

"What if it doesn't work? I will look like a deceitful person. And what about Luke?"

"Luke will have to be privy to it. It is foolproof. It can't fail."

"Of course it can fail," Linda reasoned. "I'm involved. I'm terrible at keeping secrets."

Susan had to think in more detail. "Oh wow, let me think for a minute about this."

"You take all the time you need. Don't you want to have your own child?"

Susan was happy again as she said, "It will work. It will be fine. I know it will."

"Are you going to be able to give up your baby just like that?" Linda asked.

"Knowing that you two will be great parents will make it bearable," Susan said, trying to convince herself that this would be a good thing. "Let's go tell Luke."

"We need to get you home somehow," Linda reasoned. They noticed a car approaching down the road. The two sisters did not want to be seen, so they moved back deeper into the wooded area behind the rock. As the car went by slowly, they could see it was Jim.

"There goes my ride home," Susan said casually.

"What are you going to do about him?" Linda asked.

"Maybe we can catch him," Susan thought out loud. "Actually, it would be best to stay away from him forever."

"What happened with you and Greg?" Linda blurted out in curiosity.

Susan's face sank into a tired, sad posture. "He was messing around with a waitress."

Linda had visions of him and a waitress cleaning up a mess on the floor of the restaurant. She did not press for any further explanation but did not think that was any reason to break up over. "I'll wake Luke, and we'll drive you back to town."

"You mean I can have a buggy ride." Susan's sadness was replaced with excitement.

"Sure," Linda said joyfully.

The two of them began to walk to the farm of Luke's father. They talked about the family and what their brothers and sisters were doing. Susan explained more about Jim and what he was all about. They were getting close to the farm when Susan doubled up, clutching her stomach. "Oh my," she said. Her eyes were wide open, and her voice shaking in agony. Susan slowly fell to her knees, clutching at her stomach.

"What is it?" Linda asked as she bent over her sister.

"Pain!" she yelled as tears filled her eyes. Linda had to pull her to get her off the road. She helped her sit with her back against a signpost.

"What is it?"

"I don't know," Susan said with agonizing effort.

"Stay here. I'll get Luke." Linda left in a hard run, which was strenuous when wearing heavy, stiff shoes and a long, thick skirt. She frantically ripped her shoes off. The rock on the road tore at her feet, and the grass was thick and wet.

Quick and quietly, she entered through the front door. She ran up the stairs two steps at a time and flew down the hall to their bedroom, where Luke was in bed sleeping.

"Luke, get up." She shook him. Luke quickly sat up with a wild look on his face, his hair sticking up wildly. Linda shook him to make sure his head was properly activated to the reality of the situation. She placed her hands on both sides of his face, making eye contact. "Listen and don't ask any questions. Get the buggy and go down the road to the north. Run the horse." He appeared to be unresponsive. "Hurry now, and be quiet, but hurry now!"

"What," he said blankly. He began to stir.

Linda stuck her face in front of his. "Get the buggy and run the horse down the road to the north. Susan is hurt bad."

She ran out of the room, down the steps, and out the door quickly and quietly. As she started to run down the road, she yelled out, "I'm coming, Susan."

"Hurry," Linda could hear Susan faintly yell back to her. She could hardly understand or hear her through the pounding sound of her stocking feet and her heavy breathing. Her feet were raw and numb from the gravel. She knelt down next to her. "Luke is coming with the buggy. I told him to run the horse."

"You shouldn't run the horses."

"I know, but this is important."

"I'm bleeding," Susan said.

These words sent chills down Linda's back. She could see a darkened spot in the crotch of Susan's pants. She looked down the road and figured it was taking Luke a long time to get there.

"It takes time to hitch horses," Susan said then grimaced with pain.

"Ya," Linda grudgingly agreed. Several minutes passed in silence as Linda held Susan's hand and rubbed her head gently. "I'll kill him if he's fallen back to sleep."

"No you wouldn't." Susan chuckled then gasped in pain. She clutched Linda's hand when the sound of a buggy cut through the thick night air.

"I see him. He's not running them," Linda said angrily. "Well, at least he hitched up Frances. She is the fastest horse we have." She saw him whip the horse to get her to run.

Linda knew Luke never whipped a horse or showed any mistreatment for an animal in his life. She was proud of him for whipping the horse regardless of his feelings. It proved to her that he cared so much for her that he would do something he detested for her. Linda stood up and began to wave her arms to get his attention. Frances didn't want to stop, but once she did he jumped out and joined his wife.

"What's happened?"

"She's bleeding. I believe she is having a miscarriage. We need to get her to the hospital right away." Linda reached down to help Susan get up. "Help me," she addressed her husband angrily. He instantly assisted his wife in lifting Susan up into the buggy. The two of them picked Susan up and got her into the buggy. It was obvious that Luke had not taken much time to dress. His pants began to fall down because he had not thrown his suspenders over his shoulders; they dangled behind him. He had also grabbed his straw work hat instead of a black, brimmed hat.

Susan noticed that he did not have any shoes on. "You are so sweet. You didn't even put on shoes."

"I brought them though." He pointed down at the floor of the buggy. He started the horse off in a strong trot.

"Run her!" Linda demanded frantically.

"She won't make it to town if we run her," Luke tried too explained.

"Yes, she will. She will have to make it," Linda demanded.

"Linda," Susan yelled, "he is right. Now will you just relax. You're driving me crazy." Linda quieted down and sat back like she had just been chastised. "It's nice seeing you again, Luke," Susan said calmly. She was curled up as best she could in the cramped backseat. They hit some rough road bumps that caused Susan to scream in pain.

"Take it easy on the bumps," Linda sternly told her husband.

"You want me to slow down?" Luke asked sarcastically.

"No, I want you to go faster. But take it easy on the bumps."

"It's dark. I can't see the bumps."

"Well, look for them and see them anyway."

"Good gracious, Linda," Susan said, "just let him take care of the driving."

The buggy began to slow down. "What are you slowing down for?"

"Sharp turn," Luke said, hoping not to upset his wife. They had come to an intersection where they needed to make a left turn.

There wasn't much said for several minutes. Susan was showing signs of passing out. "Don't leave me," Linda said. Susan opened her eyes and forced a weak smile. Linda could see that her pants were now soaked with blood. She began to pray out loud. Luke continued to press the fastest trot he could get out of Francis. He looked down at Susan and decided to whip the horse, and Francis broke into a strong run.

When they approached the hospital, Linda directed Luke where to take them. She saw a glowing sign. "Emergency entrance. Go over there." When they pulled up to the double doors, she yelled out, "Help us, please!"

Linda jumped out of the buggy and started to go to the doors. She saw a woman's face in the window and heard a muffled voice saying, "There's a horse and buggy out here."

The door swung open as Linda was near it, and a man came out and asked, "What can we do for you?"

"It's my sister," Linda said urgently. "I believe she is having a miscarriage."

The man and the woman quickly walked to the buggy and looked in at her. Luke had gotten out of the buggy and held the horse still. The horse was panting and sweating from the unusual workout. Luke feared that Francis might falter if he didn't get her to walk soon to cool down. Linda was now in a daze. Everything seemed to be moving in slow motion. She saw the man grab a small black box that he had attached to his belt and put it up to his mouth. He spoke into it. "We need a roller at the ER entrance stat."

There was then a bodiless voice that came from the black box, "We're on our way."

Several seconds later, there were two men dressed in dull-green, loose-fitting garments busting through the doors, rolling a bed with white linens on it. The woman who seemed to be the most interested in Susan said, "She has a weak pulse and is unconscious. Probably because of the sudden loss of blood." The four hospital people gently picked Susan up and laid her carefully onto the rolling bed. As they started to roll her past Linda, the woman asked, "Do you know her blood type?"

"I don't know."

"How far along is she?" one of the attendants asked.

"I don't know."

"Bob," the nurse addressed the man with the small black box, "you better get someone from the lab up here right away."

Bob grabbed his little black box once again. "We need lab work ER stat."

"Affirmative, lab work ER," the bodiless voice from the box said.

Linda followed them as they wheeled her sister into the hospital, Luke close behind her.

"Ma'am," a hospital attendant politely addressed her. They pulled a curtain around Susan, and the door shut in Linda's face. She could no longer see or hear what was going on with her sister.

"Ya," Linda responded finally.

"Would you like to come in here, please?" The attendant gestured toward the room across the hall that had a big window, and she could see a desk in the little office. "My name is Janet. I have some questions that I need to ask you."

Janet got her a cup of coffee and asked her several questions that Linda did not know all the answers to. She was in a dream as she worried about her sister and watched Janet punching little buttons on a board. As she received the answers to questions, she would punch the little buttons that would create little letters on a glowing screen in front of her.

Janet was confused why someone would know so little about their sister. "You are her sister, right?"

"Ya." Linda was very happy to be able to answer a question.

"Why don't you have a seat in the waiting room." She gestured across the hall.

Linda looked around blankly. "That room over there, with the pictures on the wall?"

"Yes."

Linda stood up to leave. "Thank you." She saw Luke come into the hospital. He walked over to her as she began to walk out of the little office.

"Ma'am," Janet addressed Linda, "you forgot your coffee."

Luke looked at her strangely as Linda picked up her cup of coffee. "What's that?"

"Coffee," Linda simply stated.

"You drink coffee?"

Linda held up the cup. "Apparently, I do during emergencies." The two of them went out and sat down to wait for the doctor to tell them what was happening with Susan. Linda picked up a magazine that was on the coffee table. It was an issue of *Better Homes and Gardens*. Linda was amused and intrigued by many of the pictures in the magazine.

A few minutes later, Janet came over to them. "Ma'am, I will need a signature that will authorize us to treat your sister."

"They haven't been treating her?" Linda desperately asked

"Well, yes, of course they have been," she said sympathetically. "This is only a formality. Your sister has been getting taken care of since she arrived."

"Oh." Then she remembered to add "thank you." She signed the paper. She took a sip of coffee and instantly remembered why she never drank it. She had tried it a few years ago and recalled the nasty bitterness. "Maybe it just takes a little getting used too." She shook her head. "It will take a lot of getting used too. Here." She held the cup up to her husband. "Help me out here." He tried it and looked a bit disappointed. "It is awful," Luke said as he pushed it away.

An hour later, a doctor came out to see them. Linda stood up. "Please sit down." He gestured for her to sit. He then sat down next to her. "You're her sister, right?"

"Ya," Linda said anxiously.

The doctor spoke calmly to comfort her. "She will be fine. She lost a lot of blood. We had to give her a transfusion. She had a miscarriage and lost the baby. We will have to do some testing, but I believe she may always have trouble carrying a baby. In other words, she will continually have miscarriages. But we will do some tests to make sure." He took a deep breath. "She will have to stay here for a few days. She is heavily sedated. When they get her into her room, you can go in to see her." He looked at them both. "Any questions?" The two remained silent as they shook their heads.

CHAPTER ELEVEN

The Need for a Child

"I need to go home to do our chores," Luke kindly told Linda. "You stay. I'll be back."

"Ya," Linda gratefully acknowledged.

Linda knew she would not be able to keep this a secret from the families. She knew that both Luke and she would be punished for their involvement.

"Luke," she called to her husband. He turned silently around to listen. "Could you tell my mother what has happened?"

He nodded. "Ya."

Susan had been given a sedative so she could rest. Linda stayed and sat quietly next to her bed. Linda dozed off in her chair from time to time. She was asleep in a very uncomfortable-looking position when Susan woke up.

Linda's head was kinked in a very awkward looking position. Susan leaned over and weakly reached out to try and tip Linda's head into a much more comfortable position. She was unable to reach her head, and the weakness forced her to give up the attempt. "Linda."

Linda's eyes popped open, and she leaned over to Susan. "Hello—"she brushed Susan's hair with her hand—"you had me so scared."

"Me too," Susan said softly.

"You should take it easy for a while."

"I can do that," Susan agreed, and then she solemnly asked, "I lost the baby, didn't I?"

Linda was sad to say, "I'm afraid so."

"There goes our great plan," Susan sadly expressed.

"It's all right," Linda comforted her.

"I'll have a baby for you yet. I'll get pregnant for you real soon."

Linda tried to smile and patted Susan's right hand. A tear trickled down her cheek, but she did not blink or quit smiling. Despite Linda's attempt to hide her emotions, Susan could sense that there was something wrong.

"What's wrong?"

Linda clutched her arm. "Nothing. I am just worried about you, is all."

"What happened?"

"You had a miscarriage."

There were several minutes of silence as Susan closed her eyes, and her head sank back into the pillow. Linda laid her head on Susan's chest and remained silent for several minutes.

A nurse came into the room and noticed Susan was awake. "Oh, you're awake."

"Yes, I am."

"You should have called us," she said. "I'll be right back."

The doctor came in a few minutes after the nurse had been in. He then explained what happened and what will probably happen in the future. He suggested she get an operation to prevent getting pregnant in the future. Susan was strong and took the news very well while the doctor was there.

The nurse smiled. "I'll check with you later. Just push the button if you need anything."

Linda asked, "What does she mean push the button?"

"Must be something like a remote on a television."

Linda looked up to the black box on the wall she knew was a television. Susan said, "There must be a remote around here somewhere." She shuffled around some papers, cups, and a tissue box before she spotted a small panel with many colored buttons. "Here it is," Susan said excitedly. "Take a look at this, Linda." She pushed the red button, and there was a crack, and light suddenly emanated from the big, black box on the wall.

Linda watched the television as it formed up a picture. The people in the television said, "Today, the Britons announced the Queen was undergoing an operation for an ingrown toenail." Suddenly, the picture changed into something completely different. There were several dark-skinned men chasing an orange ball on a wooden floor. The picture changed once again. There were two colorless men standing in front of a building. "Oh, this is *The Andy Griffith Show*. It is so funny, especially Barney. He reminds me of Ben Mangrich, skinny and frail."

Linda moved closer to the television that was hanging on the wall in the corner of the room. She could see the two men in the picture. Their lips were moving, but there was no voice connected with them. "Are they with the laryngitis?"

"No." Susan pushed a button on the panel, and a voice grew in volume until words could be heard. "This is a remote control. It controls the television."

The conversation continued between the sisters. Linda could not stop watching the pictures that were appearing on the television.

Luke found his way to Susan's room. When he came in, he saw that his wife and her sister were both crying. He quietly took a seat on the other side of Susan's bed. Susan hugged Linda's head as she again laid it on her chest. After a few hours of small talk, Susan said, "You better go home with your husband. He has been kind to allow you to stay with me this long."

"It is important for you and Linda to be together. I am in no hurry to go," Luke said.

"You are so sweet, Luke, but you both should go. You both will be in enough trouble being with me."

"Do you have a place to go when you leave here?" Linda asked, hoping she wouldn't go back to Jim.

"I think so," Susan said. "Trish will always let me crash there."

"Not back with Jim," Linda responded angrily.

"I may have to, eventually."

"Do you need money?"

"No, I'll be all right." Susan looked to the window. "I have some money saved up."

Linda sensed Susan was not being completely honest with her. "We have some money we can lend you," Linda said as she glanced to Luke. Luke briefly showed an agitated look but changed quickly to an agreeable attitude.

Susan smiled. "Thank you, but I will be fine. I sure do miss you."

"I miss you too." The two of them embraced once again. They turned to leave the hospital room when their mother stepped into the room. All four of them were silent.

Their mother looked to Linda and said, "You should go now and not see your sister again." She said in a manner Linda felt she meant it. Linda walked out without a response and did not look at her mother. "Please close the door." Luke closed the door as he left. Luke intended to close the door softly, but Linda slammed it shut.

Clara looked back at the door when it slammed, thinking that Luke had slammed it. Luke looked at Linda. Linda opened the door slightly. "I slammed the door, not Luke." She turned to her husband. "Are you happy now?" Luke was silent and simply nodded. Linda felt angry with herself afterward.

"Hello, Mother," Susan said weakly but excitedly.

Her mother did not respond to the greeting. Instead, she picked up the blanket Linda had been using and began to fold it neatly. She then laid it neatly on the chair at the side of the bed. She said with somber sympathy, "What happened?"

"I lost a baby," she said quietly with humility.

"I didn't know you had gotten married," she stated this knowing she would not know anything about her daughter's situation under the conditions of their relationship.

Susan hesitated just a moment before answering, "I'm not married." Susan told her, expecting her mother to chastise her way of life.

"You are a fine example of a tramp," Clara snapped out. Susan hung her head in shame. Clara felt angry at herself for her last statement. "I am sorry. Can you forgive me?" Clara asked.

Susan was caught off guard by this statement. "I should respect your position and not have expected you to be pleased with my turning away from my parents' way of life. I let you down and humiliated you. I am very sorry."

Clara stared at her for a few seconds before saying, "I love all my children, even the ones that have strayed." She took her hand and touched Susan gently on the cheek.

"I'm not the only one that has left." Susan had overheard her mother talking to her father about a sister of hers that had left the faith. Susan was sure her mother did not know she knew.

She responded quietly, "You are the only one of my children that has left."

"My older sister had left the Amish faith in very much the same manner that you did." Clara's eyes began to glisten with tears before she solemnly spoke, "I saw her one time a few years after she left. It was at an auction sale in town. I wanted to say something to her, but I didn't." She fussed around with Susan's blanket once again. "Our eyes met a few times. She looked like she wanted to talk to me, so I turned away from her. I wished I had talked to her." She reflected back in time as Susan waited to let her mother reflect. "That was nearly twenty-five years ago. I wonder what she is doing now?"

Susan felt her mother was melting her hardcore Amish belief. "Maybe it is not too late to find out. What is her name?"

Clara shook her head. "I would have no idea. She probably got married and has a different last name."

"Well, what would her first name be?"

"Eleanor," Clara said.

Susan got an idea to try and find her aunt. It would give her a relative that she could talk to, maybe even have a relationship with. "Why are you telling me this?"

"I want you to understand why I am here."

Susan smiled slightly. "Well, I appreciate your consideration." Clara picked up the blanket on the chair, sat down, and placed the blanket on her lap. They talked about what was happening and how she could not have children.

As Susan finished telling her what was happening, her mother quickly responded, "Will you please come back to us? With confessions and communions, you may be in better graces to be baptized in a few years."

Susan let her mother finish before she firmly said, "No, I can't go back."

"Look at what this world has done to you. Why can't you see that?"

"Why can't you accept my wishes? I don't want to just go around cooking and cleaning all my life. I want to explore and do something that makes a difference," she explained.

Susan sat back and fell silent. Clara spoke, "I am sorry if I upset you." I only was having a mother's dream of being a part of her daughter's life once again. I am proud of you in many ways, yet I am afraid for you because I am not there to help you through life. It makes me feel like I'm a failure."

"Mother, you are not a failure. It was my decision to leave. You did everything you could to get me to accept your way of life. Your way of life is not bad. I loved being Amish. I just needed more," she said.

Her mother leaned over and placed her head on Susan's chest just as Linda had done. She left her head there as she spoke softly. "I do love you." She took a breath before she continued. "I am so sorry that you can't have children. I wish there was something I can do or say that will make things better for you."

"You have made things much better. You came to see me when I needed you most," Susan said as she began to cry. "I miss you so much, and knowing that you don't hate me will give me peace of mind."

"I will not be able to see you again, at least under regular circumstances," Clara said. "It doesn't mean you should get into trouble just to get a chance to see me."

Susan chuckled weakly, "I won't, Mother. I promise."

"I want to ask you for one favor," she said with great feeling, "please don't try to see Linda anymore. It can only cause her grief."

Susan understood that what her mother was asking was a good idea. Linda now had a husband and a place in the Amish culture. She might not be able to have children, but she was happy, and Luke seemed to be a wonderful man. "I can't promise you anything."

When Linda left Susan's room, she found her younger brother, Paul, sitting out in the waiting room near the nurses' station. "Paul." She walked toward him. "Susan will be delighted to see you. She will be impressed on how big you have grown."

Paul looked around. "Mother said I can't see Susan."

Linda stopped and thought silently. "She may be right. You could get her and yourself in trouble if you were to see her."

"I would like to see her though. Could you tell her that?"

"If I ever get to see her again myself, I will tell her." Linda sat down in the next chair to him. "I take it you drove Mother into town."

"Ya."

Linda thought he was acting very strangely toward her. "Are you afraid to talk to me?"

Paul looked around. "Sort of."

"I understand," Linda said sympathetically. "I take it Father did not want to come?"

"No, he didn't," Paul said. "He was very upset Mother came. He said we should have nothing to do with Susan, and she got what she deserved."

Linda looked at him. "What did he say about me that makes you so nervous?"

"He thought you should be shunned for your contact with her, and you would get all of us in trouble with the community."

"Well, we'll go now so you won't get into trouble for talking to me."

"Really, Linda, I don't care if they do make a fuss."

"Thank you, but we are going anyway. It's been a long night." She kissed him on the cheek.

The following week, after the afternoon Sunday service, the bishop approached Linda and Luke. "It is good to see you both here today. How are you?"

They were caught by surprise and afraid they might be in trouble for their involvement with Susan. "We are fine, Bishop," Linda said apprehensively.

Luke quickly added, "It was a wonderful service."

"I enjoy talking to the wonderful faces of those that can stay awake during one of my sermons." He smiled as he looked directly at Luke. Luke's face turned red as he recalled dozing off a few times during the bishop's two-hour sermon. "It is all right, my son. I didn't notice you catching a few z's."

"Well, you must know now," Luke squeamishly said.

"Ya." The bishop smiled.

Linda confidently said, "He is very sorry, Bishop, and I assure you he will never fall asleep during one of your wonderful sermons again."

"I know he won't." The bishop looked seriously at Linda. "We need to have a discussion with the council."

"Both of us?" Linda asked. She had hoped Luke was not in trouble.

"No, just you, Linda." He appeared to be evasive when he was talking to her.

Linda went with the bishop willfully. She knew what to expect and was ready to take any punishment the council gave her. She was ready to speak calmly and with respect to the laws of the Amish community.

The bishop led her to a large bedroom where there were several elder council members sitting and standing around. She noticed there were no other women in the room as the door shut behind her. She was apprehensive and knew they were going to lecture her then put upon her a burden of punishment for her relationship with Susan. The bishop gestured for her to sit in a chair. She sat down stiffly on the edge of the chair.

"Relax, Linda," said an elder wearing a wide-brimmed hat and the longest gray beard in the room. She reacted to the kind words by sitting back in the chair.

"Linda," the bishop said kindly, "we have a request of you that is important."

"As you are aware," one of the elders she knew as Schwartz said, "we are people of great tradition and faith. But we are in small numbers in many different areas of the world. Each charter has many families, but in time, our bloodlines become intertwined." He entangled his fingers together to symbolize interaction. "Inbreeding becomes a problem and a necessity." Linda became uncomfortable with the conversation. She remained silent and listened carefully to make sure she was not misunderstanding the course this conversation was taking.

Schwartz added, "I find this somewhat awkward to tell you this, so please bear with me." Linda thought if he was awkward with this conversation, then she must be headed for a great embarrassment. He continued, "There are times when a married couple isn't able to have children. We use these unfortunate times to bring in new bloodlines." Linda was beginning to understand that the purpose of the conversation had to do with their inability to have children.

"It is very discreet, my dear," one of the other elders said sympathetically. "No one outside this room will ever know. Very few of us know that these procedures take place."

Another elder added, "You will not know the father, and he will not know who you are." Linda began to understand what they were saying. She was embarrassed, offended, and frightened. She could feel her face flush red with embarrassment. Were they actually trying to get her to have sex with a perfect stranger to start a new bloodline?

The bishop began to explain, "We hire a man of good character—"

"Stop," Linda said softly. "You want to stud me out like I was some"—she had to think—"broodmare?" The fact Linda spoke to the council before being asked a question startled them. They looked at each other, wondering which one of them would answer her question.

Finally, one elder named Joseph, who had not spoken yet, spoke out. "It is one way, if it needs to be done. Our main function in our lives is to have families. A couple that has no children is not fulfilling their need for fornication."

"You want to have children, don't you?" the bishop asked her.

"Of course I do," she said, indifferent to their reasons for having her there. She thought they were being very callous about her feelings on the matter. She was nearly ready to speak out when the bishop clutched her shoulder, and she remained silent.

The first elder spoke up, "It is nothing to be ashamed of. You will be performing a great service to the Amish community, your family, and your husband. It will be quick, without humiliation. Your child will be strong and healthy."

She could not remain silent any longer. She leaned forward and, with great force of determination, said, "But the child will not be my husband's child, which means that child will not really be mine. You are asking me to do something that will…" She was stumped as to what to say. She knew it was showing weakness if she didn't finish her thought, but the thought evaded her. After several seconds, she sat silently back into the chair.

"Linda," the bishop said calmly, "take two weeks to think about it. Come up with some questions to ask. We will meet with you then and make the final arrangements."

Linda was lost in thought as she got up to leave the room. The bishop opened the door for her to leave. She was having trouble keeping her emotional distress in check while leaving the room. It had been a short conference, and Luke jumped up from leaning against the wall just outside the room. He could tell Linda was distressed. He was sure she had been chastised for seeing Susan.

When Luke asked her about the meeting, Linda would just shake her head. "I cannot talk about it. It is fine, nothing major." Luke knew Linda had always been open and honest with him.

Clara could see that Linda was upset. She did not want to talk to her mother about the situation. It was too embarrassing. Later, when they were alone, Linda talked to her mother about the perceived situation. Her mother was reluctant to believe the situation presented to her. Regardless of the thought, she was in support of the council and very unsympathetic.

Clara reasoned, "My child, I would be honored to be able to sacrifice my body for God and the good of the Amish faith," Clara told her daughter, knowing she would have trouble dealing with it herself.

Linda heard her say the words but did not believe them. "You would honestly tell me you would allow the invasion of your body by a man you did not know then turn around and live with yourself as you deceived your husband and family to believe the child you bear is your own flesh and blood."

"My child—"

"Quit saying 'my child,'" Linda spoke out defiantly. "That's the difference. I am born of my mother and my father, not my mother and some Yankee Doodle from the English community."

"Linda," her mother calmly said in hopes to soften Linda's demeanor, "don't you want to have children?" Linda walked away in silence.

Later, as Linda lay in her bed next to her husband, things seemed so peaceful, except for the words of the elders and her mother ringing in her head. "You have no choice" and "It just makes sense" haunted her thoughts. She was just beginning to come to grips with the reality of the situation when suddenly she had a thought that could buy her some time. The doctor had said becoming pregnant was not an impossibility but a highly unlikely event.

When the next meeting with the council took place, she was determined to make a statement before they could talk to her. She was summoned to a bedroom after the meeting. She stepped into the room and saw the same faces she saw two weeks earlier.

She did not wait for a welcome but spoke quickly, defiantly, and with a speck of sarcasm. "I will be honored and obliging to your request of having a child in any manner you wish. However, I will only do it after a reasonable attempt at motherhood in the traditional manner ~~that~~ has been tried. Therefore, I will meet with you one year from now to further discuss the situation. And if I am not properly impregnated by my husband, we will proceed with the studamentation of my body." She turned around and walked out of the room with no discussion allowed by the council on the matter.

The elders looked at one another befuddled by the statement and the new word she sprung on them—*studamentation*. They felt their authority had been stepped on, and they were appalled that this young woman would dare mock the proceedings in this manner. The bishop finally said, "Well, until next year." There was a murmur throughout the room as they reluctantly agreed.

Several elders mumbled out, "Did she say studamentation?"

"Ya."

"Where did she ever learn such a word?"

"I have never heard it before."

"I don't believe it is a word."

"I guess we have no choice but to do as she requested."

"That was no request," Abraham responded. "She demanded it."

"Ya," all the council members nodded and chuckled.

Abraham spoke to the bishop. "What about telling her she isn't going to be studded like a broodmare?"

The bishop answered, "You can try to catch her if you like. I am too old. Besides," the Bishop reasoned, "thinking that way may be of great encouragement for her."

For the next several months, Linda and her husband prayed to God to bless them with a child. Linda tried every way she could to get pregnant, often to the bewilderment and delight of her husband.

After eight months, Linda was becoming more desperate to get pregnant. She had talked to Susan a few times on other ways to get pregnant. Susan was appalled and impressed with her sister's techniques. She did supply her with pregnancy testing kits, which, disappointingly, always showed negative.

After nine months, Linda was close to giving up hope. One night, she saw on the back page of her father-in-law Abel's newspaper a picture of a man that looked like Allen. She tried to read the heading that was at an awkward and crinkled angle. She awkwardly tipped her head and shoulders to read it. "Recent Graduate," she read before Abel moved the paper down.

He chuckled as he spoke. "You shouldn't read the paper, especially that way. It is full of the devil's words."

"You are reading it," she implied playfully as she stood up. She found herself slightly lightheaded from the sudden movement and stepped back dizzily.

"See what I mean," Abel told her.

"That wasn't because of the newspaper's devilish words," she said, smiling.

With a smile still on his face, he said, "I know what to read and what not to read. I only get it for the market reports." Abel folded the paper so she could not read it. "And the advertisements."

Linda saw an advertisement for women's lingerie, which he was just looking over. "I understand," she said.

Later that night, after everyone had gone to bed, Linda went quietly downstairs to find the newspaper. She had to know if the picture was Allen. She found the newspaper, tucked it under her night garment, and with lantern in hand she made her way across the yard to the little barn. It was a calm, cool late spring night with a heavy dew in the grass. The crickets were making a strong call in the fields. Once she made herself comfortable in the little barn, she turned the lantern up and read the story.

> A recent graduate of Bronca University will open his new business as a local construction contractor. Allen Bernard Barber will open his business here in town. He graduated Jefferson High School here five years ago. He attended Bronca University and received a degree in engineering. Although Barber has an engineering degree, he has taken on several small remodeling jobs around town for the past four summers. He wishes to expand on that business to building bigger and better projects. "If things go well, I will plan to hire several workers to assist me," Barber said.
>
> He already has contracted to build a home for the mayor, whom he had done some work for in the past. "I have to make my mark somehow. So I have to start by building some houses. I hope it will eventually lead to bigger buildings," Barber said.

Allen is a single man on the rise in our humble community. Check out his advertisement for barber construction in this very newspaper.

His status of being single sent her into a whirlwind of thoughts. She thought if Allen were the man the council chose for her, it wouldn't be so bad. She laughed at her thought. She was impressed with his advertisement. She did not dare cut out his picture until Abel was finished with it.

The following week, she contacted her sister to plan a visit. That Saturday evening, Linda left to visit her family. She stayed there for only an hour before leaving to meet her sister at the rock. Susan was not at the rock when she approached it. Linda slowed her pace down to give her sister more time to show up.

There was a car coming down the road; it wasn't a car that she recognized. She tried to ignore it and continue down the road past the rock. The car was an old rusty thing with a woman in it. As the car approached, it began to slow down. She could then see it was Susan.

"Get in," Susan requested. Linda ran around the car and got in. She had trouble securing her belt, so Susan had to help her.

"So what is it you want to do that makes our meeting so urgent?" Susan asked.

"I need to get pregnant."

This did not surprise Susan since Linda had been trying for several years to get pregnant. "Well, you have been trying your best, haven't you?" Linda had not told Susan about the council's plan.

"You don't understand," Linda said. Then she proceeded to inform her of the whole situation. "I have eight weeks to get very pregnant, or they will do it for me."

"That's sick," Susan said disgustedly. "All right, I'm with you so far. We can dress you up and get you laid, girl."

"You're sounding more like Trish all the time."

Susan blankly shook her head. "I don't know what is wrong with me."

Linda blurted out, "I want to have a baby with a man of my choosing."

"Wow," Susan said. "Well, you will have a great selection at the Pedigree Lounge. We need to talk to Tasha."

"I want Allen."

"Allen Barber." Susan chuckled. "Haven't you gotten over him yet? Besides, he has turned into a real hunk."

"Hunk?" Linda questioned.

"Aah"—Susan thought of how to explain it—"a good-looking, popular guy with the ladies."

Linda was puzzled. "But the article said he was single."

"He is," Susan replied, "but they are at his door wanting to be with him. Do you really think he is going to choose you over all the others now? I mean, do you really think he would remember you as Tanya or as Linda? He has so many others to choose from." Susan really didn't know what Allen's love life was like, but she didn't want Linda to pursue him.

Linda was not sure. "I think he would. I only need him to have relations with me. Not marry me," Linda said with unusual cold emotion. She had never approached a man in any way to have sex. It will be uncomfortable for her to be with another partner, even if it was Allen.

"Linda, I can't believe you are saying this. It is so unlike you," Susan said.

"I am desperate to get pregnant," Linda frantically told her.

"What about Luke?" Susan questioned. "You technically would be cheating on him, you know."

"Well, of course he should never be told. What would be the difference if I were to get pregnant by a stranger in some sick ritual or by someone I know and respect?"

"Do you love Allen?" she asked tentatively.

Linda was confused briefly by the question. She did not know how to answer or how she really felt. "I don't love him. I hardly know him, really." She had to convince herself she did not love him. She tried to justify her actions by thinking that she could love both men.

"Then why are you so sure he should father your child?" Linda did not respond. "You don't know if he has some terrible mental problem that may be passed on to his offspring. Maybe he has really bad eyesight. What if he recognizes you later? What if he doesn't want to have sex with you?"

"He doesn't wear glasses," Linda fumbled out meekly.

"Maybe he wears contacts." Susan got excited about the idea. "Why don't we get you hooked up with a sperm donor program?"

"What?" Linda responded.

"A sperm donor program takes the sperm of different guys, and they implant the sperm into your womb," Susan said excitedly and sprung her hands into the air. "Voilà, you're pregnant. No cheating, no direct relations with a man, quick and clean. What more could you ask for, sweetie?"

"Sounds lovely." Linda liked the option but found it less exciting for some reason.

"We should talk to Tasha. She works at the hospital's clerical office." Susan shook her head. "I don't know why I didn't think of it before."

"Ya, months ago," Linda lazily responded.

"You're going to have to stop saying ya. You need to say yes or yeah."

"That will be tough."

"Just for tonight," Susan said. "You did it before."

They went to Susan's apartment above a small paint store in the business district of the small town. The apartment didn't look very nice from the outside. It was old, and the concrete brick on the outside appeared to have several patch jobs. "First, we'll give Tasha a call on the phone and see about getting you into the program."

The apartment was better inside. Susan had it tastefully designed in yellow-and-red flower curtains with nice pictures on the wall. "You mean they could do this tonight?" Linda could see there was a small kitchen and a small table. There were two doors, one of which went to an indoor little barn, and a bed.

"No, we will have to make an appointment I'm sure." Susan picked up a white banana-shaped item, poked at it with her finger, then placed it next to her head. Linda remembered that it was a phone.

There was a tall vase-looking thing that had a white hat on it. Susan reached up inside the hat and appeared to be tickling it. There was a click, and light suddenly glowed from it.

"Tasha," Susan said happily, "it's me." Linda heard some very faint voices. "I am fine, thank you." There were more voice noises before Susan talked again. "Tasha, Linda is here with me, and we were wondering about how to go about getting into the sperm donor program."

Linda could hear some laughter from the phone. As Susan talked to Tasha, she felt embarrassed that this discussion was taking place.

"Great! ... Really. Susan then said sadly, "That long ... There's no way to speed things up. Even if it were an emergency ... Well, there could be an emergency. Then we need to get her knocked up now, tonight." Then Susan started to tell Tasha the story of what the council was doing to Linda. Linda gestured for her not to say anything more about it. "I'll talk to you later. Thanks. Bye."

"Not good?" Linda asked.

"It takes months, and you need a complete physical to qualify as a recipient."

"Well, it's back to Allen."

"Yes." Susan gave up trying to talk her out of it. "I'll help you. I hope you won't live to regret what you are trying to do."

"I'm sure I will regret it someday."

"So," Susan slurred out, "where does he live?"

"I don't know where he lives," Linda said. "Should I just drop in on him?"

"No." Susan picked up a yellow-and-white book. "You call him and set up a date."

"Me, call him?" Linda was frightened at the thought of calling Allen.

"Yes, we'll get his number, and I'll dial his number for you."

"I don't know how to talk on the phone," Linda squeezed out.

"There's nothing to it. You just talk into the mouthpiece like you are talking to them if they were right here in the room."

"Really," Linda timidly said without any comfort in the thought.

Susan looked through the yellow-and-white book. "It's not in here."

"Do you get the paper?" Linda asked her as she remembered the article and advertisement in the paper had a number to call.

"No," Susan responded casually as she remained in deep thought.

Linda said, "The advertisement he had in the newspaper had a number to call."

"That would make sense," Susan said. "I'll go find a newspaper. Go through my closet for clothes you might want to wear. You will probably want something provocative." Susan left Linda in her apartment alone. Linda looked around the apartment curiously. She opened a door that had several sets of clothes. She was not sure what to wear that would be provocative. There was a knock on the door, which she thought was Susan. She opened the door to find Jim standing there.

CHAPTER TWELVE

Happy Family

Linda was stunned for a moment. Then she said, "I am sorry. Susan is not here." She began to close the door politely on him. He put his foot down to stop the door from closing. Linda saw a benevolent smile grow on Jim's face. "Please come back later."

"I think I found what I want," he said as he pushed Linda back into the apartment and closed the door. He continued to step closer toward Linda, forcing her to retreat hastily past a chair and lamp. He started to unzip his light-blue jacket. Linda was petrified. She thought of what she could do. She looked for anything she could use to strike him with. The most menacing thing she could see was a broom in the kitchen area.

He removed his coat and, with a benevolent smile, he moved closer to her. Susan stepped into the apartment and saw what was happening. "Get out!" Her defiant voice cracked the tension in the air. Linda shook in fright and relief while Jim didn't jump or turn around. He continued to stare indecently at her. He slipped his jacket back over his shoulders slowly. He then turned and walked out without saying anything.

Linda was relieved and angry. "I thought you weren't involved with him anymore?"

"I didn't think numb nuts knew where I lived." Susan casually searched the paper.

"How did you even get involved with him in the first place?" Linda asked.

Susan wasn't proud of some of the decisions she had made in the past. She certainly wasn't very proud of her relationship with Jim. "I was an idiot, desperate, I suppose."

"Well, I suppose I shouldn't talk, considering what I am about to do."

She stopped turning pages in the newspaper. "Well, I got a number that should get a hold of him." Susan picked up the phone. "Do you know what you are going to say?"

"Are you kidding? I am about to call a man that twists my heart, whom I haven't talked to in years, on an invention that I don't know how to use. I have never approached a man like this before." Linda finished her statement. "Of course, I don't know what to say."

"Okay, we had better call him now before it gets too late." Susan laughed. "I wouldn't be surprised he doesn't want to see you."

"Of course he wants to see me."

"You really think you made such an impression on him five years ago that he will drop whatever plans or babe he may have to see you, the one that ran out on him and didn't tell him who you really are? He thinks you were just using him to get a good laugh."

"Then why are you helping me?" Linda asked her angrily.

"I want you to get this out of your system and face reality," Susan admitted. "Besides, I'm your sister."

"He said I was very special to him," Linda defended herself.

"They all say that so they can get some." Susan gave her a loving, sisterly smile and a pat on the shoulder.

Linda wasn't sure what she meant. "What do you mean 'get some'?"

"It means they want a kiss at the end of the night. Anyway, I'll dial." Susan picked up the phone and began to dial. Linda panicked as she dialed. Suddenly, Susan thrust the phone into Linda's face and then stayed close to listen.

Suddenly, there was a click, and there was a man's voice saying, "Hello, thank you for calling Barber Construction."

"Huh," Linda forced out awkwardly.

"Huh," the man's voice returned.

"Huh," Linda said once again stupidly. Susan quickly grabbed the phone from Linda.

"Is this Allen?" she asked.

"Yes, it is. May I help you?"

"Sorry about before. I was hiccupping uncontrollably, Allen," she addressed him as she looked at Linda, rolling her eyes.

"Yes," Allen said.

"This is Tanya," Susan said, hoping he would hang up on her. "Tanya Tucker. Not the famous singer, of course."

"Tanya," he said with great excitement, "where are you? Can I see you?"

Susan was surprised by his quick response to see her. "Well, I was just in town for a day, and I wondered if you would like to get together? I mean, unless you are busy or if it would cause any problems with anyone you might be involved with?"

"No, I would love to see you again," he said. "Where are you? I'll come get you."

"I will need a few minutes to get ready," Susan explained, knowing they would have to frantically get her ready to see Allen.

"Fine," he said. "Shall I pick you up in an hour? Does that give you enough time?"

"That's fine. Pick me up on the corner of Mott and Chatham."

"That sounds cheap," he said. "How about at Teachers' Park by the river?"

"All right," Susan agreed. "I'll be wearing a red sweater."

"Don't worry. I remember how you look." Then he finished with a serene manner. "Your beauty is etched in my memory."

Susan was flattered as if he was talking about her. "Well, I'll see you in an hour then."

"Yeah," he said excitedly, "I'll see you then."

"Good-bye, until then," Susan said seductively while trying to keep a straight face.

"Good-bye," Allen responded.

Susan placed the phone down. "Boy, is he whipped."

Linda suddenly was concerned. "Is he all right?"

Susan chuckled lightly. "He is fine, Linda. I'm sorry. When I say he is whipped, it means he really likes you. You can do anything you want with him. Just be careful." Linda didn't completely understand what she was trying to say.

Tasha showed up just then. "Let's get things rollin'."

Tasha and Susan spent the next hour frantically getting Linda dressed and made up into Tanya. When they had finished, there was a knock on the door. Susan apprehensively went to the door. Linda watched Susan put her face up to the door as if she were trying to see through it. "It's Trish," she calmly said as she opened the door.

Trish swept into the room. "I just saw numbnuts parked out in the street."

Susan walked over to the window and looked out through a slightly drawn yellow curtain. "You remember my sister, Linda?"

"Sure," Trish said as she approached Linda with her arms out to hug her. They hugged and then joined Susan at the window. "You look more beautiful than you did five years ago."

Tasha looked her over. "We aren't dressing you for the objective at hand, though."

"What do you mean?" Linda asked.

"Well, the objective is to get him in the sack," Tasha said. "We should have dressed you in something more slip-out-off. You know, more cleavage showing, more leg maybe." She unbuttoned another button of Linda's blouse and then pulled open her shirt, showing more cleavage. "This will tell him that you are receptive of a kiss or two. That is all you need to get things rolling."

"Thank you," Linda replied quietly, knowing Tasha was an authority on getting men.

"You want him to take you to dinner and drinks," Tasha suggested.

"Drinks?" Linda quizzed her.

"Yeah, that might be just the thing to loosen him up for sex," she added. "Oh, and you should appear to have had enough but not too much."

"A drink," Linda said in wonderment.

"Yeah," Susan said.

"What kind of drink?" Linda questioned. "Lemonade, coffee?"

Susan smiled. "An alcoholic drink."

"You mean…"

"Yeah," Susan answered, "our parents would call it devil's water."

"I can't drink that," Linda explained.

Tasha shook her head. "You must, or the whole thing is for nothing. Guys try to get girls drunk, but in your twisted situation, you want him drunk. So you need to fake being a bit tipsy. You know, throw out your inhibitions."

Linda looked at her. "I can't deceive him."

"Why not? They do it all the time trying to get us girls to sleep with them," Tasha said with a twinkle in her eye. She got starry eyed. "Oh, the good old days."

"Are you leaving the Amish life?" Trish asked Linda.

"No, she just has a date with Allen Barber to get pregnant," Susan explained.

"You're kidding." Then she recalled the past. "That's right, you two had an affair."

Linda wasn't sure what she meant. "We talked a bit." Then she put the two together. "Oh, of course we had the fair."

"Oh sure," Trish said. "He is going to be a tough one to get." Trish looked out the window to see if she could see Jim lingering about. "I had to sneak in the back way so Jim wouldn't see me. I hope he doesn't find you again."

"He already has," Susan said distastefully.

Tasha sadly shook her head. "Sorry."

"It's time, Linda," Susan said. "I'll show you the back door so you won't be seen."

"All right," Linda said with a shaky voice.

"There are a few things we have to go over," Tasha said. "If he asks if you have protection, tell him that you have an IUD and you're on the pill. If he wants to put on a condom, you tell him that you would rather he didn't. It's the best. And be sure to stop him from going for any safety measures such as withdrawal." Linda was stunned silent by the instructions she was given. "We had better stop talking about it. I am getting horny," Tasha added. Linda's eyes grew wide, afraid she might see horns grow out of her head. She thought it was unlikely, but this different world had so many strange surprises.

She was shaking nervously as she followed Susan down the stairs and out the back door. Linda took a deep breath as she began to walk along the sidewalk toward Teachers' Park.

"Good luck," Susan said.

Linda could also hear Trish say, "I don't believe this is happening. I never thought the two of you would conspire to get her pregnant using Allen this way. I feel so privileged and thrilled to be a part of it."

She began to have second thoughts of making Allen a father without him ever knowing. But these were desperate times for her. Why should she punish Allen for a problem that she had? She stopped, took a deep breath again, and decided to go back to

Susan's. She turned around and came face-to-face with Jim. "Oh my," She squealed.

He looked at her as if he knew who she was. "You live in the same building as Susan Hershberger?"

"I"—Linda knew if he recognized her, it would be a disaster—"I don't live near here. I don't think," she said in anguish. "I don't know many people in the building yet."

"There are only two apartments in the building." He knew she was lying.

"I'm just visiting." Linda tried to salvage the situation. "I've heard her through the walls a few times. That's all." Linda turned around to walk farther into the park in hopes to get away from him. He grabbed her roughly by the arm.

"I know you," he said angrily.

"I have never met you before," Linda said forcefully as she tried to break away from his grip. He increased his grip on her and turned her toward him. "Let go of me," Linda pleaded.

"I know you. You're her sister," he said with a smile of joy.

"No, I'm not." Linda began to cry. "Now let me go."

Another male voice calmly interrupted the altercation. "Let her go." There was a flash of a fist connecting with Jim's face. Jim's large body dropped sprawled out on the ground.

Linda looked to her rescuer and quickly recognized him as her Allen just as he said, "Wow, was that a lucky punch."

Linda drank him in with her eyes. He was gorgeous. She noticed he was smaller than Jim, but he filled out his shirt firmly. He no longer had the boyish look about him. Linda was relieved and excited to see him. "You always come to my rescue." She fell into his arms.

Allen was puzzled. "I don't recall ever rescuing you before."

Linda quickly thought. "Well, at the fair and in my dreams."

"I am in your dreams?" The thought intrigued him a great deal.

Linda took a second to make sure she said *yes* instead of *ya*. "Yes, all the time. Let's get away from numb nuts before he wakes up."

Allen chuckled at the reference of Jim being numb nuts. "I'll go along with that." Allen took a kind hold of Linda's arm, and they briskly walked deeper into the park. Neither one of them wanted Jim to wake up soon. He was proud that he flattened Jim with one punch, but he knew Jim could really beat the crap out of him. She didn't want Jim waking up telling Allen who she was. "It is sure good to see you again."

"It is good to see you as well," she said with a loving smile. "Let's go sit by the river, where no one can see us, especially numb nuts."

"Yeah, I don't believe I could be lucky enough to get a second sucker punch on tubby numb nuts." Linda felt so comfortable with Allen she nearly forgot she was married to a fine man. "I haven't eaten yet. Would you like to go eat somewhere? Then we can walk and find a secluded place."

"Ya-es," Linda agreed.

"Do you have a particular place you want to eat?" he asked her.

"You know the area better than I do, so you should choose where we go."

"All right." He thought briefly. "How about pizza?" Linda had never had pizza before, but she had heard of it. It sounded like an interesting food.

"Sure." She looked around to see Jim was gone. They approached a large red vehicle with big rubber wheels. This truck had writing on the side door, Barber Construction, and a series of numbers under it. Allen escorted her around the tall red vehicle. She read the words *Dodge Ram* on the side of the vehicle.

He opened the door for her to enter the passenger side. She stepped up into the truck, and he shut the door. She frantically fumbled around to get her seat belt fastened. She thought back. Tasha's concept. "Boy meets girl," she said out loud.

Allen heard as he got in. "I am glad to see you know how it works." He thought that statement was rude to her, so he explained further, "I mean this belt system is defective. I seldom have anyone riding with me, so I just haven't gotten it fixed."

"Oh," Linda said with some relief.

They went to Mama's Pizza restaurant. "I have a surprise for you." He dug into a compartment between the seats and pulled out a small, clear plastic box. He removed a silver disc from it, shoved it into the front wall of the truck. He then turned a small knob, and a woman's voice accompanied by other musical instruments broke out around her.

She looked at Allen confused. He was smiling. "I got every one of her CDs now." He steered his truck around a few corners, and they ended up on a wider street. Linda looked at the plastic case and read "Tanya Tucker." She felt flattered by his connection to her fictitious name. The lights downtown reminded her of the fair.

It was only a few minutes before they pulled into the parking area of Mama's Pizza. When the truck stopped, Linda pushed the button of the seat belt. Her seat belt flew back into the receptacle quickly. It frightened her just a bit, yet she was amused by it. She knew there had to be a latch or lever somewhere to open the door. She panicked just a bit as Allen was making his way around the truck to her door. He walked around the truck to her door and opened it for her.

He said, "I'm glad you waited for me. I wanted to show you that I am a gentleman."

"Of course," Linda said, relieved by the gesture. Linda had not been in a worldly restaurant before. She accompanied Allen with her arm wrapped around his arm. She was not sure if she did it for affection or in fear of getting separated. They were escorted to a seat in a secluded corner of the restaurant.

The windows allowed them a fine view of the parking area and the main street. The waitress had given them a shiny three-page plastic book. Allen began to look at the book. She quickly realized the booklet pictured and described the different foods they had to offer at this restaurant. The food looked very well cooked and colorful.

"Do you like meats, or do you want veggies?" Allen asked. He was not sure if she was a vegetarian or not.

"Meat," Linda said timidly. She wasn't sure why he had asked the question.

"Pop, beer, milk?" he asked.

Milk was the only thing she recognized. "Milk," she answered with confidence.

"Would you like some breadsticks or garlic bread?"

"Do they have white or wheat bread and butter?" Linda asked.

Allen hesitated a moment. "I don't believe so. I could ask if you would like?" Allen thought it was a slightly odd request.

Linda sensed she had asked an odd question by Allen's reaction. She also looked around the rest of the restaurant and did not see anyone else with white bread at their table. "I mean, garlic bread will be fine."

"With melted cheese on it?"

"Yes, please," she answered enthusiastically. She liked cheese and bread, so it actually sounded good. She looked out of the window and saw a car streaking by with red-and-blue lights flashing from the top of it. Her eyes popped open, and suddenly, the car screeched with a whistle. She had a quick flash of fear when this happened. "What's happening?" she asked nervously as she pivoted in her seat to follow the flashy car.

Allen was surprised by the question. "It's just the police stopping someone that doesn't know how to drive." Allen realized Linda was truly someone who was not normal. He did not fear her, but he was concerned about what he was getting himself into. He began to think she was from another planet for real, like she had claimed.

"They shouldn't be driving if they don't know how to drive," Linda said innocently.

"You're right, but to get permission to drive, they must pass a test. But even after passing the test, many of them refuse to follow the proper rules that are set up to safeguard the rest of us." Allen looked at her strangely. "Where did you say you come from?" He was hoping that she had matured some since the last time they had met.

Linda was petrified by the offhand direct question. "I come from another planet," she threw out and then laughed. Allen smiled but was troubled by the lack of a truthful answer. "Tanya, I really need to know."

"I know you do, and you deserve to know," Linda said honestly. "I'll tell you later. Please forgive me, and be patient." She had a fleeting thought to tell him everything, but she suppressed the thought.

"Of course, I forgive you," Allen answered respectfully, showing some reservations. She appeared to fit the characteristics of a person from another planet. Someone that was unknowing of many of the simple things. He thought if she was from another planet, why was she so defenseless against Tubby Boy Jim? Coming from another planet, you would certainly have some defensive apparatus, like a ray gun.

A skinny, young lady with short, black hair came to their table. She was carrying a small notepad. Linda noticed she had metal things protruding from her face. There was a round silver thing above her left eye. There was another one on her chin and two on her nose, one protruding out each side of it. "Are you ready to order?" she asked.

Linda couldn't help herself from looking directly in the lady's face. But it was Allen who spoke to her. "Two milks, garlic bread, and a medium pizza. Pepperoni, sausage, with extra cheese."

"Do you want the bursty crust or regular crust?"

"Regular," he said as he peered at Linda for confirmation. It was obvious Linda was curiously looking at the girl's face of metal, so she was no help in making a decision. The girl grabbed the menus and walked away.

Allen was debating whether or not to explain the piercings to her. The young woman brought their milks and two small plates with forks on them. She later returned to their table with a basket of fat bread. Linda started eating the bread as if she were at a noontime meal and very anxious to get back into the fields. Allen was surprised she was gobbling down the bread.

"So how have you been?" Allen tried to get a conversation started.

"I have been fine. And how have you been?"

"Fine."

"So are you an engineer now?"

"I have an engineering degree."

"Tell me all about it," she requested, eyes gleaming with excitement.

He was not sure she would understand anything he said, given the fact she knew very little about anything. The two of them continued to have small talk. Linda tried to keep control of the conversation so Allen would not ask her any questions. Once in a while, she would avoid a question by pointing out something for him to look at.

Once Allen started talking about his business, he rambled on for several minutes. When she got Allen talking about his business, the young girl carried over a disc-shaped pan with a thin-looking multicolored and textured pie. She placed the pie in front of Linda, who looked at her with empathy and asked, "Do those things hurt?"

The waitress looked at her strangely for a few seconds before realizing what she meant. "Oh, my piercings." She smiled. "They did at first, but now I don't even know I have them."

"Why would you do that to yourself?"

The girl shrugged her shoulder. "I don't know. Maybe because my parents forbid me to do it." She shrugged again. "My friends had some, so there you are."

"Really," Linda said excitedly. The waitress went on with her work.

Linda looked at the pie on the table with great wonderment. "Wow, doesn't that look good. Is she going back to get yours?"

Allen raised his eyebrows. "Are you hungry enough to eat it all?"

Linda looked over the pizza. "I really don't think so. Would you help me?"

"Sure," he said happily.

She started to cut into the full pizza still in its original pan. Allen noticed what Linda was doing but decided to ignore it. He took the spatula and scooped up a slice and put it on his own plate. Linda noticed she must be doing it wrong, so she told Allen a lie. "It is a family thing. We try a piece first and send it back if it isn't good." She finished getting her bite into her mouth. It was very hot and burned her tongue a bit. She tried to hide the fact by waving her arms and hooting like an owl. The whole restaurant noticed her actions.

"Yeah, you got to watch that first piece. It could be hot."

"Ish fing," she tried to speak with her mouth partially open, trying to blow air over the bite in hopes to cool it. The last thing she wanted to do was spit it out with Allen watching her. Her eyes began to tear up.

With sympathy, Allen said, "Sorry, I didn't warn you soon enough." Linda nodded. "Then we won't need to send it back?"

She nodded again and worked the piece of pizza down her throat. "It is very good." She took the spatula and placed a slice on her plate.

The conversation died out as they both ate their pizza. Linda found it to be a very fine-tasting pie. When they were finished, Linda piled up the dishes and stemware together, picked them up, and started to take them back to the kitchen. As she had gotten a few steps from the table, Allen asked her, "What are you doing?"

"I was thinking I would take the dirty dishes to the kitchen while I go to the little barn." Her voice faded to a silent whisper by the time she said "little barn." She quickly returned to the table, placed the dishes down, and sat quietly in her seat. She was considering telling Allen everything about her. She was feeling very stressed and afraid of what she was doing. "I'm sorry. I'm just really nervous." She was not sure Allen heard her say "little barn." She knew Allen had been amused by her reference to the outhouse as the little barn when they were children.

"They'll come to get the plates and clean up. We pay them to do that," he explained.

Linda's eyes widened. "Oh no, I have no money with me."

"Did you think I would let you pay?" Allen smiled broadly. He then reached over the table and clutched her hand. "Don't be nervous." He was suspicious of who she was with the 'little barn' phrase. He looked intently into her eyes.

She looked around and saw a sign of a stick woman and a stick man. "Sorry. I recently read a book about an Amish family, and they referred to their outhouse as the little barn. I thought it was cute, so I use the phrase sometimes." She pointed to the signs in hopes of getting an affirmative reaction from Allen. "Restrooms."

He nodded. "You use the door on the right."

Linda looked at him and smiled, proud that she knew something. "I knew that."

Later, as Allen drove the truck out of the parking lot, he suggested, "There is a second show at the theater about to start. Would you like to go?"

She was not sure what he was talking about, so she said, "No, I want to go to your place. It sounds very nice. I want to see your pet fish." She said this in a matter-of-fact tone. It was getting late, and she needed to get things rolling along. She still had to seduce him, get away from him, change clothes, then get back to her husband before it got too late.

He was caught off guard by her request. "Well, if you're sure that's what you want to do." He thought they would be alone in a private place together for the first time. He began to get a bit nervous about the situation. He thought she might expect him to make the moves on her to have an interaction. He wondered how to make the moves on her without making her feel slutty. They were older now, and it wasn't like they were complete strangers. This helped his confidence in any action he might feel necessary to achieve the goal.

"I have a UID, and I'm on the pill. I just thought that you would want to know that," Linda said, just as she was instructed by Tasha.

Allen was shocked she would be so forward about her intentions. "Well," he stammered, trying to be polite and unassuming, "it makes things more comfortable knowing that." He had not thought of her as a sex-crazed woman before. But now, he knew she was, and he wasn't totally sure that he liked it. But his hormones were acting up with the thought. He hoped she was this anxious because it was him and not that she did it all the time. He was in such deep thought that he ran a red light. Of course, Linda was not aware of that fact. Luckily, no one else knew of it either.

When they arrived at his apartment, Linda tried to act sexy. She decided to unbutton one more button on her blouse. She grabbed his arm and squeezed it slightly, just like Tasha instructed. She walked and talked like Tasha had told her to.

Allen could tell she was either very nervous about her action or her pants were too tight. The way she was acting would indicate to him that she hadn't had much experience at it. In either case, he fell deeply in love with her and all her pretenses. He calmly took control of the situation. He was very gentle and looked for any signs of her reluctance.

They were face-to-face in the darkness. He placed his arms around her waist. Linda was both frightened and excited. She had dreamed of this moment many times in the past, but still, it was awkward. He pressed against her body, pulling her tightly against him. He slowly placed his lips on hers. Linda, with a rush of passion, closed her eyes, tilted her head slightly, and they kissed.

When things calmed down, Linda was able to get away from Allen without having to tell him much about herself. She snuck out after he had fallen asleep. She hurried away from his apartment and in the direction she thought her sister's apartment was. She quickly found the park where they had met. As she walked back to Susan's apartment, she became obsessed with her anger toward herself. She felt dirty, shameful, trapped, abused, frustrated. She knew in her heart that as much as she loved Luke, it was Allen that she truly loved.

CHAPTER THIRTEEN

Controlling the Joy

The next morning, Linda took out the testing kit she had hidden under the drawer of her dresser. She tucked it under her clothing and went to the little barn to test herself. She waited impatiently for the test results. She began to cry as the test showed a negative result. She tested it once again the next day and came up with the same results. She thought of how difficult it would be to arrange another night with Allen.

One month later, Linda and Allen were together again. Linda showed up at his doorstep. Allen was glad to see her but was angry with her quiet escape a month earlier. Eventually, Linda was able to calm him down and assure him she had very deep feelings for him.

After making love once again, he concentrated on staying awake in order to keep her from getting away while he slept. He firmly was insisting she come clean with him. "Listen, sweetheart, we have made love twice, and I don't know much about you. I think it is about time you be honest with me. Let's start with your real name?"

Trish had told her what to say to get past this interrogation. "We have such a good thing going here." She tried to create a tear as instructed. "Let's not ruin it." Even though Linda was beginning to cry, Allen was becoming more frustrated and angry.

Allen was starting to get the impression she wanted him for selfish reasons. He could not believe she only wanted him for sex. He wanted to be with her because he loved her. He wanted her to be with him the rest of their lives, not a part-time love affair. He wanted to take her out, show her off, call her every night, have a regular relationship.

"So I am just a sex toy to you," Allen said sternly. "If you haven't noticed, I love you. You're the only girl I have ever loved in my adult life. My life has been haunted by your memory for the last five years. Making love to you is like"—he had to pause for a second as he thought—"making love. It isn't just sex to me. It is the most wonderful feeling and experience to love someone and be so close and personal with them and only them. I don't want anyone else in my life except you." He was ready to spill every bit of his feelings. "You have to stay and be my wife."

"Stop!" Linda yelled. "I am so sorry. This was not supposed to go like this." She hesitated a moment. "I,"—she shook her head—"I do love you very much, more than anyone else, but we cannot have a regular relationship."

"You're married, aren't you?" he asked strongly. Linda could not answer him. She could not lie to him with such a direct and invariable question. She was cornered, so all she could do was hang her head and cry. She had committed adultery, and it sickened her greatly. He knew what the true answer was. "This is the first answer from you that I truly believe." He took a deep breath and firmly said, "Get out." She began to cry uncontrollably but did not move. Allen's anger grew, but he kept his voice to a low tone. "Quit with the act, and get out of here." She could not bring herself to move. She was hurting someone that she truly loved. "Get out," he yelled. He nudged her shoulder to get her to move. She slowly and quietly gathered her clothes.

"It," she spoke between sobs, "wasn't supposed to happen like this. I love you, Allen."

"I don't want to hear about it," he said sternly. "Just get out, and never come back."

"It isn't what you think. Please let me explain," she pleaded with him. She wanted to tell him everything. She knew he would understand.

"No," he said very harshly. "Get out!" He had no interest to hear her explanations. Sobbing uncontrollably, she got her clothes on and left. She had never been so ashamed in her life. If she did not get pregnant that night, she was doomed to be studded like an animal.

When Linda got home, she snuggled up with her husband in search of love and security. Luke was surprised at her tenderness so late at night. He embraced his wife lovingly for the rest of the night.

When she tested positive for pregnancy, Linda was emotionally confused. It was the result she wanted but distressing at the same time.

Linda's mood swings caused Luke's parents to talk to Luke about Linda seeking guidance from others. Luke seemed to understand his wife's emotional fluctuations. He thought for sure it had something to do with Susan. One night, he asked her about things with Susan. Linda would insist things were going very well for her sister.

Luke trusted and loved his wife very much. There were many times Luke's family had often spoke harshly of her to Luke, especially his mother and father, who had never trusted her since the episode with Susan and the miscarriage.

Luke would defend her firmly while showing respect to his parents. The thought of divorce in the Amish community was very rare but did take place from time to time. For Luke, it would never be an option. However, there were times Luke got the feeling they would have encouraged him to divorce her if they had their way. They were sure she would eventually be excommunicated.

A few weeks later, her mother asked Linda to come visit her. "Linda"—Clara lovingly touched Linda on the cheek—"I want you to experience being a mother. I want you to go to the council and agree to their wishes. It is for the good of the community, Luke, and for you."

"I do not wish to speak about it," Linda told her. It would be just a few more days until she could expose the pregnancy. She could arrange for a doctor's appointment to verify the pregnancy and put part of this nightmare to rest. On Friday, she and Luke went to the old outhouse where a community phone had been placed and made an appointment with a doctor in town for the following Monday.

She went to the Sunday meeting with delightful thoughts; she would soon be able to let everyone know her secret. Her plan seemed to be working well, except for the sick feeling in her heart for the two men that were denied the truth.

She thought to herself, when she announces her pregnancy, everyone will think she was with child who had the blessing of God. It would make so many people happy. She couldn't help but think good thoughts about the situation. Luke sensed the possibility but did not want to get his hopes up.

The couple was in one of the exam rooms, anxiously waiting for the doctor to come in with the test results. A few minutes later, the doctor came into the office. He smiled broadly. "Congratulations, you two have created a baby."

Luke was so excited he stood up and silently fisted his hands in the air. Linda smiled and urged her husband to get control of himself. She asked, "I'm sorry. Could you go over that again?"

The doctor looked at her strangely and said, "You are going to have a baby." Luke stood up and fisted his hands in the air once again.

"I just wanted to hear it again. Thank you," she explained.

The doctor went over certain things that they need to do or not do. When he had said his last, Luke stood up, and the two shook hands vigorously. He turned to Linda, who realized that it was time to go.

When they returned to their home, Luke leaped out of the buggy and sprinted through the barnyard, screaming at the top of his lungs. "We're with child! We're with child!" Luke's family members, young and old, streamed out of the house, barns, and seemingly everywhere to greet the happy couple.

There were handshakes, pats on the back, hugs going all around. They had a happy, extra-loud dinner for that noontime meal. Linda felt much better about herself seeing how happy her husband was.

She soon asked her husband if they could go and inform her family as well. They were excused from any after-dinner chores for the afternoon. Luke's parents encouraged the young couple to stay for dinner at Linda's family's home. The reaction of Linda's family was much the same as it was for Luke's family. The evening meal was generally a much quieter meal, but this day, it was an extra-happy occasion, and the conversations were running wild and loud.

Linda's mother was especially excited about the news. She wanted to sit and tell Linda what being pregnant was like. She talked on and on about it while Linda's mind began to wander back to Allen and how she had cheated him out of fatherhood. When she had a few moments to herself, she composed a small note for Susan.

Three weeks after her pregnancy was announced, the bishop of the charter stopped to see Linda. He asked for her to accompany him for a walk. They went to a corner of the horses' stables where it appeared to be more private. He expressed his thrill that she and Luke were going to have a baby as if it were a great blessing from God. Linda listened and acknowledged that God was great and she is forever grateful to him for his blessing. The bishop and Linda prayed to their Lord together.

He also went over with her the things she must confess before the communion that was still a month away. Linda acknowledged her transgressions and understood the benefits and the consequences. He wanted her to understand the situation. She was tempted to tell him about her affair with Allen very briefly and then dismissed it as a secret she will never reveal to anyone.

Linda convinced Luke's father that she wanted to read the paper so she could get some recipe ideas from it. He would sometimes give her that section, but most of the time, he would just give her the whole paper when he had finished with it.

Linda had refrained from seeing Susan but had written a letter back to her once through the metal pipeline. Linda saw her sister for one afternoon a month. They would normally sit in a park near Linda's home and talk about things that were happening to the family and what was happening with her.

On February 26th, Linda had a wonderful baby boy they named Mathew. He was six pounds ten ounces with the deepest brown eyes to match his mother's. He had thick, dark, curly hair like Luke's. It was good to have an appearance that resembled both parents. She really didn't see any significant resemblance to Allen.

Mathew was treated as a special child, getting more attention than most children. Linda was aware of this. She did not like him getting all the attention but was pleased to observe that her child was not aware of it. Luke and Linda made fine parents and fine members of the Amish community. Both sides of the families embraced the child with love. Mathew was a small boy for his age, but he was blessed with a big heart for everyone around him. Linda was sometimes haunted by the comments many people made on how he was so much like Luke. Linda did nothing to encourage or discourage the comparison.

As he grew a little older, he noticed the attention but conducted himself properly as he was taught by his parents. He played and did what chores he could with great enthusiasm. He ate well but continued to be smaller. Some of the other children, mainly his cousins, did not always treat him well. They knew he was treated differently, like someone special. They would sometimes not allow him to play with the same rules everyone else played by. They would make fun of him or call him a freak of nature.

Linda continued to see Susan once a month but never asked her about Allen. Linda would convince Susan to take her for a ride into town from time to time. Susan drove by a nice new home one time and informed Linda that it was Allen's house. Linda looked it over intently. She had mixed feelings as they passed by. On one hand, she hoped to see Allen, and on the other hand, she was afraid to see him.

Susan was regretting driving by until she saw Linda's intense interest. "I'm sorry," Susan said. "I probably shouldn't have shown you that."

"I'm glad you did."

"Does it bother you?"

"No," Linda said firmly. "I am very happy with the way things are."

Linda requested to go by the house once in a while. One day as they drove by, a very beautiful pregnant woman stepped out of the front door and started to walk toward a vehicle in the driveway. This was the first time Linda had seen anyone outside the house. The moment that Linda had seen the woman, she quickly turned her head away.

"What is with you?" Susan asked.

"What do you mean?"

"You know what I mean," she firmly stated. "You really need to get over him. He is not a part of your life. He cannot be a father, brother, lover, or anything. You want to go past here every time we drive around, why?" Linda was silent. "It just tears you up inside. I know you think he is your real true love." Susan talked with passion. "You have chosen the path of your life. Like our mother would say, you have rolled your own ball of string. You need to forget about him."

"I know what Mother has said," Linda said angrily, "more than you do."

This struck a string deep in Susan's heart. She had wanted out of the Amish way, but it was hard because she still loved her family. Susan has never regretted leaving the Amish life, yet she wanted so much to see her family, especially her mother. She had accepted the idea she could not see her family without causing a problem for her family members. It was only once in a great while that it really bothered her, and this was one of them. Linda's cold remark brought her pain in her heart. "I rolled my own ball, and I have done the best that I can for me. Maybe you think I did this for selfish reasons, just like you thought of yourself when you decided to have a baby from another man," Susan sarcastically finished, "not your husband."

Linda was angered by the attack. "I didn't have a choice!"

"Yes, you did!"

"Well, I didn't think I had a choice!" Linda spoke harshly. "I made the choice to have a child with someone I wanted to have a child with, not some stud man that a group of grumpy old men picked out." Linda was on fire. "I didn't let my body be invaded by some Jimbo Numbnuts like you did. I went out and chose the man I love. The man I thought best to be the father of my child. Besides, I still embrace my parents and the proper way of serving my God."

Linda's words cut deep into Susan's heart, but she did not address it. "You could have said no."

"I thought they would have forced me to be studded," Linda said. "I really hate that word. I don't know why I use it."

Susan pondered a thought then asked, "Why do you constantly use it to describe your situation?" Susan's tone calmed down, easing the tension.

Linda calmed down. "I don't know. Maybe it helps me to cope with what I did."

"If you had a choice to do it all over again, would you do it any differently?"

Linda said firmly, "No, I wouldn't have changed a thing." Susan got a very satisfied look on her face and began to smile. Linda noticed this look and asked, "What?"

"You did the right thing. Remember, I was there helping you in your venture," Susan said with a swagger. "I think you just need to be reminded of that once in a while."

Linda rolled her eyes. "Oh, thanks." Linda was upset that Susan thought getting her all upset was a good way to make a point.

"That's what sisters are for," Susan said. "Also, if it makes you feel any better, the pregnant woman was his sister."

Linda was truly relieved but did not want her sister to know. "Don't matter to me what he has."

Susan dropped Linda off close to her home. As Susan pulled away in the car, she yelled out to Linda, "I love you."

Linda mouthed silently back to her, "I love you too."

As she walked down the road toward her home, the three-and-a-half-year-old Mathew came running out of the house toward his mother. Linda was overjoyed to see him and received her son with open arms.

Susan had driven down the road and turned around. As she went by the house, she saw the two embracing in the yard. She was touched and very sad for herself. She thought back to when she was pregnant wanting to give her child to Linda. If she could have, maybe things would have been better for everyone. Susan started to cry, realizing she would not be able to have the feeling of love with her own child. She still wanted to have children very badly.

Her friends have slowly been getting married, and a few of them have had children. Tasha was getting married in a few weeks to Phil. Trish was married and would be having a child in a few months. She herself is still working as a waitress and living in a lovely small apartment. The restaurant Susan worked in was not doing very well. She had not been making as much money as in the past. Her bills had been getting tougher to pay. She was behind in her car payments, and she has not been able to keep her cupboards full. She always indicated to Linda during their visits that things were going well for her.

She has not had a meaningful relationship with a man since her botched relationship with Jim. She seemed to feel indifferent, unworthy of having the love of a man. She also knew when someone in the charter was having trouble financially, the charter members would do what had to be done to assist the troubled members. She began to question her decision to leave the Amish community, but it was too late to try to get back into the Amish faith.

She stopped at a rural park on the way back home a short distance from where she and Linda would meet. There was no one at the park, which suited her since she wanted to be alone. Susan got out and walked around the area. She sat on a picnic table with peeling paint and started to cry. The wind blew through her hair, causing it to slap her in the face once in a while. She spied a rusty old butter knife in the dirt on the ground near her. She picked up the knife and brushed the dirt off as best she could. She placed the knife on her left wrist and ran it gently across her wrist. She did it again, but this time, she used more force. She kept doing that, pushing down harder each time. The knife left an impression but did not cut the skin. She slashed faster and harder until she finally stopped in a frantic rage. The knife barely broke the skin. She threw the knife on the ground and cried with her head in her hands.

As she sat there with her back to the road, she could hear a buggy on the road coming toward her. Susan did not move but tried to get control of her emotions. She wiped the tears from her eyes and cheeks with the long sleeves of her blouse. Her back was to the road, and she did not look up to see the buggy. Just as she felt the buggy would pass, it stopped. She heard a voice call out, "Are you all right, ma'am?" She turned to see an Amish man in a buggy.

"I am fine, thank you," she said weakly. She did not want to show her face in case it was someone she knew.

The man thought she looked familiar, so he studied her carefully. "Susan?"

She looked back at him more carefully this time in hopes of recognizing him before she replied. "Ya."

"I haven't seen you in years," he said. He flipped the reins to the horse to drive the buggy down into the frontage road of the park. He tied the horse loosely to a branch on a nearby tree. Susan would have been excited to be getting the attention of the fine young man, except the man in the buggy had a beard, which told her he was married. His beard appeared to be short, so she knew he had not been married very long.

"Do I know you?" she asked.

"I would hope so," the man said. "Remember when Wally knocked you over when you took my ball?"

"Paul!" she yelled, reaching out to give him a hug. He hugged her without reservation. After several seconds, the two broke apart as they looked at each other. "How could I not recognize you," she said, hoping to find a forgiving response.

Paul pointed at his beard proudly. "It's my beard. And it has been a long time."

"You got married," she said happily.

He shyly looked away. "Ya."

"And who did you marry?" Susan knew who he had married but wanted him to tell her.

Paul had a look of disappointment. "I would have thought Linda would have told you.""Freckled Frances," she blurted out happily.

"Hey, she doesn't have freckles anymore." Then he added, "Well, not as many."

"She doesn't?" Susan kidded him.

"No," he said, "she is very beautiful."

"Well, I am sure she is." Susan said. "So are you working for Father?"

"No, I am working for Isaac."

"That's right. Father gave him the whole farm," Susan said sadly. Many times, the farm could be expanded over the years and parts of it distributed to other sons.

"It is all right," Paul said. "Isaac will be giving me a portion when I turn twenty-one, just like he did for Aaron."

They continued to have a good conversation. Susan worried Paul might get into trouble for talking to her. Paul did not seem to be very concerned about the possibility of getting into trouble. After half an hour of priceless conversation, Paul said he had to go before he was missed. Susan understood, but she made him wait while she hugged him again.

When Susan got back into her car, she was feeling much better about herself and the life she had. She decided to change her life for the better from that day forward. She enrolled in a nearby tech school for secretary/office assistant.

Mathew continued to mature while helping his father milk cows, clean pens, mend fences, and plow fields. One day Mathew was leading the horse, Mo, while his father worked the plow behind them, and his foot got stuck in the mud. The horse stopped in order not to step on Mathew. Luke was unaware of this and continued to urge the horse to move forward, using a harsh tone in his voice. Mathew yelled out to his father for assistance. Luke felt appreciative of Mo's efforts to protect his son. He assisted Mathew out of the mud then patted and hugged Mo's head while asking for forgiveness. Mo leaned his head into Luke in an affectionate manner.

Observing his father's interaction taught Mathew that his father was a caring man and treated animals like family. He wanted to be like his father. He enjoyed working with his father and doing other things like going to the general store. They would buy the necessary items, and they both would get their favorite candy. Mathew grew close to his father.

After a few tough years, Susan was able to graduate at a small, nearby college. She watched the paper for jobs she wanted. One of those jobs she responded to happened to be as an assistant for Allen's construction business. His business had been growing, and he could no longer keep up with the books and administrative part of the business.

Allen had a girlfriend, Julie, who was an interior design graduate. She was assisting Allen with administrative duties but had her own business to deal with as well. Julie contacted Susan, and she was soon working for Allen. Susan adapted to the job very well and was an important part of the business.

As the years passed, Susan found herself very happy now with her life. She had not dated anyone in years, but her life was full and exciting. In time, she understood why Linda was so infatuated with Allen. He was truly a fine man in so many ways. He had the right combination of sentimentality but was still rough in character. He had a joyous, overwhelming sense of humor. He was very confident and optimistic about any project he attempted. Susan had no romantic thoughts or feelings for

Allen. She was too good a friend of Julie's to even consider the possibility of coming between them.

Susan was able to keep her job working for Allen from Linda. Susan found it difficult to tell Linda about her job without exposing the fact she worked for Allen. She got good at inserting fictitious names in her stories of work. She did not want to deceive Linda but felt it was the right thing to do.

CHAPTER FOURTEEN

The Power of Water

When Mathew was ten years old, he was out in the fields with his father during a heavy spring rain that lasted for several hours. They were herding the cattle away from a stream that was swelling quickly from the heavy rain. The rain came down harder than Luke had ever known. He knew there was a danger of losing several heads of cattle in the swelling stream. The cattle isolated in a low-lying area. Luke was sure it would be flooded soon. The area was surrounded by wet, muddy slopes the cattle would have trouble climbing. There were cows with calves that were destined to be caught in the waters.

"Mathew," he yelled to his son, "stay here, and when I move them up the slope, keep them moving to higher ground. Don't let them bunch up."

"I understand," he replied, nodding his head.

Mathew remained near the top of the slope, ready to direct the cattle as they came up. Luke was circling the cattle and herding them toward the slope. They were reluctant at first, but Luke managed to get them moving. Mathew took hold of the first cow's collar, which had a tinkling bell, and led it to the top of the slope and away from the stream.

Most of the cattle followed along slowly. They were confused and scared with the heavy rain, slippery slope, and thunder that cracked from time to time. One mother and her calf separated from the others. They were heading back down the slope toward the stream. Luke raced back down to redirect her up the slope. Her calf was right behind her when she slipped in the mud, knocking her calf into the swelling wild current of the stream.

Mathew had returned to the top of the slope, waiting for the rest of the cattle to come up. He saw the cow fall in the mud and knock the calf into the water. The calf would have no chance to survive in the raging stream. He watched as his father jumped into the stream, reaching out for the calf. Luke had no time to waste if he had any hope to save the calf. Mathew lost sight of his father, so he decided to go down the slope to see if he could help or at least get the mother to come up.

The calf was hung up on some branches along the bank of the stream. Luke was up to his chest in rushing water. He had one arm around the calf, and the other was pulling on the branches, trying to reach the bank. Mathew knew it was a very dangerous situation, especially since his father did not know how to swim. It appeared to Mathew that his father was struggling for his life, yet he still held on to the calf.

Mathew looked around and saw a large branch near the bank. He ran for it in hopes to use it as a rescue pole for his father to grab. It was large enough to do the job but too large for him to handle. With all his strength, he swung the branch around over the water. But his father and the calf were not there. He quickly, without thought or delay, ran down the bank looking for him. It was difficult for him because of all the bushes, trees, and rocks that lined the edge of the stream. The branches lashed out at his arms, legs, and face. He could feel painful lacerations on his face.

He saw the calf struggling in the current farther downstream. He saw the white head of the calf caught in a clump of limbs on the bank. Mathew continued to look for his father as he ran to the calf. The calf was still alive, struggling with the rushing water and the tree limbs it was tangled in. The rain was getting into his eyes, making it very difficult for him to see properly.

Mathew looked frantically around for his father. He wasn't sure if he should continue downstream to look for his father or stop to rescue the calf. He started to work the calf out of the entanglement when he thought he saw his father slip past him facedown in the water. He left the calf, who was nearly out of the brambles, and ran farther downstream in hopes to get ahead of his father. He caught another glimpse of him coming down the stream behind him. He felt he had just enough time to crawl out on a strong branch that hung out over the stream.

He hung on tightly to the branch and worked his way out into the stream. He had just gotten out into the stream when the body of his father slammed into him. Out of desperation, he grabbed for his father. He was able to get a grip of one of his suspenders. Mathew gripped as hard as he could at the suspender. It tugged on his arm so hard it felt as if it were ripping his arm off. Mathew could feel the branch shift and feared it would give way from the bank, taking him and his father with it.

He hung on for his life as water flushed over his face, causing him to gag. His fingers were being pried open by the force of the water. He did not have the strength to pull his father out of the water, nor could he hold on indefinitely. He frantically tried to think of a way to pull him out. Suddenly, Luke's body shifted and pulled the strap of the suspender out of Mathew's determined grip. He could only watch as his father floated away from him. The body rolled over, and he saw his father's mournful, deathly looking face. It startled him to the point that he turned his head. Water rushed over him, gagging him again.

He quickly realized he was in mortal danger. The branch he was on seemed very unstable. He inched his way back off the branch onto the bank. He made one last look to see his father, but he did not see him. He was exhausted from the ordeal.

He went back to find the calf, which he was able to save from the same fate as his father's. The rain suddenly stopped as Mathew solemnly made his way to the house. He wanted to run to get help, but it would have been too late, and he had not the strength.

He found his grandfather and told him solemnly his father had been swept away in the stream. His grandfather told him to ring the big bell and gather the rest of the family. His grandfather ran off toward the stream to fetch his son from the stream. Mathew rang the bell as he cried. He told the family members as they gathered around him. Several of Luke's brothers took off after their father to the stream. Linda, who left the wet dishes in the sink when she heard the bell ringing, came running when she saw Mathew ringing the bell.

When he saw his mother running toward him, he stopped ringing the bell and started to run for her. His tears stung the lacerations on his face.

Linda saw the red cuts on his face. "Mathew," she screamed, "what's wrong?" Linda looked over his shoulder, expecting to see her husband close behind.

"Father drowned," he squeezed out before succumbing to realization.

Linda looked at him with pleading eyes. "No!" All he could do now was cry. She knew he was telling the truth. She grabbed hold of him, and they went into the house together.

Luke's mother greeted them at the door with great concern on her face. "What has happened?"

"He says Luke drowned," Linda said solemnly, knowing this was not a sugarcoated way of telling a mother her son might be dead. Luke's mother was stunned and slowly walked out the back door in hopes to see her son walking through the fields. There was no sign of him, so she returned to help Mathew. Linda still was expecting Luke to come around the barn any moment.

Linda was silent for a few seconds. "Let's get you over by the stove." She placed a blanket over him. "Tell us what happened."

Mathew took a few deep breaths and then quietly told the two women what had happened. The two women sat in calm silence as they listened.

Luke's father came in calmly an hour later. The women looked to him mournfully, hoping to hear good news. He removed his coat and hung it on the hook near the kitchen door. He came over to them solemnly. "We found Luke. God has called him to his side."

The three of them burst into tears. Grandfather then spoke calmly and quietly to them, "The boys will be bringing his body up soon. They will take care of him."

The funeral was held at a neighbor's home. Susan had let Linda know through the pipe mail that she was very sorry, and she would have liked to be at the funeral.

It was a sad time for everyone. Luke's family treated Linda like she was their own daughter, yet she felt as though she was an outsider now. What was important to her was not how she felt but how Mathew felt. He grew up living with Luke's family, and that is where he would be most comfortable.

Her feelings for Luke were now more evident than they had been in the past. She realized how much she truly did love him. Now it was too late to let him know that. But in reality she did let him know. She had always been a good, loving, and affectionate wife, and he knew it.

Linda spent more time with Mathew, in an attempt to let him know she will always be there for him. Mathew continued to work hard on the farm, but was very quiet.

It was a sad time for several days, but each day got slightly better. Life had to go on, and Linda needed to be strong to help Mathew deal with the loss.

Susan was in the office of Barber Construction working on payroll when Bobbie, Allen's sister, came into the office. Bobbie was a delightful girl with long, brown hair. She smiled pleasantly, showing off her perfect, white teeth. "Hi, Susan. Is my brother around?"

"No, he is at a job site right now."

"Which one?"

"The one on eighth street."

"All right."

Bobbie just stood there for a moment. Susan noticed she was contemplating something upsetting to her. "Is something wrong? You look sad about something."

"Yeah," Bobbie said halfheartedly. "I just found out I am being deployed overseas."

"Deployed? Oh no!"

"Yeah, I have to report for special training next month, and I don't know what to do about the kids."

Susan thought it was awful to take a mother away from children. "How can they do that to a family?"

"Oh, it's my fault. I volunteered. And I'm okay with that. But I want the kids taken care of properly." She shook her head. "I'm technically still married, but he is not going to do it. My mother is really not able to do it. The only one left would be Allen. But he is so busy with his business. It would be a burden on him."

"I certainly can help. I mean I can take them places, feed them… It could be a combined joint effort between us all. It would be fun." Susan was actually excited to assist in being a part-time parent.

"I hate to ask him to help me out."

"You know he will do it."

"I know, and he will sacrifice himself and business to do it."
Bobbie sat down and thought. "The kids like him, and since their
father ran out of the picture, they have gotten closer to him. To
live a year without a parent around will be hard for them. This
would be a major change in Allen's life. Can he learn to nurture
children just like that?"

"Let me call him and get him over here. You just stay right
there." Susan took the initiative. "We'll hammer things out right
now, and then you won't have to worry about it."

"Thank you, Susan. I really need some support right now."

Allen rushed back to the office unaware of the true situation.
It was portrayed to him to be urgent and involved his sister. He
came into the office. "What's up, sis?"

Susan spoke for her, "She's being deployed overseas, and
we were hoping that you would take the kids in and be a
stand-in papa."

It took a few seconds for the news to sink in. "I was afraid you
would have to do this. I'm surprised it hasn't happened before
this." He looked at Bobbie. "Brandon is worthless. Mom can help
some. Julie would certainly help. She talks about having children
someday and likes children."

"And I will certainly do what I can," Susan added.

"See, we'll do fine. I'll call Julie and let her know. I think she
will be excited." Allen dialed her up. "Julie."

Bobbie shook her head and said to Susan, "She isn't going to
like this."

"Why?"

"Too self-centered," Bobbie snarled.

"Yeah, hey, Bobbie is getting deployed overseas, and I am taking
the children in. Would you like to move in more permanently and
help me out?" Allen put his finger over the mouthpiece of the cell
phone. "Add a little sugar." His smile faded. "Well, I thought it
would be fun to play parents for a while. Well, yeah. I mean can't
we just try it for a month or two?"

"Told ya," Bobbie said.

"We don't need her that badly. We'll be fine," Susan reassured her.

"Yeah, okay it will be fun. All right, love you. Bye." Allen nodded. "She is completely on board."

Bobbie laughed. "It really didn't sound like that."

"Well, it took a minute for her to realize what was going on. Then she was cool with it."

Bobbie was apprehensive about his optimism but was willing to be positive about the situation. "I will do the best I can to prepare the kids and tie up any loose ends before I go."

A month after Bobbie had left for training, Allen came into the office with a somber demeanor. Allen had trouble adjusting to being a parent to the two little girls. They were very good, well-raised children, but they had some trouble adjusting as well. Susan could tell that things were more upsetting than usual. "You okay?"

"Actually, yeah, with a big footnote." He forced a grin.

Susan squinted,. "What happened?"

"Well, yesterday Alicia dared Caleb to jump from the table on a bouncy ball and see how high he would bounce. He flew into a shelf and broke two of Julie's Precious Moments figurines. She went ballistic on them and told me that it was them or her. She said, 'I know it's them, so good-bye.' And so off she went. Her last words were, 'Don't call me ever.'"

"Is Caleb all right?"

"He's fine."

"What's a bouncy ball?"

"I don't know what the real name is for it, but it is a big ball with a ring on it. You sit on it and bounce around." Allen shook his head. "She really didn't want to be there anyway."

"I'm sorry, Allen. How are you doing?"

"Ya know, I'm actually relieved. It hasn't been a pleasant relationship since she moved in."

"Your mother watching the kids?"

"Yeah."

"Good."

"Do people still hire nannies? I have got to get some help."

"Well, why don't I plan to come over after work each night to cook and clean up some?"

"Thank you, Susan. That would really help until I find a permanent solution. So, I want you to place an AD in the paper for a nanny. Put in all the information you think necessary to get results."

CHAPTER FIFTEEN

The Working Girl

Since the death of Luke, Linda had felt out of place at her father-in-law's family home. They continued to treat her very well, as if she were their own child. In the back of her mind, she thought they were nice because she was Mathew's mother. Both sides of the family were encouraging Linda to live with them. It was getting less than cordial between the families. Linda and Mathew were stuck in the middle of the two families feuding. She had an urge to move back to her family's home, but things were different there since Isaac was running the farm. She needed to do what was best for Mathew.

One night, as she looked through the newspaper, she noticed an AD for a nanny. The man placing the AD was a busy businessman who needed help raising two young ladies. She felt this could be helping another family and herself at the same time.

Linda went over in her head again and again what she should do. She certainly wanted to stay practicing the Amish religion. However, she felt like an outsider in Luke's family, and it could be taken as an insult if she went to live with her own family. Luke's family is the closest family Mathew knew, and moving him might disrupt his stability. Linda read the advertisement once more and thought how wonderful it might be if she were to get a fresh start on her own. It would mean living with the English and surviving in their world while practicing the Amish faith. Other Amish members have done it.

She thought about how it might affect her son. She could home-school him and keep the faith going with a rigid routine. She would assign him chores but not quite like the ones on a farm.

As she lay awake that night in bed thinking about it, she decided to apply for the job. If she got the job, she would do it. If she did not get the job, she would have to decide which family to live with to start the healing process.

The next morning, after breakfast chores were completed, Linda set out for the neighbor's modern farm. It happened to be Trish and Tasha's parents who were still operating their farm. Their son Justin had married and built a house on the property. The Hostetler family had often asked them for a ride into town. Therefore, it was not a surprise to them when Linda asked for a ride into town.

It was a cool, damp, dreary day, and a mist kept her face damp as she walked. The farmland was obscured by a moist, foggy haze. The only noise she heard was the steady crunch from her heavy shoes on the gravel road. She felt nervous, hollow, and lonely.

Justin was planning to go to town anyway. "I need to find a pay phone," Linda requested.

Justin was not sure he could find a pay phone. Since the emergence of cell phones, payphones had been becoming scarce. "I have a cell phone."

Linda had never used a cell phone, but she was receptive of the idea. "Sure."

Justin reached deep into his hip pocket to pull out the small, metal device. "What is the number you want to call?"

She memorized the numbers.

Justin steered the truck with his left hand while he punched buttons with his thumb. When he finished dialing, he asked, "Are you ready?"

Linda took a deep breath. "Yeah."

He pushed one more button then handed her the small phone. She looked at it blankly, so he held it up to her ear. She could hear the blurts of the outgoing ringtone. Justin was not sure if she knew what to do. "Wait for someone to answer."

Linda nodded to assure him she understood. "It's ringing."

"Good," Justin replied.

"Hello... Hello." Linda said.

"What did they say?"

"We're sorry, something, something, blah, blah, blah."

Justin chuckled for a moment. He took the phone from her hand cordially. "I'll dial it for you." He asked her what the number was again; she told him as he dialed. The phone began to ring, and he quickly thrust the phone in her face.

She was slightly unnerved by this but recovered as a voice raptured out. "Hello."

"Hello," Linda said. "I am calling in regards to an advertisement for a nanny."

"Yes." The voice coming from the phone sounded excited. "I would like to meet you. When would it be convenient to meet?"

"Well, I am free right now," she told him.

"Now?" the voice questioned. "Yeah, sure. Can you come to my home?"

"Yes," she answered.

"My address is nine-eighteen Walnut Tree Lane. It's not very difficult to find. Do you think you could find it?" the voice said.

"I hope so," Linda said. "It is nine-eighteen Walnut Tree Lane," Linda repeated so Justin could hear. Justin nodded to her that he could find the place.

"All right, see you in a few minutes. Good-bye," the voice finalized the conversation.

"Good-bye," Linda responded. She was happy to get off the phone.

When Justin turned down a street, she remembered Allen's house was a big, blue house and was on this very street. She began to think that maybe it was Allen looking for a nanny or maid. But she knew Allen had no children.

Justin interrupted her thoughts. "There it is."

Her fears were confirmed when she looked at the blue house. Justin stopped the car, and he looked to her. Linda hesitated to get out. Justin felt Linda was having second thoughts about this venture. "Are you sure you want to do this?"

"No," Linda said. "Give me a minute." She thought quickly. She would be in a very precarious situation. Should she go up there or forget the whole thing?

Suddenly, as she thought about it, a curtain pulled back from the door window, and a man's face that did not resemble Allen's peered out at them. Before Linda could react, the man stepped out of the door onto the front porch to greet her. Linda was relieved that it wasn't Allen. *Allen must have moved recently*, she thought. She started to get out of the car. "Do you want me to wait for you?" Justin asked her.

"No, I will get a ride from my sister later." Linda smiled at him. "Thank you very much for the ride, Justin."

"It is not a problem. I can wait or come back," he said. "Wait, here is my number." He quickly scribbled a number on a piece of scrap paper. He handed it to her.

"I'll be fine. Thank you so very much for everything."

Linda got a burst of confidence as she walked up to the house, until she slipped slightly on the wet grass. "Wow, be careful," the man waiting for her on the porch said. He stepped down to the sidewalk and held his hand out in a gentlemanly fashion. "Hi," the man said. "My name is Dave."

"Good morning, Dave," Linda returned. Dave attempted not to be surprised that she was Amish. He held the front door open for her. She entered without another word. "Come on into the kitchen," he said. When they entered the kitchen, Linda saw a man with his back to them, spreading butter on toasted bread. There were two young girls sitting at a table, eating breakfast.

Dave said, "This is Allen. He is the one who needs a nanny for his two great, little nieces." Allen turned around and saw the horror-filled look on Linda's face.

Allen was also surprised to see that his applicant was an Amish woman. "I'm sorry if I startled you," he stumbled out. "I must look completely hideous." He knew he looked a little rough, having not groomed himself yet that morning.

"I…" Linda hesitated, stupidly tongue-tied. She knew she had to blurt out something very quickly. "I was just surprised the children could not butter their own bread at this age." Linda knew the moment she said this she had blown any chance for the job. She had just insulted Allen and the children. However, seeing her fears of Allen being the advertiser had come true, she was not sure she really wanted the job.

Allen noticed her eyes looked very familiar to him. He had really only known the one Amish girl, Linda, from his childhood. Her eyes were very much like hers. It had been nearly eighteen years since he had seen her, and he was only twelve at the time. "What is your name?" Allen asked, hoping the answer would be Linda.

Linda thought quickly. "My name is Mary." Linda regretted saying it the second she said it. "Mary Hostetler." She was not sure why she used her sister's name.

"Well, I am glad to meet you, Mary," Allen said. He was very disappointed that she was not Linda. He handed the youngest girl, Allison, the buttered bread he had just buttered. "This is my niece Allison." She was a petite, little girl with pale-colored skin and blond hair. She had a few freckles on her cheeks and pink ears. "And this is my niece Alicia." She had long, blond hair. She was wearing large teal glasses that looked much too big for her face. Her skin tone was darker, and her face was thinner than her younger sister's round face. "She likes wearing those silly glasses."

"Hello," Linda greeted them.

"Hello," the girls said together and laughed. "We must be sisters," they said together as well. Linda had to chuckle a bit since they reminded her of Trish and Tasha.

"You're dressed funny," Alicia stated.

"Alicia," Allen said, trying to politely indicate to her the question was rude.

"I am Amish," Linda told her. "We do dress differently, don't we?"

"I'm sorry about that, Mary," Allen apologized to her.

"Don't worry about it. Children have a tendency to be the most honest people." Linda then added, "They are also the ones who can be honest and get away with it." Linda was very pleased to meet them. She thought they were adorable.

"Why do you dress that way?" Allison asked.

"Well," Linda was happy to explain, "we believe that God creates the beauty in the world, and we humble ourselves not to challenge the beauty of his creation. We wear plain, dark-colored clothes that cover ourselves." Linda was proud to explain to the girls the reason for what she was wearing. Then she humbly addressed Allen, "I am sorry that I spoke of your nieces needing to butter their own toast. I must try to understand your culture is different than mine."

"Different, but you are correct," he said. "They normally do, but we are running a bit behind. I guess I just want to baby them for a while. They miss their mother."

Dave interrupted the two, "Well, it looks as though you two have hit it off nicely. I should be going."

"See you later, Dave. Thank you for dropping by."

"It was very nice meeting you, Mary."

"It was very nice meeting you, Dave."

Allen began to explain, "Let me tell you what will be expected of you." He went over to the kitchen sink to place some dishes in it. He turned to lean against the kitchen counter. "Oh, please sit down." He gestured for her to sit at the kitchen table.

Linda, who had been standing, sat down on a cushioned armchair on wheels. When she sat down, the chair spun and rolled unexpectedly. She lost her balance slightly before regaining control. "Oh my," she said with an amused smile. "I didn't expect that." She and the girls laughed.

She leaned back in the chair, and it tipped back just a bit, scaring her. She made a startling scream. "Oh my again!" And she sat up briskly. The two young girls tried to suppress their laughter, but a couple of snickers came out. Linda recovered from her fright and laughed along with them. "That was a ride," she said excitedly. Once she regained her composure, she sat up straight, rigid, and afraid to move.

"Please relax," Allen pleaded with her. Linda slouched slightly, being careful not to lean back. She soon found herself sitting up once again as she listened. "I need someone who can be here by six thirty in the morning to get breakfast for the girls and me and then clean up. I need someone to get the girls to school or stay with them when they do not have school. You will need to get the girls after school, prepare the evening meal, and tidy up the house. You will be in charge of purchasing groceries and other essentials to perform those duties. I will give you some signed checks to pay for whatever you need. You will generally have the weekends off, unless I need you to work on Saturdays. In time, I will have your name added to an account at the bank so you may write checks or use a debit card for payments."

He stopped to reflect at what he had said. Linda wanted to ask what a debit card and checks were. She had only dealt with cash in the past. And she, being a woman, did not deal much with the financing. She got up out of her chair and began to clear the table of the lunch plates and glasses. The kids ran off to another room.

Allen was a bit uncomfortable when Linda started to clean up the kitchen. "Mary, you don't have to do that."

"Well, I'm here, and there is work to be done."

"Yes." He agreed with her to some extent. He then continued his statement, "But I really don't think this arrangement will work."

"Won't work?" Linda wanted to pump some water into the sink, but the pump in his kitchen was so tiny. She did not think it could possibly pump enough water. She raised the pump, and water gushed out, spraying water everywhere, but as she pushed it back down, it stopped. It had been a long time since she had used a faucet like this. She turned to Allen. "Do you have an apron? I didn't bring one this morning. I actually didn't think I would be working right away."

Allen did not think she understood what he was trying to say. "You will have to find a way into town each day. You will need to have a car to take the girls to school or get to the store," Allen said, trying to be honest, yet he wanted to be considerate.

Linda asked, "How far away is the school?"

"About six blocks."

"What's that, about a half mile?"

"Four-tenths of a mile," Allen responded.

"That's a fine walk for children to make. I used to walk a mile and a half to school every day," Linda informed him. "How far away is the grocery store?"

"Now that is about a mile," Allen said.

Linda wanted to clean the dishes, so she looked for some soap. "Does your family own one of those children's red wagons. I see them sometimes when I come to town. They are so cute. I believe they say Red Flyer on them."

"I don't have one of those."

"We'll need to get one," Linda said. Allen was beginning to get the feeling Mary was taking control of the situation. Linda was determined to get this job. She knew it would be impossible to get a ride in every morning. "I will move in tomorrow when I come."

Allen had not expected a live-in maid and babysitter. "Well, I haven't given you the job yet. And I hadn't expected to hire a live-in nanny/maid."

"You can cut my wages in half for room and board if you like." Linda reasoned.

"No." Allen was getting frustrated. "I need a regular person."

Linda looked at him with the greatest look of disappointment. "You're going to fire me on my first day." She tried to pump the faucet again. It spurted out again. She was not used to not having to pump vigorously to get water out of a pump faucet.

Allen got up and slapped her hands away from the faucet playfully. "Stop it. Let me show you how it works." He pushed the handle up slowly until the water flowed out evenly without gushing. "You just push up on the lever, and it works. You don't have to pump the water up from a well." Allen would be uncomfortable having an Amish woman living with him. "See what I mean. You will be lost on how things work."

"Well, you have already taught me how the faucet works. Other things will come along the longer I am here." She was happy it was Allen who advertised for a nanny.

Allen was unable to force Linda to acknowledge she was not the person he wanted to hire. He gave in to the idea she had given herself the job. His voice resonated with a surrendering tone when he said in a semi-sarcastic tone, "Maybe I better show you how to use the toilet."

"Oh, I know how to use the indoor little barn."

Allen stopped in his tracks. "The little barn?" Linda was petrified.

She was able to calmly say, "Ya, it is just something we call the outside bathroom or outhouse." As she looked out the window above their sink she said, "You live so close to your neighbors."

Allen studied her for a moment then shook his head. "I am sorry, Mary. I thought I might have met you before. But that can't be the case, can it?"

Linda shrugged. "Some people say we all look similar. Amish people, I mean."

Allen looked at her intensely. "It is more than just looking alike."

"Well, I would have remembered seeing you, I'm sure," she said, trying to end the course of the conversation.

Allen dropped the subject for now. "Maybe I should show you how to use the dishwasher."

Linda chuckled loudly. "Allen, I have been washing dishes since I was five."

"Yes, by hand," he said, "you probably have never used an automatic dishwasher." He pointed to a large, metal door in the bottom cupboard to the left of the sink.

Linda stepped back to get a better look at the dishwasher. She tilted her head from side to side, looking at it. There was a row of buttons across the top of the metal door. "Well, look at all the fancy buttons." Linda portrayed herself as not being impressed by the machine.

"They are to adjust the cleaning cycle to accommodate different types of loads," Allen explained as he began to point out some of the buttons.

"I don't mind doing them the natural way." Linda turned away from the dishwasher to the sink once again. "I like to know the dishes are truly clean." She had the dishes nearly rinsed and ready to be washed. She looked under the sink for a bottle of dish soap.

"I spent six hundred dollars on that dishwasher. I want to use it," Allen pleaded.

"All right," Linda said in pretense sarcasm. "I will try to learn how to use it. If it makes you feel better." She smiled pleasantly.

"Okay, just as long as you know that I am the boss around here." Allen felt that the authority in his own house was slipping away.

"Of course," Linda said. "What kind of a man isn't in charge of his home?"

"Good." He showed her where the dish soap was.

As Linda continued to do the dishes by hand, Allen decided to show her how to use the automatic dishwasher another time. She had finished the dishes when she heard a cricket in the living room. She was surprised to hear a cricket inside a house. She heard it again, and then it stopped.

She heard Allen in the living room appearing to her to be talking to himself. "Hello," Allen said. Linda peered around the corner to look at him. He looked like he was talking to no one but had his hand over his ear. She figured out it was a cell phone. "Yes, I picked someone. Well, they picked me." He was silent for a moment as a smile grew across his face. "You got the packet from Cosmos? Bring it on over." He froze for a few seconds then excitedly said, "Oh, you're almost here. Great. You can meet the new nanny-maid. Yeah, bye."

Linda figured he was talking on a cell phone. "Sounds like good news."

"Could be," Allen said. "It is the answer to a bid we have been trying for. My assistant is on her way over with it."

"He is coming over now?" Linda asked.

"It's a she," he corrected her.

Linda's stomach lurched up into her throat. "A girlfriend."

"No," Allen said. Linda was relieved at the news. Allen went out the front door, apparently wanting to meet the woman. Linda put the finishing touches on cleaning up the kitchen. She had wiped the kitchen table down and scooped up the crumbs from the table into her hand to throw into the garbage. She then realized she did not know where the garbage can was.

She heard the front door close and a female voice speaking to Allen. "They wouldn't have sent such a fat package if it didn't contain a contract and full specifications." Linda quickly flicked the crumbs into the sink and stepped out of the kitchen to greet the woman. She gasped when she saw her sister, Susan, standing there. Susan's smile faded quickly when she saw Linda. "Oh my." Susan composed herself quickly. "I mean, oh my, you are already working."

"Susan, this is Mary, my new live-in maid," Allen said.

"Live-in maid?" Susan's eyes widened with the introduction.

Allen turned to Linda. "Mary, this is Susan, my personal assistant."

Linda assessed Susan's demeanor before she spoke. "I thought I was the nanny-maid."

"Mary, is it?" Susan coyly asked.

"Ya, Mary." Linda looked at her with the greatest hope that Susan will go along with her.

Susan took a few seconds to assess the situation before suggesting, "We should call her the house operations manager or HOM."

"That would be appropriate," Allen agreed then suggested, "HOME for short. For home operations manager executive." Allen smiled at Linda. He thought the title would give her more pride in her work. "How does that sound to you, Mary?"

"Home…" Linda said as she thought about going home and forgetting the whole thing,

"How about HOMEE?" Susan needled her just a bit.

"Susan," Allen sternly said.

"I apologize," Susan halfheartedly said.

Linda thought for a moment to be clever and break some of the tension in the house. "I will be happy with the title of 'Amish lady, little ego, not stupid, making absolute impressive dinners or ALLENSMAID for short," Linda spouted out quickly, without giving much thought to her words making any sense.

Susan and Allen both stopped to think about the words and how they matched up to so many letters. They debated between them for a few minutes as Linda turned away and began to re-clean the kitchen. Allen, who could not remember all the words, finally looked to Susan. "Amazing."

Susan hadn't figured out what it was either but went along with it anyway. "Yeah." She looked over her shoulder toward the kitchen. "What was that again, dear?"

Linda had no idea what the words were she had just spoken. "ALLENSMAID. I am Allen's new maid."

She was impressed yet cautious of what Linda was up to. Linda had always been so honest in her life about everything, except when it came to Allen. She cared for both of them and did not want to see this mess up their lives. She knew Allen and Linda were meant for each other.

Allen took the package from Cosmos and walked away to sit at the living room couch. Susan went into the kitchen to confront Linda. Susan silently mouthed, "What are you doing?"

"I need a job," Linda replied. Susan rolled her eyes as she looked back out into the living room to make sure Allen was busy looking over the proposal.

"We'll talk later," Susan informed Linda sternly.

"I know we will," Linda said happily. "You are going to give me a ride home."

Susan smirked playfully. "What makes you so sure?"

"I will insist." Linda smirked back.

CHAPTER SIXTEEN

The First Day on the Job

Allen came into the kitchen excitedly. "We have got it, Susan."

"Great," Susan said excitedly. Allen and Susan sat down at the kitchen table to look over the specifications. Linda decided to stay for a few minutes and find out what all the excitement was about. She really had no choice now since she planned to get a ride back home from her sister, who was now engaged in a business situation.

"Mary, is it?" Susan asked her in mock arrogance.

"Ya," Linda answered in a casual manner.

"Would you please get me a cup of coffee," Susan said then added, "with cream please."

"Of course," Linda replied extra politely.

Susan wanted to torment her sister more than she already was. "How about you, Allen, would you like a cup?"

"No," he said as he studied the stipulations of the contract. "Thank you."

Linda knew Susan was having fun ordering her around. Linda searched through the cupboards for a cup. She opened several cupboard doors before she found several on a shelf. Linda began to look for a smaller silver pot. Susan kept one eye on Linda struggling trying to find a kettle to heat water up with.

Allen put the contract back into the full-sized envelope. Then he began to study the plans for the building. His mind was buried in the plans, so he was unaware of Linda's plight. She began to look for a small kettle or glass pot and a jar labeled coffee.

Susan noticed Linda was trying to accomplish the task but was going to fail miserably. She got up. "We'll just make instant coffee for now. It will be much faster." Susan went to a cupboard in the corner of the kitchen and opened it. She twirled a shelf around and found a jar with a red label on it. It read Folgers Instant Coffee. "Fill both cups with water and place them in the microwave. Push these buttons." She pushed some buttons as she read them off. "Two three zero then push this one that says start." The microwave gave a little bang and began to hum quietly. "When it dings, take the cups out." She pointed at the jar of coffee. "A teaspoon of coffee." She pointed at another jar. "A teaspoon of powdered cream, and I want a spoonful of sugar. Then stir and serve hot. Got it, dear."

"I got it," Linda responded with a piercing glare.

Susan sat down next to Allen once again. "Oh and, Mary, the other cup is for you." Linda watched the microwave count down in numbers until it hit zero and there were three dings. Susan then got up again, out of habit, to get the cups. Linda did not want to feel worthless, so she quickly said, "I can do it. I remember what you said."

"Take a teaspoon of the instant coffee and put it in each cup. Stir it slightly and bring it to the table," Susan instructed her.

"Susan, isn't it?" Linda playfully addressed Susan.

"Yes," Susan said.

"I remember your instructions."

"Oh, of course you do, Mary. I'm sorry."

Linda brought the cups to the kitchen table, but before she could set them down, Allen blurted out, "No, don't put those on the table. Leave them on the counter." Then he mellowed his tone. "I don't want it spilling on the plans."

Susan chimed in, "Just leave the spoons in the cups and go about your business. Thank you." Linda obviously knew that Susan was playfully treating her like a common servant. She gave Susan a lovingly nasty look and went into the living room to clean up in there. She was frustrated on how the carpet looked so dirty with lint and paper. She started to pick up the visible trash on the floor. After several minutes of this, Susan noticed her obsession to clean the carpet. Amish homes did not have carpets. Their floors were wood or plain-colored, non-patterned tile or linoleum. Susan got up and, without a word, went into a closet in the hallway. She brought out a nonelectric carpet sweeper.

"Here, sweetie," Susan said. "Just move this along the floor, and it will pick up the lint and other stuff. You may have to clean out the retaining box once in a while." Susan flipped a small lever, and the sweeper seemed to come apart. She remembered seeing one of these apparatuses at an Amish neighbor's home. She remembered they used it because they did not want to take their rugs out and beat them clean.

Linda had just started to clean when Allen approached her. "Mary, you should take the rest of the day off. Go home and get ready to come back Monday all fired up to work."

"All right," Linda answered disappointedly. She stopped pushing the sweeper.

Allen then added, "Do you need a ride home or something?"

Linda announced so Susan could hear, "I would like to visit my sister and get a ride home with her."

Allen continued to look over the plans but was curious about her sister. "She is not Amish?"

"No, not anymore," Linda answered.

"Can I give you a ride there, or do you want to call her?" Allen asked.

"I think I will call her. I do have her phone number, if I may use your telephone," Linda said loudly so Susan would hear.

Susan suddenly jumped up. "I've got something out in the car I have to get. I will be right back."

"Darn, I'm not sure how to use this phone," Linda indicated for both to hear.

Allen looked up from his papers. "Susan, could you help her out?"

"Sure, not a problem." She grudgingly reversed course to assist Linda. "Push the talk button, wait five seconds, then dial her numbers, slowly."

She started to leave as Linda began to dial her cell number. "No, no, no. Too fast." She glared at Linda, as if daring her to continue to dial. Susan ran toward the door, nearly tripping on a footstool. Allen had buried himself in his plans and was not aware of the strange events. Susan just got out the door when her phone rang. She walked toward her car as she dug her phone out.

"Hello," Susan said casually to show she was not flustered by the call.

"Hello, my sister," Linda said.

"Well, hi," Susan emphasized the name, "Mary! What are you doing? Why couldn't you be…yourself? Why…Mary?"

"I'm not sure yet, but it needs to be this way until I am sure."

"This is really dangerous, Linda," Susan said. "Does Mother know what you are doing?"

"No," Linda answered. "I'm sure she would have a problem with it."

Susan snickered. "You got that right."

"I really can't talk right now, but we can talk later while you give me a ride home."

"You're going to get in trouble with the council."

Linda was not sure what to say, but she had a burning question. "So what are you doing...there yourself?" She nearly said *here* but was able to change it to a belated *there*.

"I will talk to you later about that."

"Like when you take me home," Linda said.

Susan sighed, "Yeah, how about if you make believe your sister can't pick you up so your real nonexistent sister, who is the assistant to Allen, offers you a ride?"

"Fine," Linda said. "Talk to you later. Bye." Linda stalled a few minutes before going into the kitchen. Once Susan was back in the kitchen, Linda told them, "Well, my sister is on a date with her best friend's husband, and she can't take me home. She is so immoral. I just don't know about her anymore."

Susan forced out a benevolent smile. "Why don't I pretend to be your slutty sister and give you a ride home."

Allen broke away from his studying of the plans to say, "I'd feel better if you got a ride."

"All right." Linda was happy to get a chance to talk to Susan privately in her car on the way home. Susan took a few sips of her coffee before she put it down in the sink.

Linda and Susan were on their way out the door when Allen added, "Susan, be sure to be back here as soon as you can please."

"Yes, of course," she replied.

As soon as they were both out the door, the two spoke out with the same questions. "What are you doing here?" They looked at each other; neither one was in the mood to say it.

"I wanted a job," both of them answered together. They both laughed at each other.

"Why work for Allen?" both of them said together once again.

"That's enough of that," Susan stopped the conversation as they continued to chuckle. Both of them went silent, waiting for the other to say something, afraid they might say the same thing at the same time.

Finally, Linda spoke, "I didn't know it was him. I just saw an advertisement for a nanny in the paper, and I answered it."

"You're going to just screw him up more than he already is. He just lost his girlfriend. The children don't have their mother for a year. They don't need you coming in and making things complicated," Susan badgered her sister.

Linda answered in great distress, angered that her sister would think she was there to hurt anyone, "I don't want to hurt him. I didn't know it was him when I first contacted him. When I got here and knew it was him, I was already here. I couldn't just run away."

"Now you know," Susan said. "Get out now."

Linda wanted to change the subject, so she threw the question back to Susan. "Why didn't you tell me that you were working for Allen?"

Susan was on the defensive and answered, "Because I thought you would badger me for information about him." Linda stared at her blankly. "I just didn't think it was a good idea."

"How long have you been working for him?" Linda asked with great curiosity.

Susan was hesitant to answer but knew she had to answer, and answer honestly. "Five years"—she hesitated a second— "maybe six."

"You told me you worked for a finance company and a man named Peter."

"Well," Susan said, "we give them a lot of business. So I kind of work for 'em."

"Do you love him?" Linda asked her bluntly, her big brown eyes stared intently.

Susan's face went scarlet red, and then she said, "No, I don't."

Linda raised her eyebrows. "Your words do not match your tone."

"I said that normally," Susan defended. "Here, I'll say it in a different tone. No, I'm not." She continued using different tones. "No, I'm not. No, I'm not. No, I am not."

"All right!" Linda capitulated. "It's not the tone in your voice," Linda coyly said, "but the tone in your face."

Susan asked coyly, "How can my face have a tone?"

"I don't know, but it just does." Susan rolled her eyes. Linda added, pointing a waggling hand, "Your face is red like you were caught with a hand in the cookie jar."

Susan chuckled at the analogy, "Who cares if I have my hand in a cookie jar?"

"The cookie jar is Allen."

"Oh, I see your theory." Susan started up again, "No, I'm not. No, I'm not. No—"

"I got it, you're not in love with Allen. So it shouldn't bother you if I work for him." Linda raised her eyebrows. "Think about it, Susan, we will be closer together this way. And maybe I will leave the Amish life for good, like you have always wanted." She did not intend to quit the Amish faith, but if giving Susan the impression helped to get her on board, then so be it.

Susan smiled. "Oh, stop it. We can work together. But you can't mix work and pleasure."

"You remember that," Linda said sternly.

"Just remember, sweetie, you are working for him as well." Susan raised her eyebrows. "How are you going to live with him without exposing who you really are?"

"Maybe I should tell him who I am."

"Are you going to tell him who all of you are or just one or two of you?" Susan asked sarcastically. "Why didn't you just be yourself? Why Mary? You would be Linda at least."

"I don't know." Linda swooned. "I panicked. Maybe I just wanted to have a fresh start and not be distracted. Besides, he said some really nasty things to me way back then."

"He hadn't seen you in nearly twenty years." Susan rethought her statement. "Well, he would have thought he hadn't seen you in nearly twenty years."

"You may have been right," she admitted cautiously.

"And what about Mathew?" She continued to chastise her sister's judgment. "I love you so much, Linda, but this is not good. You really have to think about where this is going. Your lies will catch up to you and hurt everyone, especially Mathew. How will he feel if he ever figures out Allen is his true father?"

"I will protect that secret to the death, and so should you."

"How long do you think Allen can be fooled? He will eventually recognize you as Tanya. Then he will put together the fact your son is the right age to be his son." There were several minutes of silence as Susan made the turn to head out of town to take her home. Susan added, "Do you need me to come get you Monday morning?"

"Yes please," Linda said.

"You had better keep saying ya. You're playing an Amish woman now." Susan sighed. "The less you look or act like Tanya, the better." Susan shook her head. "I still don't understand why you couldn't be Linda this time."

"I know. I just didn't have time to rationalize what was transpiring."

"See, you are going to mess up his life again."

"That is not my intention."

"But you are. Amish. What difference would a name make?"

"You weren't there when he told me to get lost twenty years ago," she spoke meekly. "He was mean. It is best to have a completely different identity so we can have a fresh start. So if he does figure some things out, he would be so confused that things would work out."

"Do you realize how stupid that sounds? It doesn't make any sense."

Linda gave up in frustration. "I know. I just panicked."

"Great."

"All I know is, I want to do this. I need to do this."

Susan shook her head and laughed. "Sweetie, you are headed for a brick wall. And you are making me an accomplice in this diabolical charade, making me lie to my boss. Are you happy?"

"I'm so sorry," Linda said with true remorse.

"It's all right. Once he finds out, maybe you and I can start our own restaurant or something," Susan said. "What are you going to do with school and Mathew? He needs to continue in school."

"I thought I would home-school him," Linda said.

"You may have trouble with the authorities," Susan said. "They may not allow you to do that without a teaching certificate."

"It is our religion that will protect us," Linda reasoned. "I need to give Mathew a good father figure, and Allen will fill that role nicely."

"Father figure?" Susan snapped back. "What is wrong with Luke's brothers and father?"

"You're the one that tried to get me to join you in the worldly world. I just want to keep my faith in God as Mathew and I have been. Why are you so against this now?"

"You're moving into a worldly single man's home. Do you really believe the Amish community will continue to embrace you after that?" Susan took a deep breath and then continued, "There are only a few weeks left until summer vacation. See how things go through the summer. Allen does need help. He hasn't had any good responses to the ads."

"Well, he just started looking, didn't he?"

Susan informed her, "He has been looking for weeks. You are the first that actually qualified."

"I went there determined to get the job," Linda said. "So what you are telling me is that I didn't have to be so obnoxious in getting this job."

"Oh no, you needed to be as obnoxious," Susan chuckled.

Susan stopped the car to let Linda out. Linda had one last thought. "What did he mean by fired up?" She tried to remember how he said it. "Mary, you go home now and get ready for Monday so you can get 'fired up' for work."

"Oh," Susan laughed. "It means you have the job, and he wants you to come to work on Monday excited and ready to work."

Linda said with some relief, "Good, I was just confused somewhat."

Since Luke had died, Linda had taken it upon herself to have nightly conversations with Mathew. That night, she told her son, "Mathew, I know this may be different for us, but we are going to live in town with a man that needs our help to raise two little girls."

"No boys?"

"No, just two lovely girls."

"How many acres do they have?"

Linda chuckled slightly. "They don't run a farm, just a household."

"We have to move there just to help some girls?"

"Ya," Linda said, "they are motherless for a while and need help."

Mathew was sympathetic but wondered about his situation. "I just lost my father, and you want to go away from his family."

"It does sound rather ridiculous, doesn't it," Linda admitted. "We can try it for a while. Who knows, maybe they can help us deal with our loss."

"No boys though, huh?"

"No, sorry. No boys."

"He has the two little girls working with him to run the household?"

"Ya."

"He now has to do woman's work himself and work the fields, but he has no fields." Mathew reviewed while looking for a confirmation.

"Ya, sort of, maybe." Linda decided to explain in more detail what to expect. "Well, they live a little different than we do."

Mathew was happy staying with his father's family and would have been happy to move in with his mother's family. He also found a great deal of comfort in what his mother portrayed for their future. He agreed that they must go and help this poor family survive.

"So, we are going to move on with our lives. It will be different, but I believe in time it will be a benefit for both of us."

"Will I be able to come here and see everybody once in a while?"

"Absolutely," Linda said.

"Will I be able to do chores at the man's home?"

"I think we will be able to give you some chores to do," Linda said. "Are you upset with me for doing this?"

"No," Mathew said as he chuckled slightly. "It will be different, that's for sure."

"That's the spirit," Linda said. "You're just like your father."

Mathew reached out to touch his mother on the cheek. "Do you think I will be able to meet my Aunt Susan?"

Linda was surprised that Mathew knew about Susan. "You know about Susan."

"I heard you and Father speak about her sometimes."

"I don't know if you will see her or not." Linda was not sure how to handle that.

"I would like to meet her."

"We'll see," Linda said.

Linda apologized to the two families that they were leaving to live in the city. She emphasized that this was something she had to do. The families remained silent as the two of them left. Linda got the feeling they considered turning their backs on them.

Susan showed up at the four corners right on time to pick them up. Linda helped Mathew into the car and got him strapped in with the seat belt. He was excited to get into the bright-red car.

He had seen cars drive by appearing to be going faster than the fastest-running horse ever. He was about to ride in one of those fancy fast carriages.

Susan looked back at Mathew, knowing he was her nephew and the closest thing to a son she might ever have. Linda did not hide anything from him concerning his Aunt Susan. "Mathew, this is a friend and business associate of my new boss, Susan. Susan, this is my son Mathew," Linda said.

"Hello, Mathew," Susan said happily, nearly about to break down in tears.

"Hello, Susan, it is a pleasure to meet you." He reflected for a moment. "I have an aunt named Susan." Susan, who was unaware he knew anything about her, quickly looked at Linda. Mathew saw the reaction Susan reflected. He studied Susan's face or what he could see of it. He could see Susan carried some resemblance with his mother. "You're Aunt Susan!" he shouted with excitement. He was not sure, but he wanted it to be Aunt Susan.

The two sisters looked back at him while they smiled. It was a great relief for them that he figured it out. After a signal from Linda, Susan acknowledged, "That's right. It is very nice to meet you."

Mathew struggled, twisting and pulling himself out of the restraints of the seat belt. He jumped up and hugged Susan around the neck. Susan kept her mind on driving but was very pleased with the affection from him.

"Get back into the harness, Mathew," Linda directed him. He squirmed and twisted to get back into the seat belt.

"I have a few things that we need to keep secret," Linda said. "Allen, my new boss, thinks my name is Mary, and Susan is not my sister or your aunt. We're playing a trick on him. It will be fun."

Susan looked over to Linda, shook her head and gave her a disdainful look. Linda looked at her with shame in her eyes. She realized she was deceiving Allen and involving her son as an accomplice in the lie. She realized the deception was out of control. She could not stop now without possibly losing her job. She could not bring herself to tell Allen who she really was.

Mathew took the news with some wonderment. He looked at his mother blankly, assessing the situation before he spoke. "This is really going to be fun."

Susan looked at her sister and rolled her eyes and quietly said, "Like mother, like son." She shook her head. "You two." She took a deep breath, "Poor Allen."

Linda seriously said, "We will take good care of him and the girls won't we, Mathew?"

"And you will not lie to him about anything else?" Susan chanted out.

"I promise," she agreed. "Just remember, I also do not want to hurt him or the children."

They pulled into the driveway of Allen's home. Allen came out of the door and walked toward the car. "Hello, Susan," he said as Susan opened the driver's side window. "Jerry from Cosmos called. They want to meet us at one today. We need to get the final figures and adjustments done this morning." He ducked his head down a bit to see Linda. "Mary, I'm sorry I can't stay to help you get settled in. The girls will help you get adjusted." He then looked back at him. He was puzzled at first but quickly figured it out. "Is this your son?"

"Ya, his name is Mathew," Linda proudly announced.

"Can't I be someone else too?" Mathew asked.

Susan and Linda burst out in laughter to hide the reference to the changing of names. Allen had other things on his mind and did not respond. He did take the time to help Linda and her son with their bags and showed them their room.

"We'll find a fitting place for Mathew when I get home tonight." He shook his head and added, "Mary, I am so sorry that I have to leave."

"It is all right," Linda said. "We'll get along."

"There is no school again today. They are having parent-teacher conferences," Allen said. "I'll be going to Alicia's at four today. So I will be home when I get done with that. Probably around five. Don't worry about making anything for dinner. I'll stop and get some chicken somewhere or something." He then walked through the kitchen and into the family room, where he met up with Susan, and out they went.

Susan looked back at Linda. "Good luck, Mary." Susan had a slight teasing smile on her face. Linda tried to suppress her smile.

Linda had some reservations about being left alone that morning. There was a small box on the kitchen table that was speaking to an invisible person in the room. She remembered a similar sensation when she went into Trish and Tasha's kitchen years earlier. It appeared that the children were not paying much attention to the words coming from the box. The electrical items on the counter she had seen the other day appeared more menacing today.

Linda and Mathew changed into their work clothes. Then Linda went downstairs to find the two young ladies sitting at the kitchen table. "Good morning."

"Hi, Mary," Alicia said, "we're hungry." Alicia was wearing yellow slacks and a dirty-looking old, orange shirt that had a colorful rabbit on the front. The shirt looked to be much too small for her.

"I will make something," Linda said, clearly ready to dig into her work. "Is there anything you would particularly like to have?"

"I want Pop-Tarts," the messy-haired Allison said.

While Linda was looking intently at her hair, Alicia noticed her looking at it. "Uncle Allen tried to put ponytails in her hair. But her hair is too short."

"It wouldn't be so short if you hadn't cut it," Allison complained.

"You wanted me to cut it."

"Ponytails?" Linda wondered as she looked more carefully at her hair. Mathew also looked intently at Allison's hair. "Where did he get ponytails?"

Alicia tried to explain, "That's my point. He didn't. He can't do ponytails or pigtails."

Linda had no idea what Pop-Tarts, pigtails, and ponytails really meant. "All right, Pop-Tarts," she said. She began to open the cupboard doors in search of items that could be used to make tarts. She quickly learned where some items were stored in the cupboards. The two girls did not offer her any help even though they knew she was not aware of what Pop-Tarts were.

Allison said, "Dad said you were stupid." Linda was hurt at first, hearing these words.

"He did not," Alicia said quickly. "He said that Mary is not accustomed to certain things, and we should help out as much as possible."

"If we have to help her, then she must be stupid." Allison asked, "What does *accustomed* mean?"

Linda turned to her and said, "I live a different style of life than yours. Therefore, there may be some things I won't know much about." She then smiled pleadingly. "Such as, I have no idea what a Pop-Tart is."

"We know," the older Alicia said smiling. "You looked right at them a while back."

"I did?" Linda looked back toward the cupboards.

"Yeah,"—Alicia pointed—"that door there."

Mathew came running into the kitchen. "Mother, their outhouse is in the house!"

"I'll show you how to use it later," Linda said.

"He doesn't know how to use a bathroom?" Alicia asked.

Allison proudly stated, "I was potty trained when I was two."

Linda said, "We have a different kind of bathroom. Allison, maybe you could show Mathew how to use it."

"Sure."

Mathew was embarrassed to have a little girl show her how to do something, but he needed to use it. "All right."

Mathew quietly said as he followed Allison, "Do you call it the in-house?"

Allison answered politely, "We call it the bathroom."

"Why do you—oh," Mathew said, "because there is a washtub in here. Mother," he called to Linda, "they have a washtub in the"—he had to think for a few seconds—"bathroom."

Allison pointed at the toilet. "You go potty in there and then pull down on this handle to flush." It did not seem very sanitary to him since it appeared to him to have such a small retainer for the waste product. He was used to a broad board with a hole leading down into a massive abyss. He also noticed that this in-house outhouse did not smell like an outhouse. She pulled the handle, and a roar of water swirled around inside the bowl. Mathew's eyes widened when she did this. "Got it?"

"Ya," Mathew replied, but in the back of his mind, he wondered that this was magical and certainly could be a product of the devil. He thought if this was the devil, he was sure welcome to whatever he could give him.

Allison left the bathroom. Mathew turned and caught a glimpse of himself in the mirror. He was startled for a moment. Then he began to study himself. He made faces at himself and smiled in amusement. There was a smudge on the mirror. He noticed there was a roll of paper next to the devil's hole. He took some of the paper to clean the smudge off the mirror.

Linda looked inside the third-door cupboard, but did not see anything that said Pop-Tarts.

Alicia spoke up after letting Linda search for a while. "They are actually called Toast'ems on the box. Allen said they were cheaper than the real Pop-Tarts. But I don't think they taste as good." Linda quickly recognized that box and pulled it out. "It is good that you can read," Alicia added.

"Well, I'm not stupid like your uncle said," Linda said jokingly.

"He didn't really say that," Alicia said. "Allison is just saying that 'cause she is stupid."

"Nobody is stupid," Linda said while opening the box with the tarts in them. The tarts were wrapped in aluminum wrap. "Where is your scissors?"

"In the junk drawer," Alicia said as Allison sat back down at the table.

"Junk drawer?" Linda questioned blankly.

"Yeah, the drawer you put all the crap stuff," Alicia said. "Tracy's mom says that every house has a junk drawer." She then pointed to a drawer at the end of the counter. "Allen has three junk drawers. Didn't the place you come from have a junk drawer?"

Linda opened the drawer and looked inside of it for the scissors. "This drawer does look very familiar. We just called it the drawer. She found the scissors and used it to cut the end off one of the packages of two tarts. She looked to Alicia and asked, "You don't eat these cold, do you?"

"No," Allison said. "You put them in the toaster."

"Oh." Linda looked around for something that had the word toaster on it.

"Don't you people eat toast ever?" Allison asked.

Linda was amused by the question. "We cook our toast on the stove. I'll get a toasting rack sometime to show you."

"The toaster would be much easier." Alicia pointed to the white metal box.

Linda looked on the counter and saw a metal box with white sides. There were two elongated holes on the top and a lever on the end. "Oh, I see."

"Let me show you," Alicia said as she got off her chair to help. "Place the Pop-Tarts in the slot." Linda put the tarts in the slots as instructed. "Then make sure the thing there"—she pointed to the pointer—"is pointed to *pastry*. Then push the button down." Linda turned the pointer to the word *pastry* then hesitated a moment. "That button there, push it down." Linda pushed it down, but it popped right back up again.

"Push it down all the way until it hooks," Alicia explained. Linda pushed it down harder, and this time it stayed down inside the metal box.

Linda was very interested in what was happening inside the toaster. She leaned over the opening on the top. She could feel the heat on her face as she looked inside. Then she tried to see if the tarts were cooked properly. "How do you know when they're done?" she asked anyone that was willing to answer her.

"Better watch it carefully, or it may burn up," Alicia said.

"What should I do when I need to get it out?"

"Just pull up on the button," she told her. "Keep waiting. It hasn't been nearly long enough." Allison looked at her sister, and Alicia gave her a glare. Allison understood that Alicia was playing a trick on Linda.

Linda stared closely inside the toaster when it suddenly popped. This caused her to jump in fright. Alicia and Allison laughed uncontrollably. Mathew had come down the hall just as his mother jumped, causing him to flinch as well. He started to laugh at himself.

She admitted to herself that she must have looked silly jumping like that. Linda laughed along with everyone else. "That was a bit funny, wasn't it?"

As she pulled the tarts out of the toaster to place on plates, one of them tore apart and stayed deep in the toaster. Linda picked up a silver butter knife that was near the toaster. She began to poke the knife inside the toaster to dig the lost piece out of it.

Suddenly, there were sparks flashing and shooting around the toaster. Linda screamed and pulled her hand away, leaving the knife in the toaster. Linda started shaking with fright.

"That was epic," Alicia excitedly shouted.

Allison began to cry with fright.

Alicia felt bad for Linda. She was afraid Linda might think she was playing another trick on her. "I didn't know that would happen, honest!"

Linda was scared but was able to compose herself to speak. "I know you didn't," she calmly comforted Alicia. She then addressed her son. "I am fine," she lied. Her heart was pounding with fright, and her hand had been burned. "Mathew, can you moisten a dishrag for me please." Mathew saw a clean, dry dishrag on the counter, and he went to the sink to pump some water. He lifted the pump, and water splatted out into the sink. Then he pulled down the lever, and it stopped. He tried to pump it properly, spurt stop, spurt stop, spurt stop, the faucet went.

Linda said, "It's automatic Mathew. Up is on, and down is off."

He tried it again and it worked properly. "Wow, that is wonderful."

Linda had burns on her hand from the sparks, but she wanted to make sure Allison and Alicia were fine. Linda carried Allison over to her son and asked him, "Could you hold the rag on my hand there please." She held out her hand, showing him the burn marks.

Mathew grimaced slightly when he saw his mother's burns. "Are you really all right?"

"It will be fine," Linda said. They could hear Alicia on the phone with Allen. She spoke calmly to Allison as she walked over to Alicia.

"Allen," Alicia said, "Mary just blew up our toaster. It was epic. Sparks were flying everywhere."

Linda held out her hand. "Let me talk to Allen please." She did not want him to think the house had blown up as Alicia was making it sound.

Alicia handed the phone to her, who tentatively spoke into it. "Hello, Mr. Barber."

"What is going on there?" Everyone in the house could hear him through the phone. Allen was angry to be getting a call just minutes after arriving at the office. He had a lot of preparation to do before one o'clock that afternoon, and this was not what he needed.

"Well, I am not sure what happened," Linda said very calmly. "I was trying to get a piece of tart out of the"—she had to think of what to call it—"toaster, when there was a spray of sparks, like what a log might do in a fire, but much worse." There was a moment of silence as she listened to Allen talk to her on the phone. "Well, nobody got hurt. It was all quite exciting." There were a few moments of silence as she listened to Allen again. "All right, that is downstairs?" Linda asked for confirmation. She continued to listen and then looked at Alicia. "Show me where the laundry room is downstairs," she requested of Alicia. She put Allison down. "Please sit here with, Mathew."

Allen gave her instructions on the phone on how to trip the breaker in the breaker box. Linda was successful, but she had left the knife in the toaster, so the sparks flew once again, sending Allison into a frantic screaming fit. Allen could hear her over the phone, so he decided he had to come home.

"He is coming home to fix it," Linda informed them sadly. She felt like she was bungling this opportunity, and Allen was angry with her. Allen had not been gone an hour, and the house was already a disaster. The two young girls had lost their appetite for the Pop-Tarts. One was frightened half to death, a toaster was fried, and Linda had some rough burns on her hand. She decided this was not going to get her down.

"Bread and butter, anyone?" She made the girls butter sandwiches, orange juice, and milk. She was not sure to do that she was certain wouldn't cause a disaster of some type. It would take too long to bake anything, and she was not sure how or if she should try to do anything with the stove. It had very few similarities with the stove she was accustomed to.

Soon, Allen burst into the house. "Where's the flashlight?" he demanded. Alicia ran to him with the flashlight. "Thank you, honey," he said calmly as he gave her a quick hug and a quick smile. He stomped over to the toaster and said, "You never dig around in a toaster when it is plugged in." He unplugged the toaster, pulled the knife out of the hole. He glared at Linda. Then he went downstairs, flipping the light switch.

Linda looked at the girls and smiled. "He is very good at fixing problems."

He came back upstairs, looked at Linda. "I'm sorry, but this isn't going to work." Linda understood what he was saying, and she could not blame him. She halfway expected to be asked to leave, but it still hurt to be fired on your very first hour of your very first day. She was not knowledgeable about many things of this world and felt lost and out of place. She could not expect him to leave her there caring for the children after this. She knew that next time she did something stupid, it might result in someone getting seriously hurt.

CHAPTER SEVENTEEN

Learn, Teach, and Experience

Alicia was horror-struck. "What," she said angrily, "you're going to fire her for that?"

"You can't, uncle Allen," Allison chimed in pleadingly. "Don't you remember the time you started the grease fire when you were going to make popcorn?"

"How can you remember that? You weren't even born yet," Allen said in a petty defense.

"Mom told us," Allison said plainly.

"And the tree in the backyard that you cut the limb off." She stopped to let the story sink in. Alicia reminded him. Allen looked at her as if he did not understand. "The limb that nearly hit Allison when she was a baby," Alicia said.

"When did that happen?" Allison asked.

"When you were a baby," Alicia said. "I heard Mom telling Julie when she gets mad at him."

"That was then. This is now," Allen said.

"I have more, uncle Allen," Alicia said.

Allen shook his head and then looked at the children. He curled his lower lip just before he started to nod his head. He turned to Linda. "Okay, I'm sorry," he said. "When I get home, I will show you how to use the more complicated things around the house. Just try not to use anything mechanical in the house for the rest of the day." He started to leave but turned around to address Linda once again. "If you haven't been properly trained and checked out on anything, don't touch it."

The house remained silent as he left for work to prepare for his important meeting. Linda was delighted to have another chance. She spent the next hour looking over the house. She went from room to room, learning where things were. Allison followed her around, explaining what things were. She was relieved when they found the cleaning materials. Linda knew what to do with those items. She was delighted to have something constructive to do later after the tour of the house.

Allison seemed to enjoy helping her and took her self-appointed duties very seriously. "That is a broom. That's a mop to scrub the floors. That is the vacuum cleaner." Linda knew what many of the items were but allowed Allison to feel she was doing an important job.

Linda was looking for a pencil and paper to make a list of items to get. The first thing she wanted to put on the list was pencil and paper.

Allison soon was disinterested in telling Linda what each of the items around the house were. She decided to join Alicia and Mathew in their bedroom. The girls had separate bedrooms before their mother left, but now, Allison did not want to sleep alone. Alicia shared the same feelings but never let on to anybody. As long as Allison wanted to stay in her room, she had no reason to reveal it.

Allison wanted to watch their favorite soap opera. They had not seen the soap opera for some time, so they had to catch up on what was going on. Alicia showed Mathew how the television worked. He was very intrigued by it. Now he was strongly being encouraged to watch the television by these two younger girls he had just met. He wanted to be polite, so he watched with them.

Mathew watched with great interest every commercial or program. The two girls filled him in on the story line of the soap opera. He seemed to understand, but he could not comprehend why people would have their lives exploited in this manner.

"So," Mathew recapped, "Anita is married to Henry, but she is having an affair with Charlie. But Henry's brother will tell on her unless she steals something from the firm."

"That's right," Alicia said excitedly. "You're getting caught up quickly."

"Why is she having an affair with Charlie if she is married to Henry?"

"Because they are in love," Allison told him dreamily.

"And isn't the firm going to know that she is going to steal something from them? Wouldn't they be watching the television and see what they are planning?"

"Those kinds of guys don't watch television at this time of day. And if they did, they certainly would not be watching a girly soap opera like this one," Alicia informed him.

"How can they not know?" Mathew could not understand. "Someone that knows them would certainly tell them."

"You'd think," Alicia shook her head. "They can be pretty quiet about things like that, if they want too."

"Yeah," Allison added. "Besides, nobody likes them."

Mathew sat quietly and continued to watch the show. Alicia then interrupted the silence. "I think that Henry is going to find out that someone is going in for the stuff. He is going to bust it wide open and catch his own wife in the act." The show ended soon after that. Mathew started to get up to leave. The two girls grabbed him and dragged him back down to the bed. "There is another one on after this one. The next one is the best." Alicia began to fill him in on the next soap opera. The younger girls made themselves more comfortable on the bed while he continued to sit on the edge politely.

There were two rings of a bell that rang throughout the house. Mathew looked around, wondering what the ringing was. The two young girls jumped off the bed and ran down the hall into the living room. Linda, who was studying the vacuum, looked around to find the source of the ringing bell. She curiously followed the two girls into the family room and watched them go to the front door. Alicia opened the front door.

"Ginger!" she yelled out.

A teenage girl made her way into the house. She was average size with very beautiful long, brown hair. She reminded Linda of the two sisters, Trish and Tasha, when they were teenagers. Alicia and Allison gave this girl hugs of affection.

"Hello," Linda greeted her politely.

"Hello," the girl said, "you must be Mary?"

"Ya," Linda responded as Mathew appeared in the living room, curious about all the commotion at the front door.

"I am happy to meet you. My name is Ginger." Ginger put her purse down on the couch and walked over to Linda near the entry to the kitchen. "Allen called me and wanted me to come over and give you a hand today."

"Oh," Linda said, "of course. I appreciate the assistance." Linda was a bit embarrassed to have a teenager sent to help her. "I was just about to clean the floor. I know this is used, but I don't know how to use it."

"Oh yes, the complicated vacuum cleaner." Ginger walked over to it. She felt the fat pouch of the cleaner. "The bag needs to be emptied." She tilted her head a bit. "It is the toughest, dirtiest job, but you will have to learn sometime."

The three younger children retired back into the bedroom to watch their soap.

Linda reached down and squeezed the pouch that Ginger had felt. "Oh, it feels full and squishy, doesn't it?"

Ginger nodded her head. "Yeah." She walked toward a closet in the hallway. "I'll see if I can find an empty bag." She dug around in the closet until she found a bag. "Here's one." She showed Linda how to change a bag in the vacuum. The old bag was puffing out dust that got into Linda's nasal passages. She began to sneeze uncontrollably. Ginger tried to keep up. "Bless you, bless you, bless you, bless you, dido, dido. Sorry but I got to do this." She pinched Linda's nose and rolled her fingers.

Linda sneezed once again, spraying Ginger with spit and snot. "I am so sorry."

Ginger leaned away with a disgusted look on her face.

"Well, that was my fault, trying to stop the normal human bodily function." Ginger chuckled at herself. "It usually works on my brother." Linda sneezed three more times. "Bless you," she said in frustration.

"You can wait," Linda said then sneezed twice, "until I am done."

"You must have allergies?" They looked at each other anxiously, waiting to see if she was going to sneeze again. "They are getting further apart. That's a good sign."

Ginger took the dust bag out to the kitchen to dump it in the trash can. Linda did not sneeze for nearly two minutes.

"I believe I am done sneezing."

Ginger said with great finality and relief, "God bless you."

"Thank you."

"Now plug it in," Ginger directed her to plug the vacuum in.

Linda was not completely sure what she meant by plugging it in. She carefully looked at the plug end of the cord Ginger had handed her. She remembered Allen taking a cord like this to the toaster and pulling it out of the wall. Then she studied the wall for a receptacle of the plug. A few seconds later, she found a receptacle in the living room. She took the plug in her hand and fit it into the wall.

Ginger showed her she needed to turn on a switch on the vacuum to get it to operate. Linda switched on the vacuum. There was a terribly loud, annoying sound from the vacuum. The bag she had just put into the vacuum filled up instantly with air and emitted a small puff of dust.

Ginger yelled out so she would be heard over the noise of the vacuum, "That's normal. Now just move it around on the floor!"

Linda shut the vacuum off and was relieved that the annoying sound had stopped. "That is very loud," she said.

"Yeah," Ginger agreed. "You don't want to run it when someone is trying to talk on the phone."

Mathew, even though he wanted to continue to watch the television, felt guilty he had not done any chores all day. He went out to the living room and asked his mother. "Is there some chores I can do?"

"Why don't you go out into the barn and see what kind of tools are there? Maybe organize them," Linda suggested so he would feel more useful.

Mathew went to the window and looked out. "Where is the barn?" He could not see one anywhere out back.

"It's just a small one, attached right to the house," she explained. "It is where they place their automobile."

Mathew went out through a door out the side of the kitchen directly into a barn. He looked around. He noticed that Allen had a great collection of tools. He was impressed with his collection. But nothing impressed him more than the big blue-and-silver truck inside the barn.

Afterward, Ginger showed Linda how to use a can opener and how to turn a burner on the electric stove. They cooked chicken noodle soup from two large cans for everyone's lunch. Linda was amazed at how the stove worked. It was different to have cooked up a meal quickly and easily like that. She was surprised how cool the kitchen was after cooking. It was not a very substantial meal compared to what she would normally prepare.

She knew Mathew would be expecting a great meal of meat, potato, and vegetables later. He had looked at the pathetic soup meal as though he was being punished for something. He accepted what he thought was a punishment for being lazy all day watching television.

She questioned how to use the oven. Ginger briefly showed her how a sequence of buttons being pushed would heat the oven in a certain way. Linda felt like a failure all day, not knowing the simplest of things in order to clean the house and cook a proper meal.

Allen called to talk to Ginger during the afternoon. He asked Ginger to order pizza to be delivered to the house for dinner. He was going to pick Alicia up for the teachers' conference. After the conference, he would drop Alicia off at home and go back to the office to work. He had to work out a few matters before returning home.

Ginger, who was playing with the girls in the living room when the noise of the garbage disposal sounded and heard the mousy squeak from Linda, yelled in to Linda, "That's the garbage disposal! It's no big deal!"

Linda peeked around the door of the kitchen. "What does it do?"

"You put leftover garbage, like food scraps, into it. It will chop it up and dispose of it. Thus the name of garbage disposal." Ginger then added, "Don't put your hand in there. It grinds up anything that goes into it, even small bones and stuff."

Linda began to realize that these automated things could be very dangerous. There were always dangers on the farm but not as many hidden daggers as there were in this house. She understood the Amish belief that these things were tied to the devil somehow.

Allen stopped by very quickly to pick up Alicia for her conference. Alicia came through the door a half hour later. A few moments later, the doorbell rang again. Linda looked around again before realizing that it was someone at the door. Alicia ran to the door, opened it, saw it was the pizza delivery boy, then ran back into the bedroom yelling, "Pizza's here."

Linda greeted the pizza boy, "Thank you." She shut the door before paying.

"Mary," Alicia said, "you have to pay the man."

"Oh," Linda said. She opened the door to find the boy still standing there, not knowing what to do. He hated to have an argument with an Amish woman.

"Ma'am," he said.

"I'm sorry. I'm new at this."

"It's fifteen fifty."

Alicia grabbed a twenty-dollar bill in a jar on the kitchen table. She ran it over to Linda. "Give him this and tell him to keep the change."

Linda handed it to him. "Keep the change."

"Thank you," he said and walked away.

After dinner, Linda was in the kitchen cleaning up when Allen arrived. Linda greeted him anxiously. She was disappointed to find him not alone. Susan was with him. Allen presented her with a Red Flyer wagon. "Thank you." Then she asked politely, "Is there something I can get you for supper?"

Allen very kindly responded, "No, thank you. Susan and I had dinner in celebration of a great new contract we will be finalizing in a few days." Alicia and Allison came running out of their bedrooms to greet Allen and Susan. Linda noticed they were almost as excited to see Susan as they were to see Allen.

Allen proceeded to show Linda more about the house and the way things worked. He dug up an old mattress and set up a small area in the fully finished basement for Mathew to sleep. He apologized to Mathew several times for the poor conditions, but he said the next weekend he would build Mathew a proper room.

He showed him how to release the window in the basement to allow him to escape in case of a fire.

When he was showing Mathew the garage, he noticed Mathew's interest in his truck. "Three hundred forty horsepower," Allen blurted out. Mathew's mouth dropped open for only an instant as he briefly tried to imagine three hundred forty horses pulling this truck. Mathew then realized Allen couldn't be really talking about real horses. He then remembered a scene on the television earlier in the day. He saw a truck similar to this one chasing a herd of wild horses. The words spoken by the television said, "With three hundred forty horses, you can do this."

"Do you really chase horses with this?" Mathew asked excitedly. The commercial he had seen looked like something he would really want to do.

Allen began to smile and laugh but stopped so as not to embarrass Mathew. "I don't, but some people do, out in the West, where there aren't as many people or fences." Allen noticed the tools had been changed around and sorted nicely. "Huh, things seem to be a little different out here."

Mathew quietly said, "I'm sorry."

"Don't be sorry," Allen said as he opened up the drawers one by one to look inside of them. "You did a very good job. It may take me a while. Well, actually everything is arranged so well that finding what I need will be very easy."

"My father always liked to have his tools sorted out well so he can scan the box or wall for what he needed quickly," Mathew said. "Like these drawers, if we were to put in dividers so everything isn't thrown in anyplace, we could sort things out much better."

"Yeah," Allen agreed. Then he had a fine thought. "Would you like to do that?"

"Ya, I would," he said excitedly.

While Allen was out showing Mathew the garage, Linda and Susan had a chance to talk privately. Susan opened the conversation, "It is different here, isn't it?"

"Ya," Linda said as she sadly looked to the floor while wiping her hands on her apron. "I never felt so lost and useless in my life."

"I was afraid of that. Allen told me what happened this morning. He blames himself more than he does you," Susan said. "You are very capable of doing this job. Look at me. I was able to adjust."

"You have been here for a long time."

"But I had to adjust the same way you are now," Susan explained. "I was once in the same position you are. It took time, but I had one thing in my favor. I didn't continue to embrace the Amish faith. That will complicate things for you."

"I don't want to lose the faith," Linda said.

Susan reasoned, "You don't have to lose the faith. But, it will be tough to properly practice it here. There are too many things that will contaminate your efforts."

"I might be able to adjust, but I don't believe Allen will be as patient as he needs to be. I can't really blame him. He has to think of his family. I could have done something stupid and killed them all," Linda said sadly.

"Li—Mary," Susan corrected herself quickly, "you are overdramatizing things a bit, aren't you?"

Linda looked around the kitchen, especially at the charred toaster and the wicked-sounding garbage disposal. "I don't think so."

"All right," Susan agreed. "Well, let's discuss your plans for tomorrow." They discussed what to plan for meals the next day. There was school the next morning, so Linda had to work around the girls' school schedule.

The children were in bed an hour earlier than usual, as Linda had encouraged them. Susan left after she and Allen put the children to bed. Allen came out to the kitchen and sat down at the island as Linda swept the floor. "I understand you are not familiar with the gadgets that we use. I do know some things about your culture. I once had a good friend that was Amish."

Linda's heart leapt, and her stomach dropped when he mentioned knowing an Amish person. She was sure he was referring to her. She was hoping he would not say anything more about it. Allen soothingly said, "I do want you to stay and give it a go, if you would, please?"

The words excited her since she was not wasn't sure of his feelings about them being a part of their lives. "I would really like to stay. The children are adorable, and my son seems to get along with them. I would very much want to help you with the children."

Allen chuckled at the hidden proposal, "Well, I am anxious for you to take part."

"I am sorry, Allen. I didn't mean that you haven't been a good parent or person. They are obviously very well raised and loved."

"That would be because of their mother." Allen reminisced sadly that his sister had gone to serve the country. Linda did not interrupt his thoughts.

"She is a very special lady, I am sure," Linda comforted.

"Yes, she was."

"What has happened to their father?"

"He was a crackhead dealer that the feds were after, so he fled to the Phillpines."

Linda was lost at what he meant, "Wow, that sounds awful."

"Here is a check that I signed. You can take this to the store tomorrow and get whatever we need for food and supplies at the Piggly Wiggly Food Mart."

"Is there something Mathew can do around the yard to keep himself busy? He will get lazy on me if he stays idle for very long."

"The lawn needs to be mowed and clipped. But I better show him how to use the lawn mower tomorrow when I get home. I have actually already given him a project for tomorrow."

"Oh good," Linda said. "He could do that in the morning. We will be studying in the afternoon."

"We may have to look into getting him into school here. I don't know exactly what the truancy situation is for Amish living in town," Allen said. "I will have Susan check into that in the morning."

"It is the same as living out of town," Linda said. "I am impressed that you have taken such interest in his welfare. I am also wondering why you have accepted Mathew and me. From your demeanor earlier today, I got the impression you didn't want us here."

"Well," Allen struggled to explain, "Susan seemed to be fairly familiar with Amish and indicated that in time, you would certainly be the best servant a man could ever find." Allen knew right away his statement was not accepted well by Linda.

"I am not a servant."

"Oh, yeah." Allen apologetically said the letters as Linda mouthed them, "A-L-L-E-N-S-M-A-I-D."

"Very good," Linda said playfully. "And what do the letters stand for?"

Allen shook his head slowly and apologetically said, "I really have no idea."

"Neither do I." Linda laughed.

Allen proceeded to show her how to use various appliances around the house. Linda was most interested in how the stove operated. "So tell me how to use this contraption over here please."

"Well, bring yourself over here and let me school you on the operation of a genuine electric stove."

Linda smiled. "I want to hear all about it, every little thing about a genuine electric stove."

The next morning, Linda and Mathew both got up at 5:00 a.m. She felt confident using the stove that morning to cook sausage, bacon, and eggs. The aroma of breakfast cooking in the morning brought back memories of Julie, who used to cook a fine breakfast. Allen was drawn into the kitchen wearing boxer shorts and a T-shirt. "Coffee. I got to show you how to make coffee."

Linda tried not to be offended or embarrassed by his casual appearance. She looked away from him. "Good morning."

"Good morning, Mary." He looked past her, spying the breakfast cooking. "This is a bit early for us."

"I'm sorry. I didn't know what your schedule was." She tried to look at him as he stood in his boxers but could not do it without a trace of embarrassment.

"What's the matter?" he asked just as he figured it out. "I'm sorry. I wear gym shorts to bed. I'll change into something more cover-up-age, if that will help?" He trotted off back toward his room.

He scooted past Mathew, who was coming in from outside the back door. "He must have had to go bad," Mathew said to his mother, thinking Allen had to use the bathroom.

Linda chuckled, "We had better get used to some really strange things taking place around here."

"Is there still hope for them?"

"Of course. There is always hope." Linda asked, "Could you get the girls up please?"

"Mother," Mathew pleaded, "I really don't want to go in there. They made it clear that I should stay out of their room unless I am invited."

Linda could understand Mathew's dilemma. "I'll get them up. Could you watch the bacon please?"

"Me?" Mathew questioned, thinking it was beneath him to be forced to do women's work. He was afraid to watch the bacon on a strange stove in a strange house with strange people.

"Just for a moment."

The girls were reluctant to get up. Linda thought she could entice them to get up. "I made bacon, sausages, and eggs."

"Yuck!" Alicia spouted out.

"Milk or orange juice?" Linda tried to get them excited. There was no response. "Bananas, Pop-Tarts." She desperately thought.

Allison said, "I'm turned off to Pop-Tarts right now."

"Food works on boys," Alicia said.

Linda joked, "Frosted sugar cookies."

"Really?" Allison said excitedly.

"No, I'm just kidding."

"Don't do that!" Allison said angrily. "Grown-ups aren't supposed to tease kids."

Everyone ate well, and they were ready for school and work an hour before they actually needed to. Linda started a conversation to get everyone telling each other about the day they expected to have.

After Allen left for work, Linda and the girls set off for school. Mathew stayed home to work on his project he and Allen had discussed the night before. Linda pulled a Red Flyer wagon behind her as she walked the girls to school. Both girls attended an elementary school just a few blocks from the house.

They did not seem to mind walking with Linda, even though she was wearing her full Amish apparel. They drew many strange looks from the other children, which did not surprise Alicia. They also drew strange looks from the parents. Alicia liked Linda but was uncomfortable that everyone was looking at them. She got on the bus as fast as she could to distance herself from Linda.

Linda overheard one of her friends ask, "Who is that lady you were with?"

"She is our new housekeeper," Alicia said.

"You have an Amish housekeeper?" the little girl asked.

"Yeah."

The conversation did not bother Linda personally. She felt deep sorrow for Alicia, who remained silent. She could see Alicia's anguish as her face appeared in the window of the bus when she sat down.

Linda briskly pulled the little red wagon to the grocery store. She had been grocery shopping before and was fully capable of getting the things she needed. She left the store with her wagon full of goodies. She did not get everything since the wagon could only hold so much. She figured she had to go back the next day to get more.

After unloading the groceries, she cleaned the house for the rest of the morning. Then that afternoon, she searched the yard for Mathew but did not find him. She eventually did find him in the girls' room watching a soap opera.

"Hello, Mother," he said quietly, knowing he was in trouble.

"What are you doing?"

"I am watching a soap opera."

"A what?"

"A soap opera." He tried not to get into too much detail since he wasn't sure how to explain a soap opera.

Linda was confused. "Is it an advertisement for soap?"

"No." Mathew labored for more words. "It's really a story of how people mess up their lives and stuff." He used the remote to turn the television off and began to leave the room.

"Why would you watch that?" Linda asked.

"Because Alicia asked me to so I could tell her what happened when she gets home," he said with a forced innocent smile.

"Since when do we do what an eight-year-old girl tells us to do?"

"She is one of our bosses, isn't she?"

Linda only shook her head and thought he had a point. They went through his lessons for the day. Linda then had him help make bread. He kept muttering about women's work. But she paid no attention to his verbal anguish. She watched the time so she would not miss meeting the children.

When she returned with the children, she had them do their homework first; then she put them to work cleaning their rooms. Linda told them that once they had it clean, it would be much easier to keep it clean each day. Alicia was not happy with having to clean her room. She refused to say a word to Linda the rest of the day.

Allison made a comment that her mother has possessed Linda somehow.

Linda and Mathew served up a dinner that the Barbers were only used to being served at Christmas and Thanksgiving. There were buns, vegetables, potatoes, fruits, and the most delicious, tender roasted beef. There was gravy to use if they cared to. The children were hungry and ate like it was a feast they had never experienced before.

Once they had finished eating, the children started to run off to their rooms. Linda said forcefully, "Chores!" The two girls stopped in their tracks and returned to the kitchen to clear the table. Allen was impressed that they did this so willingly. They cleared away all the plates and put away the butter, milk, and bread, threw away the old napkins, and even placed the chairs smartly around the table. Then they ran off to their rooms before anyone could tell them to do anything else. Linda smiled in amusement as they ran off.

Linda spent the next hour and a half cleaning the kitchen. She stuck her head out into the living room, where Allen was watching a television show. "Would you like me to pack leftovers for your lunch tomorrow?"

Allen was used to getting a burger at a local fast-food place or not eating at all. He was caught off-guard by the suggestion. "Yeah, sure, I could try it once," he answered happily. He thought that the meal would not be as good as it was tonight, but it had to be better than the usual hamburger. Linda continued to clank around in the kitchen for a few minutes. Allen got up and joined her. "Mary," he said in a serious tone, "you have been working all day. Why don't you take a few minutes to rest. I know Amish don't work all the time, do they?"

"Not all the time, but nearly all the time," she told him.

"Sit down and relax for a few minutes. I would like to talk to you."

"Fine, I will, but let me finish up a few last things." Linda went back into the kitchen and clanked around for a few more minutes. She then came into the living room, still wearing her apron. She sat down on the couch. Allen sat in a reclining chair, which reminded her of her father-in-law. Both appeared to sit in the chair to relax while reading. Allen started the conversation. "I once knew a little Amish girl when I was younger."

"Really," she said and then quickly tried to change the subject. "You may want to show me how to use the washing machine in the morning or right now." She began to get up out of the chair.

"No," he said, "I can show you later." He continued to tell her about the little girl. "She would be about your age by now, I would guess." Allen began to chuckle. "In fact, the first time I saw you, I thought that you might have been her."

"Really," Linda said again with a sense of curiosity and fear. She was curious about what he was going to say and fearful about what he was going to ask.

"Linda Hershberger, do you know her?" Allen asked with great anticipation.

Linda answered apprehensively, "I know her."

"Tell me about her." Linda did not want to get into this conversation. She knew that once she was involved in the conversation, she would have to lie to him. She again searched for a way to change the subject. "Just curious," he said. He could tell that she was not very happy discussing it. "If you don't want to talk about her, that's all right."

Linda sensed that it meant a lot to him to talk about her. She then became very interested in what he was thinking. She also thought he deserved some consideration from her since she had mistreated him so badly in the past as Tanya. "Tell me, why do you want to know about her."

"You don't really want to know about it. I was just curious as to whatever happened to her." He said this in a very heartfelt way that impressed Linda.

"Oh come on," Linda began to entice him to talk. "Really, tell me. If your reason is sound, then I might tell you about her, or at least what I know about her."

"Well, you might enjoy this story," he said.

"I'm sure I will."

"This is between us. You won't use it to hurt or make fun of her in any way, will you?" Allen asked her honestly.

Allen moved to the couch next to Linda. "I went to a creek one day on my grandfather's farm. I was fishing there when this Amish girl pops out of the bushes and proceeds to fall into the creek. She fell in the deeper part of the creek, and I didn't see her come back up. So I dove in after her. She was wearing those heavy shoes, and they stuck in the mud at the bottom of the creek. She was just inches below the water. I pulled her out, and her shoe stayed in the mud." He paused a moment. "I dove down to get her shoe for her later."

"So you saved Linda's life," Linda concluded. She thought it interesting that he neglected to tell her he had fallen in before the Amish girl Linda had fallen in.

"Yeah," he said proudly. "She was afraid to go home with her clothes all wet."

"Why?"

"I think she thought she wouldn't be allowed to come to the creek for solitude anymore. Anyway, her visits to the creek seemed to be very important to her," he said.

"Could be," Linda reasoned.

"Well anyway," he continued, "I got her a blanket to stay warm. Eventually, her clothes dried, and she went back home. But we made arrangements to meet the next day."

"Her clothes," Linda questioned, "how did they dry when she was wearing them?"

"She removed her outer layer and hung them up on branches of trees," Allen said with some embarrassment. "I turned my back of course."

"Of course. That was very gentlemanly of you." Linda smiled as she recalled.

"The next day when I went to meet her. We had a great time. She had brought some sandwiches and they were good. We were just kids, but it was different."

"So what happened between the two of you?"

"We saw each other for a few weeks. She was really fun, and I felt so comfortable talking to her. It was the greatest time of my life. Then one day, out of the blue, her mother came to my grandfather's farm and requested that I never see her again."

This was news to her. She had not known that her mother had talked to Allen. "Did you see her again?" Linda asked anxiously to get more information.

Allen explained, "I talked to her brother, and he told me that she had been beaten by her father for seeing me. But she still insisted on seeing me. I couldn't let her get caught and beaten again. So her brother and I arranged for her and me to meet again. He brought her to a place where we could meet one last time. I had to tell her that she'd better not come around looking for me again. I even had to say some terrible things to convince her that I didn't want to see her again." Linda could recall that night vividly having reminded herself of it for the last twenty years. She had always thought he did not mean what he said. Now it made sense to her. He was doing it to protect her from further harm. It was very hard for her to keep from crying, but she managed to fight off the tears. Instead, his eyes began to tear, and one tear trickled down his face. "It was the worst day of my life." He looked at Linda. "I didn't understand it then, but I felt like I got kicked in the stomach."

"Me too," Linda said quietly.

"You too?" Allen asked.

"I mean, I know the feeling," Linda saved her secret. "So you never saw her again."

"I never talked to her again," Allen sadly said. "That's why I am interested to hear about how she is. If her life turned out to be wonderful like she had planned." There was a brief pause before he added, "I remember she wanted to have lots of children."

"You really did want to see her, but never let her know that," Linda said solemnly.

"I didn't want to mess up her life." A tear trickled down Allen's cheek. "I was stupid not to tell her the truth. But I didn't want to get her into trouble. I did try to get her to understand that seeing me wasn't worth it."

"You should have let her make that decision herself," Linda said.

"No, she would have taken the chance to see me and risked being beaten or killed by her father," Allen said.

"Do you really think her father would have gotten that abusive to her?"

"I don't know. I have never met him. But it wasn't worth the risk." Allen reasoned.

Linda wished she had known that before. She did not want to reveal anything more than that.

Allen was silent for a while. Then he said, "I am very glad she is fine and healthy. I knew she wanted to have children so badly. I figured she would have had her ten by now."

"Ten would be a healthy family indeed. She is still young enough to have more children. Who knows what life has in store for her."

"So you are only going to have the one boy?"

"You never know." She shrugged her shoulders.

"Are you going to be able to meet another Amish man that isn't already married?" he asked earnestly, concerned for Linda's happiness.

"You never know," Linda said. "There is an occasional divorce, of course. However, if one gets divorced, they are usually viewed as a risk when getting remarried."

"Well, anyway, I am glad she is well."

"I'll keep you posted, if you like, if I hear anything concerning Linda."

Allen looked deep into Linda's eyes. Linda was afraid for a moment he might recognize her. Her fear was dashed when he said, "Do you think it would be appropriate to send her a message?"

Linda's heart skipped a beat. "It wouldn't be a good idea. I mean, what would be the benefit of contacting her now?"

"No benefit I guess," Allen spoke sadly. The two remained quiet for a few minutes before he spoke again. "The meal tonight was wonderful. I don't think I have ever had a better meal other than Christmas at my grandmother's."

Allen added, "Mathew did a great job organizing my workshop area. He is a fine boy. You have done a wonderful job of raising him."

Linda smiled appreciatively. They watched the television until the present show was over. Allen found the girls to put them to bed. He also told Mathew what a great job he did on the workshop. The house lights were turned off, and silence spread throughout the house.

It was the earliest the Barbers had gone to bed ever.

CHAPTER EIGHTEEN

Too Close for Comfort

The days went along with some interesting situations that Linda found herself involved in.

There was the time Linda wanted to get a farm animal. That was one thing she missed most living in the city. She went out to a farm and bought several chickens so they could have fresh eggs. She and Mathew spent an afternoon building a chicken house. Allen was not very pleased with the chicken-wire fencing and small chicken house in his backyard. He was appalled by the mess and the clucking of chickens. He had trouble getting his appetite once the smell crept into the house. He was not sure he was allowed to have chickens in town. But Allen had more things to be worried about than the city ordinance. There was the mob of neighbors who didn't appreciate this latest development.

He would not have let the chickens stay, except for the fact the children wanted them so badly. Linda missed the sound of a rooster in the morning, so she purchased a rooster named Spike. Allen made it very clear to Linda that she was not supposed to get anything else without checking with him first.

The children eventually changed their minds about the rooster because he would attack them and chase them around the backyard. Spike considered the backyard as his domain.

One day, Allison was angry at Alicia, so she locked her out of the house from the back door. Alicia was screaming and running for her life when Allison asked Linda, "Mary, is there anything I can do for you?"

"Ya," Linda said without looking up. "What's all the screaming about?"

"Oh that," Allison answered. "Alicia was playing with Spike."

Linda smiled. "I knew you two would enjoy having chickens."

"Yeah, they have been great entertainment." Allison smiled, remembering how Alicia was scurrying around the backyard.

When Alicia came inside, she grabbed Allison firmly by the arm. "Come along, my little sister."

"Mary," Allison began to plead, "she is going to kill me."

"I know," Linda responded calmly. "She won't hurt you too badly, I'm sure." She gave Alicia a stern look, making sure she understood she was not to carry the payback too far.

A few days later, the two girls were trying to lock up Spike in his house, but in their haste, Allison accidently closed the door on the pursuing Spike and broke his neck. Allison felt bad about it, but Linda was the only person truly disappointed.

Later that night, Allen was busy finishing the last touches on Mathew's room in the basement. He was delayed in coming up to tuck his nieces in for the night. Linda took the opportunity to sit on the children's bedside and talk to them. Allison asked Linda, "Mary, do you suppose God will forgive us for killing Spike?"

"You didn't kill him on purpose. It was an accident. There is really nothing to forgive," Linda comforted Allison.

"Really?" Allison asked.

"Yes, really." Linda's smile assured her forgiveness.

Allison hugged Linda in gratitude. Linda could sense Alicia wanted to hug her as well but was hesitant. Linda leaned toward her, and Alicia hugged her as well. Allison said, "You remind me a lot of my mother."

"Yeah," Alicia agreed.

"I bet your mother is very sweet and beautiful," Linda said to them. She felt a bit uncomfortable with the comparison to their mother.

Allison began to cry. "She is, but I am beginning to forget what she looked like."

The girls would get calls from their mother once in a while. This would usually result in a night of sadness at the house.

Even though the Amish didn't embrace photographs, Linda was aware the English did. "Do you have any photographs of your mother?"

Allison looked funny at her. "Pictures," Alicia said.

"There is a picture of Mommy on the fireplace shelf," Allison said.

"Alicia, why don't you go get the picture," requested Linda.

Alicia did not hesitate to get the picture. Allen was coming up the basement steps as he saw her excitedly run back to her room carrying the picture.

Alicia jumped into the bed, cradling the picture so it would not get damaged. "That's our mother," she said. "She has the most beautiful blue eyes."

"Oh, they are beautiful," Linda said with true passion. "She has a very nice smile." Allen stood out in the hallway just outside the room, eavesdropping on the conversation. Linda asked, "Why don't you tell me about your mother?"

Alicia asked, "You really want to hear about our mother?"

"Ya," she responded honestly.

"She is always happy," Allison offered quickly.

"Yeah, even when she was sick, she acted happy," Alicia added. "And when she was sick, she still took care of us. Except when she had a miscarriage."

"Your mother had a miscarriage?"

"Yes, that's when the baby falls out too early. Now she can't have any more children."

"She would always tuck us in," Allison said sadly. "She might read us a story or tell us one she made up. She would lay down with us and just talk about things." She went silent for a few seconds. "I miss her," Allison said as she started to cry. "Allen, has been really great to try and be a mommy, but he isn't Mommy."

"He does a really good job of playing a mother." Alicia began to cry. "I shouldn't cry."

"Why not?"

"It will make him feel bad," Alicia said.

"Why do you think he will feel bad?" Linda wanted to know.

Alicia was reluctant but she explained, "I know he is sad about Julie leaving and if we get upset and cry, he will feel bad."

"We all need to cry. That is God's way of helping us deal with our emotions, both happy and sad feelings," Linda explained.

"Even Allen?" Alicia asked. "He is a man. They shouldn't cry, should they?"

Linda explained, "God did not give woman the only right to have emotions. Men need to cry as well. But boys are not supposed to be as emotional as girls."

"So we shouldn't hold our feelings back?" Allison asked. Allen made himself more comfortable listening by sitting down with his back against the wall.

"Uncle Allen, needs to cry as well. It will help him to accept things," Linda said.

"We just call him Allen," Allison informed Linda.

"Yeah, we called him Uncle Allen for like the first month we were hear, and it was just weird. So he said to just call him Allen," Alicia further explained.

"I have an idea. We should place a couple of pictures of your mother right here next to your bed. When you go to bed, you should talk to your mother, telling her everything you did that day."

"Do you think she will hear us?" Allison asked.

"I believe she will be able to feel it in her heart." Linda tried to comfort them.

"I'll go first," Allison said excitedly. She looked at the picture of her mother Alicia was holding on her stomach. Allison took several minutes to talk to her mother. She ended her loving message with "I love you, and I miss you so much."

There were a few seconds of silence. "Are you done?" Alicia hugged her sister.

"Yeah," Allison answered solemnly.

"Good." Alicia went on for several minutes, telling her mother everything she could think to tell her. "I love you, and I will talk to you every night."

"Do we say amen?" Allison asked.

"Let's say a prayer to God and end it with an amen." Linda said a fine short prayer, and they all ended with "Amen."

"Do we have to wait to talk to her at night only?" Alicia asked.

"You can talk to her privately anytime," Linda answered Alicia. Linda got up to leave the room to find Allen. She just about tripped over him when she entered the hallway. "Oh wow, sorry." He quickly arose, eyes wet with tears. She could see that he had been listening.

"That was very nice," he said, looking at her strangely.

In the next few weeks, the big contract with Cosmos forced Allen to spend less time at home. He would often miss dinner, but he always made a point to be home an hour or two before the children went to bed.

Linda took more responsibility for making decisions around the house. Many times, she would ask Ginger's mother or Susan for advice. Linda spent much more time with the children, thus, becoming very attached to one another. Susan and Allen spent a great deal of time together.

Linda and Allen would often have conversations at night concerning the house and the children.

Linda knew that in the Amish community, it was accepted practice that work took up a great deal of time. However, the family was always working together. She could see the effect of his absence in the demeanor of the children.

Allen took a few minutes to talk with Linda. "I know I haven't been there for the children like I should. It has been tough, and I am so tired."

"Allen," Linda addressed him seriously.

"Yeah." He leaned back in his recliner and closed his eyes.

"I really think you need to stop working so much," Linda said. "The children need you more than ever before."

"I give them quality time every night."

"I know you do. But that isn't enough."

Allen shook his head lazily. "I have too much work to do. This is the first big job I got, and I need to make sure it goes well."

"Are things not going well?"

Allen yawned. "Things are going excellent. I'm afraid things will go sour if I let up." There was a pause, but just as she was going to speak, he started talking again. "It has been hard hiring enough men to work. Many apply for the job and quit two days after they start. I don't really think they want the work. We have a new computer system, and that has been hard to set up. I spend the evenings trying to figure out the computer or fix all the problems."

He remained silent for a few seconds, and Linda saw this as an opportunity to say something. "Are you the only one that can fix the problems?"

"No," Allen said in frustration, "I just don't like to be delayed the next day."

"Who is your second?"

"Second?"

"Who orders people around when you're not there?"

Allen laughed, "Nobody."

"Doesn't Susan run the computer?"

"Yeah." He knew she was making a good point. He was trying to do everything, and he didn't need to. "I see where you are taking me."

Linda had the obvious solution for him. "If you would hire some young Amish men, you will have a nucleus of dedicated workers. You find a good man to be your foreman."

Allen thought for a moment. "Don't the Amish occupy most of their time on their own farms?"

"Many of the young men want to work other jobs so they may make money for themselves," Linda enlightened him.

"Really?"

"Ya, really."

"I'll see about getting in touch with the Amish tomorrow."

"So will you try to make more time for the children?" Linda asked, trying to get a commitment.

Allen knew he needed to make more time. "Yes, I certainly can, and I will. I just have been running things top to bottom from the start. It is hard for me to trust others to do it." Allen smiled at Linda with great affection. "Thank you. I am very glad that you came along to help me. It has been a great comfort knowing you are taking care of things here."

A few weeks later, Susan stayed for dinner. She was excited to eat a good home-cooked meal like she and her mother used to make. "That was a wonderful meal, Mary."

"Yes, it certainly was," Allen agreed. He then assisted Susan out of her chair just as he had assisted her into the chair. The two were not officially dating, but by their mannerisms, Linda considered them more than just work acquaintances.

Allen was spending more time with the children since their discussion. The little girls ran off to their rooms, leaving Linda in the kitchen cleaning up and Susan with Allen in the living room. Mathew stayed to help his mother.

The children and Allen spent their time talking to Julie. Then he went out to sit with Susan. Linda had finished cleaning up the kitchen and was now sitting in a chair, knitting quietly. Susan and Allen sat on the couch close to each other. Linda continued to knit as they talked quietly together. They would laugh and joke around. Susan was loyal to her sister, but she and Allen had gotten so close working together, that they were like siblings. The scenario made Linda sick to her stomach.

As Linda was contemplating going to bed, but she wanted to monitor what was going on between the two of them. On the other hand, she did not want to be a witness to it.

"Guess what?" Allen asked.

"What?" Susan replied anxiously.

"I have decided to make you office manager."

"Really?" Susan was surprised by the offer. "But I am the only one in the office now, so I am already the office manager."

"Not anymore. Tomorrow you are to hire an assistant."

"Wow." Susan gave Allen a big hug. "Thank you."

Linda was very happy for her sister getting a promotion, but she did not like the hug that Allen was receiving from her.

It was a relief to Linda when Susan got up to leave. Allen escorted her to the front door. Linda did not watch them, but she heard Allen giving Susan a kiss.

Allen only kissed her on the cheek, but Linda was not aware of that fact. She quickly finished putting away her knitting stuff and started to leave the room.

"Linda," Allen addressed, stopping her hasty retreat, "can we talk?"

Linda quietly and without facing him said, "Yes, of course." She fought off the strong desire to cry.

Susan gave Linda a kind smile. "Good night, Mary."

"Good night."

Allen gestured for Linda to sit. "Sit down. We haven't had a good talk lately."

"No, we haven't," Linda unenthusiastically answered. They sat down on the couch next to each other. Linda was very uncomfortable. She was afraid her feelings for him may be revealed through her jealous actions.

"I need your advice," he started the conversation.

She replied in a mocking manner, "All right, tell me all about it." She expected the conversation to be about him and Susan.

"Well," Allen started, "I need to talk to someone. I am so confused. I have figured that I have really loved three women in my life. Not including my mother and my sister of course."

"Of course," Linda replied with a fake smile.

"The first one was your friend Linda from twenty years ago, when we were just twelve."

"Really," Linda said. "I might have known from the way you talked before about her."

"Yeah, I know we were only twelve, but there was something really special between us. We just clicked when we were together. Well, so I thought we clicked anyway. Maybe she didn't think of me in the same way. I still remember the hurt look on her face when I said nasty things to her."

Linda was warmed by the thought that he really did have strong feelings for her twenty years ago. "She may have felt that way about you as well, but being Amish, it would have placed her in a very difficult situation."

"I can understand that." He thought for a moment. "Maybe I only thought I loved her because—I am ashamed to say this— but she was the first girl I ever saw naked." With these words, Linda had trouble controlling herself. She could feel the blood rushing to her head and felt that she was obviously blushing.

"How did you see her naked?" She remembered he had his back turned and a blanket between the two of them.

"I snuck a peek when she changed after falling in the stream."

Linda slapped him right on the face. She had some frustrated anger built up in her that was coming out. The thought that he and her beloved sister would do this to her gave her a reason to want to punish him.

Allen was surprised but not upset by the slap. "Well, I deserved that from Linda, but not from you. I didn't see you naked."

"Linda isn't here to defend her honor. It is a thing with the Amish. We take the place of the offended in cases like this," she lied.

He wanted to redeem himself to minimize the actual incident. "There really wasn't much to see," he said. Linda smacked him again hard across the face. "What was that for?"

"You just insulted her."

"She was only twelve. She hadn't developed yet. Now stop slapping me. It hurts." He rubbed his face. "It was twenty years ago. Ever hear of the statute of limitations?"

"No," Linda said, not caring what the statute of limitations was. "What else do you do to the ones you love? Probably snuck a peek into her bedroom too." She remembered when he snuck around the back pasture the day after she had seen him at the fair. She paused for a few seconds and then said, "Pervert."

Allen was embarrassed. "I didn't sneak peeks in her bedroom. Even if I did, I wouldn't tell you about it now," he said as he rubbed his face where she kept slapping him. He was not sure if he wanted to continue with the conversation. "Well, anyway, we separated, and I never saw or heard anything about her until you told me about her."

Linda then calmed down. "So Julie your ex-girlfriend was your second love, right?"

Allen was silent. "No, I didn't love her."

Linda slapped him again.

"What the hell was that for?"

"Carrying on with someone you didn't love and for saying *hell*."

"I hadn't even said *hell* before you slapped me. What has gotten into you?"

Linda held her hands up away from Allen. "All right, I promise I will not slap you again." She realized she wasn't mad at him for what he had done in the past but for what he did earlier with Susan. She was convinced he would be claiming Susan as one of his three loves.

"No, Julie came after my second love."

"Oh." This intrigued Linda. "So go on," she urged him.

"Well, there was this girl I met at the county fair just after I graduated high school." This struck Linda right in the heart. "She was beautiful. She was funny. She was sweet and had a great air of innocence about her. We seemed to click."

"Like you and Linda clicked?"

"Not exactly, but very similarly," Allen said. "It was different. I guess it was because we were older then. I could see in her the same things I saw in Linda, but she was all grown up. She reminded me so much of her, so when I fell in love with Tanya, I realized that I also had loved Linda. Does this make any sense at all?"

"No, but I love it just the same. Well, it appears to me that you just fall in love with everyone you meet, don't you?" Linda badgered him.

"No." Allen shook his head. "I met a lot of women and never fell in love with them."

"Now, go on about this Tanya girl. Like, how long did this affair last?"

"It was hardly an affair," he said. "We saw each other twice in two weeks." Allen shook his head. "I know it is the funniest thing. It is like a magical thing."

"Magical?" Linda inquired.

"Yeah," he replied. "I was devastated when she never came back."

"Did she promise to come back?"

"No," he said sadly. "She told me she would never come back. It was a very touching scene." Allen's eyes began to tear as he lay his head back on the couch. "She was so plain and cute in so many ways." He started to chuckle. "She got sick on the rocket ship." He got a great big smile. "I thought it was the cutest thing that ever happened."

"You thought that was cute?" She could only remember how awful she felt, both physically and emotionally.

"Yeah," he said, "because she did it and was so embarrassed, yet she was so cool about it." He looked over to the window. "She never had pizza before. Who in this world never had pizza before their eighteenth birthday? She never had pop before either. It was like she came from another world, and she claimed she came from another world." He got very sad. "I nearly died when she told me she would never return."

"Never saw her again?" Linda asked with great interest to see what he was going to say about her return years later.

"Oh yeah," he said, "she popped back into my life just to tear my heart apart again. She calls me up one night out of the blue. We go out a few times. Then I find out she is married."

"Why didn't you try to find her?"

"I did try. I checked every place I could for her, but it was like looking for a needle in a haystack. I talked to Trish and Tasha, who were her friends, but they just laughed and wouldn't tell me anything. Well, they said she came from the planet Amishia or something. I knew her name wasn't really Tanya Tucker, and now, she is out there getting a good laugh on me." He chuckled again. "Well, that was over ten years ago. I should have gotten over her by now."

Linda felt terrible for what she had done to him. "It was very cruel of her. You did not deserve it." She felt that he owed her a slap on the face. She was impressed Trish and Tasha kept the secret.

"Don't take it so seriously," Allen comforted her.

"I just feel so bad for you." She started crying. She felt very guilty. "And I just slapped you for something that wasn't that bad. Well, you shouldn't have peeked at Linda anyway."

Allen was touched by her sentiments and wanted so much to hold her. He was not sure he should hug her. He might lose control of his emotions. "It's all right, really. I deserved to get slapped. I eventually got over Tanya." Allen tried to comfort her with some kind words, "It's all right. I'm over her. I have found that I can truly love again."

"Really?" Linda weakly squeezed out. "Julie?"

"Julie was great." Allen spoke of her as if he did love her. "I loved her very much, but it wasn't the same kind of love."

"How do you mean not the same?"

"Well"—Allen had to think of a good way to explain it—"Julie was the perfect woman, except she was intolerant of children. Allen reflected about her for a few moments. Linda remained silent. "But the level of love I felt for Tanya, especially, was unattainable by any other woman. I guess Julie might have been the one who came closest. She came into my life years after Tanya left for the last time."

"So Tanya must be the woman you compare all your women to?"

"I guess Julie was caught on the rebound. She seemed to be the answer to all my wants and needs." Allen realized what he had with Julie was special in its own way.

Linda did not know what *rebound* meant. She had to remember she was Amish and actually playing an Amish person and would not be expected to know. "All right, go on. So Julie was not one of your great loves, but you loved her very much." Linda thought again. "Maybe you loved her more than you thought before because you hadn't completely gotten this Tanya out of your mind. Therefore, your comparison is invalid."

"But I did love her."

"You loved her very sincerely."

"Yeah." Allen liked the way she put it.

"So Julie was not your third great love?" The two of them looked down the hall

toward the girls' bedrooms to make sure they were not listening.

"No," Allen said. "My third love is something I cannot possess, a love that I cannot acknowledge to anyone ever."

"Why not?" Linda asked bluntly.

"We are too close, and it would be inappropriate for me to talk openly about it to her."

"Who is it?" Linda asked, anxious to hear but afraid just the same.

"I can't tell you who it is," Allen said. "It only means that I can love someone else. I just have to wait for the right one at the right time in the right situation." Linda looked at him strangely. Then he added, "It's not going to happen, is it?"

"Maybe once every thirty years." Linda was remembering a line she heard on one of the daytime soap operas. She shook her head. "I have to stop watching soap operas."

Allen looked intently at her. "I think you know who it is I am talking about."

"Ya, I know who it is." Linda got up off the couch, knowing he loved Susan, and she went to her bedroom, leaving Allen sitting on the couch.

CHAPTER NINETEEN

The World Comes Crashing Down

As soon as Allen left that morning, the two girls started jabbering away at Linda. Alicia blurted out, "Mary, you have to let him know."

"Let him know it is okay," Allison said. "I think you would be the prettiest girl if you were to put on some makeup and eye stuff."

"What?" Linda replied.

"You would be the prettiest woman," Alicia said.

"Yeah, prettier than Julia Roberts," Allison said. Linda had no idea who Julia Roberts was but perceived the comparison as a compliment.

Alicia had a great idea. "We should get Ginger over here. She knows about makeup."

Mathew made his way to the kitchen table and began to help himself to the bacon and sausage. Linda gave him a kindly look. He quickly said a brief prayer, blessing God and asking for forgiveness. When he finished, he began to eat aggressively.

"Hold on, ladies," Linda said. "What are you talking about?"

Alicia explained, "Come on, you have to let Uncle Allen know it is okay."

"We heard you two talking last night," Allison confessed.

Confused about what they had heard or thought they heard, Linda started probing their precious little minds, "You were listening in on our conversation?"

Alicia said, as if the procedure was practiced all the time, "Yeah."

"He will like you better than Julie once he sees you all made up pretty." Allison batted her eyes.

"What does Julie have to do with anything?" Linda asked.

"You need to watch some of these soap operas, Mary," Alicia said. "They are very informative for the ones battling for love."

"I think you two have been watching too much television," Linda said as she got up to clear the table.

"We didn't learn all this from television. We learned it from our own life's experiences," Alicia said. "We have had our battles."

"You are only nine years old." Linda shook her head. "Besides, I am not competing for your uncle against anyone."

"But you must show him," Allison begged.

Linda asked, "Show him what?"

"How beautiful you are," both girls said.

Linda looked at them questioningly. "What makes you think he has any feelings for me?"

"I see the way he treats you," Allison said.

"And the way he looks at you," said Alicia. "He tries to hide it because you're Amish, and he feels he is being naughty or something for having those thoughts."

Linda was astonished and frightened at the thought that Alicia may be right in her observation. "What thoughts?" Linda asked her inquisitively.

Alicia rolled her eyes, not believing Linda did not know. "Sex."

Linda immediately began to blush that such a young girl would use such a word so willingly. "Please don't talk like that."

Alicia explained, "Why? You see and hear about it all the time on television and YouTube."

"We both know where babies come from," Allison added proudly.

"Another good reason why we should get rid of the television. It spouts the devil's word." Linda looked out into the family room, hoping to see the television burst into flames from the wrath of God.

Allison looked up from her cereal bowl. "Don't even joke about that."

Alicia added, "I hope Allen doesn't want you."

"Yeah," Allison agreed.

"You would sell me out for the television," Linda implied.

Alicia said, "And you base that assumption on…what?"

"Allen and I had a nice talk last night. He pretty much said he has found the woman he wants to spend the rest of his life with, and that person is Susan."

"No, it is you," Alicia said.

"What is it that makes you think that?"

"Ugh," Alicia grunted as her head fell back on the chair. "We just told you, it's the way he looks at you and treats you." She began to shake her head. "He never treated Susan that way." Allison looked up from her cereal bowl again and nodded in agreement with her sister.

"So he looks at me and treats me nice. He is nice to everyone. He is a very loving man." Linda looked at their unconvinced faces. She then looked at her son, who had remained quiet throughout the conversation.

"They're right, Mother," Mathew added. "He does treat you differently."

"That's because I am here taking care of his household needs, and I remind him of someone he held dear to his heart many years ago." Linda turned her back to them all and began to run water into the sink to clean the dishes. "And being Amish, some people are uncomfortable around us. He feels the need to be on his best behavior. Bring your plates around when you are finished."

There were a few moments of silence before Alicia, who was hesitant, said, "You are the third love, Mary."

Linda did not say anything for a moment as she began to cry. "You didn't see him kiss Susan good night, did you?"

"I don't have to see him kiss her," Alicia said, "because he has kissed her many times on the cheek." Linda realized she had not actually seen them kiss passionately before. She was beginning to believe the two little girls could be right. Besides, she possessed two-thirds of the women he has loved.

"If he loved her, he would kiss her on the mouth," Allison added, "like they do on—" She stopped before she said television. She did not want to give Linda anymore reason to get rid of the television.

"It's true, Mother," Mathew added, after taking the last bite on his plate. "That's the way they do it all the time on television."

"That is enough," Linda said as she began to run water in the other tub of the sink to rinse the dishes in. "And you are not watching anymore television, Mathew."

"Why do you think his third love is the forbidden one?" Alicia asked her bluntly.

"I don't know," Linda said as if she didn't care. But deep down in her heart, she knew she needed to find out.

"Because an Amish woman would not be allowed to marry a worldly English person," Alicia said. "Am I right?"

Linda stopped everything she was doing. She stared out the window into the backyard for several minutes. She did not notice the gray skies and the pile of wood chips Mathew had created when he chopped the logs up. The three children waited silently for her to do something. Allison eventually got up and brought her bowl over to the sink. She placed the bowl awkwardly in the soapy water, and the splash woke Linda from her deep thought.

"Has he actually said anything to any of you?" she asked.

Alicia spoke up, chuckling, "Like he's gonna to tell us." Alicia tried again. "All right, just try dressing up as a real woman and see how things go. If he makes a move on you, then we'll know. And if he doesn't make a move on you, then we'll know."

"Dress up like a real woman? I am a real woman." Linda knew if she dressed up, he would certainly recognize her as Tanya. She knew Tanya was one of the women Allen claimed to have truly loved. She thought that it would not be fair to him to make him choose between Tanya and Susan. Once he found out she was also Linda, it would be two against one. Accept the two were big, fat liars, and Susan was not. Accept Susan was the co-conspirator sister of the two big fat liars. "Oh, God, what have I done?"

She felt so stupid and tired of the make believe world she had created. She was not proud of the position she found herself in, but she was anxious to resolve it. She knew the truth would come out eventually. She wanted to get on with a real life. She owed that to Mathew, Allen, and Susan. What would Allen do? Would he figure out that Mathew was his son, how would he react? And how would that affect Mathew?

"Take the leap," Alicia interrupted her whirling thoughts.

"And accept whatever the consequences," Linda resolved out loud.

Mathew quietly got up so he would not disturb his mother and left the kitchen to go work on the log splitting he had been doing for the last several days.

She was enjoying the life with Allen and the children. But, she had to make things right. Her stomach turned with both excitement and terrible nervous pain.

"All right," she interrupted the tense silence, "we'll do it today."

"Great." Alicia flew off her chair and ran to the phone. "I'll call Ginger and get her right over here."

"Wait!" Linda shouted. This prompted Alicia to stop in her tracks and turn around. Linda pointed to her cereal bowl left on the kitchen table. Alicia stepped back into the kitchen, picked up the bowl, and took it to the sink. Then she tore off into the family room.

Allison asked, "Do we have to do it now?"

"Yeah," Alicia said, "Uncle Allen will be home in, like, eight hours. It doesn't give us a lot of time."

"But I have all this housework to do."

Allison looked around the house, which was spotless. "What needs to be cleaned?"

Alicia looked back at her as she waited for someone at Ginger's house to answer the phone. "We'll do it while you're changing over to the real woman."

Allison looked at her with the most disgusted look. "Are you including me in that?"

Alicia addressed the phone first. "Hello, is Ginger there please?" She then turned to her sister and yelled, "Yes, you too!"

Allison looked up at the clock. "We better be done by eleven o' clock."

"That will be an incentive to work harder," Linda said.

Alicia yelled to Allison, "Forget the soaps on television. We have our own soap opera going on right here."

"Yeah," Allison said excitedly. Allison began to clear the table and wipe it down. Alicia talked to Ginger on the phone. She came into the kitchen. "Ginger will be over in an hour."

Alicia went directly to the back door and yelled out to Mathew, "Mathew, get your butt in here."

Linda looked at her. "Try to be more ladylike in your speech please."

"I'm sorry, but *butt* is better than *ass*."

"Ya, that would have been worse, but unnecessary just the same."

Mathew came in, and the girls convinced him he was a man but now was the time to help with women's work. Mathew was reluctant, but they told him it was important to his mother, so he joined in with less fuss.

They were nearly finished cleaning the kitchen when the doorbell rang. Ginger walked into the house, carrying several boxes and a bag. Alicia instructed Mathew, "You may leave now, Mathew. Go back to your work outside splitting the wood up. This is ladies only now."

"Make up your mind," Mathew spoke coarsely. Suddenly he got curious. "What are you going to do?"

"I will be looking a little different later," Linda told him. "Don't be scared. Just remember I love you, and no one will interfere with us."

He leaned over, hugged his mother and then got up to leave. As he was leaving the room, he quietly said, "This could be an interesting day."

He regretted not telling her he loved her too. He determined that he didn't need to tell her; she already knew.

The three young ladies sat Linda down on a chair in front of Alicia's mirror in her bedroom. Ginger released Linda's hair from the bonnet she was wearing. Down flopped beautiful long, silky, straight, brown hair over her shoulders.

Ginger ran her hand through her hair. She shook her head. "We need to cut off your split ends." Linda was a bit apprehensive but was resolved to trust them.

"Your hair doesn't want to curl very easily," Ginger said.

Alicia said, "I'll get some of Julie's clothes." Julie left several outfits behind.

"Allen might recognize them. That would not be good."

Linda tried on some clothes of Ginger's mother she had brought over. Ginger said as she looked at the clothes, "My mom is way fat."

"Yeah, you wouldn't be able to turn Dad on with these clothes. We need to go shopping," Alicia said happily.

Linda asked, "How far is it to the store you want to go to?"

"It's downtown," Ginger responded.

Linda looked around for her shoes. Alicia figured out Linda was thinking about the long walk downtown. "We don't have to walk. Ginger can drive us."

"I'll drive," Ginger said loudly.

Linda slipped back into her Amish clothes. Linda yelled out back to Mathew, "Mathew, we are going shopping. Would you like to go along or stay here?"

There was a yell from the backyard. "I'll stay, if you don't mind."

Linda put her hair back up into her bonnet. She gathered the money she had, and they left the house for the downtown business district. They went into Lovely Jolene's Clothing downtown. They were greeted quickly by a fine-looking young woman. She looked at the group with some wonderment. She was surprised to see Ginger bringing in an Amish woman.

When they walked out of the store an hour later, Linda was wearing jeans and a white blouse. She could walk along Main Street now, and no one would know she was Amish, unless someone recognized her, but according to Ginger, "No one will recognize you now."

Mathew recognized his mother right away when she walked in the door. "What? You went to some makeover joint." He did not want anything to do with what was apparently going on. The girls wanted Ginger to stay, and she really wanted to see Allen's reaction.

A half an hour before they expected Allen to come home, Linda was trying to get something prepared for the children to eat. There was an unexpected knock on the front door. Mathew, who was watching television in the family room with the three girls, got up to greet whoever was at the door. The girls curiously waited to see who it was. Linda froze when she heard a familiar female voice speaking German, "Hello, Mathew, it is good to see you well."

"Grandmother," Mathew said in English with more volume than he normally would use. He glanced back toward the kitchen before addressing his grandmother further. "It is nice to see you, Grandmother."

Linda was afraid to come out of the kitchen, but she was prepared to face her mother's wrath. She stepped into the doorway of the kitchen, the only Amish apparel she was wearing was an apron.

"May I come in?" Clara politely asked in English. She was focused on Mathew and was so overjoyed to be seeing him that she did not notice Linda.

Mathew glanced back again to his mother. Linda nodded to her son to allow his grandmother in. Mathew pushed the door open and then backed away, allowing his grandmother clear passage into the family room. Clara entered the house and looked around the room. There were two other older Amish gentlemen who accompanied her into the house. Linda recognized them as members of the council.

Clara nodded politely at Linda as she stood across the room in the entrance to the kitchen. She smiled politely at the young girls that remained silently seated on the couch. They were apprehensively anxious to watch the proceedings.

"Where is your mother?" Clara asked Mathew. He was not sure what to do, so he remained silent. Clara looked to Linda. "I am looking for my daughter, Linda."

"I'm right here, Mother."

Clara looked at her more carefully. "Linda," she sternly said. The two Amish elders were astonished at the sight of Linda in such worldly apparel and makeup.

With great effort, Linda said, "Mother, it is good to see you again."

"Well, obviously you didn't expect to see me tonight, did you?"

"No," Linda answered calmly. "You have come at a most inopportune moment."

"It is obviously a bad time for you," her mother sarcastically stated. "You have come to this place and mocked the God you have promised to serve."

"I still serve my God." Linda had to restrain herself. She did not want to cause a scene with the children present.

"By dressing as a harlot and living in the home of a man who is not your husband." Clara's face began to turn pink with rage as she spoke.

Linda was beginning to get a fire in her belly. "I live in a man's home to care for his children just as I have lived in the home of my husband's father."

"It is not the same," Clara argued. The three girls, who were smiling moments before, now sat silently on the couch and observed the spectacle unfolding before them.

Allison asked Ginger, "Why is she calling Mary, Linda?"

Alicia knew the answer. "*Linda* is the German word for *Mary*."

Ginger corrected her, "No, Amish address their close relatives by their middle name."

Allison asked, "So her full name is Mary Linda Hostetler?"

"Yeah," Ginger answered. "Now shush."

"There is no shame here in what I am doing." Linda looked down at herself, knowing this statement was completely unbelievable. "These are just clothes to cover myself. They do not block the heart and soul in which I love my God."

"Your dressing like this is the ultimate insult to the worship of your God."

Allison, who was sitting between Alicia and Ginger, whispered to her sister, "This is better than a soap opera by far."

"Shut up," Alicia and Ginger quietly said together as they both poked her.

"Well, it is," Allison said quietly in defiant retaliation.

Linda lowered her tone and asked politely, "Why have you come here today?"

Clara continued, "I came here to get you to come back. But I see that you have gone the same way as your rotten sister."

"Susan is not rotten!" Linda's tone and volume took a leap forward. Linda had never in the past raised her voice to her mother.

"It is Susan who has possessed your mind with these impure thoughts," Clara spoke sternly but with great restraint. "You are now consorting with this man that is not your husband. This is showing your son the impurities of this world. He will return with me, and you may go on giving your heart and soul to the devil."

"My soul is for my God, but my heart can be shared with another." Linda wanted so badly to convince her mother she still wanted to continue to embrace the Amish faith. "That is what you preach to me. All my life I have served my God, and this"— she gestured to her mother to look around—"has not changed that feeling. It has not changed me inside."

"It is not our way."

"It may not be your way, but it is my way."

"It is the wrong way. You are spitting in God's face." The front door opened, and in walked Susan and Allen laughing joyously. The room quickly went silent as they became aware of their guests.

Mathew was now standing close to his mother in the doorway of the kitchen. Clara and the two elders were in the middle of the family room. Susan and Allen were standing near the front door. The television was on, and there was a commercial on for Viagra.

CHAPTER TWENTY

Truth and the Consequences

The children weren't scared of what was unfolding in their family room, just confused. Alicia turned off the television. This drew the attention of one of the elders, who appeared to have been watching it. The three girls were wide-eyed and remained transfixed on the couch, anxious to witness what happened next.

Susan was horrorstruck to see her mother there with the two elders. She knew why she was there. She was surprised to see that Linda had dressed up as Tanya. She looked at Allen to see his reaction.

Allen's initial attention was drawn to the Amish men and woman standing in the middle of his family room. He saw the children sitting still on the couch. His attention was then drawn to a beautiful lady standing in the kitchen doorway. He stood in stunned silence when he saw who he thought was Tanya in the doorway. "Tanya?" he asked her. Linda was stunned silent by the whole situation. All she could do was bow her head in shame. This was much more than she had prepared herself for.

"It's Mary," Allison blurted out, so everyone heard her. Ginger and Alicia poked her to keep her quiet. "Well, someone has got to tell him who she really is." Everyone was looking at Linda, including Allen, who was realizing that Mary was actually Tanya.

Clara broke the silence. "What is this all about, Linda?"

Susan attempted a good response for her sister, who didn't appear to have the ability to answer. "It is a complicated situation, Mother."

Clara looked at Susan, recognizing her at once. When the elders recognized Susan, they turned their backs to her. Linda hung her head, took a few steps toward a recliner chair, and sat down. Her whole body writhed with the pain and shame she had brought upon herself.

Clara looked toward Linda. "I would like to hear from Linda." Linda remained silent.

Allison leaned toward her sister Alicia. "Who's Linda again?" Alicia just shook her head. "Quiet."

Allen was surprised Susan called this Amish woman Mother. The room was again silent, with the tension thicker than anyone was comfortable with.

Clara broke the tense silence once again. "Susan," she sternly bellowed. "It is your fault your sister is this way. You just had to turn her to your evil, worldly ways. She will lose salvation just as you have. What is worst is Mathew will lose it as well."

Susan felt a surge of spite. "Salvation is there for those who ask for it. What Linda does, she does of her own free will. I have not tried to influence her since her baptism."

Clara did not believe her daughter would lie to her at this point. "That may be true, but Linda would not have been lured here if it weren't for you. Look at her, all painted up as if to tempt the devil." She then turned to look upon Allen and pointed to him. "And here is the devil himself."

Allen was angered by the verbal assault and being referred to as the devil. All he did was come home and find a situation beyond his comprehension. He respected the older Amish woman, so he did not respond.

Allison blurted out, "He is not the devil. You are!" This time, neither Alicia nor Ginger poked Allison to keep her quiet.

Clara had a fleeting feeling that she might know this man. She took a few steps toward him to study him. After a brief study, she turned away and walked to the front door. She went outside and looked at the mailbox that hung just outside the front door. She returned, mouthing the name quietly, "Allen Barber."

Allen started to put together the bizarre situation. He recognized the Amish woman as his old friend Linda's mother. Linda then must be this broken woman sitting on his favorite recliner. But she looks just like Tanya. Mathew was kneeling next to his mother, Mary, with his arm wrapped around her neck and his head lying on her shoulder.

"What is this all about?" Allen asked anyone in general who might answer.

Clara began to piece the puzzle together on her own. She knew Allen was the young boy Linda had as a friend twenty years earlier. This was the same boy who she demanded that his grandparents to keep away from her daughter. Allen referred to her as Tanya when she was dressed for the devil. She looked at Mathew and gasped. It was becoming apparent to her that the miracle baby Linda had might not have been a miracle.

"Oh my," Clara calmly spoke. "Mathew, come, I will take you home now."

He hesitated. He wanted to stay with his mother. Linda did not indicate that she heard what her mother had requested. She was now shaking uncontrollably. Her bottled-up emotions were consuming her. Allen was aware that Clara was afraid of something and suspicious of her eagerness to get Mathew to leave with her.

Mathew, confused as to what to do, slowly stood up. He began to step slowly toward her, still unsure of what to do. "That's a good boy." She put her hand on his shoulder.

Allen was frantically trying to figure out what was happening. He thought to himself, *Susan is the sister of Linda. This woman is the mother of Susan. Linda is Tanya.* He shook his head to clear his thoughts. *Mary is Tanya, who used to be Amish, or still is Amish. It is Susan that used to be Amish. So Tanya is Mary and Linda. Mary and Linda have a son, who must also be Tanya's son. I made love to Tanya, how many years ago was it?* He then whispered to himself, but everyone could hear him mumbling. "Ten years, eleven years."

Clara began to pull on Mathew to hurry him along. Allen was sure that Mathew was ten years old. He looked to Linda in hopes she would verify his suspicions somehow.

Linda continued to sit leaning forward in the reclining chair, shaking violently. He then looked to Susan for a confirmation of his thoughts. Susan nodded ever so slightly to confirm to him that Mathew might very well be his true biological son. Clara also saw the nod confirming her suspicions were correct.

Allen's heart leapt, and he could not speak. He watched, horrified at the sight of his son being escorted out the front door, realizing he might never see him again, but he was frozen. Mathew and Clara were nearly out of the door when Susan saw that Allen was unable to move. She moved to block Mathew and his grandmother from reaching the front door. Clara gave Susan a stare of utter hatred. Susan remained defiant, refusing to let her mother to take her sister's son away.

Allen caught his breath and was able to force out the words quietly. He hoped that his words were forceful enough to have the impact he was after. "Mathew, go to your mother. She needs you."

Mathew, without hesitation, left his grandmother and went to his mother's side. He knelt down next to her chair. He wrapped his arms around her neck.

"What is going on?" Allison blurted out. She was again poked for speaking out by the other two girls. "Gee whiz."

Clara's lips clenched together in anger as she stared at Allen. "How dare you try to take my grandson! Mathew, come back with me." He looked at her with sad eyes. He did not want to hurt his grandmother, but he knew he needed to stay with his mother.

"His mother needs him right now," Allen said.

"His mother is in no condition to care for him now," Clara retorted.

Allen said quietly, "We will take care of him. He will be fine." Clara realized this as well and knew it would hurt Mathew to push the situation any further. Mathew looked sadly toward his grandmother, whom he loved dearly, and shook his head.

Allen walked over to her, and with great compassion and understanding for her, he said, "Mrs. Hershberger, I believe I understand some of what is going on here. I am very sorry. I do understand your position. Please give us some time to talk, and we'll let you know what is happening. I assure you that your grandson will be fine, and you will be able to see him again. I'm certain he will want to see you as well."

Clara looked at him, grateful for the words of comfort. She had one last look at Linda and Mathew. "It appears that I have no choice." Saddened by the events, Clara capitulated gracefully. "I have lost half my family." Susan stepped aside as Clara swept out of the house with the bewildered elders anxiously on her heels.

Allen turned around to look at Linda. He screwed up his face in deep thought and wonderment as to what he should do. Susan was afraid he would be mad at her, so she was hesitant to say anything. She inched closer to him, and with a soft shaky voice, she said, "Don't be angry with us until we can explain. Please."

Allen looked coldly at her, and with a slight tone of anger, he said, "I don't know what to think right now."

"I can understand that," Susan said.

"You two are sisters?" he asked her.

"Yes." She wanted to elaborate but could not bring herself to do so.

"Her real name is Linda?"

"Yes, it is."

"My Linda," he asked, "from years ago?"

"Yes," Susan assured him.

"So this has just been some great game you two have been playing on me?"

"No," she responded firmly with a sympathetic tone. "Nothing like that."

Allen raved on, "But you two have lied to me, kept it a big secret, laughing at my ignorance behind my back. The two people in this world I trusted the most. The two people that I allowed to be so involved with my nieces."

"No, Allen, it isn't like that, really." Susan clutched his arm. "She has always loved you."

He scoffed at the suggestion, "She is also Tanya, I take it?"

"Yes," Susan answered. "I know how it must appear to you. It is a complicated story. Please let us tell you what happened and why it happened."

Allen shook his head. "Not right now." He then leaned toward Susan's left ear and said softly enough so that no one else would hear, "Mathew is my son?"

"Yes." Susan pleaded with him, talking quietly in his ear. "He must never find out."

"Huh," he retorted.

"Linda and Luke couldn't have children on their own."

"Stop with any more lies," Allen said quietly.

"She didn't have a choice," Susan whispered in his ear. "She needed you."

"What do you mean she didn't have any choice?"

"She wanted it to be you."

"I don't want to hear anymore," Allen said.

Allen sat down on the couch with the children. The two girls curled up next to their uncle, laid their heads on his chest, and closed their eyes. They did not know what exactly was going on. They seemed to be content with waiting for an explanation.

Ginger got up. "I really feel that I should go now." She was interested in how things worked out, but she was afraid they would blame her for what happened.

Susan whispered to her as she passed by her, "Thank you. We'll talk later."

"Okay, good-bye." Ginger was happy to have received the kind words as she left. Susan was the only one left standing without a soul to comfort. The house remained quiet and still for nearly two hours after that.

Linda was emotionally drained and felt unworthy to seek forgiveness from Allen. She feared the consequences ahead from the result of her lies.

Mathew stayed at her side the whole time in silence, holding her hand and with his head on her shoulder. He was very confident that her name was Linda and would always be Linda, and he was fine with that.

Allen's head was spinning with thoughts and emotions. He was not sure what to do. Susan sat quietly in the chair next to the silent television, hoping to have the opportunity to tell Allen the whole story.

After a while, Linda got up silently and went to her bedroom, without making a sound. After Linda had gotten up, the two girls became more restless. It was now getting late, and Susan saw this as an opportunity to get the girls off to bed. She gestured to them to come with her to their bedroom.

Allison said, "I wish someone would tell me what is going on."

"I will try to explain it to you briefly," Susan said.

"Who is she really?" Alicia asked.

"Linda, Mary, and Tanya." Susan knew that would cause a commotion.

"We don't get it," Alicia said.

"I know. Come on in, and I'll try to explain it."

"You are still Susan, right?" Allison asked.

Susan chuckled. "That's a good start."

"That's Mary, right?" Alicia asked.

"Sort of," Susan explained. "Mary's real name is Linda."

Allison laughed, saying, "Allen thinks her name is Tanya."

Susan wanted to explain. "I'll get to all that. Give me a chance. Anyway, your father and Linda met a long time ago in a land far, far away when they were children. They were barely older than you are now." Their bedroom door went shut.

The house was silent and dark once again. Allen had not moved from the couch. He was deep in thought about how he felt about the events.

A few minutes later, Linda's bedroom door opened up, and light from the bedroom flooded the hall. She switched the light off, and the house went dark and silent once again. Mathew came up the stairs from the basement and met his mother in the hall. They were both in their Amish clothes, both carrying their personal possessions.

They silently walked through the family room toward the front door to the house. She felt unworthy of his attention and purposely avoided walking past him. She weakly pulled the front door open to leave. But the door abruptly slammed shut in her face with great force. This startled her. Allen was now blocking their path of escape. He did not say anything but peered deep into her eyes.

As her eyes met his, they filled with tears. She then looked down in shame. She could not tell whether he was angry or sad. Then she forced out with a shaky voice, "Please let us go. I am so sorry for what I have done to you." She took a deep breath, and more tears poured down her cheeks. "We will not trouble you any further...I promise." Tears were gushing from her eyes. She felt unworthy to look at him, so she kept her eyes closed. Mathew held on to her lovingly, giving her great confidence of support.

She tried once again to open the door, but Allen slammed it shut again. He continued to stand there, staring at her in deafening silence. Linda was not afraid of him physically but was prepared to endure an onslaught of verbal words that might cut deep into her soul.

Allen spoke in a forceful, compassionate manner, "You are not running out on me again. I won't let you go again." He paused for a few seconds as he moved closer to Linda. She was still facing the door away from Allen. He whispered in her ear, "I regret every day that I ever let you go." He shook his head slowly. "That is not going to happen again." He took a deep breath, and Linda still did not move. "Whoever you may be, or want to be, is fine with me. Just as long as you do it here...with us."

Linda understood what he was saying, but she could not believe it. She opened her eyes to see him looking at her not with malice but with love and compassion. "What?" She needed to hear it again to make sure she did not misunderstand him.

"To let you go now would be the biggest blunder of all." He looked deeply into her big brown eyes. "Remember our talk last night?"

"Ya," Linda said quietly. Allen pulled out a handkerchief and began to wipe the tears from her cheeks and eyes.

"It has come to my attention that you are the only girl— woman," he corrected himself, "that I have ever loved. All three of you." They both chuckled slightly. Linda continued to chuckle or sob, it was hard to tell, as they both dabbed at her tears together. "It might sound kinky, but some people like that role-playing stuff. I don't know why you did what you did, but for whatever reason, it just doesn't matter to me. I loved you then, then again, and then again." He smiled. "If it wasn't so sad, it would be funny." He thought how confusing his statements must have been to her.

He chuckled. He clutched her shoulders and turned her toward him so she was facing him. "I love you," he softly said as he leaned forward toward her. She leaned toward him, and their lips connected softly. His arms extended around her waist, and she placed her arms over his shoulders. They were then locked in a long, passionate kiss.

"I have always loved you," Linda told him softly. She felt feelings for him burst out of her as if they had been trapped within her all these years.

"Cool," Mathew said. He had been squeezed out of the embrace, so he turned around and took his bags back to his room in the basement.

Allen and Linda separated long enough to have a few words. "Why don't we take your bags back into your room?

"Should I put my bags in your room?" Linda asked.

"I would feel more comfortable if we got married first. You know, the children," Allen said. "I could make arrangements for us to get married tomorrow."

"Not tonight?" Linda asked. "I got this outfit today. It would be perfect."

"We could if we were in Vegas," Allen said jokingly.

"Let's go there then."

"I don't have enough money for tickets for all three of you." He then added, "I would really like to hear this whole story from your perspective. It must be a pretty wild story."

"Oh it is," Linda said. "Shall we start a fire and stay up all night talking about it? Then when the morning comes, we'll get married."

"We'll have to buy a ring."

"Why waste the money?"

"It's a symbol. You have got to have a ring when you get married," Allen said. "We can get an inexpensive one if you like?"

"If it makes you feel better, that will be fine."

There was a voice from the girls' bedroom, "Can we come out now?"

"Sure!" Allen said. The two girls came running out and joined in a big group hug. Susan came out quietly, not wanting to be an outsider in the newly formed family. She was happy that her sister had finally found herself and the love she will finally truly experience.

Susan silently snuck around the group hug and left the house. As she walked down the sidewalk, she felt a sudden loneliness. She would drive away from the happy family silently sulking but also very happy.

Later that night, Linda lay in Allen's arms on the couch. The fire's flames reflected brightly in their glistening eyes. The children had gone to bed, and the house was dark and silent.

Linda softly spoke, "I was devastated when you said such terrible things to me when I was Linda."

"I couldn't let you be punished because of me."

"You were so noble, sacrificing yourself. It would have been my choice to risk punishment."

"I didn't know what else to do to convince you not to want to see me again." Allen stroked her hair as she lay with her head on his chest. "I had to say those nasty things."

"I knew what you said was not in your heart," Linda remembered. "The pain I felt was from not being able to see you again."

"I thought of you all the time after that, but it had to be done," Allen said, and then he suddenly blurted out, "Hey!" He recalled the conversation they had before, which resulted in Linda slapping him. "That's why you were slapping me last night."

"What do you mean?" Linda had forgotten their conversation the night before and the reason she had slapped him.

"I was talking about you when I said Linda was the first girl I ever saw naked." Allen shook his head.

Linda playfully slapped him.

"What was that for?"

"Mary got to slap you for me. Now I get to slap you for myself, the one whose honor was impugned," Linda responded coyly.

"I was just beginning to get my life back together. You know, being able to feel for someone again. At least until I went to the fair with my sister."

"Why didn't you leave the Amish community when we met at the fair? And why were you at the fair dressed like that?"

"Susan made me go with her to experience the other world," Linda explained. "She was ready to leave the Amish community. I was trying to talk her out of it. But how could I convincingly talk her out of it if I did not know what I was talking her out of? Of course, she, on the other hand, was trying to convince me to leave with her."

Allen nodded his head slightly. "I suppose." He then scrunched up his face. "And meeting me didn't convince you to leave the Amish. You must have known I wanted you."

"You wanted me," Linda laughed.

Allen laughed. "Well, I was just a kid. You should have made your feelings known."

"Allen," Linda seriously said, "you would have still gone to college, and I would have been a deterrent."

"Maybe."

"You aren't mad at Susan, are you?" Linda asked as she raised her head off his chest to get a glimpse of his eyes.

"No, not really," he said cautiously.

"She wanted to tell you the truth the whole time. She was truly caught in the middle of the whole situation. This has all been my fault."

"I understand," he said as he nudged her head back down on his chest. They settled together even closer to each other on the couch. "Where is Susan?" They both looked around for any sign of her.

"I don't know."

Allen curiously asked, "How did you recognize me at the fair?"

"I don't know. It was just obviously you," Linda said candidly. "You really had no idea that it was me at the fair?"

"No," Allen said, "but I knew you were different and unaccustomed to a lot of things. I mean, like when you tried to eat that cookie."

"It was a cookie," Linda squealed. "Cookies are made to be eaten."

"Those weren't." Allen recalled they were cookies that received a blue ribbon at the fair. "Well, they were, but not for Joe Public to eat." "Why can't he eat them?"

Allen smiled in amusement. "There's no Joe Public. It's just a figure of speech."

"Oh, of course," she replied. She was still far from understanding many of the figure-of-speech lingo of the modern society. She was really going to have to learn it now. "I kind of remember having this argument back then, didn't we?"

"Yeah, I think it was then that I fell in love with you. Or it could have been when you lost your cookies after riding the shooting star." Allen smiled at the thought.

"That was embarrassing." Linda buried her face in his chest. "I thought for sure you would have left me then. But you didn't."

"I'm glad I didn't."

"So am I."

"The first time I saw you as Mary, I thought that it was you, which it was, until you said your name was Mary. I couldn't very well accuse you of being someone else. That would be calling you a liar." He paused a few seconds. "Interesting, because you were a liar."

Allen shook his head. "I should have been able to put it all together. But the idea of it was so far fetched I didn't think a lot about it. There was one thing that was eerily similar about the three of you. Your beautiful, big, brown eyes."

"The most beautiful brown eyes you have ever seen," Linda added with a smile. She was recalling his own words to Tanya more than once.

"Funny I would fall in love with three different women that ended up being the very same woman. That's romantic in a way, I think" Allen said. "And I kept thinking I was too easy falling for all kinds of women."

"Why were you telling Mary about the three of us last night?"

"I was trying to get my nerve up to tell Mary how I felt about her."

"She thought you were talking about Susan."

Allen nodded his head. "I tried to convince myself to fall for Susan. But it just didn't click the way it should."

"You kissed her last night. I saw you."

"No, you didn't," Allen chuckled. "I was watching you when I kissed her, and you purposely turned away so you wouldn't see it."

"Well, of course I didn't want to see you kissing her."

Allen suddenly had a question. "Why did you marry…" He hesitated, trying to think of her husband's name.

"Luke," Linda answered for him. "I wanted to. There was no chance for us, and it was expected of me to have a family. You know how I so wanted to have a big family." She got a serious look on her face. "I loved Luke in much the same way you describe your love for Julie."

"But…" He was hesitant to bring up Mathew as possibly being his son. "Mathew?"

Linda buried her head in his chest. "I had no choice," she said as she began to sob. "I don't like talking about it."

"Why?" Allen was confused. "How could you have no choice?"

"Well"—Linda knew she had to tell him—"you deserve an explanation," she calmly and confidently told him.

"You used me just to get pregnant?" he asked, half appalled and half flattered.

Linda could sense some contempt in his voice, so she playfully replied, "Yes, and you make a very fine stud." Linda patted him on the stomach. "If Luke couldn't be the father, I wanted you to be the father."

Allen wasn't sure what to think of her explanation. "I am flattered that you think so highly of me. Do you realize how hurt I was when you just popped in and out of my life like that? Don't you think I had the right to know I was a father?"

"Yes." Linda now had great concern for their relationship falling apart because of this episode in the past. "I am sorry. I have no excuses."

"I want to talk to Tanya," he said playfully. Linda raised her eyebrows. She raced into his room and back out in one of his big T-shirts. She jumped back on the couch in a childish, playful manner next to him. "Tanya, is that you?"

"Yes, it is."

"If you loved me, how could you leave me like you did?" he asked. "You let me think you were married."

"I was married," Linda said playfully.

"Yeah," Allen said sadly. "I felt really"—he tried to think of a good word to use—"yucky about sleeping with another man's wife for a long time."

Linda could sense that Allen felt guilty about the event. Linda had felt very guilty about it as well. She tried to comfort him. "Believe me, it hurt me to have to hurt you. I had hoped our argument that last time would ease your pain. Just as you had said those bad things when we were children. You wanted me not to want to see you anymore even though it hurt you to have to do it. I also was hurt and wanted to be with you back then. But it just wouldn't have worked." She took a deep breath. "I'm not trying to say that anything I did was right." She sighed. "But look at the result. Mathew would not be here today if it didn't happen. I can understand if you don't want to forgive me. And I am very sorry for using you that way."

"Mathew doesn't know?" Allen was sure he did not know.

"No," she said sadly, "everyone believes Mathew was a miracle baby. Even Luke thought so."

"Well, your mother seems to know now," Allen informed her, just in case she didn't notice when her mother was there. "What a tangled web you have woven for us."

"Yes, but I want to untangle it. That is why I dressed as Tanya tonight because I wanted to tell you everything. I couldn't live with myself any longer. I had hoped it would have been done in a more subtle manner."

Allen chuckled in angered amusement. "So I walk in to see Tanya, and that was how you wanted to tell me."

Linda squirmed around. "That was stupid, wasn't it?"

"Yeah," Allen reasoned, "it might not have been so bad if your mother hadn't shown up. It sure made an interesting event."

Linda felt bad about her mother. "Yeah."

"Why Mary?" Allen asked. "Why couldn't you have been yourself at that time?"

Linda started to shake her head. "I don't know." She took a deep breath. "I guess I just panicked." She tried to change the subject. "After you met Tanya for the first time at the fair, the next day you went to Linda's farm. Why?"

Allen looked at her blankly. He knew he had gone there but was leery about admitting to it. "What do you mean I went to Linda's farm?"

"You went to Linda's." Linda shook her head. "My family's farm. Susan and I saw you creeping around the trees near the stream. You went to the edge of the trees and watched the farm. Why?"

"You saw me there and…" Allen was desperate to turn the inquiry back into Linda's lap. "Were you spying on me?"

"We were goofing around at the stream, and you showed up." Linda was getting slightly frustrated with his avoidance of the question, so she said. "Now explain yourself."

Allen was definitely trying to avoid answering the question but felt he needed to answer. "I wanted to see Linda."

"Why?"

"Because I thought that seeing her might help me determine my feelings for Tanya and that I was suspicious that you or she might have been Linda or you." Allen smiled. "I mean, you really didn't think I bought that story about being from outer space, did you?"

"I thought it was a good story," Linda disappointedly said. "But you went along with it."

"I had this idea that you might have been Amish," Allen continued. "Well, think about it. What if I was wrong and I accused a regular girl, a girl I wanted to impress, that she was Amish?"

Linda was amused and offended by that statement. "Well, I would think that a regular girl would be flattered to be thought of as an Amish girl," Linda said with great conviction. "Oh, Mary is my younger sister, by the way."

"Oh." Allen smiled. "I see. You had to come up with a name real quick, didn't you?"

"Ya," Linda answered.

"And Susan knew all this time?"

"Yes, but she did try to convince me to tell you everything a long time ago," she reaffirmed. "She wanted me to leave the Amish life for you when we first met at the fair."

"That would have been nice," Allen agreed.

"Don't you see, Allen? No matter what we have done in the past, we should be happy for it and live the rest of our lives happy with our past. I am just glad to be here with you now, and I hope forever."

"Well"—he paused to be sure to have her complete attention— "do you promise never to lie to me again?"

"I promise," she answered casually.

"Do you promise to never run out on me again?"

"I promise."

"Do you promise never to take the identity of another person, be that person relative or fictitious?"

"I promise." Linda backed her head away from him a few inches and looked him straight in the eyes. "I promise never to deceive you in any way ever again. Even if in fun, I will not hint or suggest deception in any way that may mislead you to believe something that is not true." She smiled broadly. "Does that sound all right with you?"

"How can I believe you now after all this?" he asked, shaking his head.

"Believe me, believe me!" she yelled pleadingly as she shook his collar.

Allen could no longer keep a straight face. He burst out laughing. "But"—he paused to emphasize this point—"I can deceive you and lie to you in fun for the rest of my life." He tilted his head slightly. "This is called payback."

Linda sighed and leaned back against the couch, allowing her head to lean back on the headrest in frustration. "I suppose."

"Good, I think we will be fine then."

After Susan left Allen's home, she went to a local bar, where she sat for a few hours drinking several pops. She wondered about what was going to happen between her and Allen as far as her job was concerned.

As she was leaving the bar, she ran into their good friend, Deputy Sheriff Dave Kingery. They struck up a conversation with each other. Dave talked about his two boys, whom he had custody of. Dave and Susan walked off in no particular direction, but they would be walking together for the rest of their lives.

BIBLIOGRAPHY

Amish Life through a Child's Eyes by Alma Hershberger

Amish Taste Cooking Company–Danville, OH, 43014
Amish Heritage Publications
Amish Society by Andrew Hostetler
Copyright 1963–1968
By John Hopkins Press–Baltimore, MD, 43014
Amish Confidential: A Bishop's Son Shatters the Silence by Chris
    Burkholder
Argyle Publishing
A Woman's Journey to the Amish by Sue Bender
Plain and Simple
Harper San Francisco
Division of Harper Collin Publishers
Meet the Amish by Charles S. Rice and John B. Shenk
Rutgers University Press–New Brunswick

The Amish: People of the Soil by John M. Zielinski
Copyright 1972
Photo Art Gallery Productions - Kalona, IA, 52247

Amish Children by Phyllis Pellman Good
Good Books - Intercourse, PA, 17534

Amish Women: Lives and Stories by Louis Stoltzfus
Copyright 1994
Good Books - Intercourse, PA, 17534

listen|imagine|view|experience

AUDIO BOOK DOWNLOAD INCLUDED WITH THIS BOOK!

In your hands you hold a complete digital entertainment package. In addition to the paper version, you receive a free download of the audio version of this book. Simply use the code listed below when visiting our website. Once downloaded to your computer, you can listen to the book through your computer's speakers, burn it to an audio CD or save the file to your portable music device (such as Apple's popular iPod) and listen on the go!

How to get your free audio book digital download:

1. Visit www.tatepublishing.com and click on the e|LIVE logo on the home page.
2. Enter the following coupon code:
   63d2-0c4c-53af-cb1c-1b19-19b6-c40c-664a
3. Download the audio book from your e|LIVE digital locker and begin enjoying your new digital entertainment package today!